P9-AFC-867

CUP OF CLAY

Books by Carole Nelson Douglas

FANTASY

Six of Swords

Exiles of the Rynth

SWORD AND CIRCLET

Keepers of Edanvant

Heir of Rengarth

Seven of Swords

MYSTERY

Good Night, Mr. Holmes

Good Morning, Irene

SCIENCE FICTION

*Probe**

*Counterprobe**

**also mystery*

CUP OF CLAY

BOOK I OF THE TALISWOMAN

CAROLE NELSON DOUGLAS

A TOM DOHERTY ASSOCIATES BOOK
NEW YORK

This is a work of fiction. All the characters and events portrayed in this book are fictitious, and any resemblance to real people or events is purely coincidental.

Map by Darla Malone Tagrin

A Tor Book
Published by Tom Doherty Associates, Inc.
49 West 24th Street
New York, N.Y. 10010

Library of Congress Cataloging-in-Publication Data

Douglas, Carole Nelson.
Cup of clay / Carole Nelson Douglas.
p. cm.
"A Tom Doherty Associates book."
ISBN 0-312-85146-4
I. Title.
PS3554.08237C87 1991
813′.54—dc20 91-20934
CIP

First edition: September 1991

Printed in the United States of America

0 9 8 7 6 5 4 3 2 1

For Howard,
an agent who works like magic.

In the beginning God gave to every people a cup of clay,
and from this cup they drank their life.
—Northern Paiute Proverb

Ancient.
Earth grows older.
Shifting, creaking, straining.
Wind and wayward water batter its
mountainous spines. Fire sparks in its
hidden entrails. Inanimate, still it moves.
Mute, it grinds countless rocky teeth and belches
ardent flames. Sexless, it engenders a million
restless permutations, and an endless declension of
masculine. feminine and neuter in a hundred million
species. Old beyond Leviathan, Earth floats ponder-
ously through the empty shoals of night, life's
parasitic colony barnacled to its rough old hide.
Life is a thin, fluid skin, a narrow wedding band
of air, fire and water and mute mineral alchemy
haloing the planet against the glamorous,
star-shot vacuum of endless space.
Earth's old bones lay well-rapt in a
gossamer shroud, a mere
whisper of Veil.

QUEST SCAR
PEOPLE OF THE HORIZON
EARTH-EATERS CLIFFS
Desmeyne
EARTH-EATERS DOMAIN
Inn of the Scarlet Swan
Valley of Voices
MAP OF VEIL
©'91 DARLA M. TAGRIN

Prologue: The Red Swan

She knows it's a dream, because she's a child again, sitting cross-legged and cozy at Eli's feet, listening to stories. And it's so real, so detailed, as the best dreams always are.

"*First was nothing.*" Eli's voice, exactly as she remembers it. "*Then comes the fog like a great white bear from the North, where rainbows of night burn campfire-bright. South Wind whistles from the pit of nowhere, blows the fog apart. Brother Fire and Sister Water are born and wander from East to West until they eat the darkness and lay bare the Earth. Earth is the Mother, our rich, red-earth Mother. She lies on her back looking at sun.*"

"Is the sun our Father, Eli?"

"My story. *Father is the Sky—*"

"Oh."

"*He looks down on Mother. She faces up at him. From them come all the little peoples between.*"

"People are like sandwich baloney?"

Eli claps weathered brown hands. "People are meat for the teeth of Earth and Sky."

Eli's voice rumbles like velvet thunder in the dim cabin. In the dream, she doesn't yet know his last name. He's just Eli, and she's seen him since she was old enough to remember everything that she saw. He is like Mother Earth and Father Sky and her family's Island. Always there. Earth and Sky and Island. And Eli.

She questions each retelling, though she cherishes the familiar pattern. She is eleven now, has begun dotting the "i" in her name with a tiny, tightly closed circle—Alison—and can't be fooled easily by stories, no matter how beloved they are.

She knows that the glass mountain the knight climbs to claim the princess isn't real. Yet her imagination hoards the impossible image. How often she has pitied the gallant young suitor—and even more, his poor horse, who does all the work.

No chill, mirrored mountains, no princesses, populate Eli's

stories, the only ones actually told to her. Some people might say that makes them not as good as a book, but there are few books on the Island. There is, however, Eli. She likes his stories better anyway. She can't interrupt a book.

So she sits cross-legged at his feet, her dungaree cuffs showing the denim's pale underside—they've been rolled up thrice because she is expected to grow into them (fairy tales use words like "thrice"; that's one reason that she loves them)—and listens. She has always listened to Eli.

The brothers in Eli's tale are orphaned—as they usually are in the Grimm Brothers' fairy tales, too. Instead of hunting princesses, they stalk deer, elk, moose . . . and buffalo—ponderous, fleecy beasts, always at a misty distance, like cloud mountains that a magical steed could scale with hooves the color of rainbows. She has never seen a buffalo.

The Indian brothers want wives—what all brothers on the fairy-tale shelf of the public library get around to wanting, too. The eldest goes wife-hunting first and the others object.

"So they hold a hunting contest instead. Each agrees to slay a male of the kind he has special skill in hunting. From the hides, they will fashion quivers for their arrows."

"Is that why there aren't any more buffalo, Eli? All of them were made into quivers?"

His black eyes sink deeper into the sagging socks of skin rumpling around them. In the dream, the pupils of his eyes are strange and strong, like licorice tea.

"Once the buffalo numbered like the flowers in the field, and they were made into many things, but then they were made into nothing. That is what killed them. When a thing can be made into another thing, it is cherished. The buffalo were not cherished."

She wants to ask why, but because Eli's voice is especially thundery, she just clasps her ankles and bounces her akimbo knees until they brush the cabin's pine floor.

Of course the hunting brothers separate and of course the youngest, Odjibwa, meets a bear, which he isn't allowed to kill. So of course he kills it anyway. People in tales always do the worst possible thing, especially at the beginning. And especially in dreams.

"As Odjibwa begins to skin the bear, a red fog clogs the air. A distant human cry lures him to a lakeshore."

"Is it like our lake, Eli? Like Swan Lake? Or bigger, like Mille Lacs? You can't see across Mille Lacs."

Eli ignores her. He never cares about real places when he's telling a story, and he continues.

"There in the lake Odjibwa sees a beautiful red swan, scarlet feathers shining in the sunlight as it cries in that oddly human voice.

"Odjiwa lifts bow, pulls string to ear, and shoots. An arrow strikes the water. Odjibwa shoots until his quiver is empty. The swan drifts untouched on the silver water.

"Odjibwa runs home, gets all his brothers' arrows and shoots every one of them—into the lake, not into the red swan. Then he remembers the three magic arrows in their dead father's medicine sack. Though it is forbidden to even open this sack, he takes the arrows and runs back to kill the swan."

"If the swan's so rare and beautiful, why does he want to kill it, Eli?"

"It is story."

She knows it, but doesn't like this next part.

"Odjibwa's first magic arrow flies closer to the crimson feathers than any of the others did. The next draws even nearer, and the third . . . She wonders: Is it always the third for the same reason it is always the third and youngest brother? . . . *pierces the great bird's neck."*

"He's not going to *eat* it, is he, Eli? I know the creatures of earth are there to be eaten, but the red swan can't be a creature of earth—"

Eli's eyes shut for a moment. He has no discernible eyelashes, only a fine web of wrinkles netting his bright, dark eyes, trapping their furtive glitter that is like something round, mysterious and muddy dredged from underwater.

She doesn't know why, but the wounded red swan never dies in Eli's story, or in her dreams. Instead . . .

"It flies on ungainly wings into the bloody setting sun, crying a sad, human wail. Odjibwa follows, stopping at three villages and accepting a maiden for a wife each time."

She thinks that soon Odjibwa will have as many wives as Eli

has fishhooks. But the beautiful bride from the third village turns out to be the red swan, waiting for a warrior to claim her, just like the princess at the top of the glass mountain sat and waited.

"That was dumb, to run away," she says. "As dumb as it was for Odjibwa to shoot her swan-self with an arrow. Girls are always running away in stories."

Eli's smile reveals a dark absence rather than the usual pale presence of teeth. His eyes vanish in seams of parched flesh. He is so old, the oldest person she knows.

She taps her fingertips on the floor and studies the strange, familiar things on the knotty pine walls: snowshoes that look like badminton rackets for giants; shelves of blinking, salvaged bottles filled with fishhooks; a calendar for last year, 1969, the first year people walked on the moon . . . a dogskin she hates to notice but always does. The pelt is pale like a buckskin horsehide, and the brown-glass eyes hold an accusing glint that her stuffed animals never show.

"My story," Eli says, and begins the part that she really, really doesn't like, the part that doesn't resemble a happy ending at all, no matter how she tries to pretend it does, even in dreams. What he tells her is this:

"When Odjibwa returns home, he gives the first two brides to his brothers, but keeps the red-swan maiden. The other brothers are unhappy with their wives and try to make Odjibwa feel so bad for taking their father's medicine arrows that he'll go away to find more. While he is gone, they will take his wife, the red swan. Even in the sweat lodge the brothers scold Odjibwa, until he at last agrees to go.

"He travels far, into a cavern in the earth and down into the land of the dead. Buffalo cover the slopes of a beautiful green country and speak to him. He tells one of them of his quest, and the bone buffalo—for that is all this particular buffalo is, bleached bones—warns Odjibwa that he has come where no living man has gone.

"Odjibwa looks West and sees a bright light, like the sun. But there is no sun there. The bone buffalo says that radiance is the light of the good, who dwell here in death.

" 'And that dark cloud?' Odjibwa asks. It seems to spring up from and shadow the whole land.

" 'Wickedness,' answers the buffalo in a voice of thunder.

"Odjibwa then wanders in the Underworld and almost doesn't come back—not to the world of his people, not to his wicked brothers, and certainly not to the beautiful red swan. . . ."

All the cabin's homely, reassuring detail has vanished. Alison is in the woods, *the* woods, like Odjibwa.

Her dream-self is heading for her family's cabin along a footpath that's interlaced with switches of wild asparagus and sumac. The flashlight's ribbed silver-metal sheath warms her palm; its light shines red through the thin skin between her fingers.

Skittering wild things chide her passage. Squirrels, chipmunks, birds—owls, loons, maybe even a red swan. Or bears. Bears can swim to the Island, Petey often says in the half-tease, half-threat way of older brothers. Not wolves, though; wolves never come to the Island.

"Gotcha!"

Something dark bounds, shouting, from the brush. Something claws her sides and almost topples her. She is running, running from Petey's stupid mock attack, running from the taunting echoes of her older sister, Demaris.

Demaris in dreams always speaks in a slow, insufferable big-sister drawl. She is always fourteen and holds whispered conferences with Mom that stop when Alison comes by. Demaris wears her T-shirts with a difference in dreams and ambles to Janssen's drugstore soda fountain to meet boys. She insists that everyone call her "Marisse." Petey calls her "Demerit."

Petey jerks one of Alison's brown braids, then holds his nose, turning away. "Everything that's been to Eli's place smells."

"Does not!"

"You smell, too. Of scalps and dead meat and animal guts."

"Do not! Smoked fish, that's all."

"What you got there?"

Alison looks down to see that she's holding something besides the flashlight. "A pot I found."

"It stinks, too. It smells like it's got dead people in it. Ashes and bones and icky stuff. Get rid of it!"

"Petey! Let go!"

While they struggle, Demaris's nose wrinkles, as it does in

dreams. "Eli's weird. Why do Mom and Dad let him live in our island? I hate coming here! It ruins my social life, being stuck up here in the sticks with a bunch of Iron Range Neanderthals all summer."

She rustles into the dark, the undergrowth crackling like a Chee-tos package. Petey makes a last, rough grab.

"Hey!" Alison's glasses vanish from her face. "Give those back, Petey. I can't see!"

He retreats, laughing, following Demaris. They are gone, and owls hoot at Alison. Branches snap like bubble gum. Then the night goes still. A distant bird—a loon—yodels its long, fluttering call. Maybe it's really a red swan.

She hates her glasses. The plastic frames skid down her sweaty nose, the bows pinch her ears and tangle her hair, the lenses fog in winter and smudge in summer . . . She needs them. Alison sweeps one arm ahead, parting switches of undergrowth that could whip her eyes.

Live things rustle and chirp, hoot and snuffle, in the dark. She is running and the stories are all behind her, like the Petey and Demaris of when-she-was-eleven. The dream has caught her in that slow, sticky, long-ago summer night now, like a fly trapped in a web of melted amber. Without warning, she breaks through the undergrowth to the lakeshore, recognizing it with dread. It is still night, but a red moon turns the strip of water between Island and mainland into a crimson river.

On it Demaris hovers like a saint about to be assumed into heaven. Demaris, twenty feet offshore, truncated at the thighs, a human torso suspended on the lake's flat, shining razor's edge. Demaris floats there, motionless, while the bloody water shivers all around her.

"Come on, baby," she taunts.

Demaris wears a new two-piece swimsuit, black with tomato-red bands slashing her hips and adorning the chest so recently christened a "bust." She resembles the scantily clad apprentice of some magician who has failed at the sawed-lady trick.

Come on.

Alison stands as if frozen in a game of "Statue." Then she turns, still clutching . . . what?

She runs toward the family camp, stumbling over all the words at once, trying to shout, and only whispering. She runs, something cold and hard caught at her chest just beneath her throat, something like the icy piece of mirror that impaled Kay's heart in "The Snow Queen." She runs like the girl in the dancing red slippers; there is no stopping, not even for the fallen branch angling into her path like a bony arm, and she is sprawling—flat, facedown, the treasure she carries breaking into thick shards that carve their memory into her flesh.

Blood. Her hands guard her chest, blood smearing the knuckles, soaking her white T-shirt. She shudders, stutters, then Dad 'n' Petey 'n' Mom are there, prying Alison's hands apart and tying a dishcloth around her neck. They want her to name the place. She can't. It is all Island and all water and all the same eternal shoreline.

She lies in the emergency room in Grand Rapids, the T-shirt stripped from her budding breasts. Hands labor above her while a fluorescent light betrays every crack in a parchment-colored ceiling. The hands come closer, bearing knives. They etch agony into her skin, cut with the burning edge of a buzz saw. Pain hums in her ears. Strange faces gaze down on her. Their voices murmur like the trees—aloof and indecipherable.

She must do this thing. She must hold still despite the fear. Torches flutter hotly at the edges of her eyelashes.

A man in a pallid robe and with a thin white beard as long as a ladder leans over her. He wields the expression of an adult who will do something for her own good, and a bloody blade. A worried woman shimmers behind him, her hair as silvery as a Christmas tree angel's, her hands wrung whiter than frost. Her gown is the iridescent sparkle of snowflakes flirting with the back porch light.

Alison doesn't know these faces, though she knows this pain in her bones, in her flesh and blood. An ache begins in her stomach, a hard knot of cramp that won't go away. She can feel blood trickling over her shoulders, between her infant breasts; a slow, warm red pulse tickles down her thighs, as subtle as a snake.

She screams in the dream, but it is useless. The strangers loom over her. The pain is endless, and she is helpless. Overhead, the ceiling has become a candy-mint sky of green and lavender and light yellow. A red swan beats its heavy, majestic wings for the horizon.

She looks down to see red hair spilling over her shoulders, mingling with the blood.

Wednesday, April 10, 1991 *St. Paul Express-Messenger*

GUILTY VERDICT ENDS BLUE EARTH CHILD-ABUSE TRIAL

BY ALISON CARVER
STAFF WRITER

BLUE EARTH—After months of pre-trial publicity and weeks of painful, often graphic testimony, a Fairbault County jury returned a guilty-on-all-counts verdict Tuesday afternoon in the Blue Earth multi-generational child-abuse case.

Some courtroom observers cheered the verdict, the conclusion of a grueling investigation that has shaken this small, southern Minnesota town since October of 1990, when a sixth-grade teacher reported possible sexual abuse of a child in the Lindahl family.

Subsequent charges—and controversy—snowballed as one Lindahl child after another testified to long-standing family sexual abuse involving three generations. Despite a defense buttressed by allegations of trial-by-publicity, community witch-hunt and manipulation of the alleged young victims, a jury of seven men and five women found all six defendants guilty.

Facing sentencing Friday are clan patriarch Walter Lindahl: his widowed mother, Mary Pritzel; Walter's wife, June; their son and daughter-in-law, Richard and Janna Lindahl; and a second son, Jerome. Jerome Lindahl's wife, Deborah, was not indicted.

The verdict offers a long-awaited closure to a case that tore a town apart. Psychologists say that it will be years before the mental scars heal, especially among the eight juveniles, ages two to fifteen, whose testimony painted a devastating picture of how easily a spectacularly dysfunctional family blended into an unsuspecting rural community.

CUP OF CLAY

1

Alison's neck ached and the darkness behind her eyes burned. The phone keened for a long time in the dappled, underwater distance before she awoke enough to answer it.

"Hi, it's Mark McPherson from the paper. You were really under." The man's voice droned from fathoms below her consciousness. "Must've rung twenty-five times."

"Oh . . . hi." Mark McPherson was the newspaper's environmental reporter. Nice guy—maybe he could be more to her someday. She tried to shake herself awake, but her grogginess echoed down the phone lines. "I was dead beat. Had an awful dream."

She always had bloody dreams before her period, which was imminent, and her voice sounded clogged, not the way she wanted to sound to an attractive man in the morning.

"You've been covering a rough story." Respect tinged Mark's voice.

She pushed herself upright in the pillows. City-desk types didn't think much of Sunday feature writers like herself, no matter how many in-depth social-issues pieces they did. But writing the verdict report on the child-abuse case of the century . . . that was big time. It'd been one A.M. before she'd finished the analysis piece that would run Sunday; then she'd gone home and collapsed.

Fumbling for the bedside clock, she brought the red LED numbers to her nose. Eleven. She squinted at the window. Murky light sifting through the miniblinds advertised day, not night.

A yawn cracked her jaw, drowning out Mark's next words.

"Listen," he was saying when she could hear again, "I didn't mean to wake you, but I figured you'd be too tired to think of ordering tear sheets. So I saved a bunch of the first-edition fronts. That way you won't have to pry them out of the librarian next week. Get 'em while they're hot—and around. You look real good in forty-eight-point headlines."

"Thanks." Alison laughed, basking in the admiration of a

fellow journalist. A front-page byline was a step up for her in the opinion of a hard-news reporter like Mark. Alison's waterbed rocked as a huge white blur bounded atop it. She reached unerringly to her dog, Rambeau.

"Anyway, Alison," Mark said, "enjoy the fleeting glory. Next Monday it'll be 'What have you written this week?' " Mark's voice still droned from far away. She felt wrapped in warm wax, but a pulse of alarm agitated her sleepy cocoon. "I hope I didn't ruin your sleep."

"Not at all . . ." A serendipitious notion tangled on her mind and tongue at the same moment. "Hey, I'm glad you called when you did. I'm going up to the family island. Get away from that bummer child-abuse story. Clear my head."

"You're going up alone? Isn't that risky?"

Alison heard muffled shouting and the plastic chuckle of computer keyboards. City desk was nearing its P.M. edition deadline. Mark shouldn't be taking time to call.

"It's spring. Things need looking after, and it's my island. I own it now. I'm used to camping out there alone. Besides, I've got my big bad dog with me—a Samoyed, kind of like a white husky, so you know he's nothing to mess with. I'll be back Sunday night in time for work Monday."

"Yeah. Well, have a good time."

"Sure, and thanks. 'Bye."

Too sleepy to hang up after the click, Alison let the receiver drone on her shoulder like a purring cat. Beau's cold fuzzy-focus black nose nudged her hand. His needs got her moving while her own were still mute. She put her contacts in, fed Beau, wolfed down some low-cal toast and an apple, dressed and packed.

They were on the road before noon. She couldn't explain her impulsive flight north, except that it felt good to leave the city behind on an early April Friday, to lead-foot the Blazer and scoot up the Interstate alongside the ghost of old Highway 61 to the Island. The lowered backseats were laden with supplies: sleeping bag, Coleman lantern, her backpack and overnight gear. Her folks always meant to build an ultra-modern retirement home on the Island—a civilized, high-ceilinged redwood chapel of a place—but had died before realizing their dream. So for years the young family had roughed it, her father eventually installing a concrete pad for the family-sized tent and a semi-discreet latrine. Now, with so many Carvers gone, wrestling the big tent into place wasn't worth the energy. Besides, Allison liked sleeping in the open. And so did Rambeau. The dog hovered behind her, panting amiably in her ear, its black-lipped Samoyed smile at full tilt.

"We'll both get off the leash for a while, huh, Rambeau boy?" Alison smiled as his midnight muzzle made a pass at her nose. These "nose nips" signaled his wolf-spitz origins, yet Beau was as friendly as a stuffed white polar bear. She'd gotten him after a neighborhood rape scare, the same time she'd signed up for *taekwondo* lessons.

In time Alison had gone from leery student to a black belt whose hand chop could dissect a board. And Beau, once a sloe-eyed harp seal of a pup, had become a big beautiful dog, perfect companion for a single woman living alone in the moderately big city.

"Boy, could I have used you years ago on the Island." She roughened the thick mane ringing the dog's neck.

The Island was hers now, by virtue of her mother's will. Her brother Pete had raised holy hell, for some reason, about losing a place he hadn't visited since high school. Demaris—the name never touched Alison's mind without producing a twinge—was not around to raise anything, much less objections.

Trees along the Interstate wheeled by in boring rhythm. Alison hadn't visited the Island all winter, and she loved the place, despite what had happened there. It drew her, beyond all reason.

The farther north she went, the clearer the air became. She cracked a window, almost visible wisps of pine scent filling the Cherokee with natural incense. Soon roadside firs began jousting oaks and birches for room, their dark tops like barbed medieval lances. Red-wing blackbirds balanced on pussy-willow stalks lashing the ditches.

The sun slanted westward, elongating the Blazer's squat shadow into a Goya silhouette, warming Alison's arm through the window. Once she saw a pelican—an ungainly shape, with a beak as slack as a grandmother's underarms—plough through the flamingo-pink clouds before it sank into a twilight sea.

Only sixteen miles to the Island.

In Keewatin she stopped at Rubnik's Grocery, where her folks had always shopped. Mr. Rubnik still presided behind the gashed Formica counter.

"Hey, Alison Carver. How are the Cities?"

Mr. Rubnik spoke with an eastern-Europe-once-removed vocal sing-song indigenous to the Iron Range. He was bald, red-faced, and contentedly overweight. A deep purple bruise set like a small sun on the crescent of his left thumbnail, which was ridged with vertical lines. He never seemed to change, but of course he had.

"Great," she said. No one up here really cared about Minneapolis and St. Paul, but they thought it polite to ask. She prowled the aisles, choosing weekend perishables with practiced speed.

"Say, that was some story." Mrs. Rubnik emerged from the storeroom, tucking her black-gray hair into a net. Alison wondered where you got hairnets nowadays. "You shouldn't have to write about stuff like that, Alison, a nice young girl like you."

"The evening editions get up here already?" Alison ignored the parental push-pull of pride and disapproval in the couple's manner. Once people had known you as a child, they felt forever entitled to take liberties, even when you were past thirty. "And it's a coup to cover a story as big as the Blue Earth multigenerational abuse scandal. I started out doing an in-depth backgrounder for the Sunday paper and ended up covering the verdict when the courts-beat reporter's brother died. Besides, people need to know what's really going on around them, no matter how ugly it is. That's what my job's all about."

"Sure, we know that. What do you think this is, the backwoods?" Mr. Rubnik laughed. "We even got cable TV now, Miss Big City Reporter. You should write a story on that."

She smiled at his jokes because her parents had. Carvers had been on the Island long enough to be considered natives, not seasonal newcomers. The Rubniks approved enormously that she had kept the property—even fought Pete for it—on her parents' death.

Still, she waited for their rote caution about staying there alone. What once had ignited resentment was now a ritual comfort. Alison had lost most of the people who'd been obligated to care about her because of lifelong proximity. Even though she'd made a life for herself in the Big City, she'd found few substitutes.

"Heard bears were swimming in the lake. Bad winter. Not enough food up north." Mr. Rubnik sounded pleased that duty forced him to report such dire tidings.

She gathered her change and the brown paper bag. "Rambeau will eat 'em. He's hungry enough."

"Dog isn't enough against bears. Girl alone needs more." Mrs. Rubnik nodded at her husband's words.

"There's Eli," Alison said, as she always did.

"Indian," Mr. Rubnik grumbled, as he always did.

"Indians know bears—and lions and tigers," she couldn't help flinging back as she shouldered her way out the screen door. "Right? I'll be okay. Thanks."

She fought the tailgate open and jammed the groceries inside. The town, a thousand strong, was not quite dark. No neon beer-joint signs simmered in the twilight yet, though out-of-work men had been draining the taps since midday. Keewatin had that vacant, scruffy look of places with a low population and a high unemployment rate. A man shambled between two red-brick buildings. She stiffened to identify him—not specifically, but generically.

An Indian. She saw even from a twilight distance the torn plaid shirt and dirty jeans, the blood smudging his face. He lurched into the deserted street.

Most people on the Range considered the phrase "drunken Indian" a redundancy. Was he hurt? Heading for more of it down the beer-joint-lined street? Iron Rangers liked Indians in their places—out of sight on the Leech Lake reservation or downstate in the Twin Cities on welfare.

Alison shivered in the cooling air. Spring seemed a premature concept. With an uneasy conscience, she watched the figure stagger into the dusk. She supposed her childhood fascination with Eli had elected Indians as the obvious objects of her social concern. They had proved the most elusive, the least citified, the most distant, the least domestic of pet causes. To her reporter's persuasion, to her intelligent empathy, to her late-twentieth-century liberal conscience, they had extended a universal, stoic indifference. They lived, made love and children, worked, fought; they drank, drugged; they died, young or old, alike in one thing. They didn't need her.

Alison slammed the tailgate shut and climbed into the front seat. The vehicle crawled out of town past a shadow lurching along the curb. Her eyes burned, as they had all day, when she squinted into the distance. No urban smog haunted Iron Range country, but the evening sun set behind smudge-pot clouds; it was as if Alison viewed them through a dirty windshield.

Off the state highway, the Blazer's wheels hit asphalt, then dirt. Trees blocked the road ahead, whose curves always dodged the massed trunks, though birch switches admonished the vehicle's metallic sides. Beau's tail thudded the carpeting. His mysterious canine acuity unerringly sensed the advent of the Island.

"We'll have high water, boy," she warned him, actually warning herself of an unwelcome reality.

She parked beneath the usual pine. The rowboat had weathered another several months' interment of snow and looked as if it had crawled ashore. Sixty yards away, the Island—a smoky hunchback—hunkered in its ring of living, lapping water. She bullied the boat into the water and loaded it. Beau leaped into the prow, an absurd white figurehead in the semidark.

"So hot to get there, you want to swim, Beau?" The dog's ears pricked to the lilt of her voice.

The boat trembled on the gentle brink of ripples. The water wasn't deep between here and the Island—no more than waist-high, shoulder at the most. Even if the boat overturned, if she fell or jumped in, she could still simply walk. Any idiot would know that; there was no current here, as in a river. She could simply *walk* to the Island, for God's sake.

A spring flood had never stopped her family. Floods came as regularly as rain and would soon ebb. She knew that. She'd driven and walked this very land bridge hundreds of times. Besides, the boat wasn't going to overturn, she wasn't going to fall out, she wasn't even going to get wet.

"So. Good dog. Good dog. Just a minute."

The dark didn't bother her; lethal to wood planks, wasn't she? Could camp out alone with lions and tigers and bears, oh my, and owls and loons, too. So there.

But water.

The lake had drop-offs. Alison didn't swim. She could never stand to learn, not after Demaris. Drop-offs. It had a sinister sound, like the world breaking off at your feet—only underwater, so your legs churned nothing more substantial than liquid air and you sank, fell, dropped down . . . down . . . down. Forever. You dropped off the face of the earth and were never seen again; you drowned, and that was it.

Alison set the flashlight on the crude board seat. The evening was still, too cool for crickets, too late for bird calls, too early for the batlike passage of night hawks. Rambeau whined impatience; he had free run of the Island.

"Yes. Good dog. Yes, I'm coming. Now—"

She stepped into the boat, her legs bridging land and water for a moment, spanning darkness and wetness. The boat swayed with her weight the way a Ferris-wheel seat rocks at the very top of the curve when people are boarding below and you can see the world small and wee plunging before you and the wheel isn't really going yet and there's no exhilarating whirl, just the jerky stop-and-go motion of you rising up up up in the air and then dropping off over the circle's edge—the flat world's rim—into nothing.

"Silly." Alison sat down in the boat.

She was a good rower. Her parents had insisted their kids learn. The oars in her fists, their wooden solidity comforted her. But the unseen water below whispered that it was dark and deep and populated with things of like ilk, that it concealed a buried landscape of the dead of all shapes and species, that it was rife with sudden rabbit holes into a watery Wonderland that offered no exit, ever. . . .

Row, row, row your boat, gently down the stream.
Merrily, merrily, merrily, life is but a dream.

She laughed at her frail contralto. "What's next, Beau? 'I Whistle a Happy Tune'? Look, almost there."

The lifted flashlight illuminated friendly soil. For an ugly moment she hesitated before leaping to the gravel-strewn shore. Beau bounded out, wagging his tail in the flashlight's warm circle. She followed, heart catching until her feet found solid ground again, her Reeboks mincing back from the water's last thin lick at her toes. Pulling the boat ashore and securing it released her hoarded anxiety. Stupid, she knew, and like all phobias, terrifying.

"Can a person who has hydrophobia like dogs?" she asked Beau. There might be another name for the fear of water, but she'd never heard it.

The settling-in routine was familiar and pleasant. Once ashore on her annually isolated retreat, Alison felt oddly safe. Maybe the fear that always accompanied her arrival intensified her satisfaction in accomplishing it.

After a supper of beans and bread, she donned a down vest against the evening chill, grabbed the flashlight, called Beau and took the trail to Eli's place. Her folks had left Eli the westernmost two acres of the sixty-five-acre island. She supposed that was because Eli had been there first.

Eli was older now, but he didn't look it—or, rather, looked about as old as she had always thought him. They didn't have much to say to one another; no stories were told these days. Yet not acknowledging his presence, not apprising him of hers, would violate some unspoken bond.

"You couldn't leave earlier?" Eli greeted her on his threshold. A Coleman lamp on the table washed remembered artifacts in ripples of light.

She found herself apologizing, as if she'd been late. "I worked until one this morning. Big story. I got going as soon as I could. But you weren't expecting me."

"It's not safe at night now."

"Eli, you of all people, aren't going to turn worrywart about the Island?"

He stepped away from the door without answering, the only invitation he offered her to enter. A rifle lay on the table. She'd never seen Eli with a gun.

"Going hunting?"

He nodded to the same rush-bottomed chair she'd sat beside as a kid. "Things in woods."

"Bears?" she kidded.

Eli gave her a flat, disbelieving look. "No bears on Island. Never bears."

"Then why do you need a rifle? To fish?"

"Big fish in lake. You know."

"Come on, I wouldn't stick my big toe in there—or in any water—but the biggest sturgeon aren't more than three feet, and since when do you want more than sunfish and croppies?"

Beau pushed between Eli's knees as the old man sat at the table. Eli lightly boxed the dog's nose in greeting, then sank brown fingers into the white ruff and shook it.

"Dog still got winter coat. Winter fat. Dog lazy."

Alison was suddenly aware of the wall-hung ancient dogskin, its white pelt age-yellowed, eyeing her with a bright, brown-glass gaze over Eli's shoulder. Beau adored the old man, but Eli never called him by name. He was Dog, that was all.

The habit chilled Alison; it made Beau seem expendable, or inanimate, like the pelt. It reminded her that Eli came from a people who regarded nature in a similar, generic sense—Mother Earth, Father Sun, Brother Rabbit, and Fox, and Dog. What were the sisters? she wondered; she hadn't heard much about them. Perhaps graceful, fragile things like swallows and otters and swans.

"See anything in the woods?" Eli asked.

"The woods? Coming here? No."

Eli grunted. "You just come."

"Of course I just came, and not soon enough, I guess."

"You want whiskey?"

"Whiskey?" Eli had never offered her food or drink before, not even a smoked fish.

He shuffled to a battered cabinet that had always seemed so much a part of the background that she'd never imagined it being opened. She smelled the cabin now, a potpourri of old ashes, smoked fish, worn leather, wet wool. She saw it all with a reporter's clarity—yet the cabin seemed like no place she had ever been before, as if it had shrunk, or she had swollen.

Eli put two glass tumblers on the table—former olive jars. He discarded nothing he could use. *"That which cannot be made into something else is not cherished."* For the first time, Alison understood.

Two inches of Old Crow splashed into each container. The bottle was two-thirds empty. Eli a drunken Indian? No, just Eli, perhaps being more Eli with her than he had been before, as if she weren't a child anymore.

The jar glass was cloudy, the liquor's amber color burning through its haze like a warning light. She sipped, feeling tension ebb before the whiskey's fiery onslaught down her throat and esophagus, into her stomach, then her limbs—honeyed fire, humming like spring sap to all her extremities and up her brain stem into the veins of her mind.

Eli nodded and drank from his own glass.

They said nothing for a while, simply consumed whiskey in systematic swallows.

"I may go," Eli said when their glasses were empty.

"Go where?"

He shrugged. "I will leave the gun for you."

"I have a handgun in camp."

He snorted.

"A forty-four Special revolver," she said.

"He left it." The statement was a question.

"He" was an ex-boyfriend of Alison's. "Rick insisted I have it."

Eli snorted again, but then, he had never liked Rick. "White man's gun won't stop wolves."

"You said there weren't any wolves on the Island. Ever. Everyone knows—"

"Not . . . not wolves." He stared into the distance, as he had the last time she had visited. How old was he, really? Seventies, maybe. Indian-dark hair and skin made years hard to gauge.

"Look, Eli, I'm exhausted. I'd better hit the sleeping bag. We'll talk in the morning."

He nodded, dark eyes slitting finer than a horizon line.

It thundered that night, though Alison could see no lightning through the treetops and the rain never touched her. But that faint volcanic rumble echoed through this land of forest and freshwater lakes. It troubled her sleep as she twisted in the sleeping bag she'd installed on a mattress of pine boughs.

Drowsily, she decided the sound was just Beau growling at the noises the dark engendered. Yet everything around her hummed with expectancy: the ground, the wind lacing the pines, the lake tensing its liquid skin into a snare drum. Some invisible percussionist was sending scalding hisses of ripple after ripple ashore. The distant whiff of storm-sulfur wreathed Alison's face like smoke.

And her eyes burned behind the shutters of her lids, as if seared by fires that she could never see while awake.

October 11, 1986 *St. Paul Express-Messenger*

BALI LOW—OWNING YOUR OWN PRIVATE ISLAND

BY ALISON CARVER
STAFF WRITER

SWAN LAKE—We all dream of owning our own island.

Well, I've got one and, let me tell you, Island-owning ain't easy. Travel-and-Outdoor Section readers may pine for a piece of North Woods with a water view, but who warns them about mosquitoes, taxes, spring floods, bad roads, latrines and a dozen other unnatural shocks that isolated real estate is heir to?

TAKE TRESPASSERS. Once I had to run off the mid-'80s' version of the Wild Bunch with only the aid of a Samoyed puppy. (Rambeau did show a burgeoning talent for chewing shoe leather. Unfortunately, my marauding trespassers were barefoot.)

Yet it's a privilege, this sense of "ownership" for what will long outlive us—land, water, sky, in knowing that the earth under your feet is yours by law. You feel violated when alien trash litters the woods or you stand on the lakeshore one day and see the imprint of a human foot not yours. . . .

2

"Looks good, Beau," she said, and it did. Despite the branches that had fallen to winter ice storms, the Island appeared shipshape.

Beneath a brown blanket of brittle leaves and pine cones, moss greened the rocks, and insects stirred invisibly—a deep, below-surface current of new life shaking the forest floor as the wind rattled its leafy ceiling. Aspens and birches thrust slender white columns to the pale blue sky. Spruce, pine and fir huddled in their worn, winter-green coats like grumpy matrons, the ground beneath them gilded with fallen needles and teeming with ticks.

Switches of alder, poplar, hazelnut and sumac bristled from the ground, ready to challenge their thicker elders for a share of the sunlight that dappled the treetops. An almost aqueous light sifted through the saplings swaying like seaweed in the breeze.

The woods broadcast the silence of the depths as well as their sense of endless motion, of a secret world in eternal shift. In clearings, crickets chirped approval of a sunbath. Beau nosed among the leaves, chased dizzying scents, and snapped at an imprudent moth flushed from the mulch carpeting the forest with a pattern of ceaseless growth and decay.

Alison enjoyed spring inspection as much as Beau did. It was too early for speedboats on the lake, their constant dirt-bike roar, the foamy slashes of their wakes washing ashore. Beau kept his nose to the ground, his slim legs flashing through the underbrush as he sniffed for rodent neighbors.

On their return, they stopped at Eli's cabin, but the old man wasn't there. He'd left the rifle and whiskey on the table. The ancient wood-cased radio was softly playing a country-western station.

Alison frowned. Maybe the old guy was getting senile, living up here all alone. She'd never wondered about his family, but it would be her job to track them down if something . . . *when* something happened to him. Eli Ravenhare. At least she knew his last name now; it had been in the will.

"Bet Eli's gone fishing, Beau. Let's get back to camp."

The dog bounded ahead, so wired with freedom that stiff front and back legs sent him pronking like an antelope. Then Beau's nose was ground-bound and he was circling through the pine needles, whimpering as he went.

"Come on!"

But he didn't come.

"You're squirrely, Beau. You'll never catch those little tree rats. Come on now!"

The dog whined and tore at the spring-soft turf, spraying dead leaves until Alison coughed at the dust.

"Beau! Come!"

This time he did.

"Eli's right. You're fat and lazy." Alison watched him pant. "Or maybe you were smelling bears."

Four yards farther, she found a mound of litter; someone had dumped the contents of a garbage can. Beau hung back and barked, front legs extended until his belly kissed the ground, wolfish white head recoiling.

"Some protection."

Alison kicked through the refuse: bones and gristle, fish skins, scraps of wood and leather. At least there were no recyclables—no aluminum pop cans or glass bottles—but how could anyone into natural foods be so careless about dumping?

"Bears again," she teased Beau, who growled and avoided the spot.

The litter mound was some distance from the shoreline. Who would have hauled it this far inland? Trespassers usually camped near the water. She headed there, Beau plunging alongside. Alison broke through the last thin line of paper birch saplings . . . and froze.

The Island's shoreline growth framed an eternal scene of mirrored water and opposite shore—a watercolor landscape of bend and sweep and ripple and ruffling leaves. Alison always knew this particular place the moment she saw it—and yet never expected it. She sighed, trying to name the subtle woodland signs that told her that this—and no other—was the spot. Was it the curve where the grass thinned, where the gravel was ground nearly sand-fine? Or the juncture where water met land and almost made a real beach?

Alison again felt sharp gravel-stones impressing her small bare feet, felt chill water lapping her mosquito-bitten ankles and heard someone shouting, "Come on, ba-by. Come on in!"

She'd never done so, and she had not that day.

Demaris had.

Alison had not . . . because they weren't supposed to swim in the lake unsupervised, not even Demaris at fourteen . . . because Alison was indeed a baby, still afraid of water . . . because even people like Demaris, who knew how to swim, could drown in a drop-off, although Alison wasn't sure why.

A loon's vibrato song juggled in its throat. Alison blinked. Demaris was gone, as she had been these twenty-one years. Sweat stippled Alison's face like gooseflesh while wind chilled her skin. No. Nothing in the lake now. Nothing out there but earth and water and air. Nothing.

And nothing then. Demaris there one moment, then only a hiccoughing patch of water and something struggling at its center, like some caught fish so eager to retreat underwater that it tears its mouth free of the hook. Air was the invisible hook that Demaris struggled to cling to, her mouth spitting her last breath through a sudden new inhalation of water that iced throat, lungs, chest.

Alison had stood as if frozen by the same engulfing chill water. Then she had turned, still clutching . . . what? How could she ever forget? Her skin recorded the tracks of that long-lost child's treasure—random red lines converging in a starburst of angry color crayon on her chest. Her family feared at first that she had been fatally wounded, there had been so much blood and so little evident cause.

They had wanted her to name the place. She couldn't then. They had all run back to the lake too late. Only now, when it did no good, was she certain. Now, she knew it instantly.

Later, after Alison's "deep cuts" had been treated at the hospital emergency room in Grand Rapids, after the men and their boats were gone and people from the opposite shoreline had come over and said, whispering, that it happened like that sometimes, that drowning victims wouldn't ever be found—after all that, Alison had brought what remained of the pot to Eli.

He had washed the fragments more tenderly than the emergency-room staff had cleansed Alison's wounds. "Strong," he said. "It held strong medicine." He kept them.

She didn't object; she loved her collection of arrowheads, but was glad that someone wanted these souvenirs, relieved that she didn't have to deal with them, bury them again.

What Eli did with the shards he never said.

Now Alison wondered where they had gone. The birch trees trembled quicksilver in the wind across one hundred and eighty feet of water, waving the small, tattered flags of their leaves. Her right hand lay flattened against her chest. She realized she'd been holding her breath. It burst free, burning. Her hand flared away from the smooth knit of her turtleneck.

"You always going to hide it?" Eli had asked long after the accident, nodding at the high-buttoned neck of her sleeveless cotton shirt.

For once *she'd* been taciturn. She'd shrugged. The scars were ugly, though they'd faded over time. Adolescence became a constant strategy of dressing around them. A dermatologist had recommended camouflaging makeup—wouldn't even wash off when she went swimming, he said, smiling.

The wound had been a more traumatic alteration than breasts and sudden blood flows. It had come all at once. Perhaps if she had accepted the scars, she would have forgotten them.

Instead, Alison held the scars to herself as she'd clung to the pot that had made them: stubbornly, automatically. She'd worn high-collared halter evening gowns to school dances; any boyfriend had to bridge the moat of her personal mark of Cain. The scar became a kind of hymen, first and natural barrier to the most intimate pathways into her interior. A romantic relationship always created an awkward moment when they both had to come to terms with her scar. Still, Alison had found men who were friends as well as lovers, even if Rick had been too footloose to settle down, and John an infatuation that couldn't hold up to everyday realities. If she was single now, it was probably because everyone was more cautious about sex and relationships nowadays. She'd concluded that anyone worth anything could pass the barrier of a scar—anyone but the bearer.

Beau was growling at the woods behind her. The sound—serious, prolonged—finally broke Alison's reverie. She turned. A rangy gray dog peered through the trees, head lowered so that its sharp shoulder blades loomed above the flattened ears. This animal growled, too, showing ragged white teeth. Beau's usual sunny smile had become a fierce, black-lipped battle grin.

Then the newcomer saw Alison. It stared at her with yellow eyes centered by tiny bull's-eyes of black irises, though she felt more like target than sharpshooter. She grabbed Beau's ruff to keep him from charging this lethal-looking stray. Beau growled his independence and snapped the air to warn her hand off, then charged sideways to keep the stranger fixed in view.

The other animal lifted its head to give them a last condescending look, then vanished behind a shadowed curtain of forest. Snarling, barking, Beau tore toward the tree line. He sniffed and paced the ground, whimpering at the intruder's scent. Leg elevated, he urinated long and loudly on the place where the stranger had stood. Then he followed the trail into the underbrush, stopping to whimper his uncertainty.

At that moment of canine indecision, Alison caught up with him and rolled her fingers into the furred fat of his neck. "Enough! You *come* with me. Back to camp. Come, Beau!"

Their return was rushed. Other foreign scents crisscrossed their path, for Beau often strained against Alison's physical and vocal commands. She tried not to think of how thoroughly their visitor must have investigated their comings and goings.

At each turn of the path, a pair of intense yellow eyes seemed to flicker from view. The low, distant thunder of Beau's growls grew constant. Alison trotted alongside the dog, comforted by the curl of his coat in her fist, by his territorial instincts that made him a formidable ally.

Another face peeked through the underbrush as she passed: fawn-colored and smaller than the gray dog's massive head, but with eyes of the same lupine yellow. Alison paused, heart drumming. Lupine. Of course—the huge head and teeth, the wide cheekbones to hold powerful jaws. *All the better to eat you with, my dear.* Not dogs, but wolves! One gray, one fawn-colored and—another furred face paused in a frame of sumac even as she looked—one black. Oh, God!

"Quick, Beau, home. Home quickly!"

She was running, Beau trotting beside her, the woods whipping by, every knothole colored, in passing, an evil, predatory yellow. She was so intent on eluding the wolves that she didn't detect the people until she and Beau had almost blundered into their camp. She pulled the dog up short beside her. They crouched in the underbrush, silent because both canine and human instinct unanimously urged quiet.

Intruders. Human. Or subhuman, Alison editorialized with journalistic irony. First wolves, now debased hippies? Come on. If she hadn't been so alarmed, she might have laughed aloud and betrayed her presence. But these people, these *men* . . . so scruffy with their lace-up boots and Hell's Angel, arm-baring leather jerkins! Like something out of an American International movie, really.

Was someone filming *Jet-Ski Nazis Must Die!* on Swan Lake? Alison rubbed her tired eyes, which only intensified their burning. Beside her, Beau's sides heaved silently. She patted his closest flank; at least the dog wasn't alerting this unappetizing array of two—four, no—*five* intruders to their presence.

And their wagon, or whatever it was—a boxcar-like affair hung with exterior grids of rushes. It was drawn by two poles, but no harness or pulling beast was in sight; maybe *people* drew it along. Amend that movie title, she thought. *Gypsy Jet-Ski Nazis Must Die!* How had these buffoons managed to get a wagon onto the Island? By pontoon?

Her knees cracked as her weight shifted, but the intruders didn't hear. Well, these bozos didn't belong here. It was her Island. Usually she ordered the occasional trespasser to leave. Usually the romantic teenage couple, or pair of Huck Finn preteen boys, did. But these were five burly, filthy-looking and—her nose picked up what Beau's must have known for some time—unwashed ruffians.

Her mind riffled through options. Images of Rick's revolver, Eli's rifle—and Eli—flicked past. Reinforcement was the thing.

She was backing out of the underbrush when a sixth figure stepped down from the crude, canvas-covered wagon.

A child! Relief lightened Alison's mind. The little figure turned the sinister into the acceptable. These overgrown hippies might be trespassers, but anyone camping out with a child, with—now, yes, another child—couldn't be all bad. Maybe the . . . wolves . . . were their dogs. Amazing what terrors an active imagination could conjure. Reliving Demaris' death had darkened her usually sharp and sensible observations.

She tapped Beau's shoulder; together they made their way back to camp undisturbed. She unpacked Rick's revolver though, and loaded all six bullets.

And it was odd—here on the Island she'd known all her life and had never feared, dreading only the water fully circling it for a short part of the year—but she felt a need for quiet as she cooked and fed Beau that night. She felt that the very aspens had ears. Beau was nervous, too, his ears lifting as if skeining for unwholesome sounds. He settled near her, long white muzzle cradled on the dainty feathered forelegs that could spring him six feet in the air. Alison tucked the revolver beside her sleeping bag.

She slept well; the piney woods were an excellent tranquilizer. Once she awoke—to hear an owl hooting—and noticed that Beau had gone. Otherwise, nothing disturbed her except dreams of drowning on dry land. She woke slowly, as always. Slowly her location impressed itself upon her: the pine boughs beneath her, the sleeping bag zipped up to her chin to shut out the cool morning air. It kept her dry as well, for a spring rain was falling. Raindrops pattered around her in a peaceful, lazy sound; she didn't even mind if her face got wet.

Her face wasn't getting wet.

Alison's nearsighted eyes opened. They were just able to see the huge gray wolfish head four feet away, staring at her. Then she noticed the lifted leg.

The animal was pissing—pissing on her sleeping bag!

She would have shot upright, except that she was wrapped like a fillet in tinfoil. The creature shook its hind leg, sniffed its liquid offering and trotted toward the woods. Alison patted for the plastic case with her contact lens gear zipped into the bag with her.

By the time she'd wrestled the bag open and put in her "eyes," the scene was entirely normal.

. . . Except for a pungent puddle of yellow liquid cooling in a cradle of canvas between her feet.

Sunday, January 19, 1989 *St. Paul Express-Messenger*

SELF-DEFENSE: WOMEN'S RIGHT AND RESPONSIBILITY

BY ALISON CARVER
STAFF WRITER

Jujitsu and the art of affirmative action?

This may not sound like a marriage made in heaven, but modern women who turn to the martial arts for self-defense are finding, of all things, philosophy with feminist overtones.

Westerners have striven for mind over matter since the Crusades; since Adam, perhaps. (He, being male, was mind, right? And Eve, being female, didn't know what was the matter. Wrong.)

"Westerners," explains Judy Phelps, a corporate lawyer, judo black belt and local NOW chapter officer, "suffer from a split of mind and body that leeches the soul from our culture."

Phelps thinks that the Oriental martial arts can heal the ailing Western split personality: "Instead of subscribing to the old Judeo-Christian psycho-sexual split," she says, "Eastern philosophers strive for unity of body and mind, spirit and matter, male and female in the dance of the universe. When that philosophy meets the physical world, it's called the dance of 'creative destruction.' "

That means, say women who practice the martial arts, that women as well as men can subscribe to the art of self-defense, which by nature must offend someone. That women, too, must be willing and able to hurt someone—including themselves—in defense of self or someone else.

3

The strangers were gone, but not their garbage.

"Stay out of that stuff, Beau!"

Alison prowled the empty clearing Saturday morning, looking for wheel tracks in the trampled grass. Obviously, the wagon had arrived before the spring flood, but how could it *leave* the Island with the lake water still high?

She ranged the Island's dense interior, finding no trace of the party, nor of any watching wolfish faces. The people had been real; maybe the wolves came from an anxious imagination.

Beau rambled away, returning with broken branches for her to hurl for him. His white form ghosted through the leaf-bare underbrush. He always dropped the stick at her feet, dancing back to brace himself for the next pursuit. The dog's playful confidence increased her own. By mid-afternoon, when she found Eli's cabin still empty, she wasn't unduly worried. She did take the loaded rifle; not a good thing to leave lying around.

By evening she had relaxed and accepted the solitude again. Going from tin can to camp fire had a way of improving chili's flavor. Alison burped contentedly, wondering why she wolfed down her food up here like she was on a deadline at her desk. Beau had turned up his nose at Gainesburgers and was off on an evening ramble. Though without any legal title, he felt as she did about the Island: It was his, he was at home here.

She opened a paperback novel that had grown dusty on her condo shelf for over a year. The murky Coleman lantern light made reading a furtive pleasure, as it had been under the covers by flashlight. No annoying bugs buzzed in its yellow halo. Alison felt as cozy as a passenger on a ponderous cruise ship, bound nowhere but afloat on her own snug isolation, her aloneness, her independence of parking lots and pay toilets and anything not of her own invention.

Something bounded into the nimbus of her camp fire. "Not another stick, boy. My arm's out of joint—hey, bring it here!"

He came, his mouth set in a smiling grimace, holding something big in his mouth. He laid it on the ground beside her and politely stepped back.

The paperback fell shut as she dropped it beside Beau's offering: a torn-off hunk of roasted meat. She touched fire-crisped flesh, still warm.

"Beau! Where'd you get this?"

He nosed it toward her.

"I don't want the greasy old thing!" The meat was obviously game that someone had caught and cooked. Maybe Eli . . . But this was fire-seared meat. Eli's cabin had a wood stove, and Eli felt no city slicker's thrill at cooking raw food over a camp fire.

"Where'd you get it, huh? Show me."

Alison started jamming things into a backpack: canteen, flashlight, contact lens packet, the revolver. She felt a need for haste, a sudden nakedness. Someone was killing things on the Island. Not squirrels; the meat had come from a larger animal. Rabbit? Beaver? Deer? Out of season. Lord, some trespassing damn fool could shoot *her*—or Eli, and where was he when she needed him?—could shoot Beau, an obvious target with his arctic-white coat.

She kicked dirt and leaves onto her camp fire, dampening its treacherous light. Something was wrong. First the brutal-looking strangers, then Eli's too-long absence, now raw meat roasted. A chili taste backed up in her throat.

She lifted the rifle last. "Okay, Beau. Go find it. Where is it, boy, huh? Where is it?"

He eyed the meat cooling on the ground but responded to her eager tone. Rambeau loved showing off discoveries.

The full moon was bright enough to paint Beau into a guiding white beacon through the woods. Alison followed him. The dog led her to the Island's center, an area she had crossed many times that day—or thought she had. Her nose picked up what Beau's followed—scents of smoke and hot flesh coupling on the chill night air. Surprisingly, the first whiff stirred her civilized stomach.

Adrenaline revved her circulation. Her sinuses suddenly cleared, as they did before a *taekwondo* competition.

Something was wrong, but she was ready for it.

Beau approached their target by circling first left, then right, always pushing nearer. Alison realized that he was keeping the meat scent ahead but placing them upwind of its source so no reciprocal odor could alert whatever—whomever—they stalked. Beau knew who; he'd seen them.

She kept the rifle pointed to the earth, the proper safety technique, and felt decidedly unsafe. Beau, belly-down, was wriggling forward. Alison crouched, too, walking on her haunches, her muscles snapping in protest.

Firelight was flickering off the trunks of the big pines; she could see figures gathered around the flames, hear the pop of fat striking fire. A deer hung from a birch limb by its hocks, partially butchered.

Alison winced. A Bambi partisan, she hated the annual parade of cars heading south for the Cities, dead deer lashed to their hoods, barbaric trophies of man's inhumanity to harmless beasts for no reason but ego. Many sport hunters rarely ate venison anymore, and what modern food hunters would eat a kill on the spot?

These men would, came the unspoken answer.

She watched them, her lips wry with disapproval but silent. It was the same rough gang she'd spotted yesterday. Their wagon sat under a fir that had shed its lower branches to a height of ten feet.

Other scents wafted from the fire's heat. No, not scents—Alison corrected herself with a good reporter's precision—stenches. The odors of unwashed clothes, bodies and teeth and unkempt hair. Alison had visited enough transient shelters to recognize neglect amplifying human smell into a stink.

The fivesome were gnawing meat as fast as they pulled it from the spit that bridged the fire, reminding her of trolls in some Hans Christian Andersen fairy tale.

Well, she had them on trespassing and killing deer out of season—and unless she was wrong, the carcass was a protected female. Great. She just had to get off the Island, get the Keewatin sheriff and get back in time to nail the bastards.

She balanced on her heels, ready to retreat, when something gleamed in the opposite fringe of forest. "Damn," Alison hissed under her breath.

Beau's ears perked. No doubt he knew, had always known.

"Damn scrounging . . . dog."

She eyed the other animal's belly-down form in the shadows. Her so-called wolves must be the men's half-wild dogs. How had Beau nipped a piece of cooked meat from these fierce guard dogs and the five men around the fire?

As if in answer to her question, the other animal wriggled into the firelight on its stomach, growling submissively. The men jumped up and began hurling stones. It dodged the rocks, dancing forward and snapping its formidable jaws. Alison recognized the black dog she had spotted in the woods. It was leaner and less furred than Beau, but its lurid eyes shone with cunning as it teased the big men who faced it.

A fawn-flick of shadow slipped from the underbrush and darted for the fire. It was smaller than the black dog, and faster. In seconds it had torn a slab of meat from the spit, lips grinning back from its teeth so they wouldn't burn.

The men wheeled, outflanked. A gray dog joined the black one to harry their heels. Then a darker shadow sprinted from the wagon—on two legs—to snatch a fallen piece of meat from the fire's edge and retreat.

"Cursed tiefs—big fur, little feet—we roast you next!" roared one of the men. The shouter lumbered toward the wagon while his friends pelted the retreating dogs. In seconds the canine raiding crew had melted back into the night's black underbelly, even the beige one with the mouthful of meat.

Alison glanced at Beau with heightened respect. Apparently he, too, had braved this gang to snag his trophy. She huddled in the brush, drawing the rifle butt to hand, fearful of a search, of having to answer for the marauding of wild dogs. But the strangers were more concerned with the thief in their midst.

The burly man returned from the wagon, a struggling creature hoisted in his grip. Alison gasped. Small legs were churning in escape motions. Human legs.

No one heard her.

"Cursed Slinkers," another man muttered. He circled the fire and squinted into the darkness.

Nothing moved.

Alison could hear mewling now, like that of a terrified child. Beside her, Beau growled softly.

"Here!" The man thrust his prisoner high above his head. "Cursed Slinkers want fresh meat, here is thing to chew upon."

A thin keening rose from within the wagon.

"Tiefs will eat tiefs," another said, laughing as the first man tossed him the little figure.

"Yawfren will need big stick to spit whole Littlelost," another raw voice suggested.

Perhaps the men only meant to frighten the child they tossed again between them, Alison thought; though every instinct told her that they were not so harmless. They spoke a debased patois she hadn't heard before. It reminded her of voyageurs, of Iron Rangers from an earlier era, of Shakespeare and backwoods imbeciles. Of *Deliverance,* the motion picture.

"Like little Oink, will squeal," said Yawfren, poking the figure until it squeaked.

Alison stood and plowed through the underbrush, Beau at her heel. The rifle was level at her hip, her forefinger on the cold steel trigger. She was shaking, as she did before addressing a high-school convocation on the attractions of the journalistic life—inside, but not in a way that reached her voice or hands.

"Put the kid down," she ordered.

The men looked at her as if she had risen from the earth itself. No one moved to release the child.

"Put the kid down," she repeated. "This is my land. You don't belong here. You could be prosecuted for killing deer out of season. I bet you guys don't even have a license *in* season. You're in big trouble."

She spoke slowly, as if addressing speakers of a foreign language. It was as fast as she could talk and still draw the shallow, rapid breaths that were all she could manage.

One man pointed as if in awe. "Spirit Slinker." He indicated Beau, who growled obligingly.

The man called Yawfren nodded. "Twice time see Spirit

Slinker. Something die tonight. Some . . . tief." He turned toward the man who held the child.

"No!" Alison warned. "I'll shoot if I have to."

They stared at her casually, as if she were mad or not quite fully there. Yawfren's big dirty hands reached for the small form so limp and still now.

Alison jerked the rifle skyward and fired.

The forest's ruffled feathers rustled. Leaves and birds, and even squirrels, scattered invisibly in the dark above them. The men cocked shaggy heads. God, are these guys dumb, Alison thought; they act as if they haven't seen a gun before. Then how did they shoot the deer?

The answer came as she examined them in the dodging fire-light—as she saw the lines of edged weapons looming above their wide leather belts, the boots tied to their calves with thongs, the raw-leather jerkins and trousers, the ax lying on the ground.

Some sort of hippie survivalist outfit, she figured, maybe with kidnapped children from failed marriages, running rogue in the wilderness. Perhaps they'd hidden out in the remote, protected Boundary Waters Canoe Area, preying on vacationers. God knew how many bones—animal and human—littered their trail.

Alison felt a familiar quickening. It wasn't quite fear, though it was like it. It was the reflex of a reporter smelling a hot—an unheard-of—story, human hackles rising; where Beau sniffed meat, she had a nose for news. Who knew how long these guys had run wild? What they'd done? Where they'd come from originally? Who knew. . . .

"Put the kid down!" she ordered again.

They finally tumbled that the creature in their grasp was "the kid." The man who held it began to comply, but Yawfren, the big dumb bruiser, walked straight for Alison, Beau and the rifle.

"Look, man, I don't want to shoot you, but I will. No court would convict me. You guys are unreal, and this is my land."

Nothing stopped Yawfren, who was about six-foot-five and as belly-broad as a Hell's Angel, who stank like last week's gym shoes and came on like a Tiger tank.

"Listen, I *will* shoot—"

The kid was being lowered to the ground—maybe a four-year-old—oh, God, the face, the filthy little face! So old, so weary-leery, like one of those kids with premature-aging syndrome, like an abuse-withered child kept far smaller than its age warranted . . . and that damn Yawfren the Barbarian coming straight on and the trigger right there, she knew where and what it was, all she had to do was squeeze it and hold very, very steady for the recoil—

Beau leaped, snarling like a bear, when Yawfren was almost close enough to grab the rifle barrel. Alison saw a long ladder of white fur springing up before her and Yawfren's big bearish hands closing on the maned neck. If he hurt Beau . . . !

Snarls accelerated around her. Lean canine bodies were dashing from every direction; teeth snapped and harried the other men. Alison had only Yawfren and Beau to worry about, a blur of shifting white and brown too close to shoot.

Beau fell back, regrouping. Yawfren didn't hesitate a second; he tore the ax from his belt, then reared and roared toward her, shouting something like "halven-beast tief."

She shot point blank.

This time the sound froze everything alive in the clearing. Wild dogs cowered, bellies brushing the ground. Beau twisted and yelped in mid-leap. The woodsmen turned to watch.

Yawfren stared, one big dirty paw clawing his gut.

Alison retreated, denying the moment past, sweeping the rifle barrel aside like a lance she forswore using. The big man fell, gargling a word before his head smashed facedown on the forest floor.

Alison looked up to explain, justify, apologize. The remaining four men fled as if eluding a demon. Even the wild dogs backed from the clearing, tails curled between their hind legs, until the dark ate them. Only the dirty, thin-limbed child with the face of an ancient angel remained. It limped toward the fallen man.

"Taker!" it spat. Then it kicked Yawfren's still leg into a spasm resembling life.

The child's condition erased everything else. "You . . . you poor thing." Alison knelt to take a tiny, shriveled hand.

It drew back with a snarl.

Sunday, April 14, 1991 *St. Paul Express-Messenger*

CHILD ABUSE IS A POISON IN THE BLOOD

BY ALISON CARVER
STAFF WRITER
(ANALYSIS)

It boggles the mind to imagine generations of children reared with abuse—then growing up to expect nothing better for their own children.

Society must constantly reinforce the taboo against child abuse for a reason: It is an ancient human failing. The family is neither natural nor infallible. That's why the innocence of children, their inviolateness, is emphasized and even sentimentalized in literature and living room alike: to make what is unthinkable impossible. Yet making the possible so unthinkable is exactly what allows us to veil our eyes, shut our ears, turn our heads and look straight past evidence of child abuse. We didn't see, suspect, couldn't believe . . . who would have thought?

We all should have.

After covering a trial as long, complicated and sensational as the Blue Earth multi-generational child-abuse "cycle" (so the sociologists call it), I can never again view childhood with the same presumed innocence I knew in my own days of baby buggies and Barbie dolls.

4

The children numbered five.

Alison lined them up before the fire. She'd had to crawl into the wagon's close, dark stink to extract four of them one by one. They hadn't resisted, but they hadn't helped either.

Only Beau's ranging presence at her back kept them still and fascinated now—that and the prone hummock of Yawfren's toppled body. Small brown hands flared like starfish toward Beau's snow-bright coat.

"Silver Slinker," murmured one—a girl, Alison thought. "Cloud killer."

"Beau." Alison nodded to the dog, amazed that her voice did not shake. "His name is Beau."

"Beau," a child repeated listlessly.

Their eyes flicked to the dead man, to the circle of wood shadows. Alison looked; yellow, unblinking eyes made a ragged amber necklace in the darkness. Slinkers, she thought, to these little ones. To me, they must be wolves; lean, hungry wolves. Competitors. She glanced to the spit of hissing meat, then to childish ankle and wrist bones swelling at the ends of pipe-cleaner limbs.

In a few messy minutes she had managed to hack off the most edible meat from the haunch with Yawfren's ax and distribute part to the children and pack the rest in case they were desperate for food later. Beau watched, head tilted and red tongue lolling, a practiced posture that expected reward.

She tossed him a hunk of meat. Beyond them, yellow eyes watched. The rifle lay within a hand span, but Alison knew that a quick, tightening noose of hungry wolves could make millimeters into miles.

She rose, the ax cocked, and picked up the rifle. Everything stiffened in the clearing—children, Beau, even the trees, it seemed. Even the dead man. She wasn't used to causing anything to hold its breath.

Alison walked to the birch and with a few ax slashes, cut the rope that held the deer's carcass aloft. It crashed to earth, still so fresh that the limbs buckled as if alive. Before she returned to the fire, she sensed the wolves pooling toward the fallen food with the inevitable silent greed of water seeping downhill.

The children ignored the so-called Slinkers, pushing meat and hanks of stringy hair into their mouths at once.

"Listen," she told them, told herself, "we have to get out of here. The other men might come back."

Eye-whites glittered like opals among mud and grease.

"You can eat, then get your things—"

Their pearly eyes consulted each other.

"From the wagon," she said, explaining.

"Nothing in wagon," a taller child growled.

"No . . . belongings?"

"We belongings."

"We have to leave the Island before the others come back." No answer, just the same mindless, mechanical chewing that echoed the wolves by the birch tree. "Have you names?"

"Names?" A light voice, incurious. Alison couldn't tell who had spoken. She felt that she faced a multiplicity of fun-house mirrors, that she'd somehow fractured into these squalid little shapes, that it was herself who answered her.

"Names. Like his—Beau. I'm Alison."

Tangled heads shook. "No names," the tallest said roughly.

"Littlelost," came a soft, tentative answer from the smallest.

Alison knelt to the ragged elfin figure, resisting the rancid smell it radiated. "You *are* very little. The Littl*est,* is that what you mean?"

"Little*lost,*" spat the child who'd kicked Yawfren, showing contempt for Alison's persistent stupidity. "All Littlelost."

"That's . . . what you're called?"

"All Littlelost!" it repeated angrily.

Alison stood. Her back ached from crouching. She was rotten with kids; let some social worker in Duluth sort it out. "Okay. Listen up, Littlelost. We have to get moving. Get to a boat. But we have to be very, very quiet, so we don't let those bad men find us. Link hands now—"

They stared at her, unmoving. "Make a line. Hold hands."

Nothing.

In the standoff of silence, Beau moved down the bedraggled line, sniffing small hands for meat. Some reached, bewitched, for the white fur. Alison winced as greasy fingers clamped into Beau's coat.

"All right. Follow the dog; the dog'll follow me. Beau."

He came, thank God, far more mindful than they. They stumbled barefoot alongside him like a set of ugly ducklings skirting their swan-white mother.

Alison bowed into the curtain of brush, holding it up for the procession to pass first. She looked back. In the clearing, Yawfren threatened no one, the dying fire seared only the still night air, and wolfish teeth flashed on the thin, pale bones of a deer. The embers would wink safely out before the yellow eyes watching her warily.

The knapsack thumped between Alison's shoulder blades as they tramped through the woods, but she was glad she'd grabbed it when she had. No way would she risk returning to her camp; the men might be waiting.

She debated trying Eli's cabin, but if rifle shots hadn't roused him, she doubted he was back. Where had he gone, he who was always there? Maybe the men had killed him, maybe that's why his cabin was empty. Maybe they had shot him—no, they had no guns, she remembered. Maybe they had killed him somehow, claiming this Island for their own, not knowing that Alison would come.

She paused, hearing Beau and his charges crash to a stop behind her. The rifle was heavy and her arm was beginning to ache. If they'd killed Eli, had they buried the body somewhere? Or . . . maybe they'd drowned him. His cabin was near the shore. No one would ever know, not like Demaris. . . .

"Come on," she ordered her troop, turning for the shoreline, hoping to hit the narrowest neck of water. She'd worry about fitting them all in the boat when she got there.

The party bored into the woods like a threshing machine through wheat—flattening and rending as they went, raising a miasma of moss, mold and leaf dust, of tiny grubs and fallen moths. Breathing became harder, or she was tired. The children trudged beside Beau, heads bowed.

Alison finally stopped. "I thought I was headed south, but we should have reached the shoreline by now. It's hard with no sun, no landmarks."

No one sympathized with her incompetence. She knew the Island, for God's sake, knew every inch. They should have reached the land's limits by now, no matter what direction she'd taken.

"The Blazer, Beau, go find the Blazer. We're going home, boy. Go on!" The dog perked up at his name, at her cajoling, play-time voice. He gamboled ahead, leaving Littlelost in his wake.

Alison reached for a small, greasy hand. "All right, let's chase Beau. It's a game. Follow Beau."

They followed, mechanically, wordlessly. Alison sensed a lightening in the darkness, a languid retreat of deepest night. Above, dead black draped the trees like funeral crepe, but she could glimpse a pale limb here, a broken branch there.

Wishful thinking? The party blundered after Beau, his white hocks just visible ahead. They stumbled and pushed forward without ever getting anywhere. They never crossed the fatal clearing again, for which Alison was grateful; they never neared her camp or Eli's cabin or any landmark, for which she was fearful.

Shadows with lolling tongues ran alongside. Alison was too exhausted to fear the wolves' escort—it was simply one more absurdity in a wood gone wild with absurdity. And then milky, silken skeins of light were threading through the branches, and shadow melted into the objects around her, which budded from the night into their full, individual forms of tree and bush.

Brightness beamed ahead, like dawn magnifying its pale sheen on water tenfold. Alison stumbled toward the tunnel of light, welcoming the mirroring water for the first time in her life, wanting to end this nightmare, this endless night and even-more-endless forest.

They burst into the tepid morning sunshine together, canine and lupine noses twitching to taste the air, children squinting their eyes shut on brazen sunlight, Alison blinking as if to shake off a dream.

The mountains looming ahead thrust their dawn-ripened spires into a foaming confection of clouds. Wind-rippled waves of green whipped toward them—long, rolling breakers of grass crested with flowers colored in a kaleidoscopic array.

A line of blossoms foamed toward their knees, but at contact it shattered and flew up into the air, releasing an odor of rotten onions. The flowers floated away petal by petal, high above the trees behind them, wind-strummed into an incessant buzzing that sounded eerily like whispered songs. Alison jumped backward, crushing grass and releasing another wave of air-borne blossoms. Pretty, stinking petals fluttered past her face like butterfly wings and tangled in her hair. She shuddered as if attacked by bats.

"What are these things? And the water! Where's the damn water? The lake."

No one answered. Beau was leaping after the winged flowers as if chasing Frisbees in Minnehaha Park. She turned. The forest loomed at her back as abrupt and solid as a wall, its known darkness beckoning.

A droning sound came from the sky, swarmed her dazed senses, sawed through her stupor. She must be . . . tired. Crazy. After all, she'd shot a man, wandered all night. Distant humming—a train of unwelcome thoughts driving toward her? Not a train . . . a plane! Rescue. A recreational pilot who could radio back their location, or a forest ranger with wings.

Alison ran knee-deep into the alpine meadow, ignoring the eerie brush of petaled wings past her face, looking up. The sky was bright, as pale as water, without color. Shadow skimmed it. For a moment she felt that she stood at the nadir of some alien element, beneath—her heart tripped, stumbled, pumped again—*water,* and watched a sting ray circle.

The shadow droned nearer, forcing her head back to keep the ambiguous shape in view. Yes, that crucifix of the air, that familiar, reassuring silhouette of outcast wings and long, lightweight body. A plane. Rescuers. Someone to explain who they were, these children and those men. Someone to explain *to.*

The enormity of the previous night's act paralyzed Alison. How could she justify what had happened? There would be a news story. *She* would be the subject of it; *she* would have to answer to the public, to herself.

Littlelost squeals erupted near her. They were nothing to the screeching in her mind, the roar of the plane that dipped to take a look at her, at a civilized woman who had killed. . . . The shadow was slicing edgewise toward her from the sky, like an accusation. She lifted her forearms to her face, crossing them.

Then whiteness instead of dark was surging over her. Sharp nails and a hurled weight hit her chest. She fell backward to the ground, Beau panting above her. A huge, dark form sliced the trees with a cutting edge of wing as bright as a blade. Sunlight knifed off a vast metal surface that wheeled into the sky again, flapping its wings. Severed branches and leaves pelted her.

Alison sat up, pushing Beau aside. *Flapping its wings.* Birds did it. Bees did it. Maybe even unsentimental fleas did it. But airplanes . . . didn't . . . flap . . . their . . . wings. Not any airplane on earth.

A half-dozen flapping shadows skewered the sky. Alison saw them clearly, now that she no longer expected to see something predictable. Circling like vultures, huge, mottled forms hummed with mechanical persistence, odd totemic faces—a hybrid of machine and insect—between gossamer wings that lifted to ride the upper air currents.

One dove again, gliding to miss the woods, slipping between them and the forest so they would be cut off, as the pilot intended. Closer it came, and there was no pilot; there was only a pitiless, gigantic dragonfly casting an endless shadow on an ocean of grass, stalking them.

Alison clambered upright. She pushed/pulled the children toward the bunched forest behind them. Beau barked and nipped at heels, thinking it a game, herding Littlelost like sheep. Wolves scattered. Sulfur scent tanged the air. Hot wind rippled the shirt on Alison's back, raising instant wetness under the pack.

The droning lifted in pitch to keen like a demented jackhammer. Beau whined and flashed into the woods. Hands to ears, Alison stumbled after, the trees above shuddering, leaves and limbs clattering down again.

Forty feet into the forest, they stopped as if one—children, wolves, Alison and Beau—and waited. Much later, when the whining had faded, Alison walked back to the edge of the wood. Leaves had fallen from the trees like pepper from a mill. Among them lay metallic flakes as large as palm fronds, almost two by three feet. Alison braced herself to lift one, but it was as light as a smoke wraith, with serrated edges sharper than the top of a tin can. She watched a wire-thin line of blood bead on her palm.

A Littlelost had joined her. "Etherion courser," it piped in a wise, grave voice. "Etherion. No use to run."

Alison consulted the hard-bitten little face. "What do you mean, no use?"

"Littlelost never fast enough. Where there are coursers, soon come Takers."

Her fist clenched shut on her cut at the thought of confronting more of the brutish woodsmen. She wasn't used to wounds any crueler than a paper cut, and once she would have glibly labeled the metal flake at her feet a refugee from a particularly overblown West-Coast wall sculpture. Here, now, it fell from the sky, one of many such sheddings from a winged thing neither bird nor beast—nor machine.

Beyond the fluttering birch leaves a blue immensity yawned. Alison scanned for shadows she knew weren't there now—floaters of the id. Dragon scales. Were they poisonous? The cut stung. Her eyes burned from looking.

The Island . . . fatigue drained down her limbs. She sat bonelessly, knees bracing her forearms, her palms open and empty except for the crease of blood across one. It wasn't the Island anymore—or it was more than Island. It was . . . mountain ranges in Minnesota? Displaced, like the Littlelost and herself?

Woodlore didn't matter here, Alison knew, studying the real and unreal about her, reassured by the trees and Rambeau, stunned by the clump of Littlelost watching her for direction and decision. She couldn't find anything familiar in all this alteration.

All she found was her self, her personal true North, marooned in an insanely exhausted state somewhere between dream and dislocation. A sullen pit of gut feeling told her that wherever she was, this place had its own rules and regulations and that she didn't know a one of them.

Alison laughed softly. It was better than crying. Beau padded over, brow furrowed. He knew something was really wrong. So did she, at last. Everything was wrong, and she finally had found the story of a lifetime: an environment so askew that she didn't have the slightest notion of how to fix it. No rewrite job would ease her alienation or erase this bizarre reality. What did she know of wee folk in the woods and slave masters with ax-girded jerkins, of waiting wolves and things that whirred in the brightness, of etherion coursers?

What did she know of fairy tales?

FIRST PLACE, METROPOLITAN FEATURE—"YOUNG POET SPEAKS TRUTH WITHOUT RESERVATION" BY ALISON CARVER, ST. PAUL EXPRESS-MESSENGER, 1982.

She is sweet sixteen, but no one threw a birthday party to celebrate that teenage benchmark; not long after, she gave birth to a son.

She holds the infant on her lap, a madonna but no virgin, that much is obvious. The child's father is absent, mysterious; she will say nothing about him. Perhaps he was a shower of gold—or a swan—or simply the sky above Leech Lake Reservation in northern Minnesota. She is as innocent as rain and keener than ice.

Her name—Becky Smith—doesn't sound Indian, but she is Chippewa, of the larger Ojibwa nation. And she is a smith—a word-smith.

WITH NO WARNING, this shy child from the selvage edge of a culture shrunk to a thin seam on the horizon of our greater, engulfing social fabric, speaks with a simple power that has seen her poems exhibited in Washington, D.C. The program was meant to encourage minority children to express themselves and their culture, but no one expected it to unearth the likes of Becky Smith:

WILD RICE

He just blew away,
That damn Indian,
Down Reservation Road
Leaving a spoor
Of broken bottles
And crushed packs of
Unfiltered Kools,
Spending his seed that sweat-lodge summer
(Wind-borne dandelion silk)
On anonymous clods of Indian earth.
You, baby
Me
Our father
He dead.

"Odjibwa travels far, into a cavern in the earth and down into the land of the dead . . . then the bone buffalo warns Odjibwa that he has come where no living man has gone."

5

Leaves crunched underfoot, sere gold and copper leaves.

Alison shuddered. Were they leaves, or were they fallen scales from a wing-borne monster?

They trod the forest's primeval dimness, safe in shadow and yet not safe. There were phantom echoes of their progress—a parallel trail of Slinkers? Or of the rabid men who'd captured the Littlelost? The children accompanied Alison as automatically as the dog did. They moved, heading nowhere, seeking something that Alison defined as "normal."

She should have realized that the season had not changed, though the terrain had, that the carpet of desiccated leaves was not the norm, even for this unlikely landscape.

What blossomed before them resembled a water-filled gravel pit. A swamp as big as a small lake, its mottled surface looked like a giant coruscated water lily the color of putrid fruit. Tortured trees fenced its unhealthy dimensions with ashen trunks. Foul odor flung itself at them—scents of decay overladen with a bitter metallic aftertaste. Beau buried his snout in the leaves, rubbing it through the brittle litter, whimpering.

Protruding from the soup of water, scum and vegetation like leftover stock bones were sharp, mechanical shapes reminiscent of those that had harried them on the wood's verge.

"We just saw them aloft," Alison said, trying to dovetail the contradictory pieces of this puzzle-landscape.

A Littlelost eyed her slantwise. "These older. Old . . . but not ripe."

"Ripe?" Alison examined the eerily still swampwater in its coat of many contaminations. A fretwork of rush bridges floated on the stagnant surface.

"Etherion pit." Only one Littlelost spoke, but all stared at the water, their eyes as old as ancient Indians'.

"Takers' place," another noted.

From their murmured catchwords, Alison was beginning to construct a scenario. "This is where the Takers were bringing you! Why?"

"Not here. Not ripe yet."

"Somewhere like here?"

Heads nodded slowly, their owners still mesmerized by the sight.

"What do you—what would you have done there?"

A grubby hand pointed. "Walk on rushes over water. Gather etherion."

"Walk on water? Not sink?"

"We are Littlelost!" one answered. "We walk on water. That is why Takers take us. To gather etherion."

"Scales; you gather the sky-beast scales when they fall?"

A tight, uncommunicative headshake from the eldest, or the biggest, at least. "First they fall. Then they rot. Then ripen. Then float. We gather what is left."

"Scavengers," she said, her mind revolting at the notion of children being forced to skim corruption off a swamp. "You mean the heavy scales sink beneath the water and rot and then rise to the surface in another form?" Heads nodded. "This etherion must be useful, but for what?" Heads shook. They had not thought beyond their servitude, and certainly the Takers didn't look like they could explain overall realities, even if they wanted to. Takers!

Alison looked around. "More Takers here?"

Littlelost shrugged. Their faces had deadened and sharpened as they surveyed a familiar abomination. Alison turned them with the abrupt authority of a nanny. "Come on! I'd rather face the flyers than their graveyards. We'll leave the forest and Takers and Slinkers far behind."

They followed her mutely, as if the mere sight of the etherion swamp had sucked their will. Rambeau growled as he trotted alongside, a low thunder that rumbled until the trees ahead finally thinned and they glimpsed a fresh expanse of empty sky. They stood warily in the open again. Alison listening to scampering squirrels and chattering birds and hoping they were what she assumed they were. The skies were blankly blue. Normal. Maybe.

"Where are we going?" piped the dirtiest Littlelost.

"We?"

Skepticism wasn't wasted on that particular Littlelost. "Big Ones know where they go. Always take Littlelost."

"You're no longer prisoners. You can go anywhere you wish."

"Not to the Rookeries." This child was so dingy that its age and sex remained question marks. "Too far by foot."

Filthy little faces nodded solemnly.

"Rookeries? Is that where the etherion coursers nest?" She'd asked one question too many. All five faces tightened into stubborn, inexpressive knots. "Look, kids, I need your help. I may be big, but I'm lost, too. I don't know where I'm going. I don't even know where I *am.*"

"We go." The Littlest insinuated sticky fingers into Alison's hand and tugged gently.

So they followed the border of the wood, dappled by alien silhouettes. Looking up, Alison detected differences in the leaf shapes. Some were huge, others tiny; none fit the palm-sized range of native North Woods foliage. Oh, Lord, she was worse than lost . . . she was dislocated!

Tree trunks glimmered with unnerving phosphorescence in the shadows, making every knot a glittering eye. The leaves that quickened to the wind high above rasped as they moved.

The party kept the forest on its left simply because Alison couldn't bear to leave a once-familiar presence. She was a child clinging to her mother's green skirts while a world of alien Big Ones loomed all around. Only, Alison's "Big Ones" were the mountain peaks bristling across the meadows. They would have been lovely had they not been so insanely out of place.

Beau gamboled on the outskirts of the party, his black-lipped, Samoyed smile revealing his sense of camaraderie and adventure. A romp. He must think they were having a nice, long, endless romp in the long, endless woods on the brink of the unthinkable mountains.

"What do they call these peaks?" Alison asked the tallest Littlelost, who came up to her elbow.

The child's face squinched so tight that Alison expected the dirt to flake and fall off. It didn't. "Mountains have names?"

"Usually. In my land, anyway," she replied.

"What's your land like?"

"Like this, but different."

"What do they call these mountains in your land?"

"Out of place!" Alison laughed nervously, fighting a sense of unreality. She shouldn't infect these waifs with her insecurity; they had their own problems. "But let's us name these mountains, then."

"You have a great liking for names." The tallest frowned.

"It keeps things in their proper places. We could use some of that now. Any ideas for the mountains? No?"

A tug at Alison's hand made her look down. "High Mountains," the Littlest suggested shyly.

The largest Littlelost spat. "Stupid. All mountains are high."

"Faraway Mountains," said another.

"And if we go there?" the tallest demanded scornfully. "Do we call them the Nearby Mountains then?"

"Let's compromise," Alison suggested, "and call them the Middling Mountains."

"What is 'compromise'?" a child asked.

"Doing not one thing, or another, but a third thing that everybody can agree upon."

"Nothing that anybody likes, then," came the answer.

"Yes. We'll be fair and realistic and do nothing that anybody likes." She smiled, but they didn't reciprocate.

She'd begun their trek with energy and optimism, even if both were forced under the alien circumstances. By midday, when Alison sat on a log to dole out cold venison, they were all tired and untalkative. She threw Beau the bones and wiped her meat-greased fingers on a fallen leaf. The Littlelost followed her example, then watched her.

"We need water, kids."

They watched her. No help there. She rose, queasy from the unaccustomed meat, but glad it had been cooked at least. That might not be possible in the future; meat in any form might not be possible. She led them on, scouring her brains for tidbits on wilderness survival. "Should have done that Outward Bound story four years ago," she muttered, scrambling up a slope. The meadowland had roughened and the ground beneath her boots was lumpy.

Grass and thistles grew knee-high now, a green, mottled carpet that hissed with wind. For a moment Alison felt as though she waded into a rising tide of water. A sudden panic made her retreat, made her look beyond the supernaturally towering pines to . . . the bald and rocky crest of a mountain.

They were *on* a mountainside already, just where the tree line thinned. Alison, suddenly dizzy, turned to see the meadow plunge away before her toward the crease of a valley. She felt about to fall off the side of the world. Minnesota was a flat-earth theorist's dream, damn it! Not a rumpled landscape crowned with tree lines and mountain peaks.

"Listen!" cried a Littlelost.

Beau's ears pricked, then he was bounding toward the trees and their dark shadows.

"Wait!" For Alison now heard what the others had: the lucid tinkle of falling water, a sound as welcoming as a hotel-lobby fountain. Her mouth blossomed with saliva as she realized how parched she was.

She ran after Beau, and the Littlelost followed. They found a waterfall, a glistening veil of liquid that tumbled like bridal tulle down a rocky scar in the hillside before it splashed over boulders to form a pool.

Beau, belly-down, was lapping from the pool when Alison arrived. She wanted to urge caution, but the sight of the clear, still-quivering water made her join him in that long, cold, wet kiss of nature.

"Great." Alison smiled as she sat up, her thirst quenched. "Drink." The Littlelost watched her and Beau, leery, hanging back. "Come on! It's all right, honest."

Finally they scrambled down and lapped up water eagerly, not getting up for a long while. Each Littlelost wiped the back of a filthy hand over a filthy mouth. Each Littlelost bore a grin of clean skin.

"Okay," she said. "If there's running water, we can take a shower. Some of us need it."

"A shower?"

Alison approached the falling water, then put her palm under it. "What on earth? It's . . . warm," she accused, turning.

The Littlelost looked innocently blank. She might have been speaking Hindustani. "Okay, a hot shower it is. Who's first?" She bent to rummage in her pack for the hotel soap she'd snitched because the small size was perfect for woodsy weekends. Now she wished for monarch-sized bars instead of her cute quartet of mini-soaps. She handed out three.

"Don't all get in line. Don't you guys want to be clean?" Silence. "Okay. Don't you want to have fun?" Silence. "Here's what we'll do. Beau is so dirty. He needs a bath. We'll put him under the water and rub him with soap, and you come and lather it here, and you here and— That's right, and you can lather yourselves up, too. Yes, the pretty white bubbles . . . right on top of your clothes and your face and your hands. Good!"

Once Beau had trotted into the warm water, pausing to dog-grin back at them, the Littlelost overcame their reluctance and plunged in after him.

Alison stepped back from the splashing water, from the circle of wide-eyed Littlelost. They were not smiling, but they were certainly fascinated. They worked the soap as she'd shown them. Bubbles multiplied in Beau's fur and on their fully clothed forms. Two birds with one bar of soap, she figured.

Beau loved the water. Beau loved the attention. He licked any face within reach with his big pink washcloth of a tongue. Alison, congratulating herself on hardly getting wet, knelt to fill her water canteen at the edge of the stream, where it flowed cool again. Who knew when she'd find good clean water again?

Then a wail rang from the soapy crowd. "I don't have any," cried the Littlest, standing alone and unsoaped at the fringe. "They didn't give me any and it's all gone."

Alison dug in her pack and pulled out a pink bar of Camay. "Here's some more. Don't cry, wash. Circle, circle, bubble, bubble; away goes every kind of trouble."

By the time Alison had made them duck under the water for a rinse and allowed them out, the Littlelost were wet, dazed and decidedly sweeter smelling. Beau bounded onto the shore and shook a fresh shower of tepid water on everybody.

"I wish," said Alison, "that the Middling Mountains would provide food as well as hot-and-cold running water. We're gonna get hungry fast."

"I find," offered the tallest. "I remember."

"Food? In the forest? How?"

For answer, he looked around. In an instant, he was up a looming fir tree, bare feet and hands flashing pale against the bark. Pine boughs shimmied as high as the eye could see—and then the child climbed even higher.

Alison shivered in the sunshine. She looked around to find the sun waning above the mountain peaks. An ague shook the boughs; then the Littlelost plopped to the ground like a ripe apple.

He scurried to them in a whirlwind of excitement. "Twist find! Twist see spiked trees. We get fruit."

They turned as one to follow their leader.

"Wait! You *do* have names! Don't you . . . Twist?"

A lengthening silence. "Only for us," said a child.

"You're only with each other now. Beau's just a dog, and I don't belong here. What are your names? I have to tell you apart somehow."

"Twist." The tallest one looked away as if shamed.

Other names came: Pickle, Faun, Rime. Except from the Littlest. Alison looked down. "No name?"

A headshake. "I'm too—" The child sought the word. "New," it said.

Alison smiled at the dirt still shadowing the tiny features, at the pale-pink bar of soap clutched like a prize in small, grubby hands. "I dub thee Camay, then."

"That doesn't mean anything," objected a bigger Littlelost—Pickle, Alison thought.

"It doesn't have to, or let's say it means 'clean.' "

"Camay." The littlest Littlelost nodded. "Camay."

Then they were gone in a bunch, off into the forest like a pack of wolves. Alison turned to her faithful but damp dog. "You smell almost as bad as a Littlelost used to. Guard duty, boy; I'm going to shower myself."

It wasn't really "water," like lake water, Alison told herself; it was simply a bit of crude natural plumbing, an overflow from a hot spring. She felt uneasy stripping off her clothes, but Beau would bark at anything that approached. The water's warmth matched her body temperature, feeling more like a balmy wind than water. It rinsed away fear and sweat, and some of the lingering guilt at having shot someone.

Alison dried herself with her shirt and sunlight. Dressed again, she went to the nearby pool to drink. Soap bubbles had floated over the rocks and collected there; snowy suds sparkled in the softening sunlight.

It was pretty, yet disturbing. A rainbow-slick of residue spun in the current of water, no longer pristine and seductively clear. Alison cupped her hands to push the soap bubbles onto the rocks. The suds oozed into crannies, thinned and burst. She banished most of the soap, but the pool still looked murky, like a farmhouse washbasin that hadn't been changed all day.

Beau bent to drink, then reared his muzzle away. He minced back, sat, and rubbed his nose with his forepaws, as he did when he got a red-pepper flake on a tidbit of pizza. Maybe the falling water would wash the suds away. Maybe by the time the Littlelost returned, the water would be fresh again.

Sunset brought worry and, at last, the Littlelost's return.

The troupe was scratched bloody, but dry and as happy as Alison had ever seen these somber children. Their trouser pockets bulged with booty, none of it too clean. Alison contemplated an apparent hybrid of mushroom and artichoke, bits of bark dotting the fleshy maroon leaves.

"P-p-pomma." Twist lifted one, peeled off the outermost scale and bit into it.

The other Littlelost did likewise. Alison sniffed her pomma, rubbed it on her jeans leg and broke off a section. It was not bad, like mushroom string cheese.

Their faces waited, all eating suspended. "Good," she said, not altogether sure. Like kids everywhere, they wanted approval, and Alison suspected they'd had darn little of it. Their faces relaxed and they resumed eating. "Sit down, like at camp. Oh, you don't know. Well, you eat and tell stories and sing around a camp fire. When you're with someone smart enough to make a camp fire. But fire might attract the wrong sort—"

"Slinkers," Faun, maybe, said worriedly.

Alison paused. She'd grown used to talking to herself while tramping the alien landscape. After their shower and some food, the Littlelost were getting almost as itchy for conversation as the hikers at Camp Minnewalla.

"Wolves, maybe," Alison agreed. "Or Big Ones."

That shut them up. After a meal of pomma and a yellow berrylike fruit, the Littlelost collapsed into a drowsy litter. Night brought more than darkness and odd sounds. It brought a chill sharp enough to remind Alison of her down-filled sleeping bag somewhere back in the woods she knew.

She called Beau and drew against his warm, fuzzy side. They all slept.

Leaves crackle under his feet, but he is moving fast enough that the noise is always too far in his wake to betray him.

Moonlight lattices the trees. The night is so cool that his breath powders the air. He pauses to listen, then strides forward again. Night chill has smothered the day's spicy warm incense, but he can still follow the reeking track of those he seeks. They have remained near—unseen, if not undetected. His gait is springy, even businesslike. Moonlight glints on his edged weapons, on the alert profile of his head.

There, on a rocky outcropping, stands the expected guard. He stops and waits, smiling. The chieftain comes first, teeth bared in a wary grin—a grizzled battle veteran, missing one ear.

They advance on each other, intruder and defender, heads lowered, circling warily without sound. The guard has left his outcropping and now keeps watch from beneath a pine. Others approach, softly enough to attack him from behind, but he knows the chieftain won't tolerate interference.

Their greeting is abrupt, uncommitted. Nearer they come toward a tacit middle ground. Wind whisks the leaves into eddies of crackling sound. It makes the short hair on their heads rise. Each sniffs for the other's fear, and neither finds it. The old gray chieftain is puzzled now, his brow wrinkling in the moonlight. The intruder is of an unmet breed. Frustration enboldens him. He charges the newcomer as his followers tighten to a loose ring around the two.

The challenger dodges, growling a warning. They stop to regard each other again. Then the intruder moves strangely. A harsh hissing sound sizzles in the night as the visitor urinates on the middle ground.

The chieftain leaps, attacks. Powerful shoulders butt, heads twist and contend. Jaws snap on collars of fur.

Then the visitor springs free and runs off. The old veteran

swaggers to where the interloper had stood, lifts his leg and directs a stream of yellow atop the first puddle.

The rest draw near, white teeth glinting, furred foreheads worried. The chieftain has not been vanquished, but the intruder's scent lingers. They will see him again.

6

"Alison's eyes go in and come out!"

The cross-eyed Littlelost known as Faun—whether it was boy or girl, Alison couldn't say—stood pointing a grimy finger. The others swarmed around. Alison could tell them apart now. Besides Faun, there were the tall, tongue-tied Twist; Rime, a thin, nearly mute child with ash-white hair; rangy, head-scarfed Pickle; and sprightly little Camay.

Dirty fingers explored besmudged mouths. Eyes swam in wide-awake whites. This ragtag bundle of ill-kempt children stared as if Alison were the oddity.

She sat cross-legged on the ground. A contact lens that she'd just rinsed with some water from her canteen was balanced on her forefinger. Lord, if she lost a lens! Still, she dare not sleep in hard lenses. So here she was: the famous eye-juggler.

Littlelost watched in solemn wonder as she propped her upper eyelid open. They must see only the drop of water on her skin, not the tiny piece of concave plastic that held it. She pushed her fingertip toward her undefended eye.

"Ohhhh," they gasped.

Blink. It was done, and she smiled at them.

"A m-m-mage," said Twist.

"Image?" Alison asked.

"You're a mage," he asserted more boldly.

"I don't think so."

"Who can take out an eye but a wonder-worker?" Faun insisted.

"My eyes never left my head."

"Can you see to the other side of the mountains now?" cross-eyed Faun asked hopefully. "Can you sprinkle my eyes and make them straight?"

"No." Suddenly the children's mistake wasn't so funny. "No, I can't. But in my . . . land, there are wise physicians who might."

"Ph-ph-physi-sh-sh-shians?" Twist tried.

"That word *is* a mouthful for anyone. People who heal."

"Where is your land?" asked shy Rime in a whisper.

"Far behind, I think."

"See, Alison is no mage! Mages always know where they are." Twist nodded authoritatively.

Alison rose, knees creaking from a night on the hard ground.

"Is your land like this?"

Alison looked sadly at Camay. "This place? No, and yes. The Island is small and flat; this is vast, and very lumpy."

"You live on an island? Only mages dare live on islands!"

"Pickle, don't get your hopes up. I'm no mage, and where I come from isn't really an island—and most of the time, I don't even live there."

"Mages t-turn into swans and fly from Rookery to R-R-Rookery," Twist said.

"I don't turn into anything. Except hungry."

That was the cue for the terrible troupe to empty their pockets. More pommas, dusted with soil particles. Alison ate gratefully. The previous day's portion had held hunger at bay until now. Despite their vegetable look, Alison sensed that these odd pine fruits were loaded with protein.

"What do you call this place?" she asked, her lips glossed with the goldenberry juice that had ended breakfast for all of them. The flavor was sharp, yet honey-sweet, and insects hovered around the bushes that produced them.

The Littlelost exchanged looks.

"This is many places," Pickle finally said, scratching his headscarf. "Desmeyne lies over the mountains, and the Earth-Eaters, who no man has seen, bide in the barrows beneath the mountains, and the Takers—"

"The Takers are marsh-miners," Twist said derisively. "They stink."

"That is their birth-bane; they stink!" Faun put in.

Malicious glee inflamed their piquant faces. The Littlelost suddenly resembled wicked sprites whole centuries young.

"No. Their birth-bane is that they have horns instead of—" Pickle stopped, leashed by an unspoken communal instinct.

"What's a birth-bane?" Alison didn't really care; she only wanted to exile that sudden rapacity—half adult, half childish—from their faces.

Rime spoke again, softly. "The flaw you are born with."

"Flaw?" Original Sin came to Alison's mind. Could these alien people follow the same theological thread that had intertwined itself with the Western part of earth's population?

Faun's pupils crossed even more. "My eyes. Twist's tongue. We each have something wrong with us."

"So do I. Or I wouldn't have to take my 'eyes' in and out, but it's nothing serious."

They stared at her as if they thought she lied.

"That's why we are Littlelost," Faun said soberly. "Our birth-banes can't be hidden."

"Camay!" Alison longed to disprove their cruel matter-of-factness. "What's wrong with Camay? Nothing!"

"Too little y-yet," Twist rebuked her. "Her birth-bane m-m-may not show yet, but it will, or she would not be Littlelost."

"Are you saying that your parents rejected you because you were imperfect? Is that why you're on your own?"

Rejected. Imperfect. Such words weren't common to exotic children in a wild place, perhaps. But another unfamiliar word caught their interest.

"Parents?" Their puzzlement was as intense as their hatred of the Takers.

"Those who gave birth to you."

Heads shook. That meant nothing to them.

"Surely you haven't been . . . alone forever."

"We are not alone. We are Littlelost."

"But, Pickle, each of you had to come from somewhere different. From parents. Don't you remember?"

Alison's questions were making them uneasy. She knew that tight-lipped look from the times she'd pushed an interview subject too hard.

"Beau!" she said suddenly. "Has anyone seen Beau this morning?"

The Littlelost's attention immediately flung wide. They

seemed to like nothing better than finding something. Off they fanned, looking—but not calling—for the dog.

Alison stared at the mountains. Snow glittered like powered sugar in the crenellations of the peaks. Pines painted zigzagging green streaks below the tree line. Distance hazed their edges. These mountains looked like the Rockies, and were not. Yet they were more familiar, more predictable to her, than these wild children were, who knew so much . . . and so little.

She thought of Earth-Eaters in the bowels of the caverns, and the mountains no longer looked so clean and sharp. Then she saw a movement on a lower slope. She crawled into the shade of a pine and looked closer: a single figure, moving inchworm-slow across a mountain shoulder.

Alison ran back to the pool and reloaded her backpack, making sure that her precious contact lens fluid bottle was tightly closed. She met the Littlelost at a clump of berry bushes, Beau bounding in their midst.

"Let's go. Hurry! Beau, where have you been? And you've scratched your nose. I'm not going to dig the cortisone out now. I'll treat you later."

Later.

Alison looked over her shoulder: The figure continued its progress along the opposite mountain. She didn't know what she ran from—or to—but she felt safer moving. Fast.

The sun, which behaved with ordinary regularity, melted softly behind the mountain to their left. In the high crags, blueberry-colored shadows thickened. Alison kept their path just above the tree line: the snows hadn't reached this low, and they could always retreat to the dubious safety of the woods.

It was cool here, despite the occasional fountains of warm water bubbling like lymph fluid from the mountain's shattered rocks. Alison rejoiced that her down vest was not back on the Island with her sleeping bag. The Littlelost were so wound around with assorted rags that she doubted they were cold.

They claimed they knew no songs, so she was leading campfire favorites as they walked. Beau scouted their flanks, wheeling away and intermittently vanishing among rocks or trees. The scratch on his nose remained a raw, red streak, but the ointment would heal it within twenty-four hours.

"This old man," she was singing, the Littlelost right with her after the fortieth chorus, even Twist singing along clean and uncluttered. *"This old man—"*

An odor descended upon them like a collapsed tent. The reek was he-goat rank; for a moment she took the crouching figure that had leaped down into their path for Billy Goat Gruff. It was gnarled, and white hair tufted its chin, head, elbows and knees. It had sly orange eyes in a gray face and wore coarse trousers and tunic, and a belt that chimed with edged weapons.

"Takers!" screamed the Littlelost, scattering like squirrels.

Other creatures thudded down beside the first—two, three, five! The bestial slant of their foreheads, the crude, unhinged jaws, the lumbering stink of human hunger, called greed—all were echoes of the rough men who had camped on the Island.

Beau sprang atop a nearby rock and barked strenuously, but the Takers paid no attention to him. They spread out, grins of unholy glee upon their homely faces, each after a Littlelost.

As they would have surged past Alison, she kicked out a booted foot to trip one. He glared viciously at her, but scrambled up and after his prey with the intensity of an entrant in a greased-pig contest. High-pitched screams among the berry bushes and behind the rocks alternated with an occasional grunt. The Takers were too many and too scattered for her to do much but run in all directions, doing no good.

She slung her pack to the ground and crouched to undo its buckles. They chose this moment to remain impervious. Sweat flattened her hair to her neck and forehead, despite the evening chill. Of course she had tucked the revolver—Rick's silly, sissy city revolver—safe deep within the pack. Yet she'd forgotten where the ammo box was, and probably she'd forgotten how to load the gun, too.

But when boots thumped behind her and a Littlelost squeal faded suddenly, Alison found her wits and jammed the copper shells into the chamber, fearing for time and loading only five. She rose, armed, and turned to look. Beau was worrying the booted leg of a Taker, who had Camay under his arm and Faun half on his back.

Twist had scaled a rock and was pelting stones at a pair of Takers below. From the woods stole the lean, canine shadows Alison had seen before, advancing on the attackers with teeth bared. The four-footed reinforcements only encouraged the Takers to unsling the axes and wicked steel slashers at their belts, Camay's captor balancing her like a sack of flour on one hip while he wielded a tarnished knife in his other hand.

"Stop!" Alison ordered.

They did, in sheer shock, and then the hullabaloo began all over. It was only by merest chance—and the Takers' obvious greedy concern that none of their forced labor perish—that no lethal damage was done . . . Beau! She lifted the revolver in the same second that a Taker hefted his glittering ax blade to embed it in her dog's skull. Dare she kill again for a dog?

The question was taken out of her hands, quite literally, as something bounded into her back. She sprawled facedown, shocked and unsure whether she'd been hurt, as she had fallen once long ago during a crisis on the Island. A black, wolfish form leaped past her and hurled itself at the ax-wielder's arm. With the wolves now joining the battle, each Taker fought a Littlelost that did not wish to be in his custody and a wolf that most intently did wish to keep him in its custody.

Alison lay frozen on the ground, aware of a burning on her chest, of scars tightening again over raw tissue, as if her wound had been inflicted and healed and scarred shut all over again. Once more she was paralyzed, unable to move, to speak, to save her sister, the Littlelost, her dog, the wolves. She couldn't breathe, understanding vaguely that the air had been knocked out of her, that she couldn't get up and retrieve the gun and shoot it or save anyone until she could draw breath again.

She felt the agonizing paralysis of dreams: as if pinned into place by no visible bonds, carved up like a sacrifice, until her very hair ran red with blood. Thudding shook the ground. She couldn't even turn to see what disaster hurtled upon her. The earth thrummed beneath her body . . . then the quake bolted past.

More boots: another Taker. This one carried a long wooden

staff. The rod began admonishing the contenders, swinging left, then right, like oars dripping madly in a race. Came cries, wails, thumps of bodies falling to rock-packed earth.

Camay was dropped but scrambled away, scrounging for loose rocks to hurl. The latest Taker was disoriented—or desperate—enough to belabor his own kind with the formidable staff. Its wood knocked knees and shoulders, jabbed like a lance into bellies and necks.

Beau and the wolves bounded back to the attack time and again, their raging snarls pounding like surf at the knot of Takers, now intent on defending themselves. The fight's close quarters brought the glinting blades dancing over targets. The sixth Taker ducked a shovel-sized ax aimed at his throat and drove his staff into a belly that collapsed like a parachute, drawing its owner down to the ground with it. Or was the sixth Taker a Taker at all?

A piercing squeal—from dog, wolf or child?—cleared Alison's head. She dug the heels of her hands into the ground, still unable to inhale but managing to push her torso upright. At last she fell over sideways, half-sitting. Her first breath was a pant. Then another. She crawled toward the revolver, gleaming black and unspeakably lethal in the ruddy sunlight. A line of shadow from the clot of Takers moved toward it also: the oncoming bar of a staff. Alison wondered which of them would reach it first.

Then the gun butt filled her hands and she drew it to her chest. The lethal metal cooled the hot, throbbing scars behind the buttons of her shirt. She turned the revolver outward, extended her arms, and aimed at the melee.

They were looking at her, all who remained. Vanquished Takers were ebbing into the shadows they had sprung from, as were the retiring wolves. But the five Littlelost stood and stared openly at her, as did Beau, as did the hooded man in their midst, the staff still raised in his right hand.

He stepped toward Alison, his face scowling with alarm and threat. "No spells, foreign mage! Or I will knock your dark talisman into the gorge behind you."

7

Alison didn't know whether to laugh or shoot.

As she debated, the man examined her clothing, which gave her time to assess him.

First, she relaxed to see that he bore no weapon beyond the gnarled greenwood staff. He was tall and limber-looking. With staff in hand, he reminded her of a pole vaulter; he had that same air of springy, deceptive strength.

But he'd never clear more than a bramble bush in his Renaissance Festival getup, Alison reflected: knee-high boots of soft, gray hide; orange leggings; tunic and vest to mid-thigh, one cobalt and one ochre-colored. An oddly opalescent mail framed his face, and a hood shadowed it. Only his bulky pack kept him from resembling a refugee from an over-colorized Robin Hood movie.

Alison lowered the gun but backed beyond reach of the staff, just in case.

"No!" the stranger shouted even as she complied with his demand to disengage the weapon.

Confused, Alison almost paused, but her right heel had already reached for the expected ground and found it absent. What happened next was a hiccoughing series of jolts too rapid to separate: her leg plunged into nothing; the gun thumped to the ground; she slipped past it, her chin momentarily level with the turf, then bouncing off it.

Sheaves of grass greased her palms as they slid through her grasping fingers. Dirt curdled behind her fingernails as she clutched the saplings at the cliff's raw edge, then she was dangling from roots no bigger around than a telephone cord, over nothing.

Beau was barking. Littlelost faces floated in surprise above her like a belt of stunned asteroids. Then the staff nudged forward as if to dub her on the shoulder—dub her doomed, for the saplings were cracking free of the dry soil. She didn't trust the man at the staff's other end, but she had no choice.

One hand exchanged a thready root for the staff's solidity. Her other hand grabbed it, too. But the grass stains had slicked her palms; though her hands inched up the staff as if climbing a rope, for every fist-width forward, she slipped back a hand's span. The toes of her boots drubbed the cliff face, seeking tenure. Then the staff was withdrawing, pulling her up with it even as her hands ebbed down the slippery wood.

"Alison!" Camay wailed like a small, lost bird.

The staff's end had nearly cleared the heels of her hands, but she was still a foot and a half below the top of the cliff. The moment of loss was peculiarly attenuated, like a Sam Peckinpah shoot-out. Would her fall look as graceful in the wide-angle camera lens?

A hand in an ochre sleeve thrust down, caught one of hers, hauled her up. Another descending hand grabbed her plaid-flannel shirt and down vest in a white-knuckled grip. The cliff edge suddenly slapped her in the stomach; then her elbows and knees were paddling for contact and she was back on solid earth, however alien, all without uttering a sound.

Alison crawled several feet from the precipice, Beau leaping around to lick her face. Finally she breathed shakily and sat back on her heels.

"Beau, settle down!" She felt like a fool for causing such a fuss. She also felt strangely light-headed. Her knees seemed unwilling to lock.

The Littlelost kept their distance, their faces squinched with suspicion, as if her peril had affronted them. Alison understood. They'd come to take her presence for granted and had only now realized that her absence would be upsetting. They probably weren't used to dependency.

Her rescuer stood above her, his fists curled around the greenwood staff, whose end reached to his shadowed cheek. She noticed that the hands that had saved her were entirely hairless. An unwelcome riff of apprehension knifed through her. Why did the mail and hood hide his head? If daylight had proven the Takers oddly subhuman, what might this man be?

At the moment, he was staring at her as if asking himself the same unpleasant question. What might she be? Then his narrowed eyes riveted on a spot below her face. "What by the Crux-master's anklebones is that—?"

He moved toward her faster than she had fallen. His hairless hands rummaged at her shirt front, and air fanned her sweat-damp throat and breastbone. Realizing that her shirt buttons had come undone during her rescue, she scrambled upright, clutching her shirt shut, fumbling for the buttons. He lunged after her, his eyes fixed upon her chest as though nothing else existed.

Great, Alison thought as an irrepressible flash of black humor lit her numbness. Just great: saved from death for a little roadside rape. Her rage flared hot from the fresh embers of fear and as quickly doused itself in icy intent. Before she thought further, before she worried whether it would work on a gypsy rover rather than on a pajama-clad sparring partner, she turned in the spinning back kick called *Momdollyo-chagi* and felt her booted foot lash into his midsection.

The blow didn't stop him, but Alison was already executing the second half of the *taekwondo* sequence, catching him off balance, teetering him on the axis of her own ebbing weight, then letting his momentum catapult him to the ground flat on his spine.

The impact made even Alison wince.

The man seemed not to have felt it. His hood fallen back, he stared up, wordless, at her shirtfront, which she hastily rebuttoned. "Just keep your hands off me," she warned, her voice a contralto rumble.

The man's stunned features were as harshly sculpted as the encasing mail, but not debased like those of the Takers. He took a deep breath, color returning to his tanned skin, as he reinstated his hood. Alison wondered how the sun had bronzed so shrouded a face.

"How did you—?" His voice sounded unexpectedly pleasant, its tones resonant. "I must see—"

"You won't see anything I don't show you," she answered with deadly conviction, "and I am well-trained to introduce you to the ground again, if you insist on invading my privacy."

She watched him weigh the wisdom of another rush at her. Was this land populated by nothing but child abusers and women assaulters? Then he dusted off his palms and pushed off the ground in a lithe, fluid motion. She edged back, looking over her shoulder this time to where the ground plunged into a hazy valley, covered with trees. Had her *taekwondo* not caught him off guard and ignorant, he'd have made a formidable opponent. Now he was acting—deceptively?—apologetic.

"Your pardon, mage, for overcuriosity," he said with visible self-control. "Some would wish to disrupt my pilgrimage. I must know with whom I have crossed paths."

"Then ask without lunging at a person first. These little ones are—"

He had turned to the Littlelost with her. "I know what they are," he said abruptly. "A thieving breed, and untrustworthy. How have you joined forces with this lot?"

"I found them in the hands of . . . of evil men, like those who fled."

He lifted an eyebrow so blond it faded into his flesh. "And the evil men?"

"I killed one"—might as well put the fear of the mage into him—"and the others fled."

"T-T-Takers," Twist put in fiercely.

The man eyed the empty meadow and nodded. "Like these who run. Takers. You do right to call them evil, even though you are a stranger. The smallest Littlelost called you, 'A-li-sohn.' I am Rowan, a pilgrim of Desmeyne. What is your land?"

She was tempted to quip, "This land is *my* land, buddy," but refrained from an all too out-of-place jest. Somehow the present had retreated into the dim past.

"The land of many lakes." She hoped this paraphrase of Minnesota's state motto was vague enough.

Rowan's eyes narrowed, but he said nothing.

"Desmeyne." Alison intoned the word as if it were as commonplace as "Des Moines" or "Dubuque" or "Detroit Lakes."

"Is . . . Desmeyne a large place? The Littlelost mentioned it."

"Large. And lovely." Rowan's voice had softened, become almost seductive.

"Good. I need to take the Littlelost someplace civilized."

"What is 'civilized'?"

"Generally a city, though there's debate on that."

"A city—take them to Desmeyne? Why?"

"They can't be left out here, with Takers and wolves—"

"Wolves?" He sounded suspicious again.

"Slinkers," Pickle translated.

Rowan nodded and examined Rambeau. "Your . . . magical aide. I thought him one of the Horizon-weft at first, but I see he is solid."

Horizon-weft? Okay, she'd been hitting them with "physician" and "civilized." "He's been with me a long time," Alison said defensively, not sure of what charge she defended Rambeau against.

"You walk with Slinkers? You must be a powerful mage."

She said nothing. If the natives thought her empowered, let them. Especially this long-limbed one, who'd rushed her within two minutes of their meeting and who might be able to overwhelm her should he decide to. Maybe this world's mistaken superstitions were her only safeguard.

Rowan bent to retrieve the pack he'd dropped to the ground before he'd rescued her. She wondered what was in it. He'd had the forethought to protect something before he risked following her into the forested abyss below. And he *had* risked himself.

Rowan slung the pack across his torso. His casual, yet fluidly controlled movements, told Alison that the burden was much heavier than he allowed it to appear. Some object protruded, long and sharp, like a rifle.

"Are you going to Desmeyne?" she asked, more anxiously than she meant to.

"In time." He turned to go.

"Might we—accompany you?" She hated asking.

He froze, his back to them. Alison sensed that she'd said the last thing he wished to hear. "I must continue my pilgrimage."

"And we must find our way off this mountain to a settlement."

He turned back, his face as closed as a Littlelost's. The pale brows almost met above the bridge of his nose. "I have no desire to travel with foreign mages of dubious powers through a landscape already overflowing with treachery, or with woodland urchins of even more dubious honesty. But the conditions of pilgrimage force me to preserve all folk from harm if they request it, and until you prove yourselves unworthy, I cannot stop you from accompanying me. But I need not linger in this dangerous spot any longer."

He marched away, the staff digging into hard ground at every stride and almost catapulting him forward.

Alison watched their only guide to civilization shrinking into the distance. No time to stand still and bewail Rowan's begruding attitude. She scrambled to retrieve the revolver and don her backpack. "Come on, then," she urged Rambeau and the Littlelost.

The children hesitated, the suspicion in their eyes a match for that which had narrowed Rowan's.

"Come on! Beggars can't be choosers, and he doesn't smell as bad as a Taker. Besides, I want to see some people in this place! And a city or a pig farm or a puddle in the middle of the road."

"Pig?" Camay asked, wide-eyed.

"Never mind, just march!"

Rowan was a hundred yards ahead, and not slowing. Alison's lips tightened as she trotted down the mountain after him. Her arms were already stiffening after her long moments of playing human pendulum, and the Littlelost, though energetic, were not tireless. But they would all keep up, because the isolation of the alternative was even more uncomfortable.

"Go on, Beau," Alison ordered the dog, trotting alongside her. "Follow that man."

He raced off, his keen black nose skating the ground for Rowan's scent.

Alison smiled. This might be an odd, alien land, and home might be distant beyond any number of ruby-red slipper heel-taps, but she had her gun and her *taekwondo* and Beau. Forget red-rhinestoned shoes; the modern weapon, the ancient dog-human alliance, and her own confidence were fast proving themselves to be a girl's best friends.

Rowan had led them up slope and down meadow, through forest and over rocks. Distant wild flowers spilled a watercolor box of exotic shades over the meadows, but Rowan's gray boots steered clear of their luminescent beauty.

Nor did he lead them past fresh water, though Beau's tongue was hanging down to his chest. Alison and the Littlelost soon grew so dry they didn't speak. Sunset melted the wild flowers into the clouds' rose-carmine light. The highest clouds, untainted by the dusky bloodletting, shimmered mother-of-pearl white against a barely blue sky.

And it was from a hilltop that Alison looked to the clouds opposite and glimpsed a strange churning in their midst. Fleecy dust devils erupted from the rosy sunset. Snowy herds thundered on cotton-candy hooves along the lurid horizon line. As she watched, a stream of vaporous humanity and beastdom paced down the sky at the edge of the visible world.

For a moment she wondered if she saw the inhabitants of *her* world, through a sunset, brightly. Then the sun shrank to a fluorescent crimson crescent against the clouds' bruised lavender, and her eyes could see only a confusion of color and shape, like looking through filmy curtains drawn against the oncoming dark. Could this be the "Horizon-weft"?

Below, Rowan's figure had shrunk to a cardboard silhouette in the distance.

"Hurry, kids!" Alison charged down the dimming meadow. Beau ran ahead, a luminescent white ball slaloming downhill. They finally caught up with Rowan only because he had deigned to stop for the night.

He acted neither surprised nor pleased to see them arrive, and had already extracted his evening needs from his pack.

"Thanks for waiting supper."

He didn't answer, instead chewing stoically on what looked like turkey jerky. With an air of skepticism, he watched the Littlelost fan into the nearby forest.

Alison settled a comfortable distance away and began emptying her backpack. First she unloaded the revolver . . . under Rowan's stolid gaze. Observation made her clumsy; the bullets clinked into her tender palm like chiming coins.

Alison ignored her witness and called Beau. "Water, boy? Where's the water, huh?"

With a prancing turn, the dog followed the Littlelost into the woods. Alison stood, the tube of cortisone cream in her fingers.

"Will he conjure it?" Rowan asked.

"What—?"

"Your familiar. Will he conjure water?"

"Maybe."

"Wildwater is a two-tongued snake. How do you know he won't find a tainted spring?"

The words were alarming, but she wasn't about to show her concern. The man's mailed head leaned back while he drank from a leather flask he didn't offer to share. The mail was as stiffly supple as corduroy, and it shone the color of an iridescent pearl in the moonlight. Moonlight!

Alison looked up. A moon indeed, spinning secondhand sunlight into sterling silver. An unearthly keening began at a distance too far to worry about but not too far to cause a shiver of anxiety.

"Slinkers. A dangerous breed." Rowan lowered his flask. For a moment Alison suspected him of silently starting the wolfish chorus to unnerve her. "If your Spirit Slinker and you survive whatever water he finds, I'll refill my bottle."

"Beau is not a wol—not a Slinker."

"He has greater powers than Slinkers?" Rowan sounded dubious.

"Not greater. Different. He likes people, for one thing. Some people," she added pointedly.

Perhaps Rowan smiled. Perhaps the moonshine merely polished his teeth. Alison blinked. The moonlight had swelled into a blinding, blue-white blanket. From somewhere in the forest, the Slinkers unraveled the silver light on a loom of high-pitched sound.

"How can we sleep in the open like this?" she wondered. "The noise . . . the brightness. The Takers."

"Better than the silent darkness under the trees and what thrives in stillness and blackness. The Takers are things of shaded forests and light-dampened caverns."

"But I thought the Littlelost knew what they were doing. They have survived in the forest."

"Yes, and they are ever up to their own good. A callous, arbitrary kind, these Littlelost. Why have you allowed them to affix themselves to your quest?"

"You're wrong. *I* insisted that they accompany *me.* And I'm on no 'quest.' "

"A foreign mage, traveling with forbidden amulets—"

"What forbidden amulets? You mean . . . the gun?"

"I know not what you call that foul article. I am merely glad that I did not see you use it against the Takers. They deserve little, Takers, but they merit better than a machine-spat death."

"You . . . you're familiar with guns?"

"You are the one who travels with a familiar," he returned.

"What do you know of machines, pilgrim?"

"I have traveled more than most Desmeynians in my year of quest. Their graveyards litter the land," Rowan said, anger leveling his flexible voice to a stern strum of steel.

"Machines don't die."

"More's the pity."

"And why . . . how can you speak my language?"

"How can you speak *mine?*"

"The Littlelost speak it as well, so it isn't just your language."

He shrugged. "The Littlelost live upon the mountain meadows and near the forests. They are suspect, but it is you who are the true foreigner."

"Perhaps."

He snorted, as a none-too-tame horse might reject an overly convenient palmful of oats. "Mages are old beyond the moon, and usually silver-haired. Some have heard stones sing and seen machines walk. You are young for such wonders, but the smallest Littlelost says you can drop your eyes into the palms of your hands and still see. Yet you are not what you seem. There is an alien air to you I cannot name. I do not doubt that you have worked wonders beyond making men fly through the air. But I do not fear you, and I will not let you or your minions interfere with my . . . pilgrimage, though Desmeynian courtesy forbids me to cast myself free of your company without good reason."

Alison reflected. She had worked wonders he could not imagine, far beyond taking contact lenses in and out. She had made machines move by shifting into gear. She'd communicated with colleague "magicians" through I-mages that glowed like phosphorescent green eels upon a black scrying board called a computer screen. Yet he did not fear her, and that could make all the difference in her survival, as well as Beau's and the Littlelost's.

She mustn't let him know that he was their only thread to a world they all might recognize if only they could reach it. She mustn't let him see that she was afraid.

All she said was, "You're right. This language must not be my native tongue." She smiled. "It apparently has no contractions."

He frowned. "That is a clumsy word. What are contractions?"

"Something your mother must have had a lot of having you," Alison muttered, but her words were drowned out by a wash of noise as Littlelost shot like blackbirds from the woods, screeching shrilly. Their hands were fat with pomma, which looked even less appetizing by the unearthly moonlight.

"Dinner," Alison said brightly to Rowan. "Care for some?"

"Dead white welt-worms! Such sickly forest growths are little better than living white welt-worms."

"There goes your chance at headwaiter."

Alison gathered the Littlelost at a pointed distance from the pilgrim, made sure the pomma was brushed reasonably soil-free, and broke it into chunks to pass around.

It looked no worse than the stringy stuff Rowan had been chewing to death, and she'd found it amazingly sustaining. In fact, she relished its bland, meaty flavor. When Beau's beautiful diamond-shaped head rose like a furry moon beyond the Littlelost's huddled shoulders, she tossed him a scrap and he snapped it down.

Alison stood up. "Water?"

Beau barked once, meaning "Gotcha," and perked his ears at the woods. Despite Rowan's dire talk of dark and silence, Alison took her insulated canteen and followed the dog. Littlelost joined them as if drawn by a piper.

Rowan was right about one thing: She hadn't noticed the forest's unnatural nocturnal stillness until now. Did raven and hare, beetle and worm, moth and owl, turn to stone by night? Even the tree branches declined to stir. Moonlight painted every leaf into a motionless fan of leaden silver. Alison felt that if one should fall, it would crash to earth like a tray.

Yet there was water—still water—in this moonlight-iced fairyland.

Alison stared with dismay at what Beau had led her to. For the first time, she worried that Rowan's doom-filled croakings—though a voice as fine as his could hardly be said to croak—had reason.

Beau's water source was a well.

8

They went waterless until daylight. Then Alison led Rowan to the well.

He put his fists on his hips. "Well . . ."

"Well?"

"You are a mage. Work some wonder to purify it."

"Then it is tainted?"

"You do not know?"

"Water isn't exactly my element."

"Ah." Morning revealed Rowan's eyes to be the color of burnt cinnamon; for the first time, their expression was spiced with furtive amusement. "Perhaps the Spirit Slinker—"

"Beau is a dog. Desmeynians keep dogs, don't they?"

He eyed the vigilant form by her leg. "No dogs, and he is not a dog. He runs with Slinkers."

"No. He is *my* dog, and he's found water. Since this is *your* land—and what's it called, anyway?"

He eyed her as if searching for mockery. "Veil," he said at last. "The whole of it is called Veil."

"Veil, as in—?" Her hands gestured toward her face.

Rowan nodded, the cinnamon eyes lost in the shadow of his generous hood, which was fashioned of the same ochre-colored cloth as his vest. The sallow shade seemed monkish and jaundiced.

"Veil," Alison repeated. "A strange name for a land."

"You are a stranger," he said with gentle condescension.

"And a stranger asks if this water is safe to consume."

Rowan's hooded shadow leaned over the moisture-darkened mouth of circled stones as he drew up the well's thong-pierced metal pot on its rattail of rope. "You need not drink it all."

"I meant 'consume' as 'to take into ourselves, in reasonable portions,' not to drain it dry."

He withdrew the brimming pot. In the woodsy shade—now murmuring with many voices, the least of which was the tongue-tied stutter of liquid lapping on damp stone—the water pooled like molten ebony. Alison dribbled it over her fingers, expecting it to stain them inky blue. No such ill luck. She lifted fingertips to nose and lips.

"Smells fine. Tastes—" Littlelost watched her, breath held, eyes elusive. "What do you think, Beau?"

He drank immediately from the pot she offered.

"Okay." Alison filled her canteen, then passed it among the Littlelost, who watched the dog sharply for a few seconds before drinking. Only when they had finished did Rowan produce and fill his travel flask.

"The, ah . . . taint could be slow-acting," Alison pointed out.

He shook his head, making the tiny metallic links of his chain mail into a close-knit wind chime. Then he intoned,

"Flame eats slow and water not.
Air blows icy and earth fares hot."

Littlelost stood as if mesmerized, heads cocked.

"And—?" Alison said.

"An ancient rime of Veil. Children etch such sayings on frosted winter windowpanes, when there is little to do but watch flames couple with tinderwood. Thus even children learn the ways of Veil. Had this water been rank, stranger mage, you would have perished at its mere kiss upon your lips."

"You let me—!"

"Could a pilgrim have stopped a mage?"

"Maybe."

"You may know much where you are known, but you are still a stranger to Veil."

She nodded. Slowly. Fought to keep her bland expression from shattering like a frost-scored window glass. Rowan's cold-bloodedness acted as a slap in the face. In Veil, were strangers no more than guinea pigs? Why bother to keep her from plunging over a cliff if only to let her dabble in possibly deadly water? Unless Rowan assumed that magical powers would save her. This guy really didn't trust or care for anything—not for the Littlelost, a wayfaring stranger, the gifts of nature itself. If she didn't need him to lead her to a place where she could find someone who *would* help them. . . .

For a moment she wondered if the water *had* been poisoned; she felt oddly removed, as if the revolving earth were a giant Ferris wheel again, and she'd been left to swing interminably in the top gondola, each seesaw back and forth threatening to untether her into thin air, where she would be violently yoked again to the ground far, far below, until she finally woke up and found this was all a dream . . . She was out cold, having a tooth pulled, wasn't she? And Camay was the tooth fairy; the Littlelost were elves who lived in the ivory palaces of her gaping mouth; and Rowan was the dentist who kept yanking ugly words like "stranger" out by the roots.

Certainly she wasn't here. In Veil. With strangers, even herself a stranger who'd shot a man, showered in a warm fall of wildwater and tasted an alien well.

Beau's cold, wet nose nudged her hand.

The others had left. Alison was momentarily annoyed that the Littlelost had followed Rowan's lead. It cemented the fact that even those unnatural allies had more in common than she had with anyone—anything—in all of Veil.

Alison shook herself loose of self-pity abruptly as Beau shed waterdrops, refilled the canteen and walked her dog out of the woods. Maybe if she pretended that this was an unexplored region of Colorado—

"It's true." Rowan sounded accusatory.

Alison blinked through the gauzy fluid floating behind her newly installed contact lens. They were about to break camp and resume their journey, but for now she was squatting by the open canteen and didn't want to overturn it. A fleck of dust had flown into her eye, and with one lens in and one lens out, her sense of distance was askew.

"What's true?" she asked ungraciously.

"You . . . you peel the fronts off your eyes, as the smallest Littlelost said." Rowan squatted down opposite her—at a cautious distance—to peer at her watering eyes. "This practice aids your vision, mage?"

"Yup," Alison said truthfully. "Oh, rats, I don't want to lose it—ah." She caught the second lens before it flipped from her fingertip to the trampled grasses.

"Of what composition is the scrying crystal?"

"A substance called plastique. It is not found in nature."

"Not like rubrock?" His hand extended a potato-sized, blue-gray stone from his pack. "You can use it if you like."

"For what?"

Rowan began circling the stone over the knuckles of one hand.

"I don't understand."

He lifted the stone to his face to make the same rubbing motions over his upper lip and jaws.

"It removes hair? Painlessly?"

"Why would one want to remove hair painfully?"

"One wouldn't, but . . ." No wonder the man was so preternaturally hairless!

He handed Alison the rock. It was feather-light for its size and felt warm, whether from friction or from some inner heat, she couldn't judge. She rubbed it over the smooth skin atop her hand, proving nothing; any hairs there were so fine that their removal wouldn't be obvious. The motion caused a pleasant, tingling sensation.

"Gosh, in . . . my land, I could make a fortune with a gimmick like this."

Rowan frowned. "It is called rubrock, and it is common in Veil, easily found outside the caves and free for the picking up, although rubrock hawkers charge a few knots for the ease of buying it in the towns. Surely your land, however distant, has means of hair removal."

"Yes, but where we really could use your rubrock is on legs."

"Legs? Your people are smooth-*legged?*"

"And faced, as you," Alison added. "Sometimes. But it's harder to get hair off legs and . . . other places."

Rowan's blond eyebrows were on a collision course with the mail sheathing his forehead. Alison could almost see shocked speculations careening through his mind as he tried to digest alien depilatory customs. After all, she found the Desmeynian male's habit of removing hair from his hands as well as his face extremely odd.

Rowan looked again at her wet fingertips. "This clear stone you use to guard your eyes, it comes from below ground? Darnellyne has a rock-crystal ring one can see through, but it is not so . . ."

"So delicate?"

"Yes. Yours is like a slice from the heart of an eye."

"Is that what people in Veil call the colored part of an eye—the heart?"

He nodded.

"That's the first Veilish custom I like."

"They—we—would not like your ways either, but we must admit that you have some powers that we do not ken yet."

"Throwing you to the ground, you mean?"

"You are slight, and I am not."

"What if I said that my prowess was a skill, not a magical power?"

"You may have reason to hide your arts, mage, but no one in Veil is so gullible as to believe that."

"No, I can see not." Alison screwed the contact bottle shut and dropped it into her backpack.

"Why Camay?" Rowan asked abruptly.

"What do you mean?"

"That is no word in Veil. She says you named her."

"Uh, in my land—"

"—of lakes?"

"Many, many lakes. Ten thousand lakes." Rowan winced, as he had not done even when she had thrown him. They seemed to have a water phobia here in merry old Veil. Well, that was one thing she shared. Maybe they had more reason than she, if some water could kill instantly.

"In . . . Lakeland," she continued seriously, as a proper mage should, " 'Camay' is the petal of a beautiful pink flower."

"Flowers!" He stood in disgust. "You would name the child

after a flower?" He loomed over her, but she wasn't intimidated, not as long as he mistook *taekwondo* moves for magic.

"Actually, I was trying to put it in terms you would understand. Camay is really a soap."

"Soap. What is 'soap'?"

"What you wash with. It makes you clean. It's what the Takers don't use. And why do you care *what* name I give a Littlelost? They're worth little to you and your people, from what I can tell."

"Still, you need not compound the damage."

"What damage?"

"Why, their infestation with birth-banes. That is the reason they run wild. They are flawed beyond repair."

"They seem fine to me. If they hadn't found food, I'd be in a pretty pickle by now."

Her figure of speech evoked the child with that name. He was a thin, hard-bitten boy of perhaps nine, who always wore a wrinkled and grimy blue scarf over his head. Camay had quietly crept to Alison's side at the mention of her name as well, like a called animal. Perhaps Littlelost were not used to being spoken of.

"What is this 'birth-bane'?" Alison offered Rowan the canteen as a social ice-breaker.

He sat on the ground while forming his answer. "Your Lakeland has no birth-banes?"

Alison sighed. "Hunger. Poverty. Disease." The other Littlelost gathered around her as for a story-telling.

"Those are—" Rowan eyed the empty meadow, looking for a word large enough for his meaning "—like air and grass, everywhere. No, we of Veil are each visited with a specific ill. No one escapes it, though many birth-banes are benign. A failed singing voice. Nails that will not grow beyond the fingertips—"

"Sounds efficient. So what's a *bad* birth-bane?"

Rowan's glance avoided the Littlelost. "Flaws that cannot be altered—or ignored. Does not your own magic-magnified vision show you, mage? Littlelost are lame of speech and limb, or of mind. Whatever the individual outer wrongness, it but mirrors an inner unreliability. They are devious, slothful, ripe with thievery and malice. When they gather near a settlement, they are driven away, else they would steal animals and food, and commit all sorts of mischief."

"Such as survival, no doubt. Where do they come from?"

Of this Rowan seemed less certain. "Some say they are the rejected spawn of the Earth-Eaters." His voice had darkened with disgust. "Others say that they are bred in pits of earth-bane, or are born of malignant, reeking flowers. These Littlelost you have collected smell better than most, no doubt some spell you have worked."

"What are these Earth-Eaters and this earth-bane?"

"Things that should never see light, creatures of darkness below the earth that reach up through the soil to taint anything they can touch. Earth-bane pits are the slime they leave behind."

"Have you ever seen an Earth-Eater?"

"No! They are an evil to be avoided, not sought."

To Alison, Rowan's remarks reeked of superstition and rumor, not of evidence. If a man believed in magic—believed a modern woman magical by her very nature—he could swallow any kind of nonsense. But she didn't have to.

Alison produced the Camay from her backpack. "Here. My smell spell—plain soap. Well, *smell* it! It won't hurt you. Or don't the folk of Veil use much soap either, along with little water?"

He lifted the bar to his nose with the leery caution of a dog sniffing a skunk. The gesture would have been funny had his ignorance and prejudices not been so serious.

"What does this object do?"

"Think of it as a . . . a soft rubrock. You rub it over yourself with water until you get a lather and you're clean and smell good."

"Ah. Bubble bath." Rowan's indignant figure relaxed. "That's better. Why must you trifle with me?"

"You really, truly call soap bubble bath? If you only knew how odd that is!"

"Your smooth, greasy stone of soap is strange to me, as Desmeynian birth-banes are to you."

"I am a stranger," Alison conceded, "and I've never seen kids like these before. Perhaps someone should ask them where they were born and just how bad their birth-banes are."

She turned to find the Littlelost regarding Rowan with the

hungry, wary eyes of those who know they haven't won someone's regard and care. Tears polished Camay's downy cheeks after all the talk of birth-banes, but the others' eyes looked too dry to have ever cried.

"Here." Angry at the effect of Rowan's disregard, Alison took the soap from him and offered the scented bar to its namesake as she would a toy, or a talisman. "What say you, Littlelost? Are you really as sorry a lot as this hooded pilgrim claims?"

They kept silent, of course, a silence neither damning nor sullen. Alison thought it was the silence of those not accustomed to defending themselves.

"Where were you born?" she asked Twist.

He shrugged. "I don't remember."

"Nobody does. But surely someone, some big person, must have told you—once." She looked around at the Littlelost faces.

Heads shook in unison.

"Never? You remember no one? Nothing?"

"Only forest," said Pickle.

"And etherion pits," Twist added.

Rowan looked up at that, his mail-framed face guarded. "What have Littlelost to do with etherion?"

"We pick it," Rime said.

"S-s-skim it," Twist corrected.

"Spin it," said Faun, "into long, thin twists, like grass."

"Bale it," Pickle added.

"And carry and cart it."

"All lies," Rowan roared, as loudly as a man shocked by the sight of his own image after long years. "Littlelost have naught to do with etherion. Littlelost do *nothing.* They are pariahs and parasites and thieves—"

"As the Takers said," Alison echoed icily. "Thieves. So what is this etherion that they have naught to do with? Besides swamp scum?"

Rowan's shock had mellowed to mere doubt. "Etherion is a rare, lighter-than-air metal. An etherion sword would weigh no more than a feather, yet cut as deep as steel. Only few and fey folk find and work it, and they say naught of their buoyant, fire-breathing arts. In Desmeyne, only the most precious things are made of etherion, and they precious few. Etherion is gathered by magic, not by outcasts. These ill-kempt scuppies here spout fantastic lies to make themselves important."

Rowan turned to the Littlelost, reminding Alison for a chilling moment of the defense attorney cross-examining the children in the Blue Earth case. "Where have you seen this etherion?" he demanded. "How do you know of something so hidden?"

Their faces had closed like clams under Rowan's accusations. Alison recognized the stubborn expressions of those who know they will not be believed whatever they say. She had seen enough of such eyes: in Blue Earth, in the faces of rape victims, of the homeless, of Native Americans.

But here she was a mage, whose eyes went in and out. She would not let Rowan's blind prejudice undercut the Littlelost. "Where have you seen it?" she asked gently. "Tell him what you told me."

"The pits," one blurted, and then they all spoke at once, in a relieved torrent, as if believing themselves now that someone else was willing to believe them.

"In the dark forest . . . quiet . . . can't breathe. We walk rush bridges over the . . . the stink. The Takers make us . . . all day, all night. We strain the slicky stuff off the top. It smells . . . we smell . . . can't breathe. It's so light, our heads, the air, the etherion . . . we almost float off the bridges. Sometimes we fall into the swamps, never get out. Pickle thought we could save some etherion and fly away. Takers follow . . . and Slinkers . . . and Spirit Slinker."

"You escaped!" Alison was astounded. "That's why you were in the woods. The Takers had found you and were bringing you back. And that terrible, dead place we saw on the way here—that was an abandoned etherion pit?"

Serious, grimy faces nodded.

"Nonsense!" Rowan stood and addressed only Alison. "You may know how to spell a man's ground out from under him, but you know little of Veil, or of Littlelost. I must walk miles this day or I will arrive too late. Follow if you will."

"Wait! I'm not packed! Why didn't you warn—?"

Rowan had donned his pack, retrieved the greenwood staff

and was vanishing into the charcoal shade that underlined the ragged tree line.

Alison stuffed her contact supplies and canteen into her pack in angry haste, scanned the ground for loose items—there were none—and scrambled after him. Once again he had rejected a chance for enlightenment and was ready to run off at his convenience, without a backward glance. Behind her trailed the maligned Littlelost.

It was only when they had Rowan firmly in sight, if not within catching distance, that Alison calmed down enough to notice that one of her party was missing. She stopped and turned back. The worn spot of meadow on which they had camped lay empty behind them. She eyed the woods and its fence of brown pine trunks, then whistled.

"Beau! Where are you? Come on! Rambeau—!"

The only answer was Camay's waifish cry, "Alison—"

Alison looked ahead. Rowan was melding with the seam of forest he followed. At least he had a destination and, to judge by his last words, a deadline. Those things Alison understood. If she and the Littlelost didn't keep up, they would lose their chance to find some settlement in—on?—this wild world.

"Beau!" she called again, loudly and hoarsely.

Alison didn't realize her panic until a white cannonball came streaking over the distant rocks. She patted Beau's back as he came to her side, then bounded away to gambol among the Littlelost. Relieved, Alison hurried after Rowan, trusting Beau to herd any lagging child after her.

9

Rowan remained where he wished to be for most of the morning: so far ahead of the rest of them that he could be considered a traveling companion only by a Silly-Putty stretch of the imagination.

Alison was happy to forgo his company. And though she had told Rowan, and herself, that she wanted to find a "settlement," in Alison's mind that oasis of civilized comfort coincided with the one inhabitant of Veil she had not yet seen: another woman. Lots of other women—who, in a vague, maternal sense she herself didn't feel capable of providing, would say "poor dears" and take the Littlelost off her hands, distributing them like orphaned chicks to various benign environments—would shake their heads at Alison's long journey, at her trials and lostness, and *sympathize.*

That's what she wanted. Sympathy and shelter. Instead, she arrived at a rock-filled river that Rowan was unwilling to cross.

That was the only reason they caught up to him; he had stalled on the banks of a boiling comet's tail of water. Alison had been so deep in her fantasies of a cheery Hobbit-town homecoming that the growing wildwater roar had barely registered on her ears.

The river had carved its runway deep between the banks, so she didn't actually see it until she joined Rowan on the brink. A constant flume of water blew past like a white-hot bridal veil. Below it twisted a silver dragon of a river, snorting mist. Ordinarily, Alison would have been awed, but ordinarily Alison wouldn't have been expected to contend with it.

"You must spell this water meek!" Rowan roared his surly greeting when she approached the edge.

"I told you. Water is not my element," she shouted back.

"This flood was not here when last I walked this way," he complained at the top of his lungs.

"What of her?" Alison yelled.

Rowan had not yet noticed the aged figure in midstream; it

seemed carved from wet rags. "She was not here then, either," he grumbled loudly. "Likely she is a mist-mirage."

Alison shook her head and retreated from the foaming current. When she was distant enough that the river's roar muted to a mere racket, she waited for Rowan to join her.

The Littlelost stood beside her with their hands clapped to their ears, having been wise enough to stay back. Beau barked and raged at the river as at an invisible freight train.

"Did you say 'mist-mirage'?" Alison shouted at Rowan when he arrived.

"Look for yourself." He pointed.

Now that the gorge was at a decent distance, Alison could see the thunderheads of spray churning high above it. Like sky-borne clouds, the mist was an eternal shape-changer chained to an icy contrail of whitewater.

Alison discerned a rerun of the albino visions glimpsed in the previous evening's sunset: a voiceless flow of humped herds of snowy bison, of horse and human forms; great sweeping wings as flocks—flocks?—of swans and eagles clove the vapor, like Viking prows cutting fog banks into shreds. Boneless finned forms flashed by, silvery acrobats bound in a slipstream of thin, watery air.

She saw dragons and dinosaurs; lambs and leviathans; uprooted trees with leaves like lace agate; medusan anemones trailing pearl-studded tentacles; pallid grasses and prairie flowers bleached to bone; smoke-and-snow leopards, and shells with fairy faces etched into their broken-china surfaces. Pale moons and stars slipped by, entwined among serpents mailed in white velvet. Everything was ghostly, yet heartbreakingly real—or it should have been.

"Do you see what I see?" she asked Rowan.

He shook his head. "Who can know?"

She turned to the Littlelost. "You see—?"

"Etherion coursers!" Twist cried.

"Rabbits," said Camay, "with fur like snow."

"A cold, white city with its towers . . . falling." That apocalyptic vision came from Pickle.

"Ash and ice and dead things," said Faun.

Amazed at the variety of their perceptions, Alison turned to Rowan again.

He spoke flatly. "Spirits. Empty beds billowing with linens. A naked silver sword borne by a woman whose skin is whiter than rainwater. A corpse not much paler than the woman or the sword. These are visions from water demons, meant to stop me."

"What does Beau see, I wonder." Alison stared at the dog, who had never stopped barking though the river's torrent had nearly drowned him out.

"Perhaps the old woman."

Alison looked again. "She's gone."

"Likely a rock distorted by the mist-mirages." Rowan frowned. "To cross is unthinkable. To go around, impossible—without my being too late."

"Too late for what?"

"Business of Desmeyne, stranger. You will lend me no magical aid?"

"For that?" Alison shook her head. "I can only suggest that we go downstream; perhaps the river widens and calms."

"Perhaps? Pilgrimage tolerates no 'perhaps.' "

But he had no choice. So Alison led the way, a disgruntled Rowan bringing up the rear.

Even the forest shrank from the unbridled river's ceaseless white noise. The party wound along the deep cut. If the boiling mist proferred more visions, no one paused to view them. Beau stopped barking. In time, the rapids' sizzle became as unremarkable as the hiss of frying meat in a skillet.

At last they reached a place Alison had been hoping for: low land that dispersed the fiery silver current into a huge, flat oval eye of dark water. Ripples lapped quietly among the roots of trees, and half-submerged rocky ledges made stepping-stones through the dim, leaf-shaded pond.

They regarded the opportunity to cross in sober silence. Alison found an eerie resemblance between this place and the deadened etherion pit they had encountered in the first forest, and guessed that the Littlelost saw the similarity, too. She realized that finding a passage across the water was the last thing she wanted to do.

"Too wet for you?" she hopefully asked the brooding Rowan when he joined them on the brink.

He honored her with a wry look. "Desmeyne is a high—and dry—city. We trust not wildwater; even spring water can be tainted. Demons delve beneath the mirror image of such unsanctioned currents. They would like nothing better than to drown a questing pilgrim on the cusp of Wellsunging."

"You may be haunted by external demons," Alison said. "Others are hounded by internal ones, and superstitions won't overcome my hang-ups."

He regarded her with confusion. Alison guessed that "hang-ups" was a concept as bizarre to him as his "waltzing in," or whatever he'd said, was to her.

"I cross," Rowan announced as abruptly as Schwarzenegger in a Conan movie.

Alison recognized single-minded macho decisiveness when she saw it. Was the dubious assistance of Rowan's company worth what she'd have to do next to keep it—cross water?

He was already striding from rock to rock, his large boots moving from precarious purchase to downright slipperiness. The greenwood staff skillfully counterbalanced the pack upon his back; she had no doubt that Rowan would cross safely.

"Well?" she asked the Littlelost.

Twist and Pickle took that as a challenge. In an instant they were leaping from rock to rock with the practiced skill of etherion skimmers, Faun and Rime at their rear.

Beau growled at his reflection in the water and wrinkled a worried canine brow. But Camay stared at the rocks, a paralysed child eyeing her worst nightmare.

"It's all right." Alison couldn't believe that she was dispensing standard adult bravado just like Rowan. "I'll carry you."

The child was lighter than Alison expected, no more than thirty pounds. At first. Even as Alison hesitated, the water lapping hungrily at the first exposed rock, she realized that the longer she waited, the heavier Camay would feel and the more unbalanced she would be on the long, zigzag pathway across the placid river.

Her leg stretched to bridge shore and the first stone. She felt as if she were stepping from the top of one skyscraper to another.

For a moment she straddled the two, her balance drawn one way and then the other, Camay an anchor that could pull her weight too far in either direction.

Then both feet were on the rock—luckily broader than the rest—and Alison desperately wished she were back on land. There she and Beau and Camay would find their way together to that most charming, rather vintage settlement she'd imagined, where there'd be warm hearths and warmhearted householders, featherbeds, and Canterbury porridge in the pot, nine days old, and someplace forever England. . . .

If she inched her way around in a circle, she'd be able to retreat.

Trying to turn proved out of the question. She had no balance with Camay in her arms and the backpack pulling her in two directions. She couldn't see her feet, only the stones just ahead of her. She gave up.

The thing to do was to just stride wide, one foot at a time, from stone to stone, and not look back. Not look down. Not see the water and the obsidian visions roiling just below its oily, dark surface: the floating bones, the human hair plaited with water weeds and the wriggling, soft things that tittered. . . .

"Okay." She hoisted Camay to get a better grip on the skinny little legs, took a breath and watched only the next stepping-stone ahead, trying to trust her legs to sense her goal and get them there.

Alison's unseen strides gobbled up the stones. Each was swallowed from her sight before she reached it, and the impact of her foot on solid rock was always a surprise, as was the jarring moment of teetering on the rough surface before her other leg struck out for another gray patch of reality in the insubstantial sea licking at her boot heels.

She heard the quick click of Beau's nails behind her, a reassuring sound . . . until she looked beyond the next stone and saw how isolated she was, how far she had to go. She also saw the wet, gray woman marooned before her like a rock—no doubt a would-be crosser who'd frozen to stone amid these treacherous footings.

But maybe the old woman needed rescue, and why not? Alison was kind to dogs and children and could aspire to leading them across, so why not an old woman, too? Just pick her up like a sack of potatoes and trip across the stones one by one.

When she reached the place where the old woman had basked like a huge snapping turtle on a sandbar, she saw ahead of her only more turgid, slick water, more matte-gray stones to step on.

Camay was whining with fright, a low keening that would have made Alison nervous if she hadn't been already petrified. No, not petrified; rather, walking on stones. There, another step, another stone, and don't look beyond the immediate distance—neither too close nor too far, just as in life—neither to beginnings nor to endings, neither to birth nor to death. Just follow the easygoing middle ground, the middle distance. . . .

She was still stepping as neatly as a goat from rock to rock when Rowan's bronzed, hairless hands caught her arms and stopped her.

"You passed the water seven strides ago."

"You waited." She was amazed.

"Put the Littlelost down," was all he answered. "I do not wish to lose more time."

And he waited no longer.

The other Littlelost waited, though. Alison lowered Camay to the ground and wiped away the child's tears with shaking fingers. Beau helped by licking Camay's face, and then Alison's.

She laughed her tremulous relief, all the self-congratulation she had time for.

They had gathered near the clearing, as if awaiting him.

One stood sentinel on a rocky outcropping, his moonlight-haloed profile sparking with the gleam of watchful yellow eyes.

The others were less visible, even to his predatory vision.

His own two-sided eyes saw through centuries now, saw them as both ordinary and extraordinary, as what they had been and what they could become.

They approached slowly, recognizing his scent, puzzled but unfrightened. One world called them wolves. Another, Slinkers. If they slunk, it was from caution and long experience of both worlds.

He watched their ages-old inspection dance, their heads lowered, teeth bared. They were ready to display submission, if required, or to attack him in one well-ordered pack.

Always adaptable, his brothers and sisters, but still hunted and hated by many of their human brothers.

They numbered five, like the senses: the grizzled, one-eared chieftain, Weatherwise; Featherstep, the yellow-furred female leader; two young black males, Quickfang and Cowlick; and the odd female out, Moondrift, a youngster whose coat was the color of birch bark and whose manner was as deferential as melting snow.

He suffered Weatherwise's thorough inspection from nose to tail and back again. The pack had two excess males already, though these had not matured enough to challenge the leader.

He, however, was neither male nor female, and more than the veterinarian's procedure had guaranteed that. He was touched now by Mother Earth and Father Sky, caught between them, neutral meat for the matching jaws of land and outer immensity. Truly crossbred.

They came to him one by one, Moondrift last, noting their differences and his sameness. They had already marked the Taliswoman as their charge by instinct. Weatherwise's urine upon her sleeping sack had not been a puzzling animal indignity, but an ancient seal upon territory the wolf felt obligated to protect—even for reasons that were far beyond his ken.

He himself, being animal-born, was not so readily accepted. Often it was easier to bond across species and sexes than within them. Now all that was moot, as these five would soon know better than any two-legged creature in any such exotic place as Minnesota or Veil.

He smiled, pleased that his present canine form permitted the expression he had so neglected in human guise. The smile unified only the highest of the creatures of Allearth: the clever-fingered apes and monkeys; the merely clever wolves and dogs; man, woman and child. Cat fanciers would include their favorite felines among that chosen few, but cats were too wise to smile.

He wheeled, giving them his flashing white hocks. His flight led them through bramble, brush and forest, over banks and meadows, and up hills and steep walls of shale. He brought them onto the empty heights, where the mountains' cold breath rolled invisibly down to the massed armies of pines below, to where only mountain goats, wolves and gods could go.

Moonlight reflected the salt-and-pepper glitter of their coats. When he stopped atop a prominent rock, like a watch-wolf, they sat on their haunches in a circle, tongues lolling and sides heaving, yellow eyes curious and alert.

Then he stood for them, stood on his hind legs like a bear, towered until his skin split and his pelt shrank to cover only his massive shoulders, and the clever canine face smiled emptily from his brow.

It was eyeless, that face. Now his own dark eyes looked down on them from his first visage as he spoke in the language that was part Ojibwa and part whimper and part wind.

"Sisters and brothers," he hissed like the wind through shark-bright fangs, "you look to the moon and wail to the stars, but I say to you, look farther than the moon, to the seam between earth and sky."

Their sharp, pricked profiles turned obediently to the horizon below, which foamed with clouds as far as the eye could see, for Veil's horizon line was always bounded by a curtain of misty air.

He spoke to them again.

"There the People of the Horizon dwell in silence and in sorrow, and there the bone buffalo leads thousands upon thousands of its kind in cumulus herds."

Their tongues lolled farther out in memory of the hunt.

"There dwell your ancestors and your seed, unless you lend yourselves to a greater need than hunting packs and moon-cries, and take upon yourselves a semblance of the Great White Spirit. You will be as I—more, but you will never be less." The last words were in warning.

And from him—the elderly shaman, with the white wolfish pelt draping his head and shoulders—from his seamed mahogany skin and gray-streaked black hair, emanated a thing of frost and dream: a white warrior of straight limb and unwrinkled aspect.

The warrior dropped upon all fours.

"I am Dog," said all three—the empty pelt, the old shaman and the young Spirit Warrior. "I have hunted alongside men; I have waited for food alongside women; I have played with their offspring. I have made the bargain that my brother and sister wolves have seldom made, and have been rewarded with fire and food and affection—and with cages and collars and blows and death.

"I ask you now to take upon yourselves those who have gone before, who have been driven as you have from your hunting grounds, who have been starved and slaughtered and poisoned and hunted to nearly the last of their kind. These have gone both gladly and sadly, knowing that an evil of such darkness as to match the depth, height and width of the Great White Spirit itself has been gathering upon the land and in the sky for centuries past.

"Mother Earth lies wounded and insensible. Father Sky weeps burning tears. We children of earth and sky, we old enemies who are too alike to hate each other without hating ourselves, we must forge a new alliance between flesh and spirit, male and female, kind and other kind.

"Brothers and sisters, you have already bowed your nature to one marked to defend what is not ours. Will you join the People of the Horizon for the last battle?"

His answer was a howl, echoed by another. His answer was a chorus of wolves, crying as they always had—out of hunger and triumphal loneliness, out of oneness with all, out of the fierce joy to be found in life and death.

Dog shrank back into his original form, became the white wolf-spitz called Rambeau, who was part that simple animal mentality, part Eli Ravenhare, and part Spirit Warrior—an emanation from the end of everything that is overseen by Father Sky, where the People of the Horizon move endlessly among the shifting clouds.

Dog, too, howled then, white mask joining black and gray and gold faces in challenging the moon.

From the foggy horizon, where the cloud-beasts paraded in ranks like a spectral Roman legion, a breath of ancient air separated like cream from milk and became the forms of men and women with long braids of hair whipping against the moon-washed sky.

And they came, the aged warriors and maidens, the old women and the young men, in a clotting, swirling company of clouds that threw veils across the moon.

They swept up the sky and down again, to touch earth in the clearing the wolves had claimed. Misty figures vibrated to the high-pitched howls. Phantom fringe shook and ghostly beads rattled soundlessly. Vaporous arms entwined the waiting wolves like scarves. Insubstantial hands grasped fur. Heads melted into heads. The wolves' fur sparkled with dew—or tears—as if showered with sleet.

One by one they broke their chorus. When they eyed Dog, they saw the stranger, Rambeau. When he regarded them, he saw wolves with ancient eyes, eyes as black as the heart of a windstorm.

He stood, tail not quite flourished over his Samoyed back. He was more muscular than they; his white fur gleamed like a wave crest in the moonlight, with a neck ruff full enough to trim a coat. He could have conquered a show ring.

His eyes remained as hungry as theirs, as dark as theirs had become, and almost as old.

Rambeau trotted off in a businesslike canine gait. The others returned to their wolfish matters. Nothing had changed beyond their lost yellow eyes, although everything had. They would be ready when needed.

10

The party stood on a precipice facing an opposite cliff. Narrow streams plummeted from either side, needles of water stabbing into the crevasse with dizzying speed. The shining, liquid lengths narrowed like braids below, yet to lean over the abyss in admiration was to invite nausea.

"We cannot cross." Alison articulated what everyone was thinking. Except Rowan. He only pointed below.

She bent over the stream that glittered past the slick stones at her boot toes before taking its icy plunge over the precipice. Fifty feet below, linking one narrow watery veil to the other, hung a woven bridge.

"You have crossed that before?" Alison was incredulous. Rowan might have few qualms about leapfrogging a lake from stone to stone, but surely a man of his size would distrust the wind-sack of hemp swaying gently below.

"No," he said, "but there is no other way."

"And we get down to it by—?"

He pointed again, to the direction she was afraid he would choose. Down. The cliffside. Alongside the noisy slipstream of waterfall.

"Beau—" Alison began.

"Then stay."

Rowan tested the security of his backpack, reached up to a leafless limb and swung over the emptiness. His flailing foot found a stony notch. His hands slipped down to the dead tree's roots, then vanished from view with the rest of him.

"You want to go back?" Alison polled the Littlelost.

"Cross the pond again?" Pickle's face matched his name. "Too much like etherion-gathering."

"There's that," Alison agreed.

Twist took her indecision for agreement and sprang over the cliff on the same springy lever that Rowan had chosen. He vanished like a monkey down a vine. The Littlelost were fearless climbers—and descenders. They quickly followed their leader, even tiny Camay.

Alison eyed Rambeau. "Guess it's just you and me, boy."

He responded with one urgent woof, an elementary sound that said, "Come on, dummy." Or, "Go ahead, chicken."

Alison grasped the tree limb and dangled a tentative foot over the rim of the cliff. It found a niche. She climbed down feverishly, aware of nothing but the grimy, rock-studded cliff face she embraced and the water pulsing past her like a silver Midnight Special.

Frequent hand- and foot-holds kept her descending, whether she wanted to or not. Though she expected to, she never heard the thin, fading scream of a body that had lost its grip on Mother Earth.

Her feet found the ground again, which felt unnaturally horizontal. Alison turned cautiously, still hugging the cliff side.

Spray spat past her cheek with thunderous speed. A matching wall of diaphanous water roared and scintillated down the opposite rock face. The cliffs drew apart as they plunged downward, which meant that the party—for all were present now—was strung out along a narrow ledge in the icy shade of an overhang. The bridge they had thought to cross proved on close-up to be a sodden fiber fretwork sagging between the dueling waterfalls. It looked far too fragile for anything heavier than a dragonfly.

Beau braced to shake his white coat free of a blizzard of water drops. Alison eyed him. "Hey, how'd you get here?"

Camay pointed to the waterfall spraying them like a giant Water-Pik. Alison could just glimpse the stepping-stones of a rocky ziggurat behind it. No wonder Beau had been so confident at her desertion; a stone stair had awaited anyone who didn't mind walking under the waterfall.

She was about to tell their taciturn trailblazer that he'd had them risking their necks on a more dangerous route than was necessary when she saw that Rowan stood oblivious and transfixed, staring at the opposite fall.

"Her again," she breathed. For a gray figure wavered on the

far end of the bridge, barely visible through the silver sleet: the phantom of the pond rocks.

Rowan didn't hear Alison over the gargling falls, or if he did, he didn't heed her. His voice lifted and uncoiled like a whip: "You, there. Go back. We must cross."

Instead, the figure edged farther onto the hempen sling spanning the crevasse.

"We cannot pass with you in the way!" Rowan's sharp bellow rang from rock and water.

The figure, now mid-bridge, inched even nearer.

Rowan's staff lifted. "Back! Or I'll knock you into the gorge and out of our way."

Alison put a cautionary hand on the staff, a mistake. Her strength was no match for Rowan's. He jerked the wood from her grip. "She's only an old woman," she said.

His glance burned like embers, cinnamon reddened to cinnabar. "I must cross soon," he shouted, "if I am to arrive in time for the Wellsunging. She could be a Crux-demon, sent in this guise. Some say that old women can change themselves into owls and wasps; perhaps more dangerous pests can make themselves into old women."

"Let her cross," Alison urged. "We can cross afterward."

"Wellsunging?" came a faint echo over the hiss of furious water. "Why did you not say so?" The figure began to retreat, painfully, each foot moving only half the length of the other.

Rowan blew out an impatient breath. "No one dare cross until the span is bare." He eyed the party crowding the ledge. "Littlelost first, then Spirit Stalker, then mage."

"How gallant," Alison noted.

Veil either didn't have the equivalent of the sea's women-and-children-first rule, or Rowan chose to ignore her comment. Once the old woman had vanished into the mist opposite, he prodded Camay onto the ropes. She darted across as easily as the older Littlelost, who soon followed her.

Beau was different; Alison had rarely heard of a dog tightrope-walking, and he had no hands with which to hold on to the guide ropes. But he touched his black nose to the hemp netting and danced across, dainty legs hitting each strand squarely, and so quickly that his paws had no time to slip.

Alison crossed next, hating the last moments when she had to plunge into a shower of pelting water, her eyes shut, hair sopping, the backpack soaking up instant weight.

She emerged sputtering beneath the waterfall on the opposite ledge, blinking at the woman, who looked like part of the rock face. She turned in time to see Rowan emerge from the downpour, his wet, bronzed face as slick as the metal hood that surrounded it.

His eyes were only for the woman. "You have caused us delay, Grandmother," he said tersely. "And how did you expect to climb the cliff on the other side once you got there?"

"Discourtesy makes a barrier more bitter than rock faces, Wellsinger, even for one as worthless as an old woman."

The woman's self-effacement irritated Alison, but she wondered the same thing Rowan did. "How would you have climbed such a sheer cliff—or the slick, under-fall staircase—at your age and . . ."

"And bulk?" The woman's facial seams puckered in self-derision, her weathered skin crackling as if dried yellow mud. Age had bent her squat and lumpy form like a willow hoop; she had to cock her head to see the smallest Littlelost. Yet the kernel of mirth in her eyes hinted of long laughter well remembered, laughter that would not wither.

"I am Sage Wintergreen," she told Alison. "Travelers seeking the Wellsunging could not have chosen a better route. Come, dry off in the cavern." She gestured to a black archway that opened onto the ledge a few feet from the waterfall. "I have passed that way, and it is clean." She eyed Rowan significantly. "The Valley of the Voices lies through the mountain, Desmeynian."

"You are certain?" Rowan demanded.

"At my age I am certain of little, pilgrim, but I have just come from gathering . . . certain items . . . in the valley. And you might be—?"

"Rowan," he snapped.

"Only Rowan?"

"Rowan." His jaw closed with a finality that reminded Alison of a watchdog refusing to bark.

Sage turned to the Littlelost, who regarded her with wide eyes, then spilled their names in a flood. "And you, child?"

"I'm no child," Alison protested. "But I answer to Alison."

"Just Alison?"

"Carver. Alison Carver."

Sage brushed a yellow-white strand of hair from her watery gray eyes. "You are not of this land."

"Yes—and no."

"Now this large piece of louthood that you accompany—" Alison looked around nervously for Rowan, but he was out of earshot, exploring the cave mouth that gaped behind them"—is Desmeynian, and no doubt. You are not. Nor are you of others I have traveled among, such as the Silvin kind. So what land claims you?"

"A land of lakes."

Sage's head shook. "Lakes harbor dead things, and living things better off dead; lakes hold rot and decay and cover the earth where it aches. You are a land-dweller, like all of us."

"Perhaps I'm just a Littlelost grown up," she answered lightly. How could she identity herself in this alien place? The truth wouldn't serve, and she wasn't used to lying—not in print, and not in person.

Sage studied her. "You are a stranger, that is certain, and have much to learn. And much to teach, if my instinct is not wrong. Not always a comfortable position to be in, as you will find. But what land claims you?"

"The . . . Island, I suppose. Only, to be perfectly accurate—and that's my job—it's really not an island."

Sage nodded. "Truth is always uncertain, contrary to common expectations. Very well, Alison Carver of Island-Not, we will go into the cavern—once the Desmeynian is convinced that it is safe enough for his precious hide—and we will have a fire and some Millennium Milkweed tea that I have saved for key occasions."

"Walking through waterfalls is special?" Alison wondered, turning to view the crystal sheet that shattered past like shotgunned window glass.

"That is not the key occasion." Sage Wintergreen's face wore a disconcertingly youthful grin. "It is *who* has walked through a waterfall and *where* that person will walk afterward. It should prove most interesting to watch."

"I have a feeling that you enjoy being mysterious, and that you won't tell me any more."

"It is one of the few pleasures left to the old. And you are right."

If the crystalline waterfall sheeting outside the cave was a picture window, slightly clouded—and the bare ground a woven sisal rug, and the smoke that escaped Sage's camp fire to swirl against the rocky ceiling an atmospheric effect—then the cave that Sage had suggested as a resting place was not too bad.

The fire, its kindling apparently collected by Sage the previous night, owed its quick combustion to one of Alison's trusty farmer matches. Sage had wanted to start a blaze by rubbing her knuckles over a bit of sienna-colored dried moss she pulled from a lumpy gunny sack tied around her waist. The moss might have worked eventually, but Alison didn't want the kids shivering wetly in the dark any longer.

The Littlelost warmed to Sage's domestic attentions and to the treats doled out from her overstuffed, capacious pockets, especially when the old woman produced something suspiciously like horehound candy. They didn't even miss Rambeau, on guard on the ledge outside by his own inclination.

The old woman's crude hospitality relaxed Alison, too. Sage Wintergreen seemed so *normal,* despite her obscure talk and here-again, gone-again appearances earlier in the day. Alison could have met her in Rubnik's grocery in Keewatin and decided to do a feature on this independent old lady who lived alone in the woods . . . except that the woods had become a cave and northern Minnesota had inexplicably been transmuted into Veil.

"Why didn't you ask the Littlelost for family names?" Alison wondered, sipping sweet-sour tea from the screw-off cup on her canteen.

"As well ask the wind for a pedigree," Sage answered. "They would not be Littlelost had they a connection to anything—kin, land, memory—that would claim them. Their very birth is their worst bane."

"It's ridiculous to label children as lost beyond redemption! They live, breathe, can even play if their poor minds aren't haunted by horrors children shouldn't know about. You people of Veil are shockingly backward when it comes to child-protection philosophy."

Sage blinked at this outburst. Even Rowan, who, hunched over, had been prowling the low-ceilinged cavern, paused to listen. Alison sipped tea to calm herself down. Her bizarre dislocation in space—and perhaps in time? Mercy, that was an awful thought!—could tilt her emotions too far at too little provocation. The tea blended the addictive-sweet and repellent-sour, like much of what she'd seen of Veil so far.

"Why take it out on the kids?" she muttered.

Sage was silent, then replaced her battered pot on the fire. "Much to learn, much to teach."

Rowan came back to them, standing slightly bent instead of sitting down. "Earth-Eaters?" He interrogated Sage, rather than asked her. Alison's ears perked up for the answer.

"No," Sage said gruffly. She began slicing something into the wide-mouthed pot that held the tea. "A Desmeynian should know that they are his kind's particular curse."

"There are other dangers, Grandmother."

"Only to those who insist on being dangerous themselves," Sage said shortly, lifting her eyes from her work to hand him a cup of tea. Oddly enough, he accepted it.

"And there is a passage through to the valley?" he asked next.

Sage nodded.

"May not others be taking it as well?"

"Perhaps." She eyed the man with amusement. "You worry a good deal about rivals, Rowan Wellsinger, for one who believes that the prize is already his."

He straightened but did not deny the charge. "Because I believe, it will be," Rowan responded with such flaring conviction that the fire seemed to burn brighter in answer. "Last year it went to Fjermuth Anglersun, and what has his possession done to stem the tide of ills that seeps into our land?"

"At least," Sage noted, "Fjermuth Anglersun has enjoyed himself during that year."

At this gentle—if mysterious—gibe, Rowan's face reddened to match the flames. He turned his tin cup of tea over the blaze, causing threads of flame to falter and hiss like snakes. "The purpose of pilgrimage is not to ensure a quester's comfort," Rowan retorted.

"Careful, my lad!" Sage's reprimand was more amused than sharp. "You'll ruin my dinner, and thus starve yet another appetite."

Rowan turned away with an expletive. It resembled no cuss word Alison had heard before. He resumed his restless patrol of the cavern, skirting Beau, who had come in and lain down among the Littlelost, accepting their sticky-fingered pats with an amiable grin.

"Let him sulk." Sage stirred her soup. Alison recognized the main ingredient: onion-thin slices of the ever-popular pomma. The food was evidently a traveler's boon, used in multitudinous ways.

Rowan had fashioned a torch by attaching some of Sage's moss atop his staff and touching it to the fire. Alison watched his Quasimodo-like shadow shrivel into the low, over-lit mouth of one of the many tunnels leading from the cavern.

"He is impatient," Sage said, "and well he has reason to be, poor lad."

"You gave him no quarter earlier."

"He was present. There is no sense in coddling those who make hard demands upon themselves."

"He follows some sort of . . . religious duty?"

"What is 'religious'?"

Alison held out her empty cup for a filling of tea soup while considering an answer. Sage tilted the whole pot to pour it, protecting her hands with bits of brown moss. Alison decided that the moss was both a fuel and a heat retardant, an odd combination of opposite properties, but this was Veil, not Minnesota. And was it still Planet Earth? An interesting question.

The Littlelost gathered together, sipping from the pot with a common ladle now that Alison and Sage had filled their cups. Collapsed on their haunches like puppies, they sprawled around the centerpiece soup and nudged each other for position. Judging by the fast retreat of faces and lips from the first sips, Alison guessed they didn't often sample hot food.

"Religion," she mused aloud. "Ritual, I guess, that calls upon a power greater than ourselves. Does . . . Veil recognize such a thing?"

"Veil recognizes powerful beings—gods who dwell above the clouds and once meddled in the doings below. But now the old gods are distant and unfelt, mere passwords to a time when people believed in them, and Veil recognizes little," Sage said sourly, "that is worthwhile. Yourself, for instance."

"I . . . really, that's a nice compliment, but I'm just a stranger. A lost stranger." The old Negro spiritual leaped into her mind. *"I am a poor, wayfarin' stranger,"* she sang softly, recalling that she was hardly the first person to be transported to another world—or to have another world impinge violently upon her own. Native Americans and the first European explorers came to mind. Who had dazzled whom the most?

The Littlelost stopped slurping to cock rapt faces at her. "M-m-more!" Twist urged, looking like an illustration of Oliver Twist, the others' voices swelling behind him with the same demand. Was he? Alison wondered. Was this echo of a book from her world just coincidence, or more?

"Really. You guys act as if you've never heard singing before."

"They are Littlelost," Sage put in, as if that explained it. "If they are to go to the Valley of the Voices, they should hear more now. Sing," the old woman ordered, leaning against a rocky outcropping and shutting thin, wrinkled eyelids.

So Alison finished the spiritual in her best high-school-choir contralto. The song's low, melancholy range suited her deep, yet sweet, voice.

The Littlelost quieted as she sang. Warmed with soup, they tumbled into a litterlike pile and soon fell asleep.

"What will you do with them?" Sage asked with hushed urgency, as if she had been waiting for the opportunity.

"Nothing. Take them somewhere safe."

"And where is that?"

"To a . . . city." She watched the old woman's eyes for a

flicker of recognition at the word, but Sage Wintergreen was as stoic as Eli Ravenhare. "A town. A settlement. Where people can take care of them."

"Why? They feed themselves, do they not?"

"Listen, they feed me! But . . . well, look at yourself. Aren't you happier among other people, where someone your age can be looked after? Surely you don't like to make your way alone through this wilderness, a poor wayfaring stranger?"

"The people in your land must be like Rowan," Sage said. "They seem to spend much time feeling sorry for themselves. The Littlelost and I are not allowed such a luxury. But then, we are not young."

"*They're* not young? How much younger can you be and still walk?"

Sage tapped her blue-veined temple with a yellow-nailed forefinger. "Here they are not young. Do not let size deceive you: little like these, large like that one"—she nodded toward the tunnel, whose mouth glowed with the heat of Rowan's torch—"who is testing his tether to the end of the line. Veil is deception incarnate. That is our religion, our ritual. You will survive here better, poor wayfaring stranger, if you admit that."

"Perhaps I won't have to stay here," Alison found herself saying. The assertion sounded childishly defiant.

"Perhaps the choice won't be up to you." Sage smiled with a private pleasure and fished the remaining pomma slices from the tea soup. They lay on her hands like pale, fleshy coins before she tucked them into her food sack for another day's use. She dumped the tea upon the flames and the cavern was immersed in darkness.

"What about Rowan?" Alison wondered, referring to his share of dinner as well as to larger questions.

"If he had wanted to share my food, which he likely finds unpalatable, he would ask. And he will not find his way out of the caverns without me," came Sage's acerbic reply. "Perhaps an old woman is good for something, after all."

Alison awoke in the not-quite dark.

Someone was snoring softly. She hoped it was that Mr.

Know-It-All, Rowan. She would love knowing something about him that he didn't know himself.

Her mind and body stretched into consciousness for a few nervous moments, sensing and identifying the irregular dirt floor she lay on, remembering the cavern, remembering Veil.

Yes, this was where she was supposed to be—assuming that it was not all a dream or a delusion—but something was wrong, different.

Smoke hung above her like mosquito netting, fragile and weightless, pale swirling tendrils, almost alive. She had seen Sage douse their fire hours before. If Rowan had returned, he would have snuffed his makeshift torch as well. So what light illuminated the smoke? Where did it come from?

Alison turned her head to one side. There were the Littlelost, tangled in sleep, Sage drowsing by her overturned soup pot, and—yes, Rowan hadn't fallen down a rabbit hole on his explorations, for his form made a long hummock in the semidark. And Rambeau must have returned to his guard-post outside.

So all was well.

Except—how was she *seeing* all this without light?

Alison sat up, the nylon shell of her down vest rasping with the sudden motion.

"Oh." The smoke swirled in soft pastel shades, like Eli's "rainbows of night, burning campfire bright." She was watching the shadow of an aurora borealis milling on the cave's adamant midnight sky.

Then she looked down and saw faint, frosty motion on the side walls. The light was generated by a carousel of capering figures turning slowly, like a miniature zodiac composed of no constellations she'd ever seen.

She identified a Quasimodo-like figure. Was it an old woman—or a grazing buffalo? A dog dancing on its hind legs—or a bear rearing to defend itself? A dragon cavorting in fiery arabesques—or a swan? A swan with a feathered third wing protruding from its back, bloody wings beating as it sank like a wounded sunset into the wisps of smoke, of hair, of memory veiling all the moving figures.

Wonders need witnesses.

Alison eyed the cluttered Littlelost; then Rowan, off by himself, as he always was. Sage was nearest—and nicest—so she gently shook the woman's bony shoulder.

Sage sat up abruptly, like a corpse on Resurrection Day. The old sleep lightly; Alison had once done a story on the ills of the elderly, and this had been one of the complaints. Unfortunately, the snoring had stopped. The source had not been Rowan, but Sage.

Alison didn't have to point; Sage immediately squinted at the phosphorescent display. They sat and watched in silence until their necks hurt. A rhythmic expectancy hung in the cavern's stale air. Alison felt that music accompanied the light-show, but she couldn't hear it.

She considered rousing their other companions and glanced at the Littlelost, noting that Sage eyed Rowan.

There was light enough for her and Sage to gauge each other's expressions in the cavern's dusk. The phenomenon was too personal to broadcast. They exchanged a smile and lay back down. Above them, the pale, phantom smoke of dream and memory drifted like angel hair.

11

Dawn did not so much come to the cave as steal into it like a thief made of light. The cavern walls were flat gray, lit by nothing but the oozing daylight.

Sage and the Littlelost chewed the leftover pomma in silence. When Alison finished hers, she used the latrine she and Rowan had shaped the previous night: a rocky trench, not deep enough to muffle its use to either sight or smell. She hated leaving an open sewer behind them, but there was no dirt to fill it with.

In the cavern, the constantly spurting waterfall outside made talk difficult. Certainly Rowan was more withdrawn than ever. After he had gnawed on some of his turkey jerky, Alison watched him automatically withdraw his rubrock and apply it to his knuckles. Then he froze mid-gesture and threw the hair remover back into his pouch with a strange, tight smile.

"Don Johnson, Jr.," Alison muttered, trying to picture Rowan with a five-o-clock shadow. Perhaps the Littlelost's disdain of grooming was catching.

Rowan ignored both her and them, turning briskly to Sage. "I explored the tunnels last night as far as I dared. They weave through the mountain like braided hair. How can you be sure you won't mislead us?"

"No one can be sure of not misleading anyone," Sage retorted. "But I know these hidden ways; traveling alone has forced me to search out dark paths."

"Do others know your paths?" he asked.

Sage shrugged. "They are here for all who would seek and follow. Few do."

"That is no guarantee, old woman."

"Are you still so foolish that you demand guarantees, young man?"

"I am still that hopeful, yes."

"If we're going," Alison interrupted, "I need to collect Rambeau."

She went to the curtain of water before the cave mouth. A glance left and right along the ledge showed no familiar white form. She edged into the filtered daylight, stung by the tiny shards of mist that seethed around the plummeting water.

"Rambeau! Come on. Come here!"

Her voice echoed soggily through the chasm. She turned back into the cavern. "Wait," she called into the dimness, where moving figures were now funneling toward a tunnel mouth. "I have to find Rambeau."

"Cannot wait." Rowan, the tallest figure, picked up his pack. She watched his silhouette ebb into the tunnel's deeper darkness.

"Rambeau!" She darted past the falling water to the exterior ledge, blinked in bright daylight, eyed the two cliff tops with her hand-shaded eyes. She expected a fanged face and lolling tongue to grin over the edge at any second.

Seconds became quarter-minutes.

"Rambeau!"

Someone tugged on her pantleg. Camay. "They go."

"All of them?" Alison asked in dismay. "Even Littlelost?"

Camay nodded solemnly.

"I just need a few minutes to find Beau. He must have wandered off."

But she knew better. If the dog hadn't appeared by now, he wasn't within earshot—or conscious. Sighing, she weighed the unhappy alternatives: remain here, scale the cliff with Camay and still not find Beau; or follow the rest into the dark, cold heart of the mountain and hope they find their way into this vocal valley that Rowan was so hot to reach.

The choice was impossible to make. As she debated, a rock broke loose from above and crashed onto the ledge. Alison jerked Camay back and stared at the rock. An iridescent black pulp oozed out of it as if alive. A stench like pus-infected coal tar permeated the air.

"Earth-bane?" she asked Camay.

The child shook her head. Alison took Camay's tiny hand and led her back into the cave. They had delayed just long enough to make either course they took impractical. Alison pointed to the tunnel she thought Rowan's bulk had entered.

"This one?"

Camay, looking doubtful, nodded slowly.

Alison needed confirmation but knew that the child was too young to provide it. As she headed for the tunnel, a glint caught her eye.

The main cavern wall gleamed with what resembled a pale lightning bolt, like a silver ore embedded in its iron-gray surface. Alison paused to examine it, seeing then that the lines had been etched into the rock. The lightning bolt's forks were really horns, and the cloud that massed behind them was the sketchy bulk of a bison.

Alison's gaze swept the perimeter. A dozen similar sketches sparkled like heat lightning against the midnight-blue underbelly of thunderheads. These were the figures that had danced in the lazy arms of the unspent smoke the previous night. People forgotten to Veil had lived here, sketched the limits of their lives and vanished.

Evidence so similar to signs of past cultures in her world soothed Alison with a saraband of convoluted wishful thinking. If Veil, too, had a past, then it could have a future. And if it had a future, then perhaps—in time—Alison's past might intersect with Veil's as yet undiscovered future, at a temporal point where she could merge back into her real-world present. She caught Camay's hand firmly in hers and bent to the portal of the tunnel.

Light penetrated these dark aortas of air through solid rock. So did wind; at times Alison's and Camay's hair lifted from the sides of their faces. Sometimes the tunnel glowed with a phosphorescent illumination as mysterious as mist. At others, the tube turned tangibly black. The air felt like a soft barrier that could smother them. Even Alison's flashlight beam, though its sudden magical appearance made Camay coo, could barely slice the darkness; it was like a laser attacking a Black Hole that sucked all of its energy into an unseen vortex.

Their footsteps were absorbed, as if falling on shag carpet, and Alison sensed . . . growths around them in the dark. Underneath their feet, beneath their hands when they reached out to find the tunnel sides, they came upon crew-cut, mossy things that strung themselves like cobwebs across the rocks.

Some passages diffused enough light from some high chimney to imbue these lichens with vibrant, carnal colors: violet and emerald, saffron and electric-blue, and the sickly jade green of decay. Alison kept her flashlight on to fade the reflections, shaded like carnival glass—gaudy and addictive.

She had hoped to catch up soon with the others, or at least to see some sign of their passage, but there was only the checkered darkness and the sense of spiraling ever deeper into the uncharted mountain. She paused to consider retreat while she might still be able to retrace their path. The darkness swirled around them like a cocooning blanket.

Camay's fingers clenched hers, driving Alison's nails into the flesh of adjoining fingers. That terrible, unquenchable infant grip. Oh, baby, Alison thought, what have I done? Am I gonna get you out of here? She had a sudden thought—an image, rather—of Rambeau, and felt another convulsive twist of grief and guilt.

A sound came barreling up the darkness. A growl.

Rambeau?

Or a cave-dwelling bear?

Someone human, or half so?

Shouts came next, and thudding sounds.

Alison didn't care if a convention of bikers were having a face-off down in the darkness. The contention gave her a goal, a sense of direction in this unstrung mess.

"Come on!" she whispered to Camay.

They stumbled forward, following the rough sounds, Alison clutching the Littlelost, the flashlight grasped in her other sweaty hand.

Darkness saw the light and swallowed it yard after yard. The tunnel neither widened, narrowed nor grew low enough to make them crawl. It just went on forever in its circuitous certainty.

Then the flashlight beam paled—and exploded as light came drilling back at them like a devouring maw, light that started as concentrated as a star and went nova. Alison ran over the rough, hard ground toward it, sweeping Camay along with her, dousing her flashlight and stowing it in an outer pocket of her backpack as she went.

The huge cave that opened before them glowed like a lava lamp. It was embellished with arched stalagmites and stalactites scattered in a pattern like gigantic croquet hoops.

Amongst these natural pillars contended a group of figures: strange men fighting with clubs; even stranger subhumans attacking on all fours like beasts, dwarves upon their backs tearing at the hair that covered their bodies in scabrous patches.

Not dwarves—Littlelost! Pickle's knotted turban bobbed up and down as the creature he had pounced upon bucked and twisted. Faun and Rime hung on to another such creature, and Twist was butting a Taker from behind while Rowan belabored him with his staff from the front. Two other men, like Rowan in mein and dress, wielded knotted wooden clubs against the dozen Takers and beasts.

Alison halted in the entrance to the cavern and dropped her pack. She bent to dig out the revolver. The box of shells—was it lost? Her nails tore raggedly as she clawed through the melange of goods. There it was. She loaded the chamber with shaking fingers.

Around her, wood *thwunked* on wood and bone. Steel sharpened itself on wood and flesh. Cries of bloodlust and pain ricocheted around the vast, stony vault.

"Stay here!" she ordered Camay, sitting her on the backpack. The child, looking dazed, obeyed.

Alison ran toward the cavern's center, suddenly realizing that the ground was slick. She slowed to cross packed earth that shone like oozing oil. If she slipped and the gun discharged, anyone could be hit. She came to Twist, riding piggyback on a creature that made a Taker look—and smell—like a dilettante. It was an unclothed cross between an ape and a hyena, covered in hair. She kicked the thing's muscular hind leg out from under it, catching Twist's confident grin as he lifted a roast-sized rock in one hand when the pair tumbled over together. Only Twist got up.

A squat bag of gray wool—Sage!—huddled against a wall under the blows of two shambling, rough-haired attackers. Alison clipped one behind the—ear? certainly it was some sort of projection—with the revolver barrel. Her almost simultaneous kick caught the other in the midsection.

She spun at the sound of footsteps, Sage safe behind her, and lifted her hands. She wouldn't fire the gun unless she had to, she thought. The figure that faced her in full battle challenge, feet braced, battle-ax raised, had blue hair that swirled like a whirlpool around its human face.

Mutual surprise at each other's alienness paralyzed them.

Something clutched Alison's left arm and dragged her off her feet. She smelled a wave of fetid breath. She spun to deliver another kick and a hand blow to the body, glimpsing a horny cranium. Claws dragged slowly down her arm as they released her, a parting gift of blood.

She grimaced, feeling the pistol butt impress the fleshy mound beneath her right thumb. Behind her someone moaned. She whirled. A Taker slid to the floor under the butt of Rowan's staff. Why didn't the bloody pilgrim carry a sword?

The two club-bearing young men repelled two of the cave creatures beyond a lurid arch sparkling with indigo crystals. From quick glimpses of these strangers—one brown-haired and bearded, the other blond—they resembled Rowan rather than Takers or bestial things. And she would welcome allies here—

Something dropped from the arch above in a rain of shattered crystals as sharp as daggers, and landed on her back like Hulk Hogan. She fell over backward, her hands and feet flailing, her *taekwondo* discipline off balance, her senses reeling from the overwhelming smell of raw meat on her attacker's breath, the feel of bloated, hairy flesh under her.

She twisted to push the revolver into the broad side of the creature. The barrel pressed in, and in, as if there were no skeleton to stop it, as if she were trying to shoot breakfast mush. . . . A resounding crack to her opponent's cranium made her own head ring. But the fierce grip on her torso slackened and she fought to get upright, at last grabbing the staff inelegantly poked at her.

She heaved up on someone else's strength and leaned over to ease the stitch in her side. Her rescuer, Rowan, was eyeing the huge, hairy, unconscious man-thing on the cave floor with some satisfaction. She glimpsed a movement above, saw something dark and shapeless dropping toward him.

The revolver lifted of its own volition, like a bird breaking for freedom out of a tree. She remembered to follow the target and to squeeze the trigger—twelve pounds of slow pressure in her forefinger. The report nearly shattered her eardrums. The gun flashed streaks of fiery red and yellow war paint amid a halo of faint blue. Smoke clouded the ceiling with an odor of sulfur.

It was as if Mephistopheles had made an overdramatic appearance at the Met. Everything stopped. In slow motion, the figure dropped to the floor, its final statement a dull and fatal thud.

Camay's thin scream echoed from far away. Alison was amazed that she recognized the identity of the screamer. Rowan stepped back with theatrical denial, as if rejecting both the danger the dead creature had posed and the beast's death at Alison's hands.

The other combatants sprang apart. As the club-bearing strangers lowered their weapons, the Takers and their bestial allies, grimly mute as they had been all along, scrabbled away into the dark of presumed tunnels and chimneys in the rock. Something touched Alison's left sleeve with delicate deference. She started, then looked down into Sage's wizened face.

"You will need tending." The old woman's forefinger stroked Alison's shredded, bloodsoaked sleeve.

Alison wanted to say that it was nothing, but it hurt like hell, she realized. Then a staff hit a club with a dull, ringing sound, and Rowan was squaring off with the brown-bearded stranger.

"Now *they* fight?" Alison was incredulous.

"It was their fighting that drew the cave wights."

"Why?"

"They are all Wellsingers." Sage smiled at Alison's confusion. "It is not serious; that is one reason they are not allowed to bear edged metal, so they will not hurt each other."

"I wish they were better equipped to hurt Takers." Alison regarded the trio with disbelief. The blond man stood politely aside, awaiting his turn at the victor, no doubt, while Rowan's staff expertly dueled the other man's formidable club. "And they won't stop?"

Sage shook her head. "It is a ritual the Wellsingers must perform to feel that they have won their place at the Wellsunging."

"The customs of Veil are mind-boggling, but I suppose a wrestling match in my world would be incomprehensible here." Sage's blank expression confirmed that. "What about the Littlelost?"

She needn't have worried. The Littlelost had gathered around Camay, hoisted Alison's pack between them and were bearing it back to her.

"We dare not wait for the end of this semi-friendly jousting bout," Alison fretted as she took the pack. "Those cave things won't stay spooked forever. Do you know a way out of here?"

Sage nodded crookedly.

"And are you . . . well enough to lead us out?"

For answer, Sage lifted her arms, palms out, until her shapeless sleeves fell back. Her arms were sheathed in leather sleeves that had protected her from the blows.

The Littlelost, beginning to bruise but looking proud of it, swarmed them. Pickle pressed close to Alison. "Beau?" he asked.

She looked at the thin, serious face, her own feelings about to spill over. Then she put a hand on the grimy scarf that wreathed his head. "He'll be along later, I hope."

Sage was right: Alison's arm needed tending, and her body suddenly ached all over. And these three supposedly well-motivated pilgrims were wasting time knocking one another about when there were worse enemies to battle, including time.

"Stop it!" Alison ordered. Her voice reverberated impressively, sounding like an airport speaker system. "Please, stop."

They didn't.

Alison wearily raised the revolver, aiming it at the glittering arch over the men's heads. She brought up her injured arm, clasped one hand over the other and squeezed the trigger again, trying not to shudder when the recoil and the report bucked through her. The flash flared an even brighter blue.

A rainbow of falling, knife-edged crystals finally parted the combatants.

"Stop!" Alison repeated. "We need to leave the caverns

before the cave wights come back. You can kill each other outside."

"We don't know the way out," the brown-bearded stranger protested.

Alison eyed Sage. "We may. You two will precede our party."

"And have you all vanish behind, leaving us to delve deeper into nowhere?" the young blond man asked indignantly.

"You'll have to trust that we are kinder company than those we jointly ran off."

"Are you bound for the Wellsunging, too?" Brown Beard asked with suspicion.

"I am now," Alison answered grimly. "Don't force me to use this . . . this magical artifact on you. We will all escape the cavern, and you gentlemen can settle your differences then."

Sage scuttled ahead. The two men followed, then came Alison and the Littlelost. Rowan, looking the slightest bit amused at the effect his traveling companion's "magical artifact" had had on his rivals, automatically brought up the rear, keeping a keen eye to any creatures that might follow.

Alison strode along, buoyed by the Littlelost's surrounding presence. They chattered, these once-unforthcoming children, about good blows and small triumphs. They compared welts like badges of honor. They boasted to her and to one another.

Alison kept thinking of the still-loaded revolver—turned to an empty chamber—now tucked away in her backpack; Twist and Pickle alternated the honor of carrying it. Once again she'd resorted to raw technological superiority in Veil; once again she felt she had tainted this strange, dangerous, but oddly innocent, land. And what was she to make of her natural allies—Rowan and his two fellow pilgrims—who'd rather fight one another than a common enemy?

And where was Beau?

Sage finally led them from the caverns onto the lip of another mountain meadow, where—after much posturing and debate—the two strangers agreed to Sage's urging and went on their way down the slope without further challenge to Rowan. Shortly after, the wisewoman's poultice of cold, tea-soaked moss was sucking the pain and poison from her arm, but Alison felt only one, untenable absence. Where was Beau? How could she live with knowing she'd left him behind?

Rowan stood apart, self-absorbed, staring at the neighboring peak. "There lies the Valley of Voices." His triumphant voice vibrated with almost operatic timbre. "An hour's walk and I will be there."

12

It hardly mattered that these mountains should not exist. Alison could imagine no better figment of the imagination in which to lose one's senses.

To anyone prairie-reared, mountains were grand but unreachable phenomena, fabulous four-color visions reserved for calendar photographs. Now she stood dizzily on a mountainside, breathing the thin, pine-ripe air in which the other peaks seemed to be suspended.

Rowan's prophecy had proven correct in all but one particular: An hour's walk had brought them only to the lip of the valley he sought. The rest of the party, mere afterthoughts, had trailed him unheeded. Rowan had paced like a sleepwalker to this peak-cradled place, oblivious to everyone and everything but his goal. Now that Alison had seen it, she could almost forgive his single-mindedness.

The Valley of Voices was formed by meadows—sweeping folds of a grassy skirt, long green swaths embroidered by floral medallions. Wire-thin waterfalls stabbed the distant sides of the valleys like icicles of mist. The air felt neither cold nor warm, yet in the nearby lake that filled an adjoining valley, small, white-sailed ships wafted across the sky-blue surface. The mini-icebergs reminded Alison of frozen cotton candy.

Every natural given seemed reversed: She could see water-borne clouds of solid cold; ice-water daggers; air so crystalline a breath could shatter it. It hurt to inhale so much beauty, though the people assembling here matched Rowan's obliviousness.

These pilgrims were a phenomenon in themselves. Ant-like hundreds topped the ridges cradling the valley: men, women and children, all of them attired in the retro-fashioned clothing Rowan and Sage affected. They made a gaudy crew, the women's full, tiered skirts composing a sherbet-shaded rainbow. While Rowan had previously seemed tall, here he was dwarfed by a number of men in smocks and trousers who moved with the slow, deceptively gentle grace of a wrestler, like Andre the Giant. And there were fairy-sized women, many of them little taller than Twist; their garb consisted of diaphanous scarves twining their delicate limbs and trunks. These scarves made a brave flutter in the breeze that buffeted the ridges and looked commonplace amid the lively range of clothing styles affected by the crowds.

Yet no one here dressed as oddly as the Littlelost, or as Alison herself, for that matter. Even so, their attire varied, with the men's garb as vibrantly individual as anyone's. Thousands of people—as parti-colored as the flowers—poured into the funnel of the steep valley.

Alison peered down the incline, its slope deceptively soft as grass brushed her knees and flowery faces winked in the wind. Having climbed so far, she didn't want to recede into this wrinkle of vegetation, this verdant navel of the mountaintops.

"We go below," Sage said and nodded once, lowering her seamed eyelids.

Rowan plunged into the green sea on his own, his hooded head bobbing like a drowning man's, his boot heels pronging turf to slow his descent.

Like Alison, the Littlelost hung back.

"Come!" The old woman stepped off the hilltop to sink into the deepening swells of grass.

Alison repeated Sage's instruction to her charges, then launched down the long green slide. She heard the Littlelost jolting down behind her but was too intent on remaining upright to turn and oversee them. The steep incline forced her to move faster and faster, until the twin eggbeaters of gravity and momentum sucked her into an unwilling plummet.

"I must be crazy," she gasped when at the bottom. Bent over, hands on knees, she panted, noticing that the swift descent had forced Rowan into the same concession. Littlelost had tumbled down rather than run, landing in a heap and grinning at the danger.

Sage showed no patience for any of them.

"Come then, if you are to join the competition." She addressed Rowan—and Alison, who ignored the implicit invitation.

The valley formed a natural amphitheater, Alison saw as she gazed around. The Greeks had refined the open-air theater, with semicircular seats raking up from the stage, to a place of auditory magic. Even today the last-row audiences could hear a whisper as clearly as if their seat partner had spoken. That was why Greek actors had worn ultra-high wedgies and large, stylized masks. Their voices could penetrate the distance like bullets, but their bodies looked so tiny to the far-flung viewers that they had to don artificial height and outsized faces.

Veil's Valley of the Voices was not Epidaurus, however lofty its situation, however primitively clever its people. Alison was struck with a sense of reverse deja vu—one of utter alienation. An amphitheater should hold draped Greeks; she should have encountered orators and actors, even nymphs and satyrs, en route here, not Desmeynians and Littlelost, Takers and Slinkers. She suddenly craved the familiar like a toddler would, running after Rowan and Sage before they vanished into the swelling mob of strangers.

"Wait!" Her voice ricocheted back upon her, growing younger and stronger with each echo.

She bitterly missed Beau and paused to search the sloping bezel of earth containing the crowd. No hoped-for canine silhouette decorated the distance. People still flowed like water down the slopes, erasing grass and the pale, scentless flowers that dotted the area, and likely erasing Alison's own specific smell, making the valley into a mixing bowl of swirling human odors.

Littlelost dogged her still—as if these often sullen, silent puppies could make up for Rambeau's guardian bulk. Camay, the runt of the litter, clung to Alison's knee. Alison lifted the girl, who was panting uncomplainingly, and draped her over a shoulder as if she were a cat.

No children as young—or as forlorn—as Camay were in the crowd; no children at all, now that she looked for them. In fact, scornful frowns perched on nearby faces like black crows, and contemptuous glances followed Alison and her ragtag troupe, pecking at her confidence. She could understand why ordinary folk might disdain these untended ragamuffins; after all, the homeless were avoided on the streets of St. Paul, too.

Ahead, the sackcloth of Rowan's hood wove in and out of sight, but Sage's baggy form had melted into the mob.

Alison hurried despite the baby-weight, yet never risked bumping into strangers. This clotting humanity swirled away from her and the Littlelost, like water flowing around stranded sticks after a rainstorm. Perhaps their noses led them.

"Here," a familiar, sandy voice cawed. Sage had settled into the gray ashes of her robes on level ground near the front row, if the haphazardly seated people formed anything as rational as rows.

Rowan had ignored her—and all of them—since cresting the valley brow, not deliberately, it struck Alison, but from total concentration. He stood yards away, straight among a milling group of men. One was Brown Beard from the cave fight, but no one seemed inclined for conflict now. An almost holy hush hung over the gathered men, magnified by the plain surroundings: a scrim of rocks clustered like figures from an unbound sculpture. Time and many pounding feet had worn the ground the men stood upon to rock and dirt—bare bones to sit upon.

"What is this place?" Alison, with Camay in her arms, sank beside Sage.

"The Valley of Voices. Listen."

Alison detected a constant susurration, like a selvage edge of surf rippling across a beach, or the wind lashing treetops before a storm, or an old LP with only a recording hiss to play. Then—sharp, sudden sounds, as hard as hail. Cries of exotic birds mingled with the white noise all around. This commotion, she realized, was the sighing echo of the crowd talking and scratching and laughing and coughing, and perhaps of the distant crystalline chatter of the waterfalls that fenced the valley.

"And the competition?" she wondered.

Sage frowned. "Hush, it begins."

Alison turned to quiet the Littlelost. They were mute already, eyes squinted at the barren place, disreputable bloody knees tented and anchored by their linked arms. Amid this tidy, bourgeois crowd, Alison felt an alien motherly urge to wash those filthy knees and clothe the urchins for Sunday school. At least they didn't smell so rank anymore.

Now a hush came *shooshing* down the valley slopes as people from rim to bottom urged each other silent. That was the eeriest sound effect of all, that sibilant wall of whispers crashing over Alison, almost wrenching her breath away. Yet she heard nothing unearthly, merely the unanimous will, the single attention of thousands of people hunched behind her on the grass, waiting for something both ordinary and extraordinary to happen.

Camay snuggled against Alison like a kitten. Beside her, Sage smiled for no reason, staring into nothing with sharp eyes.

The ceremony began. An old man, beard dripping like a ragged icicle from his chin to the hem of his gown, lifted a translucent white stone cup glittering with embedded stones. At first his voice intoned gibberish, but as Alison listened, she began to understand words . . . then phrases . . . then whole sentences. It was as if the cup were both a microphone and a universal translator.

"The ceremony be ancient, the quest untold," came the words like amber beads on a string, one almost-liquid drop at a time. "The Cup turns, a wheel upon a spoke, then comes around again. Before us, pilgrims gather, known and unknown. Sightless stars oversee our pleas, but our own unworthy ears shall judge the Cupbearer, as will the Voice of the Valley.

"So let song begin but not end here, and number our days and shout our longing and bury our dead and welcome our heir-sons and wed our mother-daughters and fill every crevice of the earth and tell our tales and banish our woes and weave garments of moonshine for our father-sons. And for the Cupbearer, let the song be only the beginning."

A tidal-wave roar answered this invocation. Alison twisted to see a pallid coldness creeping over the rim of the mountains. She felt trapped at the bottom of a slick, grass-green earthen bowl, while someone large and distant sealed the eyelids of the sky shut above her.

Sage's leathery hand clamped Alison's sleeve. "Song swallows light as night swallows day."

Then the songsters began, each man stepping forward in turn. A variety of languages swelled their throats. Alison found herself vaguely translating some words, then understanding all of them. Some men sang beautifully words that were scratched on rough parchment. Others intoned words as warm as an arpeggio on a solid-gold organ in voices that cracked and broke.

The variance in skills didn't matter. Songs and singers blended to forge one awesome interlude, each a link on a chain-mail coat of sound that was spreading and netting the valley in its icy strength. Alison hardly noticed the dark of night shrinking the vast mountain world around them to nothingness; nor did she see the luminescent blossoms mingled with the crushed grass raise cool buttercups of light to rapt faces. Where the singers stood, the very rocks pulsed light in time to their voices; young moonshine plashed each performer's feet and face.

Alison absorbed battle songs and love ballads, songs of loss and of discovery, bitter songs and raw ones. Each was the best the moment it was sung, surpassing the previous ones. She glanced to the elder on the sidelines, who nodded to the melodies as if his long white beard were a governing string and he but a puppet. Others of his ilk huddled around the unearthly ground light as though crowding a camp fire. The judges, she thought, who cannot possibly decide a winner.

Contestants' names flowed by as lullingly as their music. Some men's hair, she saw, glinted gray; others' chins were pimpled. Features varied, though some echoed one another. Two of them were recognizable: Blond Hair and Brown Beard from the Taker cavern. They were bards now, not brawlers, one a supple tenor, the other possessing a voice more powerful than polished. This was an international event, an Olympics of otherworldly vocalization. Then the old man called out—musically, of course, for no sound that dark afternoon of night rang unpleasantly—"Rowan Firemayne."

So rapt was Alison that the name hit her ears like nonsense syllables. Perhaps the gift to recognize new language had stolen her knowledge of the old. Then Rowan was shedding his hip-length cape and hood, and she sat upright, dislodging Camay, who slid unwakened to the ground. She blinked when Rowan ripped off the mail like a marathon swimmer tearing off his cap when the final shore is reached.

Hair licked his shoulders like flame, a comet's tail of flaring red and orange and copper, and violet the shade of ancient blood.

Even the pallid moonlight couldn't douse his hair's extravagant luster.

Beside Alison, a Littlelost whimpered as if in fear. She felt only surprise. Without a shroud of metal, Rowan's face looked youthfully raw. He was no more than twenty, she realized with shock. With a young man's eagerness, he opened his backpack and unveiled the strange projecting contents: a long-necked stringed instrument. Other singers had played similar things, but Alison hadn't distinguished the instruments from the singers, or from the soft swell of breaths over the hillsides and the caesura of stars frozen in mid-wink high above.

The eerie earthlight puddled on Rowan's figure, haloed his profile, focused on the swath of hair burning from deep purple in darkness to searing copper in the light.

"Firemayne, Firemayne," the crowd breathed. Alison realized that he was known here, and a favorite, that he had been journeying solely to this moment, apart from them all.

Her jaw unhinged as if to speak or sing. She kept silence instead. Rowan began singing a ballad, that much she knew, in a baritone that braided tenderness with a deep, vibrant power that made the earth beneath her quake. Rowan was the best, she decided, as she had with each latest performer. But this time she was right. Much as she hated to admit it, Rowan was best.

Then—too soon—he bowed back into the darkness and the crowd of contenders. Another stepped forward to strum a quicksilver string and bathe in that enhancing light and delight every ear with song that was too fleeting.

Alison lost track of time, or everything around her. She could hear with her eyes—heard crickets in China, if there was a China here; heard a leaf buffeted down a street in Selma, Alabama; heard a shade pulled in Butte, Montana; heard a volcano burp in the South Seas, and ice crack deep and wide in Antarctica. She heard snakes hissing through grass like prairie fire and popcorn snapping on some kitchen countertop and kittens being born in a barn and bells ringing in an island temple in the farthest East and lovers whispering in a Buick in the middle of a dark field in Iowa. She heard orchids growing and water drying slowly in the sun. Most of all, she heard no one clapping.

"Is that all?" an ordinary voice was demanding. "Is that all?"

As she thought, no, it has just begun, I haven't heard a thousandth of it . . . someone poked her in the ribs. The gesture bore the tingle of an electrical shock.

"Where are you from?" Sage was urgently asking her.

What had she told Rowan? "The . . . the Island."

Sage turned away.

Alison felt that she must be utterly truthful; in this of all places, under the spell of such music, she must be exactly truthful. "It's not an island, really. . . ."

And then another musical phrase lilted into the air, her own name being called, only not her name, though it sounded splendid in this natural amphitheater, as if it—and she—belonged there. "Alison of Island-Not," Sage announced from the dark.

"Alison of Island-Not," the old man echoed from the blinding spear of natural light, looking puzzled.

The crowd's murmur became an excited mutter of curiosity that threatened to rattle the night's peace. Alison shook her head—no!—but Sage was prodding her upright. Twist pulled the sleeping Camay off the pillow of her hip, so there was no barrier, no need to object, no reason to.

Alison rose and went to the earth's bare center. Illuminated faces blossomed like stars on the hillsides all around. The vista dazzled her. She was standing on the lip of the Milky Way, about to plunge into the shining pinwheels of deep space. She could no longer see Sage or the Littlelost, nor even the empty, now-dark spot where she had been sitting with her own shining face in place.

She turned uncertainly to the men behind her and saw Rowan. She stared at him. He stared back, his face closed, as it had been while on the road. But the moment was too imperious for either to resist. He extended something to her. She took it without thinking.

The instrument was eggshell light, a hybrid of mandolin and guitar. It had been years since she had tinkered with—what was its make?—her brother Peter's discarded Yamaha. That had always been unwieldy for her. This . . . was not. She paced with it, as though to soothe its unspoken sobs to sleep. She, the unsung alto in the college choir, never asked to sing a solo. Well.

She looked up at the faceless glimmers in the dark. "I've never done this before." Her voice came back amplified, smoothed, sounding as mellow and potent as twelve-year-old Glenlivet.

She edged the other way and strummed a chord. The echoed purity was like a hit of the world's most common illegal substance, truth. Each plucked string shattered on the shoal of the previous sound, each note amplified the others in perfect, expanding harmony, in oms and ohms of enlightened sound.

"Well," she said, nervous. No other contestants had spoken, they had only sung. No one in the audience had clapped a singer. No one else had wondered what he/she/it was doing here, Alison told herself. No one else didn't know what to sing.

What to sing? Lord, what did she remember all the way through? "Bridge over Troubled Water"? Too high later on, like the "Star-Spangled Banner." "Scarborough Fair" should fit these folks. Or "Drink to Me Only with Thine Eyes." "Puff, the Magic Dragon"?

Alison paused in her pacing—no wonder the rock stars did it; it was so damn awesome to confront a hillside of strangers and sing them something all by yourself.

She needed a song that she knew all the way through, that she couldn't mess up on this alien instrument. She found one deep in the remembered pages of her Grade Three piano book:

'Tis the gift to be simple,
'Tis the gift to be free,
'Tis the gift to come down,
Where we ought to be.

Every chord on the mandotar, every phrase, reverberated from a thousand silent throats and a million unseen stars. Alison plucked the words and notes one by one, perfectly, as she might pull raspberries, fragile enough to bleed, from a branch, or draw uncut diamonds from the shining sands of a beach.

Each sound cloned itself into a chorus, yet remained purely singular, a sob separated from sorrow by a million miles.

And when we find ourselves
In the place just right
'Twill be in the valley
Of love and delight.

The same song, yet never the same. A simple sentiment magnified by repetition into such profundity that Alison felt electric ice-water tears run down her face. She began the second verse.

When true simplicity is gained,
To bow and to bend we will not be ashamed.
To turn, to turn will be our delight,
And by turning, turning, we come 'round right.

Only two simple verses and a final chorus, yet strong enough to bear repetition, so she began the first again, then stilled the strings in mid-chord. Even this discordance echoed like universal harmony.

"Sing with me," she said, looking at the hillside on the left. She extended her hand, fingers spread. "You there." And they did, a wispy thread of sound at first that wound tendrils into a cable of interwoven voices as the words inevitability shone through.

Two lines into the second verse another bolt of serendipity struck Alison. "And you . . ." Her hand stretched toward the middle of the amphitheater. "Begin now!"

They did. Then the right side followed with the first verse when asked, and the audience was singing a round: The elegant, resounding old Shaker hymn was vaulting to the top of the hidden sky and haunting the farthest shores of night with its chorused power. Mute lightning, as if jealous, scintillated over the mountaintops.

Alison let the song fade, let each group fall silent in turn until only one still sang. Then it, too, tapered off, and finally her clear, lonesome solo softened and stilled.

Silence hurt.

13

A keening came—thin and sharp at first, as if the surrounding waterfalls were liquid crystal strings in a gigantic harp thrummed by the wind.

Echoes swelled the sound, multiplied each hollow tone into a fully freighted chord, until the imagined harp had become a bellowing organ and the very rocks vibrated around the spellbound, silent people lining the valley's slopes.

Even as the airy harp notes deepened to a throbbing bass hum, a new noise pitched its tent high above the first. This melodious, wailing soprano counterpoint that seemed to come from several sources was still sound without words, like the full-throated, soulful threnodies of wolves building a bridge of pure, prowling sound to the moon.

Alison shivered, remembering Beau bracing himself in the backyard to tilt his head like a coyote and hurl an arpeggio of unholy yodels to the night. Was he there now, among the peaks, performing a solo as she had?

If he was, he was not alone. A third sound stirred on the excited air—an emanation from many throats, endless ladders and stiles of sung syllables rather than words. Taken together, all managed a fresh echo of "Simple Gifts."

Alison was aware of no longer being alone on center stage, and for an instant she hated the idea of anyone sharing the avalanche of unearthly sound she had triggered. Rowan had moved toward her, reining himself to a sudden stop at the new sounds. Whether he'd come to attack or to guard her, he stood as paralyzed as anyone in the valley's night-black bowl, where unscented flowers gleamed like stars and rocks glowed brighter than lava lamps. So did the shriveled bearded man stand motionless, ghost-pale, where he bracketed Alison's other side.

A fourth sound hissed through the valley—not only audible,

but understandable: "Al-i-son of Island-Not. Al-i-son," the audience chanted, whispered, keened, demanded.

The elder thrust something at Alison so roughly that her hands raised automatically in defense. Into her instinctively cupping palms bloomed an ovoid of chill stone.

The old man's voice croaked feebly from her right, unheard by any but herself and Rowan. "Never have the valley's Voices spoken more clearly. Not in many years has a Wellsinger evoked them. The stranger Alison of Island-Not will bear the Cup of Earth until another year and a day sift down the stairs of the stars and we meet again to sing our fate."

The crowd's whispering stilled. Only wind wailed out of tune among the mountain chinks. Then it was over, her moment of glory, with no time for a reprise. In the bright moonshine, Alison watched the valley rim seem to creep and crawl as the silhouettes of departing people bubbled up over the edge and trickled down to wherever they had come from. The departure was silent, but swift. No one lingered. She turned to see that the disappointed Wellsingers had left in a flock to toil up the rear hillside. The self-important sideline elders, in their long robes and narrow beards, were hobbling into the audience. Even the Cup-giver had backed away, bowing into the mob, before she could thank him. No one stayed to share her amazement and her apparent triumph, save those she had come with.

"Let me see it!" a Littlelost cajoled.

"And me!"

"Me!" wailed Camay.

Alison clutched the Cup to her chest, still awe-struck as if she held a communion chalice. "It's so heavy," she said in wonder, feeling the stone warming to her hands.

"He who wins it must bear the weight." Rowan's voice had lost its sweetness. It rang deeper, riding low in the water with a full load of loss and, perhaps, envy. "I hope that you are worthy of the prize you have usurped, mage."

"Why not go on your way, Desmeynian?" Sage suggested, as if she knew he could not. "This is no longer any affair of yours."

"Apparently it never was." Bleakness sharpened Rowan's consonants, made him sound older.

Alison felt older herself, felt . . . responsible in some unnamed way. "Where do they all go—the people?"

"To settlements high and low," Sage answered. "We stand on the edge of the populated lands now."

"Then that is where I'll go, to a settlement. That's where I've always wanted to take the Littlelost."

Rowan snorted. "You start your year as Cupbearer by going against the grain, as usual. The Cup may be a master key to much of Veil, but no settlement will welcome your traveling companions."

"Which of my traveling companions will they reject—you?" she retorted, stung by yet another of Rowan's dismissals of the Littlelost and Sage, especially within their hearing.

His forebearing silence rebuked her for foolishness.

"We will go." She shook off the Littlelosts' clinging hands. They exhausted her now; carrying the Cup was enough. Perhaps all she had poured into the song, all the unspoken things that the people in the valley had quaffed from the song, had collected in the Cup. Its weight grew heavier than her heart when she pictured Beau as no more than a disembodied howl caught forever in the magical throat of the mountains. She wondered what the vessel's mystic meaning was, and whether its unnatural weight was a reminder to the bearer not to take it lightly. If it really had powers, could a woman from a different world evoke them? Dare she try?

She moved away from the rocks and their rapidly dimming luminescence, and bent to shrug her pack over one shoulder before starting out. Littlelost flowed around her like shadow eddies. Sage's slower steps tick-tocked behind her.

"Coming, Desmeynian?" the old woman called back when they'd begun climbing the valley slope.

There was a pause.

"Yes!" Rowan's answer struck Alison's ears like a hissing snake. The valley's native resonance remained remarkable even when it lay vacant under the stars, its ceremonial visitors stolen away. Did Rowan's sudden decision mean her no good? She wondered. He didn't strike her as a graceful loser, at least not of something as vital to him as the Cup.

"I could use a tankard of ale," he said when he caught up.

In the dark, Sage's laugh sounded mocking. "Don't be so glum. There's another pleasure you may indulge to your heart's content now that you have lost the Wellsunging, pilgrim."

Rowan brushed by in the dark, a large, shadowy presence intent on taking the lonely lead again, as if that position were all that was left to him.

"I thought he'd win," Alison admitted when Sage hobbled up beside her. "He seems born to win . . . something."

"He would have, had you not been there."

"Had *you* not insisted I sing! I didn't know that a prize was at stake. I didn't want to compete—for anything."

"Perhaps that is why you won."

"And you seem to take delight in Rowan's discomfort, in my winning. Why?"

"Things have always been the same in Desmeyne, and almost always the same in Veil. The time for that has gone. I have traveled paths few will walk anymore, searching out these despised things that green and grow, which I use for my potions. More grows in Veil now than complacency, and you are not the only foreigner among us. But you must learn before you can teach, and there is much that you don't know of us—or of yourself."

Sage stooped even more than usual to spur herself up the incline and abandoned the effort to speak.

The slope had indeed steepened. They all bent their backs to the climb as Sage did, even the limber Littlelost. Alison bent double over the Cup, clasping it tightly despite needing her hands free to help her scale the hill. She was deeply reluctant to release the object, as if she *must* hold it for a certain period. Her backpack weighed as much as the Cup. In silhouette she must resemble an aged woman, she thought, creeping toward her death. Would she meet it here in Veil?

They met morning on the brim of the Valley of Voices.

Sunlight was seeping over the horizon, polishing the white mountaintops and tinting the sky the shade of faded blue ribbon by the time the party scaled the hillside.

Alison stretched her cramped fingers—she could hold the Cup one-handed now; it had lightened as if partaking of the thinner air at the higher elevation. Or perhaps the symbolic weight of the night's ceremony had temporarily transformed it. Certainly it looked less awesome in daylight. She wriggled out of her pack for a rest and set it on the ground.

Rowan stood on the downslope in the tepid light, half turned away yet looking back. Alison was amazed at how his unfurled locks softened his sharp features to the mere leanness of youth, dispelling the former forbidding profile of duty. The wind riffled his incarnadine hair around his still-grim expression like a flame eating away at an iceberg.

Alison felt vague guilt for Rowan's failure, and then she utterly absolved herself. The people had chosen—apparently even the disembodied voices had chosen—her. Maybe Rowan needed a better composer, or a new lyricist. Maybe he needed an imported song. Maybe he needed a little humility, she thought wryly. Still, a loss to a latecomer, a stranger whom he'd inadvertently escorted to the competition, would be galling, Alison mused. But her overwhelming feeling now was weariness, not guilt, and certainly not triumph.

"Where's the next settlement?" she asked him. Rowan pointed, but she had to join him on the downslope to see. "High Covey," he said. "A free village, as most in Veil are, but friendly toward Desmeyne for generations."

Alison looked. There. Far below. My lord, the very model of a not-too-modern Alpine village, all peaked roofs and crowded houses, with neat patches of farmland bracketing it into a cozy crazy quilt pieced together by a Swiss Grandma Moses. Smoke—yes, smoke—curled from chimneys and draft horses labored like oversized semicolons on the picture-perfect page below. Hello, Hans Christian Andersen, I'm coming home! Or closer, anyway, to the recognizable notion of home.

She walked back to her pack and knelt to stow the Cup carefully. Perhaps getting it out of sight would end the scowl that had roosted between Rowan's blond brows since the Cup's awarding. And why were his sun-bleached eyebrows the only body hair he'd allowed to show until the Wellsunging? She must ask Sage about this at a discreet moment.

The Cup. She studied it in the swelling sunlight.

It was a chalice—a carved-stone drinking vessel as long as her hands, wrapped in copper fretwork accented by cabochon jewels as eloquent as the iris of an animal's eye by night. Vigil lights of red, blue, green, gold gleamed from these polished surfaces, even from the stem and foot. Lightning bolts of ore shot over the pale stone, glittering veins both mysterious and oddly organic.

She wrapped the object carefully in her extra flannel shirt and tucked it into the pack. In broad daylight, it seemed to weigh almost nothing.

They hiked down the hill. Alison felt like Mary Martin in *The Sound of Music.* She had her troupe of children, her mother abbess (Sage) and—Alison eyed Rowan's limber figure marching ahead with its flag of flowing hair—Captain Von Trapp? No; far too young and gaudy for the part. Still, she felt like singing about the hills being alive—except that these hills might be; about the sound of music—except that it seemed more like the sound of muses; about a thousand years—except that it was only a year and a day, and then Rowan could warble his lungs out to get the damned Cup in his possession, and she would be bloody well out of here. With Beau. Her eyes searched the distance but did not find him. By then, she hoped, she and Beau would be out of the here and now, and back in the there and then. Home.

Many hours later they neared the village, for that's what it was by any world's definition, the first place in Veil that reassuringly echoed Alison's world. True, she had to dig up black-and-white Frankenstein films to evoke it, but here it was, a place run on woodcutters and horsepower. In the sunset glow she recognized the emblem of the obligatory tavern: the Inn of the Scarlet Swan. Odd.

Suddenly she was as eager for real food as Rowan was for his tankard. And she wanted a thoroughgoing bath for herself and for the Littlelost. And a bed, and . . . and what was used for common tender in Veil? *Knots,* had Rowan said? Surely . . . not.

Their final descent into the picture-book village in the oncoming twilight evoked hostile stares from its inhabitants. Alison reflected that people who owned their appearance to a Pieter Brueghel peasant scene should not spend so much time staring at others. The Littlelost, nervous again, huddled between Alison and

Sage. Rowan strode on ahead as if his companions were an unwanted and invisible tail he had acquired in some mysterious manner.

At the inn's broad wooden door he turned to confront Alison. "You truly wish to bring these scuppies inside?" he asked.

"Yes!"

A not-too-encouraging smile twisted his lips and he shrugged and barged through the doorway.

They followed, entering a chamber steaming with the mix of a huge, hot hearth and generously padded bodies well packed in. Unfamiliar but obvious food aromas combined with the more recognizable sour after-scents of sweat and spilled ale. Good. She could use a beer, too, but doubted she'd get her usual Lite brand.

Rowan threw himself down at a table, pausing only to prop his staff in a corner and set his pack on a wallside bench. He was instantly surrounded by hale fellows well met, or what passed for them in Veil.

"A good year has gone by since you paused at the Scarlet Swan," cried a man with ears the size and shape of brussels sprouts.

"You're as rare a sight as an Earth-Eater," agreed a youth in an emerald cloak, whirling the garment's soft wool over the women and children like a green tornado as he settled opposite Rowan.

With such boisterous greetings, the benches at Rowan's table soon filled. Alison, Sage and Littlelost subsided at an adjoining table, ungreeted. And untended, for the serving maid brought a tray of foaming tankards and plopped them down before Rowan and his friends without glancing at the next table.

"And is your year of questing done at last?" The quickening pulse in the maid's voice spoke even more strongly than her ardent dark eyes.

Rowan flashed her a glance. Alison was amazed that it didn't linger. Beneath an elaborate arrangement of raven curls, the young woman's high coloring polished her cheeks to apples, and her gown bared shoulders as plump and pale as her half-revealed breasts.

"Ask me next year," he muttered, and drank deep from the tankard.

Silence hung over the once-loud group like a guillotine.

"You cannot mean that you do not have the Cup?" Brussels Spouts suggested uneasily.

Rowan looked no farther than the ebbing foam of his ale. "The Cup comes with me to Desmeyne."

"Then—" the serving maid squeezed herself on the bench between Rowan and Emerald Cape—"I can welcome you home in the usual fashion."

Alison rolled her eyes. This female was applying herself to Rowan as if she were sticking plaster. Was Veil no more than the set for an old Hammer film? In a moment a merry old chap would start patty-caking an ocarina and Rowan would dance the buxom serving wench upstairs, and they all would carouse below until the village werewolf—or Slinker—darkened the doorway.

"No." Rowan moved so abruptly that the girl nearly toppled to the floor. He rose, stepped over the bench and took his tankard to the fire.

His table mates eyed one another in naked puzzlement. The serving girl, in a pout, pulled her limp lawn blouse a millimeter higher on her shoulders.

"How strange, Trissellyn. He said he had the Cup—" Emerald Cloak began.

Alison cleared her throat. "Not quite. He said he traveled with it to Desmeyne. I have it."

The occupants of the table searched the room until they finally found Alison's eyes regarding them steadily. They frowned at her and frowned harder at the Littlelost and Sage.

"And I'd like some service," Alison told the girl.

The creature examined her with an intensity and intimate speculation that Alison had never experienced before from a woman.

"*You* have it?" Trissellyn challenged, hands on hips, a posture that lifted her bare shoulders and other anatomical high points. "Age is no barrier to competing for the Cup, but you look barely out of swaddling."

"I walk. I talk. I carry the Cup. I'd like food for my party and some of whatever Rowan is drinking for myself and my companion. Water will do for the children." While they all stared at her,

Alison bent to the pack at her feet. She set the Cup on the table. "I'll have my beverage in this."

Now she had their attention. Even the fire paused in mid-crackle. Sage chuckled low to herself, but Rowan wheeled from the blaze, his face pale against the fire of his hair. Alison felt as if she had ordered skimmed milk in a Deadwood saloon. Her hands felt suddenly cold and clammy. What if the Cup wasn't meant to be drunk from?

The serving maid flounced to the table, full tankard in hand, and drained what fit into the stone Cup. The remainder she set before Sage. She eyed the Littlelost as a kindergarten teacher might regard lice. "Water? You want to give this lot water?"

"Broth," Sage said.

The girl simply nodded, stirring her edifice of ebony curls and their interwoven ribbons and lace. "Broth," she repeated more happily, and left.

No one spoke. Everyone stared as Alison elevated the Cup to her lips. The stone felt colder. It was like sipping from the marble of a tomb. Did the Cup perhaps turn liquids lethal, like wildwater? Her tongue didn't know what to expect, or how to distinguish a normal taste from an abnormal one in Veil. A tiny sip: the thick, sweet, ale-like drink within stung like a honeybee married to the kick of a hornet. Still, she didn't feel poisoned—yet—and she quickly set down the Cup. Her lips tingled, whether from the Cup's chill touch or the heady libation, she didn't know.

Rowan approached her table, looking from her to the Cup with unnerving intensity. Maybe he expected her to keel over and he'd inherit the Cup. He finally justified his scrutiny with a question. "How will you pay for your food and drink?"

That threw her. Alison rummaged in her pack until she pulled out her eelskin wallet. He took it without asking permission, riffling through the paper money with a kind of dazed disdain.

He threw it to the table. "These pictures will buy nothing here."

"Then we'll work for our keep."

"You—and them? Will you feed them from the Cup? Let it tame wildwater for them?" He pointed derisively at her companions. Then his hands separated in resignation. His tone was cold.

"Bring the Cup to my father's house. It was never meant for common usage. I cannot allow it to be lost or demeaned. Desmeyne will pay the price of your thirst, and for these others, if you insist."

"I won't desert them."

He pulled a leather pouch from his belt and spilled several brown circles upon the tabletop. They landed with soft thuds. Alison saw that they were literally knots of lumber polished to a glassy sheen—oversized wooden nickels.

"My money is worth a great deal in—" she began.

"Lakeland," Rowan said precisely. "Home of Island-Not. No doubt. But it is worthless here, as are any assumptions you import. You must return the Cup to the valley in a year and a day, when I will have a chance to sing for it again."

"You will try again!" Emerald Cloak asked with disbelief.

Rowan nodded.

"How many others will endure another year and a day?" the man went on.

"Few," Rowan said with steely determination. "It will increase my chances. I very nearly won this time."

"But, my friend, another year—" Emerald Cloak's head shook, stirring his fair, shoulder-length hair.

"—is another year," Rowan said between his teeth. He regarded Alison. "Much can happen in a year."

She didn't understand the undercurrents, and didn't want to. Her ears were buzzing from the sweet ale, and she longed for what passed for food in this place.

Platters of it were soon thumped down before her and Sage. One large dish served all the Littlelost. They fell upon it like greedy savages.

Alison ate hungrily at first, then noticed that the pinkish meat was dry and flavorless. No greens accompanied the meal, only a beet-colored tuber with the texture of a rubber apple. She longed for a restaurant-iced plastic tumbler of water, complete with fluoride and water-treatment chemicals.

Instead, she washed down her waning appetite with another cautious sip from the Cup of Earth, and burped. Rowan watched, his cider-colored eyes smoldering. The thought of Beau sharing her North Woods camp fire drifted through her mind; so did the vision of the fireplace ablaze in her St. Paul condo, with the Sunday newspapers spread a safe but cozy distance away and a microwaved cinnamon roll waiting for nibbling on the nearby needlepointed footstool. Her eyes blinked back a sudden wet glaze.

All merriment had fled the inn at the news that Alison, not Rowan, had claimed the Cup. The men morosely nursed their tankards, and even Sage did not speak again. The fire crackled disconsolately in the room, spreading neither warmth nor light in the deepening gloom.

Trissellyn appeared at their table with a candlestick and an expression that managed to be both sullen and suggestive. "Doubtless the Cupbearer wishes to retire after such an arduous labor." She spoke to Alison but looked at Rowan, who had remained by the hearth coddling his tankard.

"Great." Alison looked down to decide what to do with the unconsumed contents of the Cup. It was empty and stone-dry. Funny, she thought; she'd barely tasted the local ale. But it did have a kick; maybe she was getting punchy after the day's events. She stood, picking up the Cup. "We all need some rest," she announced.

"Perhaps your . . . small companions could sleep in the stable," Trissellyn suggested.

"Perhaps not. Surely you can spare one room for them. They aren't particular; they don't need a private bath."

"Indeed, so my nose has noticed."

"But *I* would like lots of hot water in the morning," Alison added as she followed the woman's swaying skirts up the narrow staircase.

"In the Cup?" the maid inquired archly.

"No, in a washtub. For the . . . small companions."

Trissellyn paused, back to the wall, to eye the Littlelost on the steps below. "It should be a curiosity; never has the Scarlet Swan harbored those in such dire need of washing."

Alison understood the comment when the party arrived upstairs. They were shown several rooms; each offered a gleaming, free standing metal tub before a fireplace where a bucket of water awaited heating. The beds were heaped with quilts, no doubt plumped with swan's-down. After the long wilderness trek, Alison hadn't expected such cheery comfort.

"That first room will be fine for them," Alison said. "Sage and I can share this one."

"You will sleep with the old woman?" Rowan demanded.

"Of course."

"That is mad," he insisted. "You must sleep with me. Let her shepherd the others."

Alison eyed thc smirking maid. "I thought you were spoken for."

"I may not have won the Cup," Rowan bit off between his teeth, "but you agreed to bring it to Desmeyne. I must protect it—and you—as if in my true keeping."

"I seem better equipped to protect *you,"* Alison couldn't resist reminding him.

His face grew even stiffer, although that had seemed impossible. "It is customary that you room with me anyway; though the woman is old beyond counting for much, it still might cause scandal."

"Now you think of scandal!" Why her sharing a room with a woman was more scandalous than doing it with a man eluded Alison, but Desmeynians had odd ideas and she was too tired to argue. Besides, Rowan was right; if someone wanted to kidnap the Cup, he'd be more useful than Sage. He was pretty handy with that staff, which he might need to fend off the amorous Trissellyn.

Rowan's apparent attractions left Alison cold. He had been an annoyingly self-absorbed traveling companion so far—but she hadn't regarded him as a man in any personal sense, especially since realizing that he was barely out of his teens, for heaven's sake! Some hot catch! A self-absorbed teenager with pretensions to Cupbearing, willing to stand by and let her die of wildwater one day and willing to save her neck, if it suited him, the next.

But maybe she *should* share a room with Rowan, after all. The poor lad obviously needed protection from the predatory tavern wench.

She shrugged. "You and me here. Sage and the Littlelost next door."

As she waited at the threshold, she glimpsed Sage lingering in the passage, her well-worn features radiating an expression of immense but hidden amusement.

The chamber was furnished with two beds as well as twin bathtubs and fireplaces. Apparently the people of Veil liked their comforts.

Rowan nodded to Trissellyn, who hefted a water pail onto its hook over the fire. Sleeping was one thing; bathing was another. When the girl paused at the other fireplace with a questioning look, Alison shook her head broadly and began unloading her pack on the footboard chest.

A candle's mothlike light flitted on the rough mantel over Rowan's hearth. "You would like my assistance, pilgrim?" the maid inquired silkily.

"No," came Rowan's sharp reply. "Thank you, Triss," he added more softly. "I only want to rinse the forest mold away." There was a pause in which Alison sensed Rowan's desire to say more—and his resolve not to.

A sigh drifted through the room. Alison could picture Trissellyn's artfully propped breasts heaving. Then her skirts rustled to the door. "Quiet night, then, pilgrims."

"Quiet night," Rowan returned curtly.

"Quiet night," Alison dutifully repeated. She heard water slosh into the tub, heard Rowan disrobing. She didn't trust him or the situation enough for *that* kind of casualness. Kicking off her boots, she dumped her down vest on the chest. First she sat on the bed to take out her contacts, then loosened her jeans and burrowed under the quilt.

"You remain clothed for the night, even at an inn?" Rowan inquired over the lulling sound of lapping water.

"All the better to jump up and defend the Cup."

"They are strange in your land."

"The feeling is mutual."

She risked glancing over her shoulder, seeing only a moving shadow on the far wall, a long, bronzed arm, an aura of red hair. Veil had its definite oddities, its unearthliness—redheads without the usual pointillistic array of freckles on milk-white skin, for instance. Again Alison wondered why Rowan had hidden his blazing hair until the Wellsunging.

But she was tired, and Rowan had forgotten her—and his bitter disappointment—enough for him to hum in the bathtub, some melodic air that lullabyed her to Dreamland, as if she weren't already there. . . .

14

A hand touched her shoulder.

Alison jerked wide awake in the dark, sensing the stillness, smelling traces of spent soap.

The hand was slipping down her arm. Breath warmed her cheek. She flailed as if she'd been walked on by a tarantula, her leg flexing to find the invader. Alison's foot connected with something soft; then a cry came as her kick hurled it into the smothering darkness. Elsewhere in the room, something thumped.

Sparks flared from the fireplaces, two eyes of blurred, red-hot embers to Alison's uncorrected vision. She finally recognized Rowan lighting the mantel-top candles, his face fuzzy with sleep. The red hair was tousled like Raggedy Andy yarn over his paler shoulders as he struggled into his shirt.

"The Cup!" he growled, seizing his staff. His candle illuminated the corner where the moaning intruder had coiled into a ball.

"Triss!" Rowan knelt by the serving girl, whom Alison myopically identified by a vague snarl of black curls. "What has happened to you?"

"What *happened?*" Alison sounded as indignant as she felt. *She'd* been attacked, and Rowan was succoring the aggressor. "Your girlfriend tried to sneak in and steal the Cup."

Alison sat up, patting the floor for the contact case and fluid she always kept within arm's reach. She extracted and wet a lens, then slipped it into the proper eye.

A gasp from the corner replaced the moaning.

Alison put in her other "eye," then blinked away the veil of wetting solution that blurred her vision. Trissellyn, handsomely disheveled, was regarding her with a gaze as limpid as distilled water.

"You . . . you don your eyes?" the girl asked.

"More securely than you don a nightie." Alison eyed Triss's apparel, which was exceedingly intricate, sheer and unanchored.

Rowan had awakened enough to regard the girl with a shade of suspicion at last. "Why are you here?"

She looked away, blushing—which apparently surprised Rowan even more. He noticed the receding neckline of her gown and rather brusquely reversed the trend. Alison had to credit him for good intentions.

"Triss—?" he prodded. "You must tell me. Else we will think you had designs on the Cup."

"Not on the Cup!" she burst out, still looking resentfully at Alison. "On the Cupbearer. But that was before I saw eyes that are carried in a bottle!"

"I don't get it," Alison put in.

Rowan shook his head. "You are truly from far beyond the borders we know or have even heard of." He helped Trissellyn rise, then released her arm. "Triss is no thief."

"You deny that she was after the Cup?"

"Triss is too—" he glanced down at Triss's thick black hair; she had buried her face, childlike, in his arm "—too unthinking to steal the Cup. What would a tavern wench do with it?"

"Maybe she'd wash it," Alison said tartly, "if she's as stupid as you imply."

Rowan ignored her frustration. "Triss was simply following her nature. Since I not only failed to win the Cup, but overlooked Triss's favors, she thought you would be more receptive. You haven't beaten off an intruder, but a bedmate."

Shocked, Alison charged upright on her stocking feet. "You both are crazy. I want no bedmates, especially her!"

"And what is wrong with me?" Trissellyn's colorless eyes flashed heat lightning under her storm clouds of black hair.

"Other than being subservient to, and manipulative of, men—the worst of both worlds—and apparently insanely oversexed, not a damn thing that I can see. Certainly Rowan hasn't noticed anything wrong."

"Then why did he refuse me?"

"Ask him."

Trissellyn pouted silently.

Rowan showed signs of losing his temper as thoroughly as Alison had. "You know the rules I live by, Triss," he began. "It's why I've not set boot in the Scarlet Swan for so long. Competing for the Cup requires celibacy for a year and a day—"

"The competition is over!" Trissellyn said.

"Not for me. I will try again next year, so until then—"

"But the winner, the Cupbearer, need not spurn me!" She turned on Alison. "Have you not been long-celibate also? Are you not eager for feminine companionship?"

"Ah . . . no."

" 'No' to what?" Rowan straightened as the implications dawned on him. "You do not want Triss—or any woman—or you have not been celibate?"

"I do not want Triss, or any woman," Alison answered slowly and definitely. "As for my celibacy, what business is it of yours?"

"It is solely my business!" Rowan's extravagant hair seemed charged with the fury that suffused his face. "If you have won the Cup by fraud—"

"Surely the Cup would not allow itself to be won by a cheat," Trissellyn put in.

"No . . ." Rowan sounded less sure.

"Can't we," Alison asked, "discuss this without the distracting presence of Miss Triss?"

Rowan glanced toward the young woman. Her gown was ebbing to the verge of indecency again. He nodded, going over to hold the door open until Trissellyn undulated out, content no doubt with causing an argument even if she had failed to inspire desire.

Alison turned on Rowan. "You didn't warn me that the people of Veil are sexually ambidextrous."

"What?"

"No wonder you objected to me and Sage sharing a bedchamber! Furthermore, if you want my opinion, and if you can pry Miss Triss away from whomever she happens to pass next, why not forget this silly celibacy and oblige her before you grow too old to do it?"

"What," Rowan asked with great control, "does sexually ambidextrous mean?"

"You *have* been celibate. It means that our recent visitor will sleep with women as well as with men."

"An arrant falsehood! No such abominations exist in Veil."

"Then why would this girl come to my bed in the night?"

"Because I had refused her."

"Flexible, isn't she?"

"It is her duty to couple with guests."

"Talk about abominations—"

"And you are the Cupbearer, as I should have been, and are no longer hampered by celibacy."

"That girl does go for the gold."

"What I would like to know," Rowan continued in a narrower tone, "is why any free man would refuse her."

"Oh, I doubt many men would, but it might help if she would stick to hitting on men."

"Hitting on—" He looked so confused it was comical.

"Soliciting. Seducing. Suckering. Men. Not me."

"You . . . are not . . . men?"

"Definitely not men. And certainly not—" Alison stopped, suddenly seeing what was obvious—or rather, what hadn't been obvious at all. "Good Lord, you can't possibly think that I—"

The chamber door opened softly. They turned, mouths agape. Sage entered, her hair, silver-gold in the gentle candlelight, unbraided down over her shoulders like a child's.

"I heard . . . talk." She smiled and sat on the chest footing Rowan's bed. "Is it possible that you two have begun to understand each other?"

"I begin to question my own sanity," Rowan said between his teeth.

"Here, my lad." She flourished a small lawn sack. "I've brought a special tea that will knit up ragged nerves." Sage turned admonishingly to Alison. "It is not easy for Rowan to resist that which is as natural as breathing. Trissellyn was his manhood mate." She smiled again when Alison looked blank. "She initiated him into the rites of relationship, which Rowan renounced when he declared himself a contender for the Cup a year and a day ago."

"Sage, that's their business. I don't care if he's saving himself for a blackberry bush. But I don't need strange women creeping up on me in the night—"

"It's Triss's duty," Rowan began with visible patience, "to choose a man of her liking at the inn each night. She is a free woman—one excepted from the restrictions that rule the ladies of Desmeyne, and even the village girls destined to be farmers' or shopkeepers' wives. It is an honor to be chosen by such a beauty, and she will mate with a boy to make him a man. Such matings can continue indefinitely. Had *I* won the Cup," he finished with a certain vocal swagger, "you can rest assured that Triss would not have bothered you."

"That's it!" Alison paced, difficult to do in a chamber already crowded with furniture and now hosting three people. "You idiots do think that— Look, any wench worth her décolletage would know that I'm not a man."

Rowan was suddenly motionless. "You are not?"

"Are you all blind? Deaf? Do I look like a man?"

Sage answered. "To our eyes, yes."

"Well, get new eyes."

Rowan's were blinking as if they had been buried in a sandbox, or maybe his whole head had been, Alison thought uncharitably. He studied her boots and jeans, her shirt, her chin-length hair and unmade-up face. Alison pictured the women in the Valley of Voices with their elaborate skirts and entwining scarves, and Trissellyn's exaggerated femininity: tortuous locks, state of dis-dress, powdered and rouged face.

Rowan's gaze snapped from Alison to Sage. "I claim the Cup. It was won by deception."

"Did Alison deceive you, or were you deceived?"

"What is the difference? This . . . this creature dresses as a man. Its manner is that of no respectable woman of Veil. I took this . . . this person for a youth younger than myself, it is true, and not as well developed—"

"I still managed to toss you, mister."

"—and so did the First Father mistake the matter, else he would never have awarded the Cup to an impostor. No woman can carry the Cup of Earth. No woman can fulfill the Quests to the Four Quarters."

Sage was unshaken. "Alison is a stranger to Veil. In Island-Not, women must dress as she does. She did not deliberately deceive anyone. And what of the Voices? They have not cried out at a Wellsunging for many, many years."

Rowan was almost rabid. "This stranger has confessed to violating the terms! There has been no celibacy, hard as that is to imagine, given the look of . . . her."

Sage turned to Alison with lifted brows.

"He's right," Alison said. "I can't swear I've been 'celibate' for an entire year, although sometimes it's felt like that." How many months had passed since she and Rick split up? Last July. nine months, then, unless . . . "Unless time passes faster here and I've been away from home longer than I think." She turned to Rowan. "Oh, and I like you, too."

He turned away, leashed by the room's smallness. "I cannot believe it." His hands fisted in frustration. "This may be a Crux-conjured simulacrum sent to destroy my pilgrimage. That is a possibility I have harbored at the back of my mind all along. But even in its original state of formless muck, it cannot ever have been . . . or now be female."

"Have you not forgotten something, Rowan?" Sage rose to dip a pottery cup in the hearth's heated water, then dropped her bag of herbs inside to steep.

"What?" he asked tightly.

"The undeniable physical signs of the quest, known only to families whose members have a birthright to seek the talisman. You bear the secret marks yourself, as the Firemayne heir of your generation. Your blood paid the price of that designation. No one without it would dare contend for the Cup, for the vessel would sear the hands of such an impostor. How did Alison overcome that?"

Rowan turned, his face bright with fresh certainty. "Yes, old woman, for once you say something worth heeding." His hands clenched the shirt ties at his throat. "Now, false bearer, what say you to this?"

He wrenched open his shirt to reveal a sight that made Alison wince: deep scars carved into his chest, deliberate scars still an angry red, scars whose like she had seen only once before. Sage nodded at Alison, the piercing quality of her gray-eyed stare making clear what the old woman wanted.

Alison had only done such a thing with a sense of emotional cringing. Now she didn't feel like cringing. Perhaps it was the wonder of witnessing someone else's scars. More likely it was how, from the first, Rowan's inbred assumptions had questioned her right to exist—to sing for the Cup, to carry it, to be concerned for the Littlelost, to be what she was, the very sex she was. She knew that Rowan Firemayne would loathe knowing what he'd asked to learn. With a trace of righteous satisfaction, Alison undid the three top buttons of her flannel shirt, pushing back the fabric to reveal her own scars. They were identical to his.

In Rowan's expression disbelief jousted with perplexity, then joined it. Nerveless fingers let his shirt obscure the disfigurement he had deemed unique.

Sage approached Alison, gazing almost greedily upon the proof she had somehow anticipated. Alison's attention remained on Rowan. She *did* have a right to the Cup, to something in this world she had not chosen, even if the claim was based on a bizarre coincidence, on accident.

Rowan pushed his hands through his hair as though drawing its ruddy color off his face would cool his thoughts. He spoke them heedlessly.

"If the quest marks *are* there, and are as old, older, I can see that, *older* than mine—then . . . she, he, it is not a woman!"

Sage cackled abruptly and wrenched Alison's shirt open several buttons more, exposing her breasts to the lacy top of her brassiere.

Rowan stared, mouth agape.

Alison clutched her shirt together. For a moment her scars had acquired a surprising magical identity, were no longer the disfigurement that rode like a pock-marked full moon above the landscape of her womanhood, a wound that she always hid. That moment had fled, leaving an afterglow of embarrassment.

Rowan turned from a revelation he could not deny. "This is mad," he muttered. "The ills that eat at Veil have managed to usurp even our ancient rituals for protecting ourselves and our land. I cannot conceive of what to do in the face of such . . . impossibilities."

"Why not," Sage suggested mildly, bringing Rowan the brewed tea, "behave as no man—no hero—in Veil has ever done before, and accept them? Accept her."

Rowan regarded Alison again and shuddered. "Never."

15

Neither Trissellyn nor Rowan appeared for breakfast. The Littlelost were out foraging for wild food, having already tired of pallid inn-cooked vittles.

Rowan had not objected to Alison's finishing the night in Sage's room. She had slept far more easily there, especially after drinking the soothing tea that Rowan had rejected out of hand, saying "Herbs bear Crux-taint, like too much in Veil nowadays."

"Do you suppose," Alison mused to Sage over the Scarlet Swan's morning brew—a hearty but misguided mixture reminiscent of ale-laced coffee—"that in the night, Rowan gave up his quest for the Cup? I don't see Miss Triss around, either."

Sage shook her head. "He is stubborn, like all Firemaynes. Like all Desmeynians, for that matter. He mayhap is brooding over the fate that had him lose the Cup to one with no clan-right to it."

"In my land, possession is nine tenths of the law."

Sage's dilated, berry-dark eyes regarded Alison sharply. For a moment Alison wondered if the wisewoman had heard that modern expression before. Something of Eli's inborn skepticism seasoned Sage's look.

"Clan-right and ritual are the only laws in Veil," Sage finally said. "You are . . . anathema to all that Rowan represents. I believe you will be very good for him."

"You make me sound like a medicinal tea. You also imply that I'll be hanging around the big lug. Look, Sage, all I want is a way out of here. All I want is home. And Beau back."

The old woman inhaled the visible steam that curled up from her mug. "There are four ways 'out of here,' each harder than the last. You already hold the key to the first."

"The Cup? But how?"

"It is the means; the method remains in your hands. I do not know how it will come about, only that you must carry the Cup and learn to know it, and Veil, and yourself. Then you and the Cup will work your separate magics together. You must accept your role."

"I have no magic! And my 'role' here is being misplaced! I'm an overage Alice in Wonderland; I know you don't know what that means, but I want to go home, Sage. I want to see sights and people I know and understand. I never wanted the Cup."

"You have no choice, Taliswoman. Your vision is fresh and foreign. We need one who can make us see what we will not. The people of Veil distrust the alien; they seldom venture from the safe circles of their cities and villages, their kin and kind. Rowan is a bold wayfarer by comparison, for all his distrust, and bold only because he cannot tolerate staying tamely in Desmeyne until he wins the Cup, but busies himself with any quests that promise progress. I have seen more than most in Veil. I have traveled all the way to the Littlelosts' Rookeries and ventured deep into the wild lands that surround each settlement, where each people keeps to its own and its own ways."

"So that's why Rowan's so stubborn and hidebound! His way is the *only* one in his mind."

"He allows himself to see no others. Yet an old, unwanted wandering woman has witnessed what others of Veil will not—even the Great Water that is rumored and feared and often denied among all the inhabitants of Veil, of which wildwater is but a pale shadow. I have observed foul changes: The Littlelosts' number increases, and no one counts the missing heads among their kind; the earth blisters with rank new growths and festering sores, and the people simply narrow what they live upon to what is untainted; strangers in strange forms subvert our separated people, like the Littlelost, to their own aims. We call them 'Crux-masters' and fear their magical power and see them in every shadowy anomaly, and yet never wrestle with their reality—or the twisted reality they are making of Veil."

"You paint a troubling picture," Alison admitted. "In my own world, I'm a reporter; it's my job to point out ugly realities—and good things, if I can—so that people can change their ways, but what can I do in a world I don't understand?"

"Oh, Taliswoman, the fabric of Veil is disintegrating—not before our eyes, but in myriad, half-hidden ways. Your arrival forced a rent in this vast, invisible weaving, as others and other . . . *things* have done before you. Your presence only testifies to the rottenness of the very tissue, of the integrity, of Veil. And yet, you are the first unevil thing I have seen reach us."

"Then you know that Island-Not is not just a far land Veilians haven't heard of, but another world. I'm relieved that someone knows where I'm coming from, literally. But I'm no savior for any world, much less this one. You credit me with a lot. And all these evil things from elsewhere have preceded me? How do you know?"

"By smell. By aches and pains in my old bones. By dreams that come by day, and by dusk. By anomalies such as yourself. By the clouding of Veil's sky and water and the death I have seen breeding in our earth. I am only an old woman who collects forbidden herbs and reaps uncommon wisdom by it, that is all."

"It's hard to believe that Veil is in such straits. It seems an earthly paradise to me, were it mine. Warm waterfalls, verdant forest—Littlelost plucking nutritious food from the pines. Even the people seem healthy. Look at Trissellyn; she's robust, to say the least. Except for this superstition of birth-bane—"

"Truth," Sage put in. "Birth-bane is the one thing unavoidable."

"Everyone has flaws, but we overcome them. Besides, what's Rowan's birth-bane?"

"You have seen it. The betraying red hair. No male Firemayne is without it."

"Some people in Island-Not consider red hair unlucky, or redheads untrustworthy, but it's no physical deficiency."

"Then why does it betray Rowan's role as seeker after the Cup and the Four Quarters? He is marked in all his travels, and must defend his life if his identity is discovered. Not only must he duel rival Wellsingers, but the Crux cannot afford a Desmeynian heir venturing abroad and learning as much as one powerless old woman has. Rowan wants to be his kind's savior, and he could preserve all Veil with new vision and your help."

"He needs new vision, all right." Alison eyed Sage with suspicion. Sage was regarding her blandly. Was Sage too eager to have Alison think of her as 'just an old woman'? Was it low self-esteem in the face of the Desmeynian anti-age fetish, or was Sage protesting too much? And another thing—"Red hair is really that rare? Surely others in Desmeyne, in Veil, have it?"

Sage shook her head. "Not even a beast of the field."

"Hmm." Alison sipped the cooling beverage. "At last I understand why he hid it."

"It is good that you begin to understand him, for he will not find that favor easy to return."

"What does it matter who understands whom—or even if? Grandiose goals seem self-deceiving when there are ills right at hand to cure, like getting these kids, the Littlelost, to some safe place and finding my way back to where I belong. Just show me some ruby slippers, and I'm gone."

Sage smiled. "If you wish to see these intriguing-sounding ruby slippers, no doubt some magical artifact of Island-Not, you will have to go to Desmeyne. Therefore, you will have to travel with Rowan. I suggest you make that necessity at least bearable to him, and then—"

Footsteps approached Alison from behind, punctuated by the blows of a staff on the wooden floor. She twisted to see Rowan, staff cocked, backpack hiked over one shoulder. He paused beside their table to address them.

"I leave for Desmeyne. If you would come, follow." He turned and left.

Swayed by Sage's plea for understanding of Rowan's single-minded sense of duty, Alison didn't waste time grousing about his manners. She scrambled to retrieve her pack from the floor while Sage threw a mesh bag of potpourri to the tabletop as a tip. Alison glimpsed the newly shy Trissellyn lurking in a shadowed doorway as they left. Likely the serving maid wouldn't appreciate Sage's rare gift of sweet scent. The people of Veil were oriented to the eye, not to subtler senses. Perhaps that was why they overlooked the encroaching decay Sage talked of, Alison thought.

Outside, the long-legged Rowan was vanishing down a trail. Littlelost spurted from the surrounding trees like squirrels welcoming food-bearers. Alison was touched to find that they had found and brought food instead of begged it: fresh pomma to pad the corners of her backpack and Sage's capacious pockets.

They started after Rowan, Alison impatient at having to slow her sprightly pace to the lagging children and the sometimes limping old woman. Despite Rowan's lengthy stride, Alison would bet she could pace him step for step. What she lacked in length of leg, she had in endurance and willpower.

Sage was laughing softly behind her. Alison paused and turned, waiting for the wisewoman to huff forward.

"You see, Taliswoman," Sage said. "You can hardly restrain yourself from catching up to yon Firemayne; your fates are linked."

"I'd like to give the guy a run for his money, yes. He just charges ahead as if we didn't exist; it makes me feel like he's trying to lose us. After all, he has no time for the Littlelost and not much courtesy for you—and we don't have Beau to keep an eye on him." A wave of sadness almost stopped Alison's voice.

Sage chuckled. "Rowan may wish to lose us, but he knows better. For all his chagrin, he dare not return to Desmeyne without the Cup, even if it is borne by another."

"If he's so wild to have it, couldn't he just take it?"

Sage took Alison's arm to keep up with her already accelerating strides. "No. No, he cannot. That would violate the essence of the Cup of Earth. It gives itself to whoever wins the Wellsunging and to no other. To steal it would be to blight Desmeyne further."

"It's beginning to sound like the Holy Grail in my world, except that this Cup can get heavier when it wants to." Alison shrugged under the backpack. Although the Cup was now no heavier than a pewter tankard, its hidden presence was unforgettable.

"Have you seen and held this Holy Grail?" Sage asked.

"Are you kidding? A woman would have been as unwelcome a Grail-finder as she is a Cupholder here, according to the legends of my land. But the Grail flowed with blood, which makes it a female principle, not the assumed male one, if you ask me. Grail-hunters were a company of less-celibate-than-they-should-be knights—men warriors—who blundered around the countryside seeking salvation via self-glorification," Alison finished, grumbling.

"Your land is rich in ritual," Sage said, "but your tale confuses me, though I detect in it a certain annoyance with the ways of Firemaynes. Still, you have not seen or held this Grail as you have seen and held this Cup. It is yours for a year and day. If you use it well, perhaps you will belong to it at the end of that time."

"I don't like the idea of belonging to anything, especially to an inanimate object; it's like being swallowed by it, Sage. I've already lost Rambeau to this crazy-quilt land. It can't take chunks of my life, too. Once we reach Desmeyne and I'm sure that the Littlelost are safe, I'll be free to leave the Cup and find my way back somehow," she asserted. A spasm of regret struck even as she spoke, probably distress at parting with the Littlelost. She certainly couldn't feel bereft by the loss of a Cup, could she?

"What is 'safe'? What is 'sure'?"

Alison stopped. "You argue like an Indian of my acquaintance, all questions."

"What is 'Indian'?"

"Eli," said Alison, remembering his disappearance with a pang. Another puzzling loss. She sat down on a convenient log. "Oh, Sage, it's no use to pretend I'm going to do anything! Everything's out of my control here."

"Mayhap"—Sage bent over Alison, as if drawn to her despair as an antidote seeks poison, and patted the backpack where the Cup lay—"everything is in your control. That is the more frightening possibility, always."

"Yeah." Alison pushed herself up tiredly. No time for self-pity. Somewhere up ahead, Rowan wasn't resting; she was sure of that. "Let's get on with it, then."

Walking was a more arduous, less joyous process without Beau as advance scout, running back barking to report on the way ahead.

Sage seemed sure that Rowan had no desire to lose her company—or that of the Cup—but Alison wasn't as certain. She plodded through the blossomless meadows that were the people of Veil's chosen paths. A cloak of flowers beckoned from the distant grasslands like the inviting poppies outside the Emerald City, but Alison knew now that their color and grace broadcast a noxious stench. Only Sage seemed able to find sweet-scented growing things, and they were herbal, like her name, rather than floral.

Yet the trees and flowers looked so inviting, so picture-postcard. If Rowan's people spurned the beauties of their own land, however ill-scented, mightn't they also find no charm in the rough-edged Littlelost? Maybe Rowan was right: Her charges wouldn't be welcome at Desmeyne—whatever and wherever it was. *She* would certainly not be welcome, unobvious woman that she was, if she weren't bearing the fabled Cup.

By midafternoon the party had paused at a crystalline stream that bubbled between chinks of the rocky mountainside. The Littlelost were jousting for the honor of providing Alison with pomma, evincing a proprietariness that went oddly with their half-wild aspect.

She was growing fond of the Littlelost and would hate to abandon them to the unknown people of Desmeyne without knowing what they'd do with the children. Pickle tossed her a strange orange berry. Its tough meat was acrid but had a sweet kicker; obviously an acquired taste. Camay begged one, and Pickle obliged with a devilish grin. His reward was watching the child's small face pucker into an infantile knot of wrinkles. Camay spit out a spray of orange—directly on Pickle.

"Here!" Alison intervened in the forthcoming tussle. "Why don't you go see if you can spy Rowan?"

"Let him get lost," Pickle urged.

"He is our guide," Sage reminded them.

"Beau was better," Faun said fervently.

Alison watched through a distorted window of tears as they scattered among the trees. What was wrong with her? Loneliness or self-pity wouldn't help her to escape—or adapt to—this land in which she was marooned. She fished the Veilian vessel out of her backpack, unwound its shroud of flannel shirt and turned briskly to Sage.

"All right, if this bloody Cup is so powerful, how do I use it?"

"The people of Island-Not are direct," Sage answered wryly. "But the answer is simple. You let the Cup use you."

"Double-talk. How?"

"You could start by using it. That is one thing Cupbearers in Veil have always been afraid to do, except in a ceremonial sense."

"What for?"

"For what do you use a cup in Island-Not?"

Alison turned its pale shape in her hands, appraising it as she would if encountering it in her world.

"How would I use it? For a dinner party with one guest of honor. Or as a display in my great aunt's mahogany breakfront. Maybe donate it as a trophy for the local school's bowling team."

The honest confusion in Sage's pale eyes at this litany of alien actions shamed Alison. "No, I was just kidding. Jesting. I'd know this Cup for something special." She sighed as her thumb rubbed a violet cabachon gemstone. "Old. Treasured. I'd keep it . . . save it. Put it away."

Sage shook her head.

"What should I do with it in Veil? Use it, you said. I already drank from it at the inn, simply because everyone was acting as if you and the Littlelost and I were invisible, and it infuriated me. Then everybody thought I was crazy to do it—why?"

Sage turned to the stream bubbling over the rocks behind them. Alison raised her eyebrows, then dipped the Cup in the water and lifted it up. She paused.

"How do I know this isn't tainted wildwater?"

"You do not. Perhaps the Cup does."

Alison eyed the Cup dubiously. The contents were shadowed. She glimpsed an oily rainbow slick on the surface, which suddenly shimmered with light. She bent near. Minuscule water drops bombarded her face. The liquid had grown clear enough for her to see the veins in the bottom of the Cup and icy enough to frost the stone exterior, and it was . . . sparkling.

Surprised, feeling daring, feeling compelled to, she touched her mouth to the chill Cup rim and tilted the water toward it. Another effervescent explosion. Alison's tingling lips drew back in a smile. "It's like drinking tiny firecrackers"—Sage looked blank—"Asti Spumante, mineral water, something fizzy, as if the stream were still flowing."

"Perhaps it is power you drink," Sage said.

"It must be only a natural effusion in the water. Gas from within the land is charging it, that's all. We have water and wine like this on Earth . . . er, in Island-Not. So this is what I'm supposed to do with the Cup: drink from it."

"Perhaps." Sage's smile wearied. "I do not know. I have never carried the Cup. It is known to benefit the lands of those who have held it over the years, but you have no lands in Veil, you have no kind to bring it home to. Perhaps it will benefit no one. Or perhaps it will benefit you beyond what it has ever given a bearer before. Only you can discover what the Cup will do for you. It is your right. It is your obligation."

Alison peered into the Cup again. Exploding bubbles sleeted into her eyes, then a side-breeze buffeted her face. She blinked wildly. Her eyes burned as if particles of acid-imbued dust had lodged behind the lenses. Of all times to have contact problems! The sharp discomfort forced Alison to pop both lenses into the palm of one hand, tears sluicing down her face.

"What is it?" Sage's voice throbbed with concern.

"Oh, sometimes the wind blows dirt into my eyes." She huddled over the Cup, forced to rinse the contacts in its oddly charged water. She blinked one painlessly into place, then the other, and sighed her relief. "It's fine now." Her vision floated on a buffer of fresh water, giving everything the look of a heat haze. Sage's wrinkled face had softened to a babyish blur. Alison waited for the excess liquid to dissipate, and smiled. "Well, the Cup makes a super lens-soaking case in an emergency."

"It did not hurt you?" Sage pressed. "It should not hurt you."

"No, not the Cup. Just my . . . seeing spell giving me trouble. It happens to us Island-Not mages all the time. But my eyes feel so cool now, refreshed. That water must be really clean, or the Cup—"

Alison turned the white stone vessel in her hands, watching the water still as the last bubbles evaporated. She felt as if she cradled an ice sculpture, yet the surface was dry. The warmth of her hands, rather than affecting the Cup, was diminishing from touching it, as if the vessel leeched her human heat into its icy whiteness.

She tried to sip the water again, but it had grown so cold that its very nearness seared her lips like dry ice. She dropped it softly to the flannel, her hands chilled to the wrist bones.

"It's as cold as death, Sage. Surely a Cup of Earth would be life-giving!"

"Earth is long-forgotten stones and buried walls of ice. What grows and is heated by the sun is only the thin skin of brown and green atop it," the old woman reminded her.

"But there's a furnace deep below the dirt and rock—rivers of liquid rock, fountains of solid fire."

Sage seemed stunned. "Do you say so? You sound sure. But fire is a separate element from earth, air, and water. It would never abide within stone, no more than liquid fire would fill the Cup."

"No," Alison insisted, "heat is at the heart of the Earth. That's elementary geology."

Sage rose to her knees. "Heart of Earth? You know of the Heart of Earth?"

"The heat within, like the heart that drives our bodies."

"No! This Heart of Earth is a specific place we seek. It lies in the First Quarter. No Cupbearer has yet found it, but when one does, Veil will begin to take back its own again."

"Sage, that was just an expression I used. I wasn't speaking of any particular place."

"But *I* was! Come, we must not lose Rowan now!" The wisewoman was on her feet before Alison could follow suit, her eye-whites reflecting the pale peach of sunset melting through the trees.

As soon as Alison had gingerly rewrapped the still-frozen Cup and repacked it, she was being herded along by Sage, by the Littlelost, who'd joined in Sage's game.

Her side ached by the time they rustled through a small stand of trees and paused before a panoramic sunset conflagration. The world fell away from them into deep valleys against a wall of sharp-peaked mountains tall enough to stab the weltering sun.

Before them, Rowan was an almost-silhouette against the flagrant light, his hair lit with matching fire. He had stopped to stare into the valley, and Alison sensed that he could have been standing there—staff slanted like a scepter—for minutes, even hours. As they neared him, they quieted their steps, and then she saw what might have struck him motionless. Her eyes still seemed watery, for the world had a soft-focus look.

A carnelian city lay carved like a necklace of beads between the mountain peaks. Its towers and sky-strung bridges sparkled like precious topaz—not the yellow-brown, mock-topaz citrines and smoky quartz that pass as precious, but those true topaz gems that vary in color from brandy to sherry to palest champagne.

And rich, peacock-blue blasts trumpeted among the autumnal tones of bloody brown and gilded orange and silvered saffron. The sunset enhanced the effect, making the mountains into one, long, human-carved vein of faceted crystals—a Hyatt Regency Las Vegas to make moguls as diverse as Howard Hughes and Donald Trump drool.

"Desmeyne?" Alison asked softly.

Rowan wasn't looking at the city, she saw as she glanced at him. He had expected the city, took its wonder for granted. Instead, he was staring into the dusk-dimming valleys, where she could just see the miniature patchwork of fields and outbuildings and hummocked farmhouses.

"Earth-Eaters," he said in a rough, hoarse voice. "They've loosed the Harrow-worms."

Alison looked again. Light was plunging behind the mountains, making it blasphemy to remove one's eyes from the city's ever-changing spectacle to peer into the darkness of the wrinkled land. But she saw, amid the grid of low-growing crops, cruel as scars, wild fissures of disrupted earth puckered into gouges here and uneven mounds there. For a moment she thought the pattern mimicked the marks scarring herself and Rowan, but that was fanciful. There was no pattern below, only random, mindless destruction. Daylight would reveal the damage's full extent.

"We are too late with the Cup," Rowan said numbly to himself.

"We?" Alison thought. But she remained silent. Quibbles were out of place on the brink of this sunset-steeped city and the ravaged fields. She saw now that the Cup of Earth at least symbolized a solution for Desmeynian ills that were realer than she'd thought. If only she weren't a modern woman who couldn't quite believe in magical solutions. If only the Cup was all it was supposed to be!

The pack was starving.

Famine, then feast, was the way of wolves, but these mountain meadows were oddly bare of big game. The small, scuttering forest things could barely fuel a day's scouting for meatier prey.

Dog still ran on the pack's fringes. Beneath his thick white fur his belly had tautened until his flesh stretched drumskin-tight over his ribs. The fat around his neck had melted like a garland of spring snow. Hunger had become a constant condition, but Dog had not yet killed.

He watched the others hunt the forest creatures in a ritual of sly stalking and sudden pounce that looked like play. Then they would lie in a circle while Weatherwise, the one-eared chieftain, distributed the meager catch. From a distance, Dog watched. The pack looked like a gathering of motley German shepherds, gnawing rawhide strips in the grass.

The pack did not yet know what to make of him, although he knew each of their scents and they his. Quickfang and Cowlick, the gangly young black-haired males who would soon be challenging Weatherwise for pack-right, would circle Dog endlessly, ears low in submission so they could get near enough to sniff under the white plume of his tail, which he always carried high over his back, unlike them.

His smell was neither male nor female, so they did not attack him. Knowing nothing of the alterations routinely performed on domestic animals, they remained confused. So did Featherstep, the blond top female, and Moondrift, the immature female who was lowest on the pack's totem pole.

Dog was lower still. Except at night.

They always settled on high ground near the forest and water, long noses cradled on extended front legs, lean bodies curled to generage what heat they could against the chill blanket of dark draping the earth.

On such nights, Weatherwise often led a community howl. They cried out their hunger to the skies. They warned prey and enemies of their presence. They sang for the joy of the crisp night air tangy with smells, and for the supple rhythm of the trot, and for the peace of sleep. They did not sing thanks for food.

And so Dog, having altered them in ways they could only sense, and troubled by the deep hunger in the once-yellow eyes that now shone as black as berries, as black as his own, went one night atop a prow of lonely rock and began a solitary howl of such range and power that it seemed to sing the stars down from the skies.

Heads rose from paws. Ears perked. Moondrift, the youngest, gamboled over, having never heard such cries from her kind. Weatherwise shambled over next, undecided whether to join in or to offer challenge. Featherstep came after her mate, then the two males, Cowlick and Quickfang. Puzzled, they sat in a circle.

It was irresistible, Dog's howl. It spoke not of hunger and hunting, but of the Great Sky Herd and the People of the Horizon, the smoke of whose camp fires wreathed the moon. It teased the clouds from the sky and the light from the stars, until the pack's raised hair-tips glistened as if snow-dusted and the moonlight glittered on their pointed white teeth. It celebrated blind, wriggling litters and three-footed, old lone ones. It cried for the life in-between that was hard and sometimes happy and all too short.

Dog's howl rose so high and so piercing that the Great Milk River overflowed its sky-banks and fell to earth in a huge, white, seething waterfall, and down its frothing tide tumbled a ghostly array of game clothed in moonlight.

Came springing, fleet-footed Deer. Came the drumming, thudding mountain of meat called Buffalo by the People of the Horizon. Came Fox and Rabbit and Raven, Swan and Fish, all of them clothed in the garments of snow and fog, shining silver down the Great Milk River.

Then Weatherwise howled once, and the pack was up and running, Dog at its head, running into the Great Milk River. A mist washed over them, wetting their noses and sleeking their fur. They ran over rock and turf, after the ghostly game. No scents led them on, only the river of racing animals. They overtook the fawn and the ancient buck, the terrified doe, and the bewildered ones, who fell and could not rise. They feasted on mist and memory until they were full.

Dog's howl was only an echo in the far forest when the fog cleared. Weatherwise sniffed the alien ground and growled at the pack to remind them to be wary.

They fanned across the forest floor. The smells were rich, the same and not the same. Small, fallen leaves powdered under their paws. And then, there—fresh spoor—meat!

All business now, no consultation, only well-practiced communal instinct. Soft-footed through the underbrush, like Featherstep, as graceful as Moondrift—and there, near a stand of pale-trunked trees, frozen, waiting for them, waiting for chase and catch and fang and claw, stood a slender deer in the moonlight, watching them with grave, sad eyes.

Hearts pounded, saliva flowed. Long-denied bellies ached.

Dog spoke from the fringes, to which he always kept during pack business. "Deer has shared your hunger and fear, my brothers and sisters, and has come to aid you. Be quick and thankful."

They ran again, noses filled with scent, feet fleet, hearts racing. The chase was joyous, as fast and as powerful as Cowlick and Quickfang, the catch a communal frenzy. They rended memory and meat, drank swift and deep at the Great Blood River.

Weatherwise stood over the gift to guard the bounty and feed his pack. The usual ritual was: After him, his mate Featherstep would eat first, then Quickfang and Cowlick. Moondrift last.

Weatherwise tore a hunk of steaming flesh from the still haunch, then hurled it toward the waiting pack.

The first gift of Deer went to Dog.

The pack was at last full and content and could run for weeks with the fleetness of Deer, on the gift of Deer.

Dog roused them after long sleep and led them back across the last mists of the Great Milk River to the land that was the same as this, but not this land. Weatherwise was still unchallenged chieftain, but Dog spoke for them all, to them all. Dog promised more game, more feast, more hunger, more chase. And he promised one thing no pack had ever been promised before. He promised a task.

16

The party camped on the sharp edge of darkness that night and listened to the wolves howl.

Becausc Rowan had declared the terrain too difficult to cross by night, they had settled where they stood. He had also declared that they shouldn't risk attracting attention with a camp fire, so their only illumination was Alison's flashlight. Everyone chewed cold pomma flakes and sipped icy tea.

Later, Alison lay awake, imagining the faceted city gleaming in the night like animal eyes, listening and hoping for the one, thready howl that could only be Rambeau's. Wolfish threnodies rebounded from the unseen peaks with the force of an over-amplified rock concert, each new chorus whining low enough to raise hackles and rising shrill enough to shatter glass and eardrums.

She also heard the hiss of unseen wings hurl like knives overhead and shuddered to think that these might be the metallic flying things that had briefly buzzed her and the Littlelost near the etherion pit. But nothing came of the sound. Perhaps the etherion coursers patrolled only the pits.

An occasional breeze too warm to be Alpine spurted past, carrying a sickly sweet scent too heavy to be pleasant. Her disgruntled bones complained when she rose to the cold light of dawn to find the latrine the Littlelost had come to take pride in creating—and covering when the party moved on.

When she returned, she found that Camay had taken Rowan's place in balancing on the lip of the high ground, staring down at the pale, daytime glitter of Desmeyne.

"What is—?" the child turned to ask as Alison approached.

"A city."

"What is city?"

"A group of people who come together to govern themselves, build common edifices, trade with and protect each other." No grade-school civics-book definition, but it would have to do.

Camay's frown screwed her tiny features into an uncannily adult semblance. "Holes in the mountains? People live there? Why?"

"More like balconies and bridges over the mountains." Alison eyed Desmeyne's pallid parapets and towers. Glass, or its double, winked back blandly. "Only one more trek down the mountain and you'll be among your own kind again, people who will care for you."

"What is 'care for'?"

"They'll wash your face and comb your hair," Alison retorted, propelling the child to where Sage sat. The wisewoman had produced jars of balms from her pockets for the bruises and scratches overlaying the much-traveled Littlelost and was attempting to talk them into washing before she treated them.

"No, I won't!" Pickle was shouting, tussling with Sage for possession of the grimy scarf tied over his ears. "Don't need clean hair! Don't need clean anything."

He broke away, his face ruddy with effort, his emotion too deep to argue with. Sage shrugged her plump shoulders and said, "They are as attached to the badges of their ill care as some folk are to their most prized possessions. Like the flowers of the field, the Littlelost prefer to reek and be left alone, rather than to grow sweet enough to pick."

Alison laughed and sat by Sage to finish her pomma. Rowan, she noticed, was stripping leafy vines to fashion lassos, but she wasn't going to stir things up by asking why.

"Why do the flowers stink?" she asked Sage instead. "I haven't smelled one a bee would care to hesitate over. And how do you find fragrant herbs in a world awash in ill-scented, or scentless, flowers?"

Sage eyed Alison's pack. "Get the Cup."

Alison complied, then scrambled up after Sage, who was now limping toward the thready waterfalls plashing over the mountain's rocky ribs.

"Fill it," Sage said.

Alison averted her face from the spray as the liquid blasted into the bowl of the Cup. She tilted its lip to capture the water, then, thoroughly damp, retreated from the cataract.

"Follow me." Sage's slow-moving, iron-gray figure plowed into the long grass of the adjacent meadow.

Alison did as Sage said, at first enjoying the dry waves of sea-green stalks eddying around her knees. Then she missed the soft, sweet scent of grass. And the clouds of tiny insects. A smell came wafting over the meadow-waves: sour, sharp, yet rot-soft and sickly sweet. She would have turned back, but Sage went on until they stood at the verge of a mass of purple-gold flowers. Both were breathing through their mouths to avoid the stench that radiated almost visibly from the blossoms.

With a gesture, Sage instructed Alison to water the offenders. So the Cup was tilted to give up its contents. Droplets fell like diamonds. Alison swept her arm in a half-circle and watched diadems of dew crown the showy blooms of a dozen plants.

Oddly, the Cup felt full again, so she tossed its contents in a wider arc. Again it almost overflowed, so she cast the contents away in a graceful spray. And again. The Cup had become bottomless. She stared at Sage in wonder and emptied the Cup again and again until the meadow sparkled in the sunlight. Each drop that found a flower trembled there like a small magnifying glass on the velvet cushion of petal. The flowers shimmered in the breeze, as rich as the finest roses and more exotic in color and shape. Yet the odor . . .

"Breathe," was Sage's final instruction.

Against her inclinations, pushing open the shuttered doors to her sense of smell, Alison inhaled. The reek was gone. Not only that, in its place was a smorgasbord of scents, teasingly familiar and alien at the same time. She turned to Sage with speechless delight.

The old woman pointed at the Cup, her face wrinkled into a jovial doily, expressively sly around the edges. "Earth is dirty. Water from the Cup cleans it. Smells good."

Alison bent to pluck a turgid lavender blossom redolent of fresh linen and apple blossoms. "I want to show the Littlelost that flowers can smell good."

Sage's face saddened amid its wise mirth, but she said nothing as Alison strode through the rippling grasses toward the overlook.

Nor did she seem surprised when Alison stopped only twenty feet from where the ground grew hard and the grass grew scanty.

"The scent is . . . paling. Growing stale." Alison's nose jerked back from the flower as if it had stung her. "The putrid odor is back!" She lifted her arm as if to cast it away.

"Put it in the Cup," Sage suggested.

And once the broken stem touched the water within the Cup, the pleasing scent poured out anew. Alison regarded Sage with wonder—and despair. "One Cup to cleanse an entire meadow, but only one bearer to stand and cast all day! I can't reverse a world of ill odor by myself."

Fragrance drifted up from the flower, curling like invisible incense for the mind. Alison found the scent so seductive, so indefinable, that she wanted to walk forever clutching the Cup before her, the blossom floating on its mysterious inner sea, she inhaling the intangible beauty.

She looked up. The Littlelost had gathered around her, drawn by the sweet smell. They were stretching on tiptoe to touch the petals as fragile as panne velvet. Only Rowan stood aside, his expression an odd blend of longing and revulsion.

Then he looped his vine ropes around his staff in knots too bulky to break. "Who will anchor the staff while I explore the route below?"

"I will!" cried the Littlelost in concert, drawn to the deed of daring rather than to the act of contemplation. Alison smiled ruefully as even Sage went over to supervise. She inhaled the water-buoyed flower once more, then lifted it dripping from the vase of the Cup and hurled it toward the meadow. A breeze snatched the blossom as wind will take a wounded butterfly, leaving the odor of beauty and death in its wake.

The steep mountainside Rowan led them down was scoured raw of any growth other than stringy locks of dried root—all that remained of any plants that had tried to grow on this limestone face.

The rock's striated nature at least projected small ledges and footholds. They clambered downward, each one concentrating on the precarious passage. Now Rowan's vine-hung staff bridged them like some puppet control stick, offering seven separate strands to give them needed support on each stage of the descent—and to ensnare them in a tangle only a fall would undo. He remained above them, single-handedly holding the staff steady.

Occasionally Alison would glance to the city across the valley. It sparkled like fool's gold in the sunlight . . . and looked a bit trashy, like a garish souvenir from a state fair. She wondered why Rowan's people had chosen so precipitous a retreat, one so distant from the fertile lands squeezed between the shoulder blades of the mountains.

The rock was becoming volcanic, glassy and black, sharp and shiny. The roughness began to scrape the heels of her hands. She pictured them inching down the rock face, ants on a table leg . . . or would-be Draculas, forced to go feet-down instead of head-down like the diabolical Count.

The others' silence attested to the difficult descent. Alison could no longer picture their positions; she no longer felt connected to the others despite the common staff from which each of their vines hung. She was merely a single spider dangling over the depths and in need of four more limbs to keep herself affixed to the ever-more inhospitable rock face.

The black stone grew so translucent that she glimpsed her fuzzy reflection pressing in it . . . then she saw it was no reflection, but another's face! She gazed through smoked glass into the murky waters of an aquarium. Something alien floated there; a pallid, fleshy visage with tiny, white-pupiled eyes like eggs, a body mass so shapeless and fluid that it seemed the wings of a stingray. A pale starfish crawled over the rough glass wall to touch tips with Alison's splayed fingers clinging to the rock.

Her body jerked back to avoid the contact, but some unswervingly rational part of her mind refused to let her actually step off her rocky foothold into space.

"Climb down quickly!" someone urged, perhaps Sage.

Alison's feet and hands paddled like a swimmer's, in unison. She slid more than moved and doubted that such haste could keep her attached to the vertical surface, but somehow she found enough glossy crests of rock to serve.

When hands grabbed her legs and began dragging her down,

she almost jerked free—and free of the cliff—but the hands were too many and too insistent. Her feet touched solid ground and her weight settled bit by bit, as if distrusting the horizontal.

Alison turned to face out from the mountain. They all stood safely on a triangular ledge well over half the way down. Opposite them, Desmeyne loomed above their heads, but a downward glance showed a dizzying, still-distant landscape, where croplands lay churned up as if by a plow as big as an ocean liner.

"What did you see?" Rowan was asking.

"A face . . . in the solid rock."

"What kind of face?"

"Pale, vague, almost manatee-like."

Rowan frowned his uncertainty.

"Like one of our faces, only horribly . . . dissolved. It must be some hallucinatory property of the rock, or a distorted reflection, but—"

A harsh, leathery rustle—the rhythmic stroke/stroke/stroke of an old-fashioned, straightedge razor against a thick length of leather—thrummed around them. The escalating sound rustled toward them, crackling like nearby lightning.

Then the creature itself elevated into view: a great subterranean shadow, balancing on thin air. Gray velvet wings edged with a steely glint sawed the empty ether in leisurely sweeps.

The wings and their size were so overpowering that Alison could barely comprehend any shape beyond them. She glimpsed a central, sluglike core of hundreds of parallel, slimy black pseudopods, a maw—or an eye—pale orange against the black satin underbelly.

The thing was rising vertically above them to match itself to the mountain, to smash them between the glassy rock and the cardiac beat of its smothering wings.

"Down!" Sage pried Littlelost loose from the ledge and prodded them down the face of the cliff.

Rowan's staff jabbed at the monster, but incredibly flexible wings folded inward like fingers to deflect his blows.

Alison turned back to the rock face, saw in the shadow created by the hovering beast an entire aquarium of flat-faced white things, and slid belly-first over the ledge's lip, jolting down a rough, grazing slide that bruised her body from ankles to chin. Level ground—rock-strewn but blessedly horizontal—was only yards below.

But there remained that awful, huffing, bellows sound, and the wind sucking on them like a gigantic mouth, drawing them up through an invisible straw into the eye of the storm, the maw of the beast.

Sticky, hair-fine tentacles were weaving a net of darkness around them. Alison felt the others struggling, slipping painfully down the last yards of mountainside. She caught a flash of sky for a moment and saw a wing wrapped tight around Rowan's upthrust staff—but then the wing unwound, flinging the staff to the rocks below and drenching them all in that awful smothering shadow again.

Someone bumped against Alison's hip. A Littlelost. Twist. She grabbed a thin arm and lowered the body another notch down the mountain's rugged face. It felt like riding down an endless giant zipper track.

She could hear the creature's knife-edge wings scraping the rock; had it not been so large, so unmaneuverable an entity, it would have crushed them all long before. In the meantime, they slid down the narrow chimneys in the rocks, eluded it like pieces of sand dribbling through the neck of an hourglass, protected by their small size and their very number.

Then, amazingly, they were all on horizontal ground, groping for each other in the dusk of the monster wings. A large hand jerked Alison forward, then pulled assorted Littlelost in the same direction.

Rowan's voice came loud and blunt in the eerie, hushed shadow of the wings that slowly pulsed up and down, like lungs breathing. "Keep low so that the tentacles cannot reach us! It cannot hover any nearer to the ground, and its wings are so delicate that we could shred them if it draped them over us."

"Tentacles!" Alison pictured the small, sluglike feet and imagined them uncoiling.

"Low!" Rowan repeated, pushing her forward and snatching up his fallen staff as they passed it.

She clutched a bit of Sage's robe and they stumbled ahead together, their arms over their eyes to fend off the sticky threads.

Doubled over, they now lumbered over pock-marked earth that led to the gouged-up fields. Crossing these made Alison think of a mine field scarred with trenches. First there was level ground, where her boots trampled the green promise of a future harvest. Then, when she encountered the gashes Rowan had attributed to Harrow-worms, her ankles turned as she plunged down loose clots of clay into a trench dark with dirt. The overturned earth was damp and doughy, like a draining wound, and smelled of rotted ferns and decaying worms.

The force of their united flight pushed her up the trench's other side and across the stalks of some innocent crop that gave way again to a fissure in the earth. As they neared the center of the field, the trenches grew deeper, until running up the loose, mounded dirt that bracketed them and down, down into them and up again and over the opposite earthy crest was like running along ranks of ten-foot waves on an ocean. Camay was whimpering softly, unable to keep up. Alison paused until the sound collided with her, then clasped the child's thin body to her chest.

Alison looked up. The leaden-gray sky of tented, heaving wings was opaque, but she could see a foliation of veins branching from thick trunks into tendrils and clustered leaves; along this network poured some inner phosphorescent substance. She kept on running as fast as the ground would allow.

Once the beast's shadow lifted as the party crested a trench. Alison glimpsed a vista of unharmed farmlands and some foothills. This slice of daylight froze her companions' flight for an instant—Rowan as stooped as Sage for once, their faces grim; the Littlelost looking haunted but determined.

Then the near lip of the next trench forced them to scale a larger mound of dirt, thereby drawing them closer to the creature's loathsome underbelly, where shiny black coils agitated all along its interminable center.

"Wait!" Sage called as they plunged into the damp slash in the earth. "Wait. I might have an herb with which to repel it."

" 'Might' is not worth the risk." Rowan lifted his reclaimed staff like a mast on which to impale the monster should its dingy sails sink upon them.

But Littlelost were collapsing on the filthy earth, exhausted.

Alison slipped to her knees with Camay, her backpack swinging around to her side.

"Then get your cursed herbs, old woman!" Rowan shouted, running up the trench's other side. The wings drew up and back, as if preparing for a lunging attack.

A circle of horizon shone bright above them as the beast hovered higher; by its light Alison could see the intricate pattern inscribing the creature's wings: an olive-green, orange, and purple tracery, as delicate as the design of a stained-glass window.

"Fennel," Sage was muttering, rummaging in the numerous pockets of her voluminous robe.

"Fennel?" Alison repeated in disbelief. "In my world, that's a harmless seasoning."

Sage kept plundering her pockets. Littlelost stared up at the writhing belly of the beast and hid their faces in each other's heaped limbs. Camay quivered in Alison's arms like a frightened animal. Up on the trench rim, Rowan remained upright, questing hero that he aspired to be.

The creature paused for a moment, its wings stilled, then emitted a strangled whimper and swooped toward earth, snuffing the precious circle of daylight in an instant.

Rowan swung his staff. Alison saw slick black digits curl around it, heard the wings' serrated edges grate against the ground. A great, tearing sound, and light seeped through a rent in one wing. The smothered whimper escalated, a sound more terrible for its dampened quality.

Alison struggled to her feet, hoping to climb up, grab a tattered wing and widen the rent. Something heavy and oily thudded against her cheek and curled into her shoulder. A chopping blow from the side of her hand, and the mass quivered away.

She smelled salt and slime and sensed the wings touch ground and beat upward for air. Another shrill whine, then the wings lifted and light knifed a circle around them. The monster was fighting to lift off, with Rowan's red hair caught in a fist of tentacles.

Alison stared in horror. Rowan was already two or three feet off the ground—in moments he'd be beyond reach. She scrabbled up the slope, launched herself at his legs and held on, feeling her own weight wobbling upward. The light was like a carousel flashing all around them. Above them was the dark, engorged belly of the beast; below, the pit of earth, where Sage and the Littlelost writhed like grub worms.

Then the wings' leathery, rhythmic hiss paused, and their steely edges began collapsing toward the earth. Other tears appeared. The sky reappeared in razor slits of bright blue, clawing through the gray. Like a circus tent, the creature folded in a slow, shivering motion. Rowan plummeted to earth, landing heavily on Alison before rolling aside.

Fallen wings still thrashed, snarls rising from the ruined form. Snarls and barks and a glimpse of sharp fangs—for the marooned beast had drawn new attackers.

Suddenly the tattered wings flinched away from the trench; the people clustered there were bathed in sunlight and surprise. The thing scuttled back on its myriad feet, dragging useless wings. A white, wolfish face peered down from the mounded dirt at Alison, smiling a black-lipped grin.

"Rambeau!" She scrambled up toward him, but he danced back, out of sight. "Beau?"

By the time she worked her way atop the shifting earthen slope, the dog was a distant blur. Rambeau and the pack—a pack of wolves—were busy herding the creature toward the cliff face, where she expected it to stop, turn and be torn to bits.

Instead, it left the pack to chew upon its discarded wings as it slithered up the vertical face, greasy tentacles adhering to the slippery rock. It vanished into a solid black spot on the rock, a spot that Alison realized was a cave mouth, one of many amid the obsidian surface. She sensed Sage beside her.

"We climbed down past all those pest holes, Sage. Who knows what else lurked in there?"

"Rowan might," Sage speculated. "But he is beyond telling us."

"Rowan—*dead?*" Alison looked back to the pit. Rowan lay there, his bronzed skin pale, his hair dirt-dulled to brown. The Littlelost surrounded his still form with the helpless curiosity of animals.

"Not yet," Sage answered, "but my fennel did not rouse him."

"Oh." Alison had little faith in Sage's fennel. "It didn't affect the creature much, either."

For answer, Sage lifted a small bag to Alison's nose; its odor made a skunk seem sweet. In the distance, the wolf pack circled, then trotted away down the valley. For a moment she felt torn in two directions, human and canine. Then only the pack's white member remained faintly discernible, like a star at dawn.

Alison sighed, knowing she couldn't keep pace with wolves. "That fennel stuff stinks. If it won't wake Rowan, I don't know what will." She lurched down the incline to inspect him.

The Littlelost were living up to their name, looking desolate. Camay was wiping Rowan's hands free of orangish ichor with the hem of her tunic. Pickle sat by Rowan's head, painstakingly brushing the caked clay from his scarlet hair.

Alison knelt beside him. The carotid artery in his throat pulsed as lethargically as had the monster's wings.

"Poison?" she wondered aloud.

Sage shook her head.

"There's a well in the field," pale-haired Rime called shyly from atop the mound.

Alison looked up and smiled. Rime almost never spoke. "All right, we'll try water. And"—she pulled the pack over to work out the Cup, remembering how a sour-scented flower had grown sweet under its influence—"we'll serve it properly chilled, so you Littlelost can help draw it." Even Sage ventured out of the trench to accompany the party.

First they had to draw the bucket from the well, an enterprise that the Littlelost's combined rope-pulling efforts more hindered than helped.

"Odd that the fields are deserted at midday," Sage noted, looking around.

"Not odd." Alison filled the Cup at last and kept her eye on the brimful container as she baby-stepped forward. "This place is infested. Whatever tore up the crops was likely a cousin of what attacked us. No one of any sense would cross these fields now, which is why Rowan headed right for them."

"He could not have known—" Sage began, but Alison was already gingerly descending into the trench.

"I hope it isn't tainted," Alison said as she knelt beside Rowan.

Sage crouched to elevate his head. "If it was, it will not be now."

"You have that much faith in the Cup?"

"I have that much faith in the Cupbearer."

Alison smiled as she tilted the pale stone to Rowan's lips. Water dribbled down the side of his face. He jerked into consciousness, knocking his teeth on the Cup rim and spilling water on himself and on Alison's hands. He sat up, looking aloft.

"Gone," Sage said.

"Fennel?" he asked in some amazement.

"No, S-s-slinkers!" Twist put in excitedly. "They came again, but ran away after the big gr-gr-gray thing."

Rowan wiped his wet mouth with the back of his hand. He still seemed less than fully conscious. "That Womb-bat had its black, ugly tentacles around me—"

"Only for a moment," Alison put in quickly. "It released you when the wolves attacked."

He looked at her oddly. "No . . . inside my head. It was crushing my thoughts."

"Nothing can crush a Desmeynian's thoughts, unfortunately," said Sage, wafting her herb bag under Rowan's nose until he jerked upright and brushed her arm away in one motion, his dream forgotten. She nodded happily.

"Enough vile-smelling roots. I feel half-drowned." Rowan glowered at the Cup, then at Alison. "Hide that; you are too eager to put it to trivial use. Besides, when we enter Desmeyne, it will be best to keep our . . . quandary . . . to ourselves until I can present the facts to my father."

He pushed himself upright with his staff, then climbed to the lip of the trench to observe the city, still a trek away.

"Our quandary?" Alison asked Sage.

The wisewoman grinned as she tucked her odiferous bag into a pocket. "Our quandary," she said complacently, "is you."

16

At last Desmeyne's sheer facade loomed above them after an uneventful hour's travel. A plinth of carved red-orange rock interlarded with gemstone veins served as a several-story entrance tower. At its base were huge bronze doors as brassy as a sunset.

Alison was reminded of an elaborate opera set. Despite expanses of balconies, parapets and windows, most of the city proper was carved into the mountain and invisible. She turned to regard the opposite mountainside, still hoping to glimpse Rambeau.

Instead, she saw the cliff they had descended, a forbidding smoke-black barrier of glassy shale, pigeonholed with darker areas. It looked like rock through which unnameable creatures had tunneled for generations.

"The entrance to the Earth-Eaters' domain, or so it is rumored," Rowan commented. As she turned to him, he stretched up his staff to pluck one of several taut strings running from foundation to tower top.

A peculiar keening whined out—the kind of piercing note that can rub the hearers' nerves raw. An answering squeal of pulleys and gears within was equally distressing. The Littlelost clapped their hands over their ears, faces squinched in distaste.

A final rumbling indicated that the brazen door before them was giving way, but it took Alison some time to realize that it was slowly *descending* into a slot in the mountain.

As the barrier sank, a view of soaring upper arches rose—united by bridges and buttresses. It was like seeing the inside of a cathedral carved from the bones of a bejeweled mountain. From the gateway, a slender walkway bridged a mountainous gorge before leading to an imposing foyer paved in white quartz.

"This is a city, not a . . . a castle? A single dwelling?" Alison asked.

Rowan seemed to find her distinctions bewildering. "This is Desmeyne," he said shortly. "The women's Lofts are to the left.

There you will stay, although you must first display the Cup to my father. The Littlelost"—he turned to frown at the entities in question—"must go to the Webbings, like the other young of Desmeyne."

"We must separate?" Alison asked, incredulous.

"It is our way."

"Surely I can visit the children—"

"Visit, certainly, if you wish."

"And Sage and I must go to the women's Lofts?"

Sage's answer was swift. "I would enjoy seeing the Lofts. They must be most impressive."

Rowan's dismissing glance at Sage was more cursory than the one he had given the Littlelost. "An old woman is anathema to the maidens of Desmeyne. To see her might curdle their beauty—unless you wish to keep her as a personal servant and thus out of sight in your private quarters."

Alison raised her eyebrows at the wisewoman, who shrugged. "Yes," Alison told Rowan, "by all means assign Sage to my quarters. I'm sure she'll keep well out of the way of your beauties' delicate sensibilities. And so will we, until we manage to get baths."

"Good." Alison had meant her last comment sarcastically, but Rowan approvingly nodded his red head, which had darkened under its helmet of caked dirt. "You must let me explain our situation to my father."

"Of course," Alison agreed. "I am dying to hear how you'll describe it."

At that moment a welcoming committee arrived: two men with pikestaffs. "Young master," they murmured, bowing to the filthy Rowan. "Well-returned from the Wellsunging. The Firemayne is most eager to discover the outcome." They cast politely disbelieving eyes upon Alison, Sage and the Littlelost. "And these others?"

"Guests," Rowan said curtly. "The old woman is a servant and should be shown quarters in the women's Loft, there to await her mistress. The small ones must be sent to the Webbings, and washed. The . . . ah, other . . . accompanies me for now."

Tandem bows acquiesced to Rowan's instructions, but Alison

noticed that, for all their garb's dandified droop of sleeve and tautness of tights, the men's eyes and hands were hard and alert. They were guards first and greeters second. But what did these men guard against at this remote height, in such an imposing edifice of stone?

A guard stepped to the wall, using the intricate tip of his pike to pluck another string. The sound that tolled was subtler than the one that had announced the party's arrival. In answer, a gray-clothed woman came floating into the quartz-lined foyer like an effacing ghost, her austere face blank. Rowan repeated his instructions about the Littlelost and Sage.

"Why should we go where they say?" Pickle demanded, stepping out of the group to confront Rowan. "I want to stay here with you." For a moment the two's eyes held, and they regarded each other, Rowan with shock at the child's temerity, Pickle with disappointment shaping his face.

To ease the odd tension, Alison answered Pickle. "Desmeyne is new to us. We must learn its ways before we object to them. I'll see you all later."

"Promise?" Camay clung to the hem of Alison's shirt.

"Promise." These slightly grubby faces would not disappear like Rambeau. Here they'd be cleaned and cooked for, watched over, and schooled. Surely. Every world aspired to do that much for its children. No matter how different the social customs of Desmeyne, the care it provided had to be better than living wild in the woods.

"You will come as well," the gray woman told Sage, eyeing her journey-tangled hair askance. The gray woman's hair hid under a tight black cap. Only her hands and face showed, and both seemed blunt instruments of inexpressiveness.

Rowan turned and crossed the shining foyer floor to the main hallway, which yawned and glittered beyond it. Alison had already found Desmeyne's welcome coldly formal. She felt that she'd entered some dour convent school of a century past, where the motto was: "Every busy bee humming in its own place makes for a happy hive."

She suddenly yearned for the newsroom's usual, mad deadline bustle and cacophony: keyboards chuckling, phones trilling, city editors yelling. None would yell in this echoing hallway, not even a vagrant child. Her boot soles and Rowan's rang much too loudly on the stones in the respectful silence that seemed to rule here. They crossed many more echoing halls before reaching Rowan's father's headquarters. The Firemayne, for so Rowan said his father was called, kept his rooms in the Men's Quarters. She saw only an occasional Desmeynian, and these appeared to be functionaries and servants: men and women wearing sensible, neutral-toned garb: shirts and trousers or skirts, according to sex, but so plain that the sexual differentiation seemed pointless.

They entered the Men's Quarters through an iron-reinforced gate. The halls and rooms within were rigorously functional, as orderly as a medieval castle's—a place of wood, iron and weapons.

Rowan stopped and opened carved doors made of what looked like ivory. Alison followed him through.

The Firemayne's room was larger and more comfortably appointed than the others they had passed, fitted like a combination campaign headquarters and study. Heavily embroidered tapestries hung gathered next to the high windows; a coal fire burned in the small fireplace; and at the end of the room several men stood at a great polished table sliced from a huge redwood stump.

One of them stepped forward.

The man himself was a surprise: not tall, but a thickset, worried, middle-aged man whose once-red hair was drawn back into a gray-pink queue. And he wore the same floor-length robes as the Wellsunging elders, not the dashing attire of the young men of Desmeyne. The ruggedly dressed, middle-aged men around the table hung back with deference.

"You have seen?" the elder Firemayne asked without greeting or introduction, on spying Rowan.

His son nodded soberly, hair glowing fiery through its patina of dirt. "Harrow-worms in the fields. When?"

"When else? When it was time for the Wellsunging and we were busy here with preparations for your triumphal return." The Firemayne left the great table littered with charts, left the waiting men whose furrowed brows matched their ravaged fields. "You do have it?"

Rowan turned stiffly to Alison.

She lowered her backpack to the hard floor, then pulled the bundled Cup free. Unwrapped, the pale stone shone softly, its dull surface catching the cold mountain light lancing from the windows high above. Behind the Firemayne, the farmers dropped their charts from work-hardened fingers. Their joint sigh of relief was as soft as it was unconscious.

"With this great talisman in our possession"— the Firemayne's formal, public tone still trembled with excitement —"we can reverse the ravages of the Earth-Eaters."

"I must speak with you," Rowan said in a low tone.

The Firemayne, puzzled, looked from the Cup to his son and back again. Alison was amazed to glimpse pale blue irises, having become used to Rowan's dark-eyed redheadedness. The father, by comparison, had a cold look. At last he examined Alison, and his expression sharpened. "We will discuss restoration later," he told the gathered farmers without turning. "You can see that we have the means now."

Apparently accustomed to Firemayne authority, the men left, rattling their reclaimed charts. Rowan strode into a bright slash of sunlight, as if unconsciously seeking warmth. Alison suspected that his news would be cold comfort indeed to his father.

"You have the Cup," the Firemayne repeated with emphasis.

"Not . . . quite." Rowan lowered his eyes. "I almost had the Cup. I could feel a strange, trembling certainty in my throat even as I sang, but—"

"You have the Cup! You have brought it to Desmeyne when we most sorely need its services. The Earth-Eaters' depradations increase; the Harrow-worms have come often during your absence. I suspect the very under-cellars throb with their evil delvings. My son, the Cup can pour balm upon all our wounds, and it is here."

"It is here, but it is not ours."

Father stared at son, finally taking in the travel-stained dress, the mud-caked boots and hair. He glanced sharply to Alison. "Who is this youth that carries the Cup? Why have you allowed another to touch what you have won? Why do you require a servant to carry this most-desired burden? You are a Firemayne."

"I am a Firemayne who has failed," Rowan said quietly.

Alison had never thought to hear such modesty from those self-certain lips. "This 'youth' has sung the Cup home."

"This . . . this stranger?" The Firemayne inspected Alison. She saw in his now-hardened eyes an expectation of command that would be bitter to disappoint, especially for a son. "Who are you, usurper?"

She smiled wearily. "I am called Alison of Island-Not."

"I have heard of no such place, of no such person!"

"Until now." She remained calm, remembering that a red-head's fabled temper was likely to flare, even in an illusory land. "Now I am also called 'Cupbearer.' " She lifted the evidence of her new, and quite unwanted, role.

The Firemayne stared incredulously at his son. "How did a stranger from a place unheard of through many generations of Wellsunging usurp our hereditary right?"

"It was a contest, Father," Rowan answered with a trace of irritation. "There was no certainty to the winner. I had met the conditions, and my song seemed to lure the very stars from the sky. But Alison's song made the watchers sing, and even the Voices of the Valley. I could not gainsay the awarding of the Cup in such a circumstance. If you had been there—"

"There was no need! I sent you, my sole surviving son. All the portents were clear that the Cup would return to Desmeyne. How could you—?"

"It did," Alison interjected.

The Firemayne whirled on her, his robes swirling around his sturdy form. Alison studied the scant white goatee decorating his chin and concluded that Rowan's rubrock was a wise choice. The Firemayne pointed at her, past the Cup, to her chest.

"Do you bear the proper marks, intruder?"

"Your son said that I would be a guest here. And if you mean these—" Alison peeled back her shirt with one hand. She was becoming brazen about flaunting her disfigurement. Perhaps she was enjoying the satisfying shock and awe the sight of it elicited. For the first time, the Firemayne was struck silent.

"You see, Father." Rowan sounded resigned. "The stranger bears the secret scars. And there is something else."

"More? There can be more bad news?"

"I have ordered rooms in the Lofts."

"Why?"

"For our . . . guest."

"The Lofts? You are mad, my son."

"No, my father. Alison is female."

"No female can compete for the Cup!"

"Apparently," Alison put in, "one can win it. If you want evidence, you have your son's word. I'm not about to undo my shirt any farther."

It was as though Alison had plummeted from view through the floor once she had been declared female. The Firemayne stared at his son. "You have been convinced?"

"Yes. At least she bears the outer appearance of a woman." Rowan looked at Alison as if wishing to accuse her of—what was the word?—Crux-craft.

"As well as the Cup," Alison put in.

"What can we do?" the father demanded of his son.

Rowan exchanged a reluctant glance with Alison. "Accept what has happened, for now. I have vowed to seek the Cup again next year. Meanwhile, Alison has brought it to us. If she is willing, it may be used to restore the fields. It will be nearly as good as having the Cup ourselves."

"These are not times for 'nearly.' " The Firemayne's angry ice-blue eyes touched Alison. Perhaps the son was more progressive than he seemed, she thought hotly; consider the stock from which he came.

The Firemayne went to sit upon the table, where charts of ruined lands had so recently papered the polished surface. Agricultural disaster apparently seemed small to him when compared to a metaphysical one: Could a stranger in a strange land, a woman in a man's world, be allowed to carry the Cup of their people's survival?

The Cup rested heavily in her hands, the stone cool and unresponsive to her body heat, to the emotions simmering around it. They were neutering it now, the Cup, making it purely a thing whose possession could be debated. She recalled the mystical moments of claiming it, of hearing the valley reverberate with other voices, both present and strangely absent. Had all that come down to a petty lordlings' squabble? What had happened to the right granted by fate?

"The Cup is ours by proxy, Father," Rowan said, a touch of youthful pleading in his voice. "We are fortunate that Alison of Island-Not is willing to lend us its presence, its usage. Who is to say what tomorrow, or three-hundred-some tomorrows, may bring? I will try again to claim it."

"Yes." The Firemayne straightened until he stood without the table's support. "We will welcome the Cup to Desmeyne." He spoke only to Rowan. "We will celebrate my son's return. We will look toward a better future."

Rowan nodded. "May I take Alison to Darnellyne? I must answer to her as well."

The father's face softened. "My poor lad . . . I forget what you have lost by this. Yes, do what you must. I will tell your mother the news, in private."

Rowan bowed to his father and left as Alison rewrapped the Cup and tucked it away. When she caught up with him, he was a good way down the hall and didn't slow when he heard her boots clattering behind him.

"Your father apparently isn't as fond of women as you are," she noted.

Rowan whirled on her with unexpected and uncorked fury. "Even the Cup cannot excuse your arrogance! You violate our every custom, and you now invade the heart of our domain. To bear the Cup is a task requiring great humility. Perhaps you can honor at least that."

"Humility!" Her own ire flared. "In that case, it's a good thing you didn't win it."

His eyes darkened, then grew abruptly rueful. "You need not worry about my worthiness. From this first experience, I perceive that I will learn much humility in the coming year."

"And I perceive that I will learn much of humiliation in Desmeyne."

"In claiming the Cup, you have stepped unthinking onto ground Firemaynes have fought to attain for generations. Why should you suppose the prize would be easy to hold?"

"I have the Cup," she reminded him. "I am told it is a powerful curative."

Alison had resolved to show no awe at Desmeyne's architectural exotica, but the women's Lofts threatened to break that promise at its first test.

The way was steep, half-hewn out of the mountain's ore-laden sides, yet encased by the most refined applications of ornament. It was like climbing the slopes of some bell-jarred peak, for window walls gazed out on neighboring summits, snowdrifts and the tree line's ragged emerald hem. Yet the view was misty. Alison suddenly realized that the walls were slightly clouded rock crystal, not glass.

As she and Rowan wound up the twisting stairways that began in solid rock and graduated to elevated ramps, the air grew warmer and staler, almost stuffy. At another oversized bronze door, a child in stiff robes intercepted them.

Rowan went on one courtly knee to this apparition while Alison studied the girl; she was no more than eleven, yet hung with jewels from the top of her head to the be-gemmed sandals that weighted her tiny feet. She made a sort of living Christmas tree, or a splendid treetop angel for the towering Minnesota state Christmas pine at the Capitol Building in St. Paul. A sudden picture of how haplessly Rowan might respond to the accoutrements and customs of *her* world made Alison smile.

"You are fresh—or should I say foul?—from your travels, Rowan Firemayne," this precocious enfant terrible said in a light, piping voice. "And your companion as well." The child's upturned nose wrinkled delicately.

"My apologies," Rowan said humbly. "I have urgent news for the Lady Darnellyne. I come directly from my father."

"The Firemayne would see you so? I will tell the lady of your condition, to prepare her." The figure slipped through a child-sized door within the larger barrier, her encrusted robes rustling like the carapace of some overgaudy beetle.

"Officious Barbie-doll-in-training," Alison murmured.

"What is a 'Barbie-doll'?" Rowan wanted to know.

"A child pushed early into the artifices of womanhood."

He shrugged. "All girl-children are thusly trained here. And she must obtain permission to admit us; the Lofts are inaccessible to men except under special circumstances."

"This is one?"

He nodded glumly, starting as the tiny door snapped ajar and the overdecorated pipsqueak chirped, "You may enter."

Rowan himself drew open the huge door and preceded Alison inside. She was glad to have his long form between herself and a full view of the interior. It gave her time to absorb the sight in bits and pieces rather than in one eye-dazzling sweep.

Everything shimmered in shades of white and pastel; a mother-of-pearl gleam haloed the draperies, the stone fretworks, the curving ramps that led to chambers piled upon chambers like the rooms of a many-storied doll's house or the interior of a huge chambered nautilus.

Alison had followed Rowan two steps into the vast area before she realized that her boots no longer made any noise. A downward glance revealed that the floor was covered with white batting in which bits of mica glittered. She seemed to be tiptoeing on snowdrifts in moonlight.

Such pale surroundings should have been cold; instead, the environs were so warm that Alison itched to unbutton her shirt and tear off her boots. Sweat filmed her face. She felt sudden exhaustion. In white stone fireplaces—and they were everywhere, like spirit lamps—burning coals gave off iridescent flames. The heat haze made the exotic chambers shimmer as if viewed through melting rock crystal.

For the first time in her life, Alison felt faint. Unreal. She was tempted to grab hold of Rowan's arm, but managed to resist the urge. Stubbing her toe would have been a nice equilibrium-restorer, but who could trip on this cotton-batting carpet?

She longed for someone to speak and break the place's paralyzing spell.

In the distant chambers, Desmeyne's beauties glimmered like festival queens on parade floats, the phantom coal-light gleaming on the metallic richness of their pastel gowns. They reclined in their airy niches on divans shrouded in white furs and velvets, the flesh of their forearms, shoulders, breasts, feet and lower faces pulsating like holograms, the barbs of their bejeweled gowns spearing the phantasmagoric light.

Then a woman rose and rustled toward them—perhaps to forestall the advance of dirty boots on the pristinely veiled floor. She was tall, or seemed so under her towering headdress. Her height was unaided by footwear; bare white feet kicked forward the heavy trailing hem of her gown.

Her skin glowed as if contaminated. Her glitter-dusted breasts—barely subdued by the web of her clothes—were a plastic surgeon's dream. And her face was veiled from brow to nose, her eyes glimmering as if through a fog. They had been defined, Alison saw, by a pastel palette of metallic powders.

"Darnellyne." Rowan went to one knee again.

At least, Alison thought, this time he has some padding. She supposed that some obeisance was required of unknown "youths" as well, but she was darned if she would make it. Kneeling to over-made-up beauties wasn't her style.

"Rowan." The vision extended a lily-white (and lily-limp) hand over Rowan's sadly matted red hair, though the smile on her pale peach lips seemed not to acknowledge his dishevelment. "How good to see you again! What news? That you come so precipitously must mean that it is good. The Cup—?"

Alison produced it more quickly than before, for there was something in the woman's voice, which she begrudgingly realized was genuine, untouched by the encompassing artifice, that merited ready answers.

"Oh." Darnellyne reached instinctively for the Cup, her nails sheathed in talons of iridescent metal. The polished surfaces looked teasingly familiar. After a moment Alison identified them. The talons were of the mystical metal called etherion. Littlelost were harvesting etherion for *false fingernails?* And how had the Desmeynians acquired something that had been produced by exploitation of Littlelost's labors?

Then Darnellyne's hands curled into themselves short of taking the Cup. "It is beyond description . . . so pure, so precious." She looked down on Rowan and spoke with something like passion in her cool voice. "At last we may live the lives that were meant for us."

"No." He rose with the word, and that seemed disrespectful, for he loomed over her despite the headdress; and she looked such a brittle, fragile creature.

"But the Cup—you have it! We have it."

"Alison has it. I did not win it."

"Alison?" Darnellyne regarded her with incurious surprise.

"Alison of Island-Not," Rowan said formally. "The Cup-bearer, and a guest of Desmeyne. And . . . a woman."

"No!" Darnellyne's lips lifted in a prelude to laughter. "Rowan, you are playing some childish jest! This is not—a woman could not— It is unthinkable."

"It is true," Rowan said stiffly. "I will try again for the Cup at next year's Wellsunging."

"Another year! You cannot abide another year."

"I can, but, Darnellyne, for you—"

Her hands fluttered dismissively. Each sleeve ended in five points, and each point was affixed to the first knuckle of a finger with a translucent pearl ring, except for the middle finger on her right hand, which bore a band of clearest polished crystal. As her hands turned over, Alison saw that the sleeve fabric covered the palm and that an arcane design was embroidered onto the heart of her hands.

Rowan burst out with a certain raw self-blame, "Had I placed the Cup in your hands, your bondage would have ended."

Alison could no longer resist speaking. "This is bondage?"

They glanced at her, but it was as if a gnat had spoken. She was beginning to feel like a living pedestal for the Cup. Indeed, the Cup seemed to be taking on a life of its own in her hands.

"It does not matter," Darnellyne consoled him with sweet resignation. "At least you have brought the Cupbearer to Desmeyne, and we sorely need some succor." The veiled eyes paused on Alison long enough for a smile to reach the polished lips. "You are welcome."

"Thank you." Alison was warmed by the first civil words offered her in this place.

"I fear that she must stay in the Lofts," Rowan said with such apology that Alison longed to kick him. She quashed the urge.

"We are prepared. How could we fail to note the arrival of the ancient one?"

"I hope she did not frighten you too much."

"No, no. Her passage was swift and discreet."

Rowan shifted uncomfortably. "As for this one—"

"Oh, Alison is from a far land. Island-Not, I think you said. Since we have never heard of it, there must be unheard-of customs there." She eyed Alison's clothes uneasily. "We . . . accept the honor of keeping the Cupbearer among us."

"It may be necessary for Alison to come and go."

"And Sage, as well," Alison put in.

Darnellyne's blinks of uncertainty produced a glamorous shimmer behind her sheer, layered veils. "Our customs do not contain a Cupbearer, but the old woman is another matter. She must not be seen naked of face outside the rooms. Your niche is ready." Darnellyne pointed to a lambent opening far up the chamber's endless height. "Purest snowmelt is ready for your cleansing, if that is a custom of Island-Not."

"It sure is." Alison grinned, suddenly looking forward to privacy; then she guiltily turned to Rowan. "The Littlelost—"

"Later. All the travelers must tend their needs first."

Alison nodded. Rowan bent knee and bowed head to the imposing Darnellyne once more. She herself got a curt nod as a farewell; that suited her just fine. Darnellyne was turning, a motion that required exquisite timing and management of her various trains, veils and trailing sleeves.

Alison returned the Cup to her pack and followed her up the undulating ramps carpeted in the soft, sparkling cloth, which Darnellyne's receding hem altered into ever-new lacy patterns as wind sculpts snowdrifts.

Sweat trickled down Alison's back and midriff. Her hair felt matted to her neck. Perhaps if Sage covered her elderly face, she could do more than rot in the Lofts. Alison herself didn't know how she could stay, much less sleep, in this suffocating environment, but at least and at last she'd have someplace private where she could think.

18

Rowan, soothed by a bath and sobered by an inspection of the calluses, cuts and bruises of the journey, some of them acquired in humiliatingly unsuccessful single combat with a woman, strode on the soft-soled shoes common to Desmeyne through the glorious corridors he took for granted.

Since the night of the Wellsunging and the loss of the Cup that every instinct had told him would be his, he had walked as one numb through Veil.

Now he was home. Now his sense of purpose had been rekindled, as his hair been polished bright by the icy flow of unheated snowmelt. A dullness that had webbed him like the tentacles of that bloodsucking Womb-bat of the Earth-Eaters had been rinsed away. His thoughts were clearer than a mountain stream. And as cold and compulsive.

His father was waiting for him. Rowan knew that although the Firemayne's disappointment would not have ebbed, the coal-fire would be blazing cobalt, green and scarlet, and that dusky, heady Char would fill a bulb-necked bottle and beg to be drained first into flagons and then into throats.

At least Rowan felt more himself again, having shed the clumsy traveler's guise for the elegant, caressing clothes of Desmeyne: velvet leggings and loose-sleeved shirt, featherweight shoes of Womb-bat wing, and the ritual hand guards of gem-encrusted fur that covered the tops and palms of his hands like fingerless gauntlets. Those whose home city is contained by arching walls of transparent stone need never fear cold, sleet, rain, wind, or even fire.

The world without, necessary as a source of food and trade—and, sometimes, quests—seemed crude and distant, along with the burden of ills that leaked from it these days. Rowan sighed as he pushed open the carved Harrow-worm bone door leading to his father's rooms. A tall, draped figure that could have been sculpted from melt-stone stood before the whining fire.

Rowan, astonished, went to one knee, silently cursing the crack the joint made, bruised during his bout with Alison. Although no custom forbade his mother's daytime presence in his father's rooms, it was unheard of to encounter her here in ordinary circumstances.

She extended a hand to his bowed head. He felt the radiant draw of a power that he had felt from no other woman, not even from the always-desired Darnellyne. It was as if his mother's hovering hand held invisible strings and he still writhed to their subtle pull. Of course he had been raised in the Webbings until he was eleven. But then he had undergone the Cutting, a ritual that had made the ease-filled, idle life of the Lofts as abruptly alien as the Earth-Eaters' noxious dens deep in the mountains.

"I am sorry," his mother said. She was the only one from whom he would accept those simple words of sympathy for his failure. At least Darnellyne had been wise enough not to extend them. "Your father says that you will try again."

He rose. "Yes."

"You need not, Rowan." An edge of pleading sharpened her voice. "You are young and cannot continue to deny yourself. I understand that we have the Cup, that we can use it—"

"We do not possess it when it rests in another's hands. Besides, I have already vowed to seek the Cup again."

"Not to us. Not to Darnellyne."

"Before witnesses," Rowan said forcefully. "Strangers. And there is Darnellyne. I cannot claim the Cup-maiden without the Cup."

"Rowan, you claimed her long ago."

"Not in a way our customs recognize." He went to the fireplace as if to search the colored flames for solace.

His mother rustled behind him, in the unspeaking way of women. She brought him a cup. Perceived irony made him smile, but he accepted the Char from her bejeweled hands. The sharp, smoky liquor burned the strain of recent frustration from his throat.

"So we have a visitor." His mother glided to another part of the room. Like all Desmeynian women, she modulated her voice to be musical, soft, and as unassuming as a breeze. Not for her the low, challenging tones that could be mistaken for a Men's Quarter stripling. Her name was Zormond, but only the Firemayne used it.

Rowan returned to a sore subject. "An odd visitor. I am half-minded to think that she—it—is an impostor sent by the Crux."

"I hope you have judged her gender rightly, at least, my son. It would be a great scandal to house her there otherwise."

"An itinerant wisewoman also attached herself to our laughable party. She claims that this Alison of Island-Not is both female and Cupbearer, and meant to be both. And the creature bears the hallmarks of both the sex and the role."

"Who heeds the maunderings of ugly old women?" His mother touched the veil over her eyes for a moment. "They have much to imagine, since their lives are so useless."

"We all age," Rowan said, startled by his own words, by their tinge of inner disagreement with a doctrine of Desmeyne.

His mother's voice was light and certain, as it had always been. "Slowly, my son. We women of the Lofts have our ways to delay that eventuality. We devote our every effort to it."

"Most successfully," he said, falling into the familiar courtly ways with a twitch of annoyance. Never had courtesy seemed to ring so hollow.

Zormond moved toward him, would have stroked his hair with her soft white hand.

He shied away, as Alison's lost Slinker did from a touch too confining. Another oddity, this partnership between beast and . . . woman. Everyone knew that beasts were bitter enemies, except for the few spiritless creatures designed for bearing the burdens of Desmeyne.

"Rowan, you must not sulk."

He regarded his mother. She was beginning to annoy him as much as Alison did, for quite different reasons. "You trivialize my reaction. I have just lost the keystone of the Quests to the Four Quarters to a usurping stranger. Is no one else disturbed that this foreign woman should appear to win the Cup so handily, and that she should be so mysteriously marked?"

"You, too, are marked. I could not bear to witness the ceremony, but there was nothing mysterious about it. I was told that you were brave to the point of silence, but it is a savage ritual of blood and pain. I thank whatever gods walk the ether that only one child of mine shall have to suffer it."

Rowan smiled ruefully. "Luckily, I had no time to anticipate the honor. Before you pity me too much, I confess that I find the loss of the Cup of far greater distress. She sang last, and until she bespelled the valley, the Cup was as good as mine."

"You know that?"

He nodded. "I could sense imminent victory. However painful the path to my quest, I have also felt the certainty that its objects are rightfully mine."

"Even with the Cup withheld this year?"

"It will be mine. That is why I never hesitated to dedicate myself to it for another year."

Zormond lifted a swan-necked decanter in her pale hands and came to refill his cup. She sighed, an almost musical exhalation that stirred the thick surface of the Char.

"I am not pleased that you must go unarmed by edged steel a year longer," she said, "and that you must deny your masculine rights yet another year. They say in the Lofts that such sacrifices are severe for a man."

Rowan was not prepared to discuss that with his mother. Though she had borne him, she seemed removed from childbearing's blood and pain, and especially from the unrefined and necessary actions that precede them. "It is not myself that I worry about. I had the freedom of the village early and doubt that I shall become a never-marry by failing to win Darnellyne and the Cup. I only regret that Darnellyne's fate as Cup-maiden also remains undecided for another year."

"Darnellyne can wait, Rowan. Women are designed to wait. Even in the Twining dance we wait until the man approaches us. Much as Darnellyne has been your friend since earliest childhood, and much as she recognizes that it is her boon and her duty to wed you if you win the Cup, she is not eager for that day. Then she sets aside the tranquillity of the Lofts for the uncertainties of what comes after."

Rowan had never considered that Darnellyne might lose something by wedding him. "They say in the Men's Quarters that the agony of childbirth is as painful as the Carving. And I understand that you faced it as silent as I."

His mother shrugged, but looked pleased. "We are each enjoined to keep still in the face of our own agony. It is the agony of others that unravels us women."

"Then knit yourself together." He took her cool hands, as he could no other woman's in the Lofts, not even Darnellyne's. "I have returned with a quasi-Cup for Desmeyne, and a mystery to amuse us."

"Oh, I am eager to meet this mystery of yours—a woman who can be taken for a man. She must have to . . . to labor to accomplish such a feat."

He laughed. "It comes as naturally to her as breathing. I feel a fool, but any other man of Desmeyne—any other Desmeynian—would have made the same error."

"Then Darnellyne has no rival for your regard?"

Rowan laughed even harder. "Only Triss from the Scarlet Swan, and she is merely manhood-mate. Once I wed Darnellyne, I will give her up."

His mother's pale eyebrows raised skeptically. "No man of Desmeyne is required to relinquish his manhood-mate. Even your father—"

Rowan shook her hands admonishingly. "Darnellyne's only other possible rival for my admiration would be yourself, who never fails to consider my best interests. Do not worry, Mother; Father is disappointed, but he has already realized that Desmeyne can turn this Cupbearer to its own purposes. Alison is ignorant, a barbarous creature, you will see. Thus you need not worry about me."

Zormond drifted long fingers through his hair before he could dodge the gesture. "I am glad that you remain confident. In truth, I am relieved that you have not carried home the Cup this time."

"Relieved?"

"Maternal selfishness. You would leave that much sooner on the next quest, and the danger increases. There are signs, troubling signs . . . but I will not worry you more. Your father has ordered a banquet in the Cup's honor tomorrow. I am eager to see it, and its unlikely bearer."

Rowan felt crimson anger sweep up his neck to meet the answering fire of his hair as he stared incredulously at his mother. The banquet should have honored his achievement as a Cup-bearer, not as the mere escort of one.

Was Alison of Island-Not to usurp even his own mother's interest?

19

The suspended Arcade of Desmeyne reminded Alison of paintings of the opulent Hall of Mirrors at the Palace of Versailles. But she was in Veil, not France, and the splendor before her was equally, if not more, spectacular.

The long exterior walls were carved from sheets of rock crystal. Beyond these thick, translucent curtains wavered majestic mountain crevasses bathed in natural light. This evening, moonshine burned so blue on the distant snow outside that it burnished the hall into the glittering interior of a diamond.

The Arcade, reached by flights of wide quartz staircase, extended between two wings of the city fortress on the floor above the main hallway below—a dazzling gallery hewn from a massive motherlode of minerals. The floor blended two exotic ores into a dizzying pattern. Crossing it was like walking on a carpet braided from aquamarines and emeralds. The high, many-pointed ceiling was carved from a natural canopy of copper, which shone new-penny bright except for ancient veinings of dark azure-green.

So many brittle surfaces might have been intimidating—despite their rich coloration—had not cloths encrusted with sparkling embroidery draped the vast chamber. The whole effect reminded Alison of some department-store Winter Wonderland window display, a precipitous tunnel of gems and glitter and frost.

Her blurred reflection paced her in the crystalline window walls. She hadn't dared preview it fully in the hematite mirrors that studded the Ladylofts like silver-gray zircon cabochons. That ghostly self-image rang another mental echo—one of a highborn medieval lady in mountainous robes of brocade and ermine, except that her head wasn't capped with a cascading peak of headdress to rival the Matterhorn.

Darnellyne, generous in both wardrobe and soul, had garbed Alison in all the usual splendor of Desmeynian ladies: whispering, trailing layers of diaphanous silk shaded with the opalescent pastel powders seemingly stolen from butterfly wings.

Like the Arcade itself, this delectable, wearable web hung suspended. But instead of the pewter chains that anchored Desmeyne to the mountaintops, a filigree of iridescent black pearls and uncut rock crystal depended from Alison's bare shoulders. The be-gemmed harness hung heavy on her torso—and seemed unneeded for a gown that swirled weightlessly like opalescent cotton candy.

Alison had resisted the necessary décolletage, the exposure, until Darnellyne had lifted a glittering powder puff the size of a dandelion seedball and struck her harmlessly on the chest.

Darnellyne had then elevated a polished hematite mirror hanging from the etherion chain girding her waist. It hung unsupported before Alison's face once its lighter-than-air leash had been unlocked from Darnellyne's belt and reflected a strange transformation. Iridescent powders dusted Alison's disfigurement like fresh-fallen snow, making brutal slashes into a glittering tattoo, or a brave, gleaming necklace. Alison had never detected any underlying beauty in the marks, but she'd always avoided confronting them. Desmeyne's rituals and beliefs no longer allowed that.

For the first time, she appreciated the scar's abstract symmetry: two jagged lines like lightning bolts that mirrored each other, beginning at the out edges of her collar bones and almost meeting in the middle at her breastbone. Had her injury been purely accident—or *design,* in more ways than one?

Even the décolletage seemed another woman's, a Desmeynian woman's, though Alison was ready to dare anything to assert her femininity by now, contradiction in terms that it seemed.

She would bet that she was not the first—or the last—woman to find herself walking a contradiction in the terms in any land. But she would no longer let the men's male pride force her to march under false colors, even it meant donning an outrageously feminine garb to make her point. She'd always scorned seductive femininity as a snare and delusion for both men and women. Now she wondered if she'd made her scars into a subtle barrier between herself and her own womanliness, between herself and men.

She'd refused all jewelry, though, once Darnellyne had again latched her vanity mirror into place against her skirts. Alison especially rejected the lacy half-veil drifting over the wearer's eyes and nose, whose fragile tissues would flutter coyly at every breath or at the rare words the ladies of Desmeyne uttered in public.

She planned on saying plenty tonight.

The long banquet tables, imported into the Arcade for the evening and clothed in a translucent tapestry, had been angled into the shape of a vast M. A youthful page, his eyes glued on her talismanic scars (she assumed), led Alison, Cup held in her unadorned hands, to a place below the M's middle point, from which she had a sweeping view of the still-empty seats. Pierced balls of etherion, each lit by a glowing rock within, hovered over the long tables, rocking softly like anchored buoys. Fur-upholstered stools lined both sides of the four tables that made up the M arrangement, and Alison was seated so that she could view—and be viewed by—every guest. Or was it the Cup that was being so honored?

She smiled, sitting alone in this formal setting, and nodded regally as a youth bent to fill the Cup with a black stream of liquid that looked like oil.

"Char," the boy murmured, noticing her stare. "Much enjoyed—with caution—by the lords of Desmeyne."

Stringed music cascaded over the hard-faceted chamber—first a few plucked notes, then their echoes, until a fountain of sound sleeted against the walls. Alison spotted the musicians on tiny balconies high in the copper vault that jutted randomly from the rock-crystal walls. Some method in this madness—a heavenly constellation of musicians—created a cantata of chords that never lost the clean notes of the single instrument.

The Arcade seemed an icy and metrical environment for a symbol as homely as the Cup of Earth. Surely fresh flowers and a rush-strewn floor, a serenade of free-flying songbirds, would have been more appropriate, she speculated. But Desmeyne apparently didn't engender nature-lovers, despite the Firemayne dedication to pursuing the Cup of Earth.

The men arrived in threes, fives and sevens. Their sturdier daily attire had given way to a peacock's-tail display of deep-toned velvets and patterned silks. Most had tied their shoulder-length hair at the nape of their neck, giving a Revolutionary War flavor that their voluminous, open-to-the-waist velvet shirts, tights and knee-high furred boots belied.

Alison sipped, enjoying the black libation's smoky licorice flavor and underlying fermentation. Even the Cup had warmed to the brew. The Char oiled her throat like cough medicine, syrupy and addictive. The Cup's girdling gems deepened their hues to match the drink. No wonder Desmeynian men respected the delights and dangers of Char.

Rowan's father entered and stood behind a seat at the M's first peak, the ashes of his once-fiery hair unadorned in contrast to his courtiers' hair, which was dusted with iridescent powders.

The women arrived in a pale sunset flock, gowns fluttering like parchment pages, heads bowed under heavy headdresses, eyes veiled and glimmering lips stilled. They occupied seats on both sides of the tables that formed the M's farthest legs, so they should commune with only themselves in a haze of anonymous mystery, and the men could gaze at them.

Yet their quiet arrival enjoined the standing, chatting men to silence. Alison could understand their awe. En masse, the women of Desmeyne were unearthly; they were *designed* to be seen and not heard—not, like children, merely required to be quiet—and thus they remained intriguing.

A faintly luminescent figure wafted in late, alone, and sat down with an embarrassed flutter. Darnellyne. And Rowan marched in after her, his flowing red hair unfettered and an untamed expression matching its choler. All eyes shifted quickly away after noting the pair's apparent breach of ceremony. Rowan stopped at the M's second peak, opposite his father; then all the men came to stand behind their stools. Alison rose also, though the women remained seated. She faced rows of Desmeynian men along both sides of the M's central vee—and Firemayne pere and fils, standing at the M's opposite peaks. All eyes regarded her, but their focus was on the Cup she held at her waist.

Serving boys darted among the places, pouring Char into the men's brazen cups. The women sipped well-water in lucid flutes of glass that proved their innocuous contents to every glance.

A water bearer materialized beside Alison, his choirboy face mortified when he found her Cup already filled with the more lethal, dusky liquid. Apparently the Char had been a mistake. She smiled and lifted her Cup as chalices rose down the central vee of tables.

"Men of Desmeyne," the Firemayne began, eyeing them all. "We celebrate an event of consequence. For the first time in eighty-five years, the Cup of Earth rests in the mountainhold of Desmeyne."

"Desmeyne!" Their roaring approval shivered the rock-crystal walls and agitated the voiceless women's veils. The mute wave reminded Alison of a sea of voile hankies aflutter.

"For the first time in living memory," he continued, "Firemaynes may consider the journey to the Heart of Earth. While we hold the Cup, our enterprises will drink deep of its bounty."

Alison found herself fuming. That "we" skimmed over her presence, over her possession of the Cup, over the fact that a woman had won it for the first time in decades, for the first time *ever.* Who did these Desmeynian lords—these *men*—think they were?

The Firemayne went on. "We may try mining some of the shallow caverns untouched by the Earth-Eaters; our crops in the valley Deeps will be protected against the Harrowing-worm. We shall be blessed to the degree that we can bestir ourselves to industry and achievement. Let us welcome the Cup of Earth!"

"Welcome!" came the men's joyous reply, but not to Alison.

"And welcome as well—" the Firemayne turned to Rowan "—to my heir, who has returned with the Cup."

And the Cup*bearer,* Alison shouted mentally. These guys acted as if Rowan returning with a woman in tow, she who owned the Cup, was as good as getting it himself. Her fingers tightened on the stone stem as all eyes paused reverently on the Cup.

The Firemayne's windy self-congratulating speech huffed on. "This first and most powerful of talismans rests within the shining walls of Desmeyne, a jewel within its rightful bezel, a light against the dark of Dearth that crawls across our lands, laying sinkholes and poxes upon the fringes and borders and those who dwell in the lowlands. We of the pinnacles are safe in our cradle of stone upon the shoulders of the mountains. Long may our Cup pour bounty down our slopes. Long may my son's sacrifices bring honor and glory to Desmeyne."

"Desmeyne" and "Rowan" roared through the Arcade, mingling with the sharp-toned music until arrows of glassy sound ricocheted from the long chamber's opposite ends. Rowan remained silent and seated. Alison fumed. It was hard to tell whether his taciturn mein was from modesty or from shame at taking credit for another's achievements, or from mere heroic brooding.

In her hands, the Cup warmed. Its veins blushed ruddy, giving the white stone a pink cast that gaudily complemented the bile-black liquor within. Alison lifted it higher, a gesture that instantly caught the eyes of the men.

All of Alison's anger bubbled in her chest like searing, thick Char she couldn't swallow. Out came an impromptu toast she hadn't expected.

"Men of Desmeyne. Women of Veil." Her voice sounded clear and loud in this hard-edged hall.

At the farther tables, headdresses audibly snapped upright, jeweled swags trembling. Had a woman's voice ever risen above the banqueting tables here, any more than a woman's voice had ever lifted to sing for the Cup in the Valley of Voices?

"Here is the Cup," Alison said, balancing its foot on her left palm. The vessel warmed her clammy hands until the chill of fear was as far beyond reach as were the North Woods of Minnesota.

"The Cup does indeed rest within the environs of Desmeyne; it may indeed be blessed and may strengthen Desmeyne, but it isn't a thing of Desmeyne's. It's a guest of Desmeyne's, as I am. The Cup wasn't brought here by a Firemayne—though you wouldn't know it from the speech just given—any more than I was. It was brought here by myself, Alison of Island-Not, who won it fairly.

"And as Cupbearer, I'm tired of hearing about your claims on it, your demands, your hopes and expectations for this talisman. Maybe Rowan Firemayne would have brought it back if I hadn't been at the Wellsunging. But I was, and he came back with *me,* not with the Cup, for the Cup is mine. And I am not of your lands, I am not of your kind and kin, and I am not of your superior gender. I am a woman, a foreign female—" she glanced at Rowan for the first time "—and I hold the Cup. I'm tired of the way you see only your ritual heroics and ignore the unrespected people among you—these abandoned Littlelost, your own women, young and old.

"I am not an inconvenience that comes with the Cup, I am—" How could she make them see that her winning the Cup must be taken as a turning point, that they must give women more credit? The word had almost always been there. How wrong that Sage had to play the hidden servant and couldn't be here to hear this!

"—I am the Taliswoman! And until your hearts and minds acknowledge that, your land will find the sorest threat not from any creeping darkness beyond it, but from the blindness within its own self."

Alison lifted the Cup as a priestess might and sipped the black blood it harbored. She sat, suddenly weak-kneed, as if the velvet peony of wine within the Cup had released its full-blown fermented power only now that she had declared herself, her right to be regarded as Cupbearer.

She glanced at Rowan again. He remained stiffly sheathed in his earlier anger, though his eyes flashed resentment at her all the way down the long table. He probably thought that both she and his father were fools for claiming something that was merely not yet his, to his way of thinking. Next year, Rowan. But who could say what changes might come in a year? Look at what had happened to her in only a few days. Oh, God, maybe she'd even be home by then, with Beau, and the Cup wouldn't be her problem, her endless . . . responsibility. The thought caused an internal flutter, as if it were very wrong.

In the stunned silence, not a flute or a flagon lifted, not a Loftlady rustled or a lord stirred. The elder Firemayne sat heavily. Men along the tables followed suit. Then serving boys were sprinting behind the diners, burdened food trays held high. Aromas of Desmeyne's pallid meats and thin, hot soups ghosted through the air like smoke. Alison was served, but not spoken to. The women of Desmeyne whispered among themselves, no doubt discussing her declaration.

Alison suddenly felt as pompous as the men looked. Her

Desmeynian finery seemed as overblown as a Queen of Snows costume in the annual Winter Carnival—another orgy of civic self-congratulation, she thought sourly. Her neck was tightening from the unaccustomed weight of the gown's jeweled harness. She was glad she'd rejected the skimpy ceremonial sandals allowed the usually barefoot women, instead donning the more practical embroidered satin mules of a serving woman. Her feet were cold enough.

Once the meal had been consumed and cleared, the girl-children slipped into the Arcade. Each wore a miniature version of an elder's gown, bejeweled straps looking odd on plump or scrawny shoulders, low necklines as ludicrous on these prepubescent girls as a bikini top on a toddler.

The girls carried lighted tapers. As the music resumed, a man rose and approached a child, bowing to whisper in the tiny ear. The girl rustled over to a woman still seated at the table and waited there. Then the man came and collected his chosen lady and led her onto the floor for a dance. It was one method of singling out a woman from a group designed to remain anonymous. As other men followed, the ritual was repeated until the tables were almost deserted. The decorative little girls lined up along the walls like human torches.

The dances of Desmeyne proved to be as sedate as the ladies' fragile dress required. Couples paraded and bowed in calculated slow motion, the women guided only by the man's forefinger on the back of a flaccid hand. The male dancers reminded Alison of God on the Sistine Chapel ceiling, awakening complaisant Adams with the power of one energized digit.

But the dancers were engaging to watch, so well did they know the pattern and their roles in it. Lacking anyone to talk to, and still keyed up after her toast, Alison sipped Char generously. It coated her dry lips with a warm, pliant tar of liquor. And as she watched and sipped, an odd phenomenon occurred.

Colors intensified. The chamber no longer seemed so vast. The music's brittle tinkling sounded less like a frozen harpsichord, more like a mellow, glissando-plucked harp. Her head nodded to the music as the tables emptied and the dancers' numbers swelled.

Rowan still sat opposite her at the table's other end. When

their eyes met, she was rewarded with a burning, apparently resentful gaze. Then he rose, and without the intervention of a candle-bearing child, approached the last unclaimed lady: Darnellyne. He seemed to be in a reckless, defiant mood, ready to dare as much as she in breaching Desmeyne's customs.

They made a graceful pair on the nearest edge of the milling dancers. Alison watched them, feeling like a czarina on her isolated throne. Darnellyne was, as always, exquisite, the epitome of elegant womanhood sharpened to the finest point of artifice. Alison tried to picture Darnellyne and Rowan as childhood playmates and failed; yet she knew that they had been so only a few years before.

It surprised her that, like all Desmeynian men, Rowan was at ease in the grander garb of formal occasions, something she never would have guessed from his tight-lipped woodland days. His rampantly red hair was undamped by the glimmering powders, as was his father's; apparently Firemayne males didn't bother to embellish their trademark.

Rowan resembled an overdressed Hamlet in his full-sleeved, emerald-velvet, open-fronted shirt. Women were not the only Desmeynians unafraid of self-revelation. In Rowan's case, the shirt's deep vee framed the ritual scars that scored his chest. His had not been cosmetically emphasized like Alison's, but the light glinted from the shiny scar tissue.

How had he gotten the scars? Not by accident. She sipped another potent mouthful of Char. Her old bad dream flashed into her mind in vivid detail, as if in outright answer to her question. She felt again the cutting, saw the sparkling woman and bearded man. Not dream-twisted, emergency-room attendants—but Desmeyians carving the ritual scars into the Firemayne heir! That's why she'd seemed to have red hair flowing over her shoulders in the dream.

Alison shuddered. Could *she* have lain still while line after line had been scribed in her skin, not under the anesthesia of dream, but in drawn-out pain, blood greasing her ribs and shoulders? She eyed the Cup uneasily. Was it . . . interacting with her? The notion was as emotionally jolting as a cut. At least her mirroring injury had come in one catastrophic instant. No wonder Rowan was so proprietary about his pilgrim's role, his everlasting quests. He'd paid terribly for the right, and probably at a tender age.

Now Rowan moved in the prime of youthful pride, his long legs, greyhound-lean, pacing around the swirling intricacies of Darnellyne's skirts. He showed the fluidity of a swordsman in a ritual exercise; after all, he handled a staff with lethal skill. He'd probably be deadly if she ever taught him *taekwondo,* but then, he'd hardly stand for learning the spiritual openness required. He was too stiffly self-disciplined, no doubt a side effect of celibacy enforced on a man in his prime.

Stupid, stupid Desmeyne. Alison tilted the Cup to drink again. What good would anyone's self-denial do a world under an apparent siege of infestation, pestilence, indifference, and even alien dangers? What a waste. She eyed Rowan's lithe physique, stepping forward and back, flirting at the edges of Darnellyne's skirt but never quite touching it.

The filtered moonlight quenched the raucous fire of his hair and softened the lean angles of his face. If Rowan would only smile at his partner . . . but no, he was too serious about his ever-consuming quests to smile. So she smiled at his behavior as she savored her Char. Handsome, headstrong young man, she wondered dreamily, do you even suspect that there are worlds where women aren't bound into constrictive roles; compliant bedpartner, aloof lady-love, industrious mother and wife, and serving woman, or reviled hag?

Perhaps he wasn't missing much in the sex department, though. Even the hussy at the Scarlet Swan didn't look imaginative enough to do more in the bedroom than sigh and pout. Poor Rowan. Not really bad-looking, and not bad-hearted once you got past his manner. And not too muscle-bound. Alison eyed the swell of his upper thighs, the strong, graceful hand that rested on his belt as he led Darnellyne through the dance pattern with his other hand, the broad shoulders and the bronzed chest that the shirt hid and revealed in supple waves of green velvet.

She eyed him over the pale horizon of her Cup rim. What would good old Rowan do if confronted with a sexually liberated, modern—with a *real* woman, period? Not just publicly, but privately.

The Char clung to her lips. She suddenly felt beautiful, as she had never before felt in her life. And strong. And part of that odd new power, that scintillating self-confidence, was the revelation of her scars, her claiming of them as a badge.

For an instant she felt as potent as an empress, as if she could call Rowan over, beckon him to her bed if she wanted to, and he'd come because he couldn't resist. He'd collapse like a puppet to the pull of her magnetic female drawing power, her earthy charm, her charisma, her frank desire. And she'd *enjoy* seducing him, surprising him with her sexual assertiveness, watching his rough edges smooth as he sank into an unsuspected sensual spell. . . .

Alison blinked.

She couldn't believe it. She'd been lusting after Rowan. Rowan! Of all men. Of all boys! Her teenaged Cup-rival. Her defeated rival. Rowan, the boy from another planet. Goodness. Or, as Mae West said, goodness had nothing to do with it. Some part of her still harbored the wicked fantasy, so she shook her head to dislodge it. The room spun a little.

Her fingers loosened on the Cup. The Char had ebbed to a smug dark pool at the very bottom. Char. Dangerous and delightful. Like her thoughts. No more Char. She tried to ignore her body's signs of unseemly stimulation. Thank God thought-reading was not an accomplishment of the Desmeynians!

She looked up, startled to see a man standing beside her stool. She had not heard him approach, but men in Desmeyne went shod on velvet soles.

Her visitor was dark-favored and leanly exotic. He reminded her of a matador. His ebony hair shone like satin ribbon and was sleeked back into a discreet queue. His black silken shirt was sheer, yet encrusted with opals of incredible brunette fire so that his every breath set off fireworks of reds, blues and greens within the somber stones.

He wore black to his toes, and the shortness of his shirt and tightness of his hose made no secret of his manhood. He regarded her with a veiled expectancy that hid a fearsome hunger. And he extended a single forefinger, as though to lead her to the dance.

Oberon, she thought. The King of the Faerie has come for me. She rose in a Char-daze, left the almost-empty Cup with only a twinge of regret, and went with him, amazed that the pressure of one finger on her hand could steer her so expertly around the tables and onto the floor. Rowan would see that one man in Desmeyne was not afraid of her.

Perhaps she should be afraid of him.

20

Alison let her imposing partner lead her to the area where the others danced, pushing back her fear of the unknown as the dancers froze to watch them.

Instead, she fretted about the disposition of her elaborate dress and whether she could dance in these satin mules, or even follow the dance's steps, and who this stranger was and what had made him turn her from wallflower to focal point.

She heard gasps as they reached the floor, and then she found herself moving, forward and back, around and out, in and away. All about her the Arcade's crystal fires dwindled as if masked by the dark man's elegant presence.

He was her personal eclipse, his exquisite shadow extinguishing more of Desmeyne's overlit brilliance with every movement. Even sound retreated, except for a distant whine of wind against the rock-crystal walls.

His eyes were his darkest aspect. Deep, clinging to her like Char, *stinging* like Char, potent and hidden. She found herself breathless—not from the dance, for it was torpid, and not from attraction, for her partner was oddly impersonal despite his compelling concentration, his overt sexiness. Perhaps it was from wonder, and uncertainty.

The edges of her vision dimmed. She saw only him, saw his precise feet tracing a perfect pattern on the jagged edges of ore beneath them, saw veins turning molten and running into branched lightning. Chasms opened in the Arcade floor: thin, innocent fissures that stretched like black cats and grew to the size of canyons. The dark man waltzed her over the absences, as if they were skating on night incarnate.

Alison looked around for the other dancers.

They were distant, separated from her by the creeping fingers of the chasms. They had stopped dancing, had stopped moving, and were staring at her and not seeing her at the same time. The touch of his fingertip on the back of her hand became an unendurable pressure. She felt that she was being squeezed down into one of those depthless cracks in the floor; when she resisted, the sensation doubled.

Colors seeped from the faces and clothing of the distant dancers. Even the lapis-and-malachite floor had faded to the shade of stone-washed denim. Then all the color was gone! The world had become a vague white blur, surrounding her like a cataract.

Her head turned wildly, only to see reality melt and pale like sherbet. She caught one glimpse of unbleached, vivid-red hair, but the face that wore it was frost-pale and its owner's clothes were as colorless as a specter's.

"No!" Alison shouted, struggling to free her hand from the ice-cold finger that centered on it like a compass point piercing thin skin.

Someone laughed.

She whirled to confront her partner. He, too, had altered. He was even darker than before, blackness itself given sketchy shape and allowed to coalesce before her. He had grown taller, to perhaps eight feet, and had solidified into a dead tree trunk that bore a bizarre likeness to a man, or to a plinth of basalt carved into an Easter Island head or . . . both.

Laughter came disembodied, along with a razor-pass of wind that sliced through Alison's fragile, petaled gown to her naked skin beneath.

She stood alone on a dim plateau, a place both natural and artificial, under a moonless, starless night sky, lit only by a multihued mist swirling like gas imprisoned by a bell jar.

"No," she whispered. The faint music of Desmeyne shattered like crystal down an endless arcade of time. Around her, scarves of mist roiled, while the melody rose and fell with the phantom's approach and withdrawal. The Dance still unwound.

"Taliswoman," the dark distance mocked. It found an echo in the attenuated form before her, which horrified her by moving.

She jerked her hand back to her side, although her sinister escort's guiding finger had long since withdrawn. Her flesh felt ripped free from ice to which it had been frozen. A weeping sore—part blood, part serum—transfixed the back of her hand.

"Tali*ssssss*woman," the very air of the place hissed. She stumbled and turned, desperate to leave this nightmare scene. The ground was polished black marble, but rough-hewn like basalt, the texture of frozen midnight waves.

Alison had never felt so cold, as if blanketed with death. Her extremities were numb, and the internal warmth that fed her thoughts, her emotions, her will, was oozing away. Only a faint, pallid flame remained. She was astounded to recognize it, the afterglow of her embarrassing free-fall into misdirected lust, still pulsing through the chill carapace her body had become. She turned again and found the encroaching shadow she had presumed to dance with, a Black Hole of substancelessness. Null. Void. Vacuum and vacuousness. If it touched her, if it drew her into its implacable, empty maw— It did not even require the act of drawing, she sensed with horror. If she remained still, she drew it to herself. And yet she was so icily paralyzed by a force outside herself that only the thready beat of a secret, shameless desire remained animate in her. It felt like Char coursing down her throat, slow and seductive and heated. Like blood pooling in her veins. Like a living, breathing skein of life to which her awareness and body were normally oblivious.

No accident! The words exploded in her mind, awakening it. The Char, the Cup . . . blending into an alien and potent aphrodisiac. Love potion. Life potion. Not a thread of ignoble desire, but a rope of survival, like DNA, that even now resisted the overwhelming nullity of this colorless, cruel place, this nightmare landscape.

Alison wheeled away from the entity's featureless presence. She lurched across the obsidian waves, wondering how she could see the fault lines of deeper black riddling the surface. *Step on a crack, break your mother's back.*

She jumped over one fissure that split beneath her, and she sensed it yawning yards wide even as her body hung momentarily lofted above it. Then the merciless force of gravity drew her back down, not to earth but to a solid something, and the fissure sealed shut behind her. She turned quickly enough to see it closing upon some of the petals of her train. A tarry substance was spreading upward through the transparent fabric, soaking it to her knees.

Alison yanked the fabric, trying to wrench it free, then trying to rip it free. The insubstantial stuff resisted her efforts as well as woven steel.

Suddenly, with a sucking sound, the material loosened. She leaped to the next disappearing black wave, feeling fissures snapping at her hemline like the jaws of jet-black eels with tarry mouths. And the stench! Both chemical and organic, the blackness below belched an overwhelming, searing, toxic smell.

She raced on. The rare colored powders rose from her garb in ashen clouds, then turned as black and glittering as coal dust. She remembered another childhood proscription: Touch a butterfly's glitter-dusted wings, take away the very substance that enables it to fly, and it will die.

21

Rowan paced mindlessly through the intricacies of the Train-lacing dance, keeping his feet from tangling with the constant sweep of shimmering fabric. Mindlessly, although he knew his attention ought to focus on Darnellyne—simply in his role as a considerate partner, if not as a suitor rarely offered an opportunity to speak with her, let alone touch her with so much as a forefinger.

She moved exquisitely, like slow-flowing mildwater pooling in the shallow bell of a fountain. Her beauty was remote and fragile, her garb a mere tissue of glamour privileged to veil it. Yet he and Darnellyn had argued in the passage outside the Arcade, the first uncivil words they'd spoken in almost a decade, the first since they'd been children and knew no better.

Noisy disagreements, as all children have; a physical struggle over some object long-forgotten . . . grabbing her arm with possessive force, then feeling ashamed because of her obviously inherent weakness.

It was an irritation that the object of his pains should dare to disagree with him, even if in his own defense. Darnellyne had urged him not to blame himself for the loss of the Cup. But guilt and obligation were the twin goads that brought ultimate glory. How could she not understand that? How could she not appreciate his need to shatter long, fruitless precedent and bring the legendary artifact home to Desmeyne?

He had made sacrifices—his unexercised virility, her company—and taken risks, forcing himself into the wider world to quest for arcane paths to the Four Quarters, risks that no one in Veil had undertaken in centuries. If only she would *see* that great evil was abroad and that great measures must be taken to meet it. Some intuition was stirring in him, part Firemayne and part . . . something else, something alien.

"She is watching us." Darnellyne's voice broke upon his thoughts as gently as a shoreline wave. It wove itself into the tinkling music as a velvet ribbon might thread through broken glass. It had not always been so.

Screeches of laughter and sudden childish terror, play teetering between safety and forbidden danger, both sharing that raucous freedom once.

"Watching?" he repeated, confused by the blurring overlap of present and past, by the two-faced evocation of his and Darnellyne's mature and youthful selves. How different they each had become, who had once been playmates.

Darnellyne's liquid voice trickled on. "She . . . is an odd creature."

Rowan glanced to the bottom point of the M, where Alison sat alone. From this distance, she glittered as grandly as any Loftlady, but he was not disarmed or deceived. Taliswoman! The very word was an abominable distortion. *She* was an abomination, an unnatural amalgam of Desmeyne's strictly separated male and female. Now this "Taliswoman" was observing them with aloof, insufferable superiority. He could feel her speculative eyes upon them, her greenish gaze burning into his back, then into his ritual scars as he turned.

Her shamelessness made him feel naked. She sat open-eyed, watching him, when the ladies of the Lofts gazed through the glamorous haze of their face-veils. Since his scarring, he had viewed no woman's naked eyes save Triss's, whose gaze was too empty to require veiling, and the old witch Sage's, and now this usurper's. A potential for judgment lay in such unconcealed regard; the idea chafed Rowan like bloodthistle. How dare Alison evaluate him, weigh his worth and perhaps find him wanting?

She sat with the prized Cup before her and drank from it, while he danced futilely with Darnellyne, who would have been his had he won the Cup. *Why?* whispered his darkening mind, and he knew which matter the question pertained to. Rowan turned in the dance and spoke at last.

"She is more than odd, she is dangerous," he told the fragile Darnellyne. "You could never understand how it feels to cede the Cup to a stranger—to one who has no notion of its value—especially when that stranger is an unnatural female who will not use it in the service of Veil and Desmeyne."

"How would you have used it?"

He paused, distracted from his feelings of righteous resentment. "For more than some ceremonial trophy merely useful for bending nature to our will to make life easier! I sense that it carries a greater purpose and larger power tied to the Four Quests. I would have teased or forced that knowledge from it."

"Might not she do that?"

"Certainly not! She has no respect for our world or its ways! Forget tonight's fripperies; she dresses as a peasant farmer. She even fought with me in the woods, as might any male Cup-rival. If it were not for the scars—and that might be some Crux-guise, or the doing of that old woman, Sage—"

"I used to fight with you, in the Webbings."

Rowan paused in midstep, struck by the coincidence: Darnellyne citing their common childhood. "Children know no better."

"Perhaps we knew better than we knew."

He studied her powdered, half-veiled face. Did regret tinge her honeyed voice? Did reservation agitate her eternal serenity? Did he hear echoes of childish screeches and laughter, feel the quick, rough gestures of play when now he pinioned her remoteness with the pressure of a forefinger on her exquisite hand?

"Rowan, she is coming onto the floor! Alone!"

Did Darnellyne's voice tremble with approval? With excitement? Did she somehow . . . admire . . . this usurper, this self-proclaimed Taliswoman?

Rowan looked to where every dancer was now subtly glancing. Alison's be-gemmed hem rasped over the stone floor in a sudden caesura, a still pond between the rhythmic oar strokes of musical notes. For a moment he thought she moved toward them, toward him, and he felt a flush of mixed emotions.

But Alison stopped and turned away in that self-certain manner of hers. Though the dancers maintained their formal paces, they whispered at this breach of custom.

"She will dance with herself!" Darnellyne said in a voice of marvel. "Without waiting to be chosen."

Rowan, silent, felt that he was stumbling on a once-flat floor that had suddenly become a flight of steps.

For Alison was *not* alone.

With her was a dark, shimmering presence, stately and formidable. Rowan saw a black-gauntleted hand, heavy with the glimmer of midnight gems, poised above her pale hand. He saw the dark hub around which she revolved, managing the pattern of an alien dance with the same quick mastery she had used to overthrow him in the woods. Her proficiency even here enraged him, and he looked away, resolved to ignore her.

"She mimics perfectly the act of dancing with a partner," Darnellyne said. "She is quite extraordinary."

"You see no partner?"

"Of course not. I may wear a veil, but I am not blind, Rowan."

He was forced to look again. Alison's fey partner was even more visible to him now, though as a darkness defined by the brightly dressed dancers around the twosome. The Dark Man was a shadow-form, attired in rich black gleamings, like a fabled vein in the Earth-Eaters' caverns. His sober near-invisibility lent him a terrible potency.

Rowan's eyes riveted on Alison's scar. He remembered how fiercely she had concealed in the woods and mountains what tonight she revealed—nay, reveled in: the marks of his defeat, now flaunted. He could not gainsay Alison's reality any longer; womanly breasts—somehow more provocative than Darnellyne's perhaps because he'd glimpsed them only once before—luxuriated against the teasing containment of the Desmeynian gown.

There she passed, Rowan admitted, looking next to her naked face. And here she failed, he thought with satisfaction. Her dark hair was cut shorter than his, and she had not adorned herself above the shoulders. Her features were not unpleasant, but bereft of the veil that made a mystery of the eyes, they were not endlessly intriguing. No man would ache to penetrate this inner sanctum of her expression. No, if anything, Rowan burned to cast her to the ground in open combat. Female the Taliswoman might be, he decided; a woman that men would venerate and seek, never.

She glanced at him, an amused, assessing look that seemed to offer some secret knowledge of himself. He froze in outrage. Darnellyne's swirling gown settled around his legs like falling leaves as her hand melted from contact with his fingertip.

And some ineluctable warmth left the chamber, left Rowan.

For now he saw the Dark Man in all his dangerous glamour. The man should not be here in Desmeyne, Rowan realized; in fact, he *was* not here. Then how did Rowan see him? How did Alison? And why could not anyone else in the Arcade see him? For they did not. The others danced on, not quite unmindful, yet obviously noting only Alison's bizarre behavior, not the reason for it.

Perhaps even *she* did not truly see her partner. This thought held Rowan transfixed. He watched the couple turn and step, draw nearer and apart. And with each movement, with each split second of motion, he saw Alison's glittering gown soften and fade, saw the Dark Man's shadow grow more solid and opaque.

A few more steps together, then apart, together—and Alison's gown, her figure, would become a field of shimmering notes in a bar of cooling sunlight. For some few moments he was content to watch her form lessen, immobile despite the distant chimes of Darnellyne's voice tolling his name.

But as Alison evanesced, the Dark Man solidified into shadow. A rank odor wafted toward Rowan. The figure's very presence became a blot of mold upon the perfect fruit that was Desmeyne. This was travesty, some perfidy of the Crux—a Crux-master himself among them!

Rowan ached for the sword he was forbidden, for the song that had not quite sufficed. He ached for something outside himself to wield against this force beyond reason into which the vaunted Taliswoman was disappearing with complacent, oblivious steps.

All those around him had become statues to his mind's eye: stock-still, mute, faded, although he knew that to them, he appeared to be the paralyzed one. Indeed, he found himself lethargic, his energy leaking out of his limbs. He was the perfect spectator, and did he not deserve the role, having failed to win the Cup, to win Darnellyne, to win all Veil free of the multiplying rot that nibbled at its people?

Rowan tore himself loose of the paralyzing spell and strode toward the empty table where the stone Cup had turned the dead color of granite. He paused before he seized it, questioning his right, his safety, in doing so. What if the Cup repudiated him? Proved him as false as he felt?

His hand obeyed some instinct surer than thought. Rowan clasped the Cup, shivering as its icy stem seared into his palm like a heated dagger. He turned back to the dance. His brief absence had put apparent miles between himself and it. The people had become tiny figures stitched into a frozen tapestry. But he was long-legged and deep-lunged, and he plunged toward the remote image, pushed against the illusion of distance and torpid time, swam against a current of will-smothering power, ignored his own notions of unreality and strode through the solid wall of light and color until it shattered and became dusk.

Alison came into clearer focus as the Arcade and the people of Desmeyne faded. So did her partner: a virile man, garbed with the secret richness of the mine deeps, a man draped in night, stinking of decay.

Rowan moved closer. Pain coursed from the hand that clutched the Cup—up his good right arm and across his scarred chest to his heart. The tighter he grasped the Cup, the tighter a dark, disembodied gauntlet seemed to squelch his heartbeat, until his blood throbbed in his head with the exaggerated rhythm of life exploding into death.

The Dark Man's features and form melted into a vortex of power. Alison fought to move on the black ground that heaved as if to swallow her while her skirts were being devoured by blackness from below. Even the light about her person had dimmed into a veil of transparent swarthiness that shifted around her like a shroud.

Rowan, too, kept moving, every step pushing him harder against the punishing distance. Yet the more that some dark force resisted his motion, the less the Cup tore at his possession. Instead, he felt a strengthening power. By the time he at last reached Alison, the Cup cleaved to his hand like a grafted-on limb. It took all of his will to thrust it away—toward her, at her chest, like a blow. Her hands lifted to ward off the talisman. Her face was drained of expression, except for her eyes, which stared at him with unfocused disbelief.

But the strike of the cold stone Cup against her insubstantial flesh rang in Rowan's mind like the brassy bellow of Desmeyne's Great Door to a stranger's knock.

Her hands curled unwillingly, slowly, around the Cup's granite bowl. Warmth sparked through the Cup's shriveled veins. Its surface brightened and lightened. The adamant black emptiness surrounding them retreated. The wall-solid stench became a veil.

Alison turned with unleashed purpose—it must have been fighting for expression throughout the ordeal—and dashed the contents of the Cup against the Dark Man's fearful aspect.

An acidlike sizzle snapped in the heavy air. A long, gleaming whip of Char lashed the darkness and hissed to the uneven basalt floor. Where it touched, green tendrils burst through, cleaving glassy rock from itself.

Rowan breathed again, feeling the iron fist upon his heart loosen. His head felt suddenly hot, as if energy blossomed forth until it scorched his hair. Alison's fading face and figure exploded into vibrant color and full substance again.

They stared, unbelieving, at their feet, where grass sprouted with dazzling rapidity, turning an ebony desert into a meadow. The obsidian waves softened into a pulsing shiver of oceanic blue. Panic filled Alison's blue-green eyes, but their bodies did not sink into this almost-water. Rowan felt an unworthy stab of satisfaction amid his wonder.

Then the grass flattened and died, and cobalt waves hardened again. They stood on the dance floor's malachite and lapis lazuli, and ice shards of music broke against the Arcade's impervious crystal archway.

Rowan turned to reassess this welcome world. Darnellyne stood watching, along with an entire riveted audience of dancers. She seemed wan after the explosive color of grass and water, as did the people surrounding her. He stole a glance at Alison; she still looked dazzlingly vivid, as if she had been somehow intensified during their invisible journey to a place beyond the known boundaries of Veil.

Darnellyne, speechless, cast an accusing glance at Rowan, gathered her frail gown in her taloned hands and fled in a wash of sad glitter. Rowan's mouth opened and he stared. Something astounding had happened to him. Twain-sight. He must tell them.

. . . He tried to move in the chamber, in present reality, but when he looked down, the inlaid slabs clashed at different heights. He stumbled on the familiar floor, as Alison had on the black basalt of the other landscape. He felt like a child who had thought to walk but had not yet quite learned how.

His father approached in dizzy tandem with a second image that seemed to wobble across a black plain. Rowan felt an idiotic rush of gratitude. Yet even as he did so, he noted the Firemayne's faded coloration, his slower step and heavier form, suddenly saw him from both farther and nearer than he had ever perceived him before. And he saw that no matter how he himself might stumble, his father could no longer help him.

Then his father took the gold-embroidered ceremonial gloves from his belt and struck Rowan across the face. The blow fell in the shadow of a sudden strike from a barbed black branch. Rowan sensed that somehow the Dark Man was lashing his—Rowan's—disintegrating image. The site of the blow tingled and numbed in rapid turn, though the impact had felt no harsher than a leaf buffeting his cheek in an autumn breeze. The fact of it and that other phantom strike resonated in his heart like a door slamming shut.

"Why do you weave like a drunkard? Why have you forsaken Darnellyne to dance with that stranger, to even bring her the Cup? You have betrayed Darnellyne, betrayed Desmeyne." His father's voice rumbled from a pitiless, painful distance. "You shame me. Take that so-called Taliswoman and leave this place."

Answer. But defense was hopeless. No one had seen what he had seen, and so his twain-sight dislocated actions struck them as drunken incapacity. Staggering, he started out of the splendid chamber. A last spasm of shame told him that even in this, he disappointed his father: *Alison* led *him* from the room.

22

Alison's delicate Desmeynian hem ripped under Rowan's stumbling boots as he wheeled from one side of the hallway to the other like a blind man.

"Come on," she urged, trying to guide a hundred and eighty pounds of caroming human billiard ball on a straight line through the center of the passage. Not as shell-shocked as he seemed to be from glimpsing the alternate reality, she held the Cup tight to the center of her chest, determined not to drop it. "Walk straight."

"I can't . . . can't see straight," he complained in the dazed voice that sounded besotted.

Alison knew better. "We must find shelter," she said. "Someplace to go and think."

"I'm going to be sick."

"No! Not here!" She eyed the polished floors and pristine walls and imagined further disgrace. "Come on!"

Though he lurched in the best tradition of a drunken sailor, Alison was able to turn Rowan's random wheelings into a semblance of forward progress. Her hem, miraculously unstained, shredded in shrill increments under his clumsy steps, and the gown's jeweled harness—never having been designed for such stress—dug into her shoulders.

She piloted him by step and by stumble to the vacant Lofts, to her rooms there, despite the breach of Desmeynian etiquette. The entries to various suites glowed starlike in the still dusk. Real stars pricked the cupped hands of night above them, visible through crystal arches. They climbed the coiled staircases almost on their knees. Alison's hem tore again, and Rowan paused once on a turning to hang over the railing.

"Only a bit farther," she insisted, and he staggered onward and upward. Finally they were brushing through the layered veils that served as a door to her chambers.

"What has happened?" Sage rushed from the inner rooms.

"I was hoping you could tell me," Alison answered. "Quick! A bowl!"

Sage produced a shallow vessel of shimmering mother-of-pearl. A moment later a kneeling Rowan honored it with the fruits of his discomfort.

Alison collapsed onto a brocaded stool, still clutching the Cup, while Sage tended Rowan with self-effacing skill. Alison couldn't help but admire the old woman's gentleness as she wiped his mouth as if he were a baby and whisked away the bowl so it should not further offend.

Even on his knees, blinking at his surroundings, Rowan wove as if bewitched by a snake charmer. The red impression his father's blow had left on his cheek contrasted with the pallor that had turned his bronzed complexion to the shade of spoiled buttermilk.

Sage returned and eyed Alison's gown. "You have walked here through brambles?"

"The way was thorny in other respects," Alison said. "What's wrong with him?"

"You cannot tell me?"

"I am . . . dizzy myself. First I danced with a Dark Man: then the Arcade faded and I was in a ruined wilderness. Rowan came with the Cup. Rowan *gave* it to me, can you believe it? He thrust it upon me—here"— Alison pounded a fist to the bone between her breasts—"and I threw its contents at the Dark Man. Then the ground cracked and we were back in Desmeyne. It sounds like a dream, not reality."

"So the greatest reality always appears," Sage said grimly. "And he?"

"Like this ever since."

While they contemplated Rowan in silence, he shook his head until his hair lashed the air.

"We were never elsewhere," he said thickly. "I saw . . . both sights, both sides, at once. The Train-lacing dance and the Desmeynians. The ruined plain and the Dark Man. Both sights, as no Firemayne has seen in centuries." A hand shaded his eyes from the light. "I saw the Dark Man in Desmeyne; Desmeyne in that dark place— I see it all still."

"I don't." Alison shuddered. "I'm glad I don't. But my hand . . ." She extended it to Sage like a child.

"Ay!" Sage's recoil was instinctive.

Alison studied the perfect hole of black pasted atop her hand like an opaque mole. It glittered slightly, as had the Dark Man's garb. "I think it's . . . larger."

Sage seized the Cup from Alison's frozen grasp and tipped it over the area. A last drop of Char oozed tobacco-brown down the white stone bowl, gathered tearily at the lip and finally plopped onto the spot on Alison's hand.

She wailed at the burning pain, which was followed quickly by a cool, drying sensation. Sage wiped the spot clean with the hem of her sleeve. No mark remained.

Alison began shaking.

Sage shook her white head and then extended the Cup. Once emptied, it had refilled itself with Char. "You have both been in a dire place, whether it masqueraded as Desmeyne or drew Desmeyne to it. Only the Cup—and Rowan's quick thought to bring it—saved you." Sage stood before Alison. "I should not use the Cup, but the need is immediate. It may help him if you let him partake of it."

Alison could have used a stiff shot of Char herself, but she held the Cup out to Rowan. He had dragged one knee off the floor and was balancing his arm upon it, too weak to rise. Yet his brown eyes blazed almost carmine at the sight of the Cup extended to him so freely, when it had proven so elusive.

"I do not need your succor," he said.

"The Cup is mine," Alison replied calmly. "The succor is purely the Cup's, and the thought is Sage's."

His lips tightened, but she pushed the Cup toward them and tilted. Rowan sipped some of the Char, quickly staying her hand and drawing away. He shut his eyes for a moment, then opened them. His gaze fixed first on Sage, then on Alison.

"What happened to your gown?" he asked.

"You."

"I don't remember. The skirt was not in rags when we came to the Arcade again. Even I could see that then. But now . . . I can see singly once more."

"You saw double before?"

He nodded soberly, despite the heady Char, watching as she swallowed long from the Cup. "Twain-sight. Ever since the Arcade faded and I followed you to that black place. I have never sensed such desolation—"

"—Death," Alison put in.

"Dearth," Sage corrected.

"What?" Alison asked the question, but they both turned to the wisewoman.

"You have danced with Dearth, my children, the creature behind all the machinations of the Crux."

"We are not your children." Rowan's jaws tensed until a muscle twitched. "And I have danced with no one. It is she who stood up in company and declared herself Taliswoman, she who walked into whatever web of Dearth's was woven here tonight."

"You came there of your own will," Alison charged.

Rowan pushed himself upright, then quickly surveyed the room to make sure it did not waver. Sage bowed and discreetly faded into the inner chambers.

"What could I do?" he complained. "I saw this Other when no one else did. I saw this Otherplace. I have done something incredible. Twain-sight is a lost art. No Firemayne since the time of Vereleon has done this."

"Oh, Rowan! What have Firemaynes to do with it? I'm tired of hearing how you must live up to being a Firemayne. Sheer pig-headed pride. What has it gotten you but a public slap across the face?"

Rowan's color returned, rapidly.

"My father did not understand. And who are you to be so angry at my disgrace?"

"You're doing it again!" she retorted. "You think you own everything: failure, uncertainty, the whole earth. I looked like a fool out there, too. And I'm tired of things I don't understand, talk of twain-sight and Dearth of this and that, and Cups that can't be won by women!"

Rowan's composure was not as strong as his impulse for a good argument required. He shut his eyes and wove on his feet, then sat gingerly on a stool near Alison's.

"Firemaynes have sought more than the Cup," he said at last. "I have also sought our lost skills, arts that allow some of our kind to see two places at once, to *be* in two places at once. This happened tonight." Rowan glanced at Alison and the Cup. "It may be that in losing the Cup, I have gained a different prize." He clutched his forehead. "If I survive it."

Alison smiled to hear Rowan sound doubtful. It became him. "Listen, in my world—which is not perfect by any means, motive or opportunity, believe me—women aren't brushed aside like I've been here. I didn't even know about your damn Cup. I certainly didn't want it. But I won it fair and square, and I won't have you and your father pretending that just because I brought it here, it's as good as yours. Okay, it isn't supposed to be won by a woman, but it was, and you guys had better get used to it."

Rowan frowned. "That is why you called yourself the Taliswoman tonight, why you dressed as a woman of Desmeyne. You were throwing your possession of the Cup in our faces—"

"No! I was throwing *me* in your faces." Alison prodded herself in the chest. "Does not a woman bleed, Desmeynian? Do I not bear every cut you took upon yourself at a ridiculously early age? And Desmeyne is as hard on children as it is on women."

"That was duty." He frowned. "And how do you know *when* I underwent the Carving?"

"I . . . had a dream. And my cutting was an accident, but the result is the same."

"Accident?"

"My sister died. Drowned. I was running for help and fell on an old pot inscribed with strange markings. I was eleven."

He stiffened. "The age of marking—you *do* know! Another accident?" Then his shoulders loosened. "My elder brother died. He would have worn the scars had he lived that long."

"How did he die?"

"We do not know. He vanished. Perhaps a Womb-bat or a Harrow-worm killed him. We have long been troubled by the Earth-Eaters' foul creatures."

"My sister's body was never recovered, either." Alison was silent for a long moment. "I can still see her sinking. There was nothing I could do. I couldn't swim. I could only run for help." She sipped the Char, but its black, briny taste was no comfort.

"That is why you don't like crossing water," Rowan said with interest. "You have a weakness!"

"As do you!"

"What is that?"

He sounded too incredulous for Alison to resist a low blow. "You get dizzy on dance floors."

He was silent, taken aback by a charge both trivial and good-humored, yet profoundly disturbing. Alison felt suddenly sorry for him; he was not the firstborn, first-chosen, but a substitute. No wonder he took his role so bloody seriously. Now he sat, shamed by his father before all Desmeyne, including the delectable Darnellyne, for the selfless act of saving the one who'd wrested the Cup from him, an act that apparently had tapped some latent mystical powers.

The Lofts' flattering lights painted sunsets in his hair and fell softly on the muscular shadows of his stretched-out legs, his bared chest.

Poor Rowan, Alison thought on a new wave of Char-induced charity, or in the lethargic aftermath of great danger. What if he had won the Cup and his overbred lady? He was too young to know, really, that women as sex objects—whether kittenish tavern wench or elegant lady—are not very satisfying. But Rowan had never encountered a woman who wouldn't settle for pedestalhood or a rote tumble in the featherbed. A woman who knew how to take as well as to give.

She stood and regarded him from a pinnacle she imagined he knew well, though he had temporarily fallen from it: satisfied superiority. He was a boy, really, a rash, handsome boy who took himself far too seriously.

She offered him the Cup again. He regarded her quizzically, with dawning suspicion, but sipped from the vessel before she set it on the table behind them. Seated, his face was level with her breasts.

She combed her fingers swiftly into the long, silken hair at the back of his neck and tilted his head up. The barbs of his emerging beard shone like fiery dewdrops in the lamplight. His eyes were thinking about growing startled when she bent and set her lips on his.

Her kiss was slow and sure and very adult. She sensed his shock, his instinctive recoil, and only intensified the contact, taking command of his surprise-softened mouth, delving deep, meeting his resistance with superior insistence. Her hand brushed down his throat, across the bizarrely familiar topography of his scars and down his softly haired chest.

His hands went to her shoulders to push her away. She almost smiled when they stopped pushing and dragged the harness of her gown over the rim of her collarbones and then tightened on the soft flesh of her upper arms. When she was done, she drew back.

He stared up at her in shock, then rose so quickly that the stool kicked over behind him. And then he left, before she could fully gauge his reaction, or her own. A sound came from behind her, but she was too lazy to turn.

I do believe that I could blow that man's mind, she mused. She put her hands to her overheated cheeks. *What am I doing? He's not a man, that's the point. He's just a boy with a savior complex. I don't have to prove anything to him.*

She turned.

Instead of Sage, a beautiful lady of the Lofts glittered before her, swathed in draperies as lovely as Alison's had once been. Alison hated having a stranger witness her misbehavior. She spoke sharply. "You should still be at the banquet. And how did you get in here?"

"I was always here." The woman's amused voice was faintly familiar.

"Sage?"

The woman nodded. "I should have warned you: The Cup, when filled with the proper, or improper, beverage, such as Char, can have an aphrodisiac effect. It is a Cup of Earth, after all."

"I'm . . . relieved, but what mischief are you up to now? Your current form isn't the product of a mind-altering substance. Sage, how can you—? What are you?"

Sage smiled the same slightly superior smile Alison had just used on Rowan. "I was a lady of the Lofts once. Like them, I practiced the arts of long life and long-lived beauty. Then I saw its emptiness and left. My beauty crumbled, but my life persisted, sometimes despite myself. I can don my past appearance whenever I choose—through the diligent use, in my youth, of a forbidden root called wintergreen."

"Then why not—?"

"For the same reason that you will soon wrench off that ragged gown and go as you were, Taliswoman. The rewards of illusion are never quite enough, just as Rowan was too easy a target for your desire a few moments ago to satisfy it."

"Ouch. I'm mortified, Sage." Alison sank onto the remaining upright stool. "I behaved like a high-handed hero in a bad romance, but I begin to understand the men of my world's obsession for virgins. There's satisfaction in knowing more of life than someone else does, someone of the opposite sex who is only the more attractive for his—or her—blithe ignorance. There's a power gained in overruling the better instincts of the unenlightened. I needed to prove my womanhood to Rowan, but all I proved was that I'm not really certain of it. Especially here. Especially with him."

"Blame Char and the Cup. And what is this 'romance,' this 'enlightenment'?"

"Oh, Sage. 'Romance' is harder to explain than Rowan's twain-sight. Let's just say that it's a magical formula in my world, seldom found and seldom retained. 'Enlightened' means knowing the world beyond your own doorstep. As you do." Alison reached out to touch Sage's fragile gown. "Did you don your long-relinquished guise to demonstrate that I don't need such fripperies, either?"

"I wear my long-relinquished guise to show you that you do not require such self-deceptions. And since my honest aspect is distasteful to Desmeynians, I can use this guise to leave the Lofts unremarked. Some Loftladies are allowed limited freedom—the Firemayne's lady, for instance, and I know how to slip through the often-empty corridors of Desmeyne. But I do not need this now."

Sage's alabaster-smooth hand nostalgically riffled the petals of her skirt; even as the diaphanous fibers sifted through her fingers, they melted. By the gesture's end, the hand that dropped to her side was welted with veins and the gown was ordinary sackcloth.

Alison regarded the dumpy old woman before her, saw past the facial furrows and into the unaging wisdom behind them. "I think that Rowan's a fool for letting a farfetched tradition of quest dictate his life, but you think we're *both* idiotic."

"You are both young." Sage smiled. "It is hard to avoid being idiotic when one can move as fast and as heedlessly as the young."

Alison lifted her shredded skirt. "Come on, help me out of this. I'm tired of playing prom queen. And let's visit the Littlelost in the morning. Maybe some of us are finding Desmeyne hospitable. I hope so."

23

Rowan strode through Desmeyne's empty, night-shadowed halls, hardly noting that no one witnessed his passage. After the unfair, yet public disgrace in the Arcade, he should cringe to encounter another Desmeynian and credit his good luck that he did not.

Instead, the embarrassment of possibly meeting those who had seen him disgraced was as nothing when compared to his present confusion. The Taliswoman's overture was unlike anything Rowan had confronted before—even ever-agreeable Triss had only responded to the pace of his needs, not set a rhythm of her own.

He felt violated. His vow of celibacy had been mocked. It did not help that the shock of Alison's advances had caused an unwanted response greater than any felt in his year of abstinence. He strode faster, hoping to outpace himself.

His father would no doubt counsel him that such outrages must be expected at the hands of a disrespectful foreigner, but Rowan could hardly confess this further failing. His pace slowed; he realized that he had nowhere to go for sympathy, and no one to whom he would care to confide his confusion.

He paused, looking up and down the hall before he noticed a small door in the polished marble wall. It led, he recalled, to a cramped stairway that expanded into a secluded bubble of balcony under the curve of the roof—an entry for the crystal polishers, who clung to a network of spun-glass walkways when maintaining the translucent ceiling's clarity.

The stair and the nook had been a childhood retreat that no adult had penetrated. Rowan made his way toward it, suddenly fearing observation, and pushed his adult frame through the familiar, albeit now cramped, doorway. It was like traversing some shrunken birth canal, taking that coiled staircase. Head bowed, shoulders pressing the polished walls, he wondered if he would be wedged within and would starve in turning, a fittingly ludicrous end for a disgraced Firemayne.

But a last curl of the stairway expelled him into a tiny chamber with crystal ceiling and walls, whose solid floor concealed his presence from any in the hallway below . . . just as it had hidden Darnellyne's presence until now.

He jerked back to leave, knocking his head on the low ceiling. Darnellyne turned from watching the pale winter mountain slopes high above them.

"Rowan! Are you still—?"

"I never was," he grumbled, "but I'm leaving. You shouldn't be here alone with me—or alone at all. If the Firemayne knew that the Cup-maiden was unaccompanied and with a man, you would be in deeper disgrace than myself."

"No, don't leave." She seemed bemused. "We both used to shelter here from childhood wounds and worries. I . . . I did not want to confront the Lofts yet."

"You were wise," he admitted ruefully.

"Rowan, are you well?"

"How can I be? According to the Firemayne, I have been drunk, derelict of duty and a public nuisance, as well as a displaced Cupbearer. But why do you wish to avoid the Lofts?"

Her ever-elusive eyes grew evasive behind her veil. Rowan realized that all the women of Desmeyne were milky of gaze, their regard always filtered through a translucent medium. Alison's eyes, on the other hand, blended blue and green, like water. He had seen that quite clearly at the last, if nothing else.

"Darnellyne?" he demanded. Her averted face and hidden hands annoyed him for some reason. "Why are you here?"

"It was my refuge as well as yours! Or have you forgotten?" she burst out with almost childlike resentment.

"I'd forgotten. We shared imagined wounds once. What is yours now?"

"You can ask? You, who left me standing idly on the floor to join the Taliswoman's strange, unpartnered dance?"

"I . . . abandoned you?" Rowan had been so embroiled in the marvel and peril of twain-sight that he had failed to see how his actions might look to a single-viewed onlooker. "Darnellyne . . .

Alison had unwittingly crossed into a Crux-place, led there by Dearth itself. We were all in terrible danger. Had I not brought her the Cup, the Crux would have swallowed her whole, and perhaps Desmeyne as well."

"You left me, before all who cared to see! No one has ever treated a Cup-maiden so."

"Have I ever denied you any courtesy, however elaborate?"

"No, but once is enough."

"You do not believe that I had to do as I did, that I *saw* something no one else did?"

She paused. "I have not considered your cause enough to decide whether I believe you or not, or whether I care to bother."

The little-girl hurt in her voice reached him. Rowan was amazed to realize how much he had distanced himself from her. "Dar," he said, using their child-name, "I am sorry if I violated courtesy, but I saw a danger more dire than a Harrow-worm. I had to meet it."

"Why would you care if Alison was lost to the Crux and Dearth? Would you not become Cupbearer then, by default?"

"I do not know. One thing she says is true: She won the Cup. To desert the Cupbearer, even to the results of her own folly, is to lay open our honor, our land, our very lives, to a darker peril than any we now face. Do you not think so, Dar?"

"I suppose I do." The veiled eyes consulted him quickly. "But I would rather not think so when my pride is at stake."

He laughed, released from his own moodiness. "Do you think that the Crux's deepest threat is to our pride? Then it has won a great battle today—I disgraced, and you abandoned."

"Small misfortunes, you are right. But what has the Taliswoman lost by this?"

Rowan eyes narrowed. "We have lost countenance, but she has lost . . . confidence. Her bold toast drew the attention of the Crux. She has opened doors she did not know existed, just as she finds closed doors that challenge her inmost perceptions." Understanding glimmered at the edges of his mind. "She even—" But he could not confess that disturbing incident to Darnellyne, not to anyone. "Besides," he consoled her, as he had often done when they were young, "I am the one truly disgraced. You are merely my victim and have everyone's sympathy."

"Oh, Rowan." She shook her head and collapsed into her robes.

He was alarmed, but Darnellyne had merely sunk to the floor, her knees drawn up, to better fit the cozy space. He sat beside her, feeling the cold stone through his thin banqueting velvets, his long legs angled to meet the encroaching walls.

She sighed again. "It is so hard, being a lady of the Lofts. I long for the old days when we could be ourselves, not the roles assigned us. Perhaps that is why the Taliswoman both intrigues and angers me."

"You call her by the name she gave herself tonight; you accept that she is what she claims, even if her boldness draws our enemies?"

"You said it yourself: She holds the Cup. And, Rowan, is it true? You *saw* two places at once, *were* in two places at once? You have truly been granted the ancient gift of the Firemaynes? Your father will forgive you instantly when he hears of this."

"A high price to pay for a father's regard, Dar. The place I glimpsed was barren beyond our grasp of emptiness. The force there, the *dis*regard of all we hold dear, shook earth and sky, blasted to bits all we believe."

"Worse than the Earth-Eaters' rumored black realms?"

"Worse than anything I have seen in my journeys."

"And she has opened the door to it? And also to your new powers, perhaps?"

"Perhaps." He had not thought of that before. "Do you forgive me, at least? I have become so coiled in my own affairs that I have not looked to the needs of others. Perhaps my loss of the Cup is punishment for that oversight. Perhaps my twain-sight is, too."

Darnellyne's hands brushed at the cloud of her face-veil, though she seemed unaware of the gesture. "They would read further scandal into our talking here. You had best find your father and explain yourself. If it helps, tell him that I accept your actions. A Loftlady's opinions are worth little, but—"

"But you are not a Loftlady." He lifted her hand to his lips.

"You are the Cup-maiden, and you are Dar, whom I still know well."

"Rowan, I am *glad* that you are not Cupbearer yet!"

"But that would permit us to marry and be friends again."

"Would it? Would we ever be as we were in the Webbings? They have taken that from us, as they took us from the Webbings—you to the knife, I to the Lofts and the veil. I would rather *do* than be, but we have been given no choice."

"You do not wish to wed me?"

"I must wed the man in Desmeyne who is first to claim the Cup. Or I must never wed, if no one of Desmeyne ever wins the Cup. I must live with whatever fate decrees. I have no preferences, since any eventuality must be accepted. But the current Cupbearer is a woman, and thus my fate is delayed."

"If you wed *me,* you will not have to submit to a random fate," he argued. "I will save you from it." She was silent. "And I had not considered Alison as a forestaller," Rowan admitted. "There is an advantage in that. If I have not resolved your fate, neither have I given you up to another."

Again Darnellyne was silent, and he had much to think on himself. He rose supplely, at last ready to confront his father. Darnellyne remained seated, her delicate gown draping the cold stone floor, only the swell of her breasts beneath the jeweled fretwork revealing her as other than child.

Rowan experienced another strange dislocation, in time rather than in place. His emotions teetered wildly between that not-so-distant ignorance of childhood and the assumption of their eventual union. Dar's fiercely guarded innocence was the price and the reward. Where did the Taliswoman's kiss fit into such a foregone conclusion? Where did the dark land of Dearth lie when it did not overlay Desmeyne?

As he navigated the narrow staircase, Rowan felt cramped in mind as well as in body. He now had answers with which to divert his father's wrath, but he also harbored many questions he could ask no one but himself.

24

"Alison!"

The calls came from everywhere—high above, below, to either side—from the myriad young faces peering at her from every direction.

The Webbings lay deep in Desmeyne, embedded in the mountain's solid rock pelvis. Yet shafts of daylight from skylights high above pierced the murk.

Endless time had eaten the earth's unseen bones into a fanciful skeleton—a stranded whale turned mammoth jungle gym. Nets strung everywhere served as beds, hammocks, ladders and safety nets for the dozens of youngsters who capered over the rigging and the rocks. The Webbing's air was warm and still, a deep breath the mountain held until it became a life force unto itself. Mosses the color of agates—green, gold, blue, white and beige—carpeted the cavern floor, as tactile as crew cuts.

Yet it was a somber environment, bereft of grass, sunshine and—Alison noticed the obvious lack for the first time—animal life. Grief for Rambeau swelled within her. Then an avalanche of Littlelost rushed down the ropes, burying her regret in their own recognition and relief.

"We thought that was Beau from way up there," Faun's piping voice accused as he pointed behind her.

Alison turned. Sage wore her springtime guise in order to visit the Webbings, and it gleamed pearl-white in the filtered light.

"It's only a Loftlady," Pickle decided with the disdain of the myopic leading the blind.

Alison leaned close to whisper, "It's Sage in disguise," and pressed a cautioning finger to her lips, with a look at the vigilant Webbing grayladies.

Littlelost eyes widened; then they all nodded in swift conspiracy, giggling at the idea of fooling their overseers.

"How do you like it here?" Alison asked in a normal tone.

Silence didn't speak well for the forthcoming answer.

"There's nothing to *do* here," Rime complained, twisting nervous fingers into her skirt folds.

That's how the grayladies of Desmeyne had signaled the children's sex: through the simple device of clothing the girls in skirts over trousers like the boys'. Alison was happy to have the distinction made clear for her: Camay, Rime and Faun were girls, Twist and Pickle, boys. The faces around her were so clean without their woodland patina that they gleamed fungus-pale in the eternal twilight.

Sage floated forward. "Such handsome, pretty ones." Her sugary trill abashed the Littlelost into silence. "Is there nothing you like about the Webbings?"

"Well, we eat something other than pomma," Pickle admitted.

"And we do not work." Faun displayed palms as white and soft as her face.

"But we don't like the others," Camay said.

Alison smiled to see that the littlest hadn't grown; already the forest trek seemed half a lifetime away. She bent to heft Camay onto the crook of one arm. "Why don't you like the others?"

"They tried to take my scarf," Pickle said grimly. Despite this, his head was still tightly turbaned; he'd found a clean, if faded, blue brocade cloth—instead of a dirty rag—with which to hide his hair.

Alison smiled again. Obviously, Pickle had managed this change of headgear in his own, fiercely secret way. She was sure that no Webbing graylady had seen or touched Pickle's hair any more than she had. Kids could stoutly cling to trivial symbols of independence; just so had she once collected Indian artifacts on the Island and resisted all parental demands to give them up. "Is that the only reason you don't like them?"

"They don't like us," Pickle said.

"Maybe when you come to know one another better—"

"They talk about us," Faun said. "They say we cannot stay together. Pickle and Rime will be the first to be sent away."

"Surely not; you've all just arrived. Sent where?"

"To the Lofts," Faun said with a tomboyish sneer.

"Or to the Men's Quarters," Twist put in ominously.

"Oh, but that won't be for a while yet." Alison turned to Sage for reassurance. "Will it?"

Sage shrugged prettily. It was amazing that the same person could act so radically different at a different age. It was also annoying. Alison had come to rely on Sage for authoritative declarations on the ways of Veil, not for girlish Desmeynian indecision. Camay was staring in wonder at the erstwhile old woman and plucking shyly at the petals of Sage's skirt. Still, the guise permitted Sage to leave the Lofts unquestioned, and Alison sorely needed the advice of a neutral observer.

Besides being clean, the Littlelost looked well and oddly older. Their eyes no longer showed the haunted, hard-bitten tension that survival in the outer world had required. In its place, though, had crept a wary self-defense, a subdued slyness, that was equally childlike and therefore also disturbing.

"Did Rambeau c-c-come back?" Twist wanted to know.

Alison shook her head. "Not yet."

"I m-m-miss the Slinkers."

"They would eat you if they could!" Faun warned.

"I miss them," Twist repeated firmly.

"I miss Beau, too," Alison admitted, resting her hand on the boy's shoulder.

He stroked her burgundy velvet sleeve as if it were fur. Alison couldn't tolerate wearing the women's hampering clothing ordinarily, so Darnellyne had presented her this morning with some Desmeynian boys' castoff finery. Alison liked it very much since it was bright, loose and luxurious.

"They watch us. All the time," Twist said. "Like the Takers."

"Who watches you?"

"The big ones, and the others like ourselves but not like ourselves," he added darkly. "We feel alone, although we have never been among so many."

"That's because you're in a new place," Alison said. "I feel the same way."

"You will visit us again?" taciturn Rime asked with anxious eyes.

"Of course. And you can visit me. Surely the children here are not always confined to the Webbings?"

"Yes, but only until the time of the Parting," Sage put in.

"When is that?"

"Twelve, at the latest," she answered.

"Wasn't Rowan . . . removed at the age of eleven?"

"Ah, but that was necessity, or so I hear in the Lofts. His brother had vanished."

"From this very placc, Sage? You've heard some story?"

"They believe the Earth-Eaters took him. Lorn Firemayne, he was called, the eldest of two."

"Takers?" Faun's eyes grew as round as blue marbles. "They have Takers here, too?"

Pickle clapped his hands to his turban to protect it from any possible Takers in the vicinity.

"Not now," Alison reassured them. "Years ago. Sage didn't mean to alarm you." At the mention of the Firemayne family history, a graylady had drawn closer, the better to eavesdrop. Alison hugged the Littlelost—my, they smelled clean—and wished them good-bye. "Go on, then. Play while you can. We'll see each other again soon, I promise."

The Littlelost, unused to inaction, scattered with undiminished energy as Alison steered Sage to a caveside niche where no graylady could eavesdrop.

The young-old Sage watched with a thoughtful expression as the children clambered up the rigging. "The Lofts are rich with rumor, as you would discover if you spent more time there. Not all children go smoothly from the Webbings to Men's Quarters or Lofts. I have heard of some young women, girls, who secretly carry unsanctioned children—children who will be cursed with dreadful birth-banes for their mothers' violation of custom—and grow terrified of the consequences. It is said they go quite mad and run to the Deeps beneath Desmeyne before their wrong is discovered. They, too, are never seen again. Or their children. But this is only whispered in the Lofts."

"How awful! And the Loftladies think that such poor girls are taken by Earth-Eaters?"

Sage shrugged. "That was likely how it happened with Lorn

Firemayne, a boy of twelve, simply gone one day, and Rowan rushed from the Webbings for the ritual Carving, to take upon himself the scars meant for his elder brother."

Alison nodded in sympathy. "That's how I lost my sister; she dropped out of sight, only before my eyes. So the Firemayne decided to mark Rowan early as the Cup-quester in his brother's place before he, too, could vanish. The ways of Desmeyne can be cruel."

"The ways of Veil can be crueler," Sage said cryptically, "as you would know if your Littlelost could talk freely."

"They are not *mine,*" Alison objected.

"You have brought them here. The consequences are your responsibility."

"Sage, you grow gloomy while revisiting your youth. The Littlelost are doing fine, as you can see."

"What of their freedom?"

"What of the danger outside?"

"Danger is everywhere. It simply wears a friendlier face in civilized places."

"If I'm not satisfied that they will thrive here, I'll take them with me when I leave."

"Which will be—?"

"Soon, Sage, soon." Alison led the way to the endless flights of stairs to the formal halls, and they began climbing.

Sunlight sliced through the rock-crystal walls' striations like lasers, casting phantom prison bars of light along the stone floors. Beyond the walls, the mountain's green skirts swirled into the deep valley below, while veils of snow obscured the peaks. The passage, sun-brightened and warmed, seemed an enchanted place, perfect for a thousand cats to drowse in until they droned like honey bees. But no cats lived here. There was not even one white dog. Alison meditated on Sage's question.

When *would* she leave? And where would she go? Being caretaker of an artifact that opened up dread vistas was not sufficient cause to remain in Desmeyne, and keeping the Cup in front of Rowan was cruel now that Alison understood his inbred need for it, especially given the loss of his brother. For Rowan, to possess the Cup would be to reclaim yet another lost talisman of childhood as well as the exquisite Darnellyne, whom Alison actually liked in an edgy, distant way.

"I think I'll follow your example," she concluded aloud. "I'll explore Veil. You say the Cup is the key to my way home. Even if I don't find a way to my own world, perhaps I can find ways to serve this one. I'm used to working in my world. And you're right, I have much to learn from the Cup."

Sage, whose visage had faded and wrinkled as they entered the Lofts, smiled with her old cynicism. "Most generous, Taliswoman. But will Rowan let you leave with the Cup? Will he allow you to be so generous—elsewhere?"

"He can't stop me, Sage."

They dodged the veils serving as Alison's chamber door, receiving a pale-chiffon buffeting in turn. Within the rooms, Sage again stood dumpy and garbed in shades of beige, like a sack of potatoes.

"I am weary," the old woman said. "It becomes ever more arduous to evoke my younger self, and that self becomes more simplistic with every donning. Did you notice?"

"Indeed I did. I find you more interesting as is."

"That is why I allowed myself to age. No one expects anything of me, so I can be whatever I wish to be."

"Don't I have that option, too?" Alison demanded.

"No." Sage's features settled into a parched plain of wrinkles again. "I doubt that you do."

The Firemayne ordered Alison to his rooms after the dinner hour. She was tired of the Lofts anyway, wearied of the ladies' constant dovelike cooing in their niches, the endless rustle of their artificial garb, the furtive glimmer of face powders, the everlasting serenity.

She assumed that Rowan would be present at the interview, and felt nervous at confronting him. To admit that the Cup plus Char had affected her behavior wouldn't be easy. She brought the Cup, not daring to leave it and not willing to be without it.

The borrowed Desmeynian shirt fell open to the waist, of course, so she had accepted Darnellyne's offer of a brooch with which to fasten it. After clasping it tightly at the throat and hesitating, she pinned it shut beneath her scars. Her fingertips read the braille of the radiating bas relief. She was coming to regard it as decorative rather than defacing. Didn't certain primitive tribes consider scarification beautiful? Every accident of life could be taken as either a disaster or an ultimate asset. Had it taken Rowan and Desmeyne to finally teach her to accept herself as she was?

Alison smiled at herself in the mirror, at her retro-Sassoon chin-length bob and clean-boned, unmade-up face, at the runic-looking scar, at the shirt that looked liked something funky off the Paris runways, at the golden sun of Darnellyne's pin setting amid crenellations of burgundy velvet. Who at the *Express-Messenger* would believe this?

She took the Cup from its honorary position on the sidetable and headed out to find the Men's Quarters. But she had no sooner descended the Loft's cursive stairways and entered the common hall than a page boy approached, bowed and led her down the hall. He was wearing a shirt of brocaded velvet far grander than hers.

Judging from what she had seen, many of the children of Desmeyne became servants. Then, as personal freedom went, Desmeyne wasn't much improvement over the Takers and the etherion swamps for the free-wheeling Littlelost she'd come to know in the forest. It seemed that children didn't count for much here, Alison mused, unless they were useful for small tasks—but that was often true of children in her world, too.

As they entered the Men's Quarters, Alison noticed several men wearing short broadswords, not the dainty rapiers one would naturally pair with their elegant dress. She suddenly could imagine Rowan's chagrin at being ceremonially denied his length of steel—as well as the exercise of less visible accoutrements of manhood.

Father and son awaited her in the Firemayne's room. The tapestries were drawn across the windows, so that none of Desmeyne's airy brightness penetrated the smoke-threaded air. The Firemaynes worked at the huge table, their hands pinning the curling ends of parchment maps to the polished wooden surface.

They straightened in unconscious unison at Alison's entrance. Next to each other, their resemblance was unmistakable; father and son were battle-worn broadsword and fresh-sheathed rapier, both forged from the same family steel. Alison suspected that they would resent the similarity were it pointed out to them.

"You have brought the Cup?" the elder Firemayne asked.

"Of course." Alison produced it from the ample folds of her blouson shirt. The Firemayne's lips tightened at this presumably cavalier method of transport, but Alison was tired of lugging her backpack everywhere she went.

She set the Cup softly on the vermilion-colored wood, which glimmered in the firelight like a bloody pond. They stared at it for a moment; then the Firemayne spoke gruffly: "We wish to use it to bind our broken land. Have you any objection?"

"None. I'd like to see it put to benign use."

"The Cup will allow itself to be used only for good," Rowan put in as if by rote.

"Then its effects last night must have had some hidden benefits," Alison said ruefully.

Rowan frowned. "Effects. Last night? I told my father that I had drunk naught from it, save for the sip after I became . . . ill."

"You soon became better, didn't you?" She turned to the Firemayne. "I assume that the Cup will restore your fields?"

"That is our hope. We have never had it within our . . . reach before, so we have never tried this proposal. We ask you to accompany us outside Desmeyne tomorrow. You must handle the Cup, or it will not work."

Alison merely nodded. "There's more you wish to say." She watched the pair exchange unready glances. "So tell me."

"We have not decided—" Rowan began.

"You have not consented. *I* have decided," the Firemayne snapped. "These maps"— his tapping finger made the parchments rattle in the quiet chamber —"they are fey, two-edged things long in Desmeynian possession. Their designs change . . . as suits some spell within the vellum, or within the inks, or the hand of the ancient chart-maker. Yet as unreliable as they may be, it is high time—now that the Cup, which is the key to every quest, is in our hands—to search for the first forbidden seat of the elements. This quest will help us begin creating the great amulet to protect us all: the Heart of Earth. Or so the parchments indicate."

"But the Cup is in *my* hands," Alison pointed out.

"Exactly why you must accompany Rowan on the journey to Heart of Earth."

"Or Rowan must accompany *me,*" she said. For this she got a hot-tempered look from her proposed escort.

"She is foreign to our ways, Father." Rowan focused all of his energy on the older man. "Cup or not, she will only hinder any quest. It is too soon to search for the Heart of Earth. Wait a year and—"

"—and you will win the Cup?" The Firemayne sighed impatiently. "My son, we cannot wait so much as a month. The Harrow-worms have wracked our food supply. The Earth-Eaters now refuse to trade with us, even at the most outrageous prices. Desmeyne is turning from our stronghold into our cage. I admit that you are right: We must go into the wider world and find these places of power to forge the amulet that was foretold."

"What do you get from the Earth-Eaters in trade?" Alison asked.

"Treasures of the earth. Gems and rare powders. Metals for our weapons. The Earth-Eaters stand between us and our free use of the buried treasure beneath Desmeyne."

"And what is this amulet you mean to create?" she asked further.

"We seek a Cup of Clay wherein beats the Heart of Earth." The Firemayne's earnest tone forestalled skepticism. "This, say the parchment-border rimes, is the first step of a journey to the world's four corners, where each of the four elements—earth, wind, fire and water—have their seat. And from a handful of human clay, there will begin to form the salvation of all the people and things of Veil." His blunt finger skimmed a line of symbols more runes than letters. Rowan translated the words they represented:

He who is first shall be at last
Unmade in the Crux of a too-present past.
The heart that is human, born to Dearth,
Will beat for all time in an armor of earth.

Alison shivered. "Melancholy sentiments. Do you know what that means?"

"No," Rowan admitted blithely. "Otherwise, we would not need to seek the Heart of Earth. Something there will make these lines clear."

"You mean that you're predisposed to see meaning in whatever you encounter. You are your own prophesy."

Rowan rounded angrily on his father. "I told you. She believes in nothing."

"I don't believe in 'nothing'; I believe in the testimony of my mind and senses, the evidence of things seen, if you will." She indicated the parchments. "Not migratory maps. I believe in what's before my eyes—like an encapsulated city enforcing the strict segregation of all its people: by age, by gender, by role in life—man, woman, child, servant, farmer, lord, heir. A city enforcing a strange isolationism that's reinforced by a lot of arcane mumbo jumbo."

"Arcane mumbo jumbo?" The Firemayne echoed numbly.

Rowan had grown more used to her. "Encapsulated? Segregation? Isolationism?" he asked.

Alison put her hands to her head. "I forget. Oh, jeez. Look. You keep everyone in his or her own separate place. You keep men and women from learning to know each other, and children from seeing their parents on an everyday basis. That isolates you from each other, as your mountain city isolates you from the other people of Veil. You say a worldwide danger nibbles at your villages and fields and cities and people? Then you must go forth. Unite. Meet each other. Mingle. Work together. Care about one another."

Rowan seemed to have absorbed her message. "What about the arcane mumbo jumbo?"

"I meant . . . I'm not sure that quests or talismans or amulets are what you really need. You need each other more than you need objects with reputed magical powers."

"What of the Cup?" the Firemayne demanded. "Surely you have felt its power by now."

"So far," Alison said ruefully, "the strongest demonstration of the Cup's power would prevent the slaughter of a lot of rhinoceros and other unfortunate creatures reputed to enhance virility in my world. But an aphrodisiac isn't a priority at home, what with a worldwide fatal venereal disease around."

Father and son knit their brows in tandem. "Aphrodisiac?" muttered the elder. "Priority?"

"Rhinoceros?" Rowan repeated. "Venereal—?"

"I'm saying that the Cup has powers I can't deny, but I don't see how to use them for any real overall good. Yet. And a rhinoceros is like a, uh, a Harrow-worm, only my people worry about losing such extravagant creatures, because they don't damage us unless provoked. Venereal disease—that's what happens because we *don't* strictly segregate men and women; it's an illness that eats away the victims because of the acts between men and women that create children."

"Horrible!" The Firemayne regarded his son in shock. "I have never heard of such an abomination! Becoming diseased from the coming together of men and women? Your world is dire, beyond anything I have known in Veil."

She nodded. "I know. I wish I *could* cure all my world's ills with a Cup of Earth. But to answer your first question—so far, the Cup's effects seem trivial." She eyed Rowan. Their mutual experience on the dance floor had nothing to do with the Cup's powers, did it? She certainly wasn't prepared to admit that to them here and now. "Oh, drinking from it can give me a feeling of well-being, or cure a burn, but there are plants in Island-Not, the aloe vera is one, that can do as much."

"You speak of the foul, scented things that grow wild, that this self-called wisewoman—this Sage—gathers?" the Firemayne asked. "Rowan has told me of her dubious teas."

"Herbs and flowers grow in every world. How can you in Veil reject the natural wonders all around you—flowers, herbs, Littlelost, for heaven's sake!—yet cling to extravagant tales, magical devices and outlandish quests?"

"There are more 'natural' woes than natural wonders in Veil," Rowan put in. "You have seen little here, yet you stand ready to say much about how we should do things."

"Well, I'm not going to see more if it involves farfetched quests to mythical pulse points on metamorphosizing maps—oh, don't ask me to explain that. You use funny words I can't figure out, too—like Womb-bat and Earth-Eaters. I'll take the Cup to the fields—the damage there is clear—but the only other mission I'll accept in Veil is that of finding my way back to Island-Not or, failing that, of finding out what Veil—the world out there—is really all about, and that includes the mysterious Crux."

"You cannot take the Cup from Veil," Rowan said icily, "or all quests will come to a standstill and the blight that nibbles at our borders will bite deep into our heartlands, whether you believe in it or not."

Alison stepped to the table and reclaimed the Cup, suddenly fearing that she dare not trust Rowan to respect her title to it. Too much was at stake.

As her fingers wrapped around the stem, silence gripped the chamber. The fireplace's panting flames ceased swaying. Whatever interior air had been stirring . . . stopped. Even breath seemed arduous to draw. In the gray fringes of her sight, something moved, something born of grayness, something that engendered it. A streak of blue laser light waved like a conductor's baton over the crumpled parchments, while an odd, high-pitched hum buzzed the massive tabletop.

No human eye could follow the swift traceries of motion the alien wand executed. It seemed a fractured length of lightning, some glimpsed fire phenomenon, a flash out of an eye's far corner, an electric needle stitching faster than sound. A smell of charred wood blanketed the chamber, mingling with a fog that deepened the encroaching grayness. The three stood frozen and confused, their senses dithering between too many vague phenomena that were too agile to be pinned down.

Alison shook herself loose first, perhaps because only she realized that the odor was not that of singed wood, but of burning paper! She reached past the Firemayne's immobile bulk and placed the Cup of Earth atop the maps.

A shock as from a power line pulsed up her arm. The Cup hissed in her grip and grew violently hot. The veins within the stone expanded into blue lightning and snapped sparks as red as blood drops into the smog-choked chamber. All of Alison's instincts urged her to release the Cup, the conduit of the current searing at her fingertips. Her native stubbornness told her another story. Something didn't want the Cup on the table; something wanted to make her let go.

Opposition only intensified her commitment; reporters were like that. Her knuckles tightened around the stem of the Cup; then she curled her other hand over the first to keep the vessel planted firmly. The more physical force she used to keep the Cup in contact with the table, the more the mystical current bucked against her efforts. The maps began bouncing up and down on the wood as the table began jolting to the power of unseen forces.

Rowan cast himself full-length across the table to keep the maps from flying off. Blue light sizzled around his form, just as it haloed the Cup and Alison's clasped hands. The Firemayne drew his short sword and speared the maps to the redwood with a *thwunck* that burst like a firecracker on their ears in the oxygen-starved room.

They couldn't talk, could barely breathe. Cool blue light licked at their figures, engulfing everything in the chamber—even the fire—except for the fringes of gray miasma thickening around them.

There was nothing in the Cup to hurl at the attacker this time; it was empty, and had been so since the night before. Alison believed in it enough to wish that this were not so; to wish that it contained a full measure of battery acid that would cut through the fog like a lethal headlight, that would duel the wands of blue light and eat them to smithereens.

There was nothing in the Cup but their expectations of it.

Alison decided that the Cupbearer had better acquire some higher expectations in a hurry, and thought of the sun-rinsed, blooming meadows that the folk of Veil feared, and of wild, growing green things in Keewatin and Kennebunkport and Kentucky. She pictured the Cup pouring new growth onto the furrowed land, saw vermicellis of grass seeded among the dry clods, saw buds shooting up, saw her fingers—her fingers!—as gnarled roots haloed with root hairs, brown and contorted, saw moss gloving her arms to the elbows and violets among the green . . . she was turning into a bloody tree, rooted, channeling some verdant power into *herself!*

Rowan was still a human paperweight atop the threatened maps, the blue wands beating at his back, his father's sword an azure taper of burning steel.

Then the wands and the fog snapped out, like a light. Air flowed into the room, almost undetectable zephyrs fanning their faces: their own breaths, operative again.

A vegetable array heaped from the Cup and over Alison's arms to the edge-charred maps: leaves, roots, buds, pods, fruit. Her arms and hands felt too stiff to move, but she gradually released the Cup and drew her limbs—limbs, literally?—through the loose vegetation. Except for clinging petals and blades of grass, her hands were fine. She laughed uneasily and dusted her palms together, shaking leaves from her sleeves and skin, brushing granules of dirt to the tabletop.

A full portion of near-black soil that smelled as rich as Colombian coffee filled the Cup.

The Firemayne yanked back his sword, wrinkling his nose. "Foul, Earth-Eater scents," he complained of the Cup's new contents. "The dark clouds and the lightning smelled better."

Rowan was shuffling the parchments as if they were an exceptionally bad hand of oversized cards. "The edges are eaten, and charred spots obscure parts of the middle, but they are mostly intact."

"Did you see what came?" his father asked.

Rowan nodded soberly. "Not what—who. Crux-masters. Six of them, three to attack the maps and three to crush us against their foul presence. Yet they were not here, but in a strange place. Not land, not air."

Alison had a question of her own for Rowan's twain-sight. "What did you see when I . . . when the Cup began growing things?"

"Nothing. You were here, as solid as we. Plants began spewing from the Cup. You must have felt the outpouring. It was like a regurgitation of the hidden fruits of earth."

Alison shook her head. He'd know more about regurgitation of hidden fruits than she. "How do you think it happened?"

Rowan regarded the dirt-filled Cup with respectful distaste. "The Cup must have acted against the forces that attacked us. We had discussed taking it to heal the fields. Perhaps it *knew* what it would be called upon to do tomorrow and the shock of assault unleashed its powers prematurely."

Alison had trouble believing that. Instead, she was convinced that her mind had prodded the Cup to produce life. She had *felt* her hands and arms as roots and trunk, as conduits for a greening tide that would no more be stemmed than a birth contraction.

It had been terrifying, as if she were as much a part of mindless generation as these Crux-masters were wedded to deliberate destruction, as if blind, undead earth were a force as powerful as greed or evil intent, waiting to be drawn upon by the right person, the right . . . Taliswoman.

"Tomorrow," the Firemayne was saying sternly. "The fields."

She nodded, unable to speak, unable to confess her new, visceral fear of what, minutes before, she had intended to dismiss as a simple, symbolic, possibly stupid ceremony.

25

Twenty armed men accompanied the two Firemaynes and Alison to the fields the next day. Despite the armed guard, the grim, hopeful farmers who awaited them with their scythes and hoes, despite the Cupful of magical earth, she felt unprotected: She was the only woman.

Normally, open air would have energized her. Now she felt uneasy at being under the naked sky. Anything could dive down from it—etherion coursers near the woods, many-legged Wombbats near the cliffs. No wonder Rowan had been such a tense traveling companion; he was defying his upbringing to explore the wider world beyond Desmeyne.

Certainly Alison would never have normally found a ring of frosting-dusted mountains, a shining sun and miles of upturned earth the sinister sight it was now.

Where Harrow-worms had delved, the dirt had heaved into ten-foot-high molehills on either side. For contrast, miniature writhing garden-sized slugs still glimmered mother-of-pearl-pale in the roiled clods. An overbearing stench of dead and dying things hung palpably on the air, an unseen cloud accosting every nose. Between the trenches, the low, bushy crops looked withered from sheer proximity to such ruin.

"What must I do?" Alison asked.

"We are uncertain," Rowan admitted. "We are as unused as you to the ways of wielding the Cup. We have brought mildwater from one of the wells that refresh Desmeyne; the wells spring from far below the Earth-Eaters' impure domain."

"Sounds good to me." Alison examined the Cup bowl and its soil. She raised her eyebrows.

"Perhaps if you pour this water from the Cup onto the broken furrows— The Cup seems to work best when it dispenses liquid."

Rowan looked away, obviously remembering the time they'd both sipped Char from the Cup with such unexpected results.

Then he nodded to a man carrying an oilskin sack that looked like a full-blown bagpipe with only one pipe. As the water-bearer approached, Rowan advised Alison, "You had better scale the mound before you fill the Cup."

Alison eyed the formidable slope of unstable dirt, then her hand that held the Cup. Rowan extended his hand to pull her up the incline, and the water-bearer followed. Their boot heels sank into the reeking loam, but they managed to wade their way upward.

Atop the mound, Alison had a clear view of the Earth-Eaters' hole-pocked cliff opposite. The armed men in the field faced this quiet expanse watchfully.

"The Womb-bats, like the one that attacked us before, will not likely come," Rowan said. Wind riffled his hair into a horizontal torch-flame. "We also have archers, so there is little to fear."

"Can't you make that 'nothing'?" she asked as the man poured water atop the dirt in the Cup. Black mud boiled over like hot coffee and she jerked the Cup from the stream.

Then Alison edged down the trench into the inner scar of the battered earth, some ten feet deep. A charnel odor resonated between the banks of soil. She prayed she'd see no disinterred bodies on her journey, then started along the twenty-foot-wide furrow, dribbling the Cup's contents onto the dirt behind her.

"Is not some invocation called for?" Rowan shouted from the top of the bank.

"Listen," she yelled back, "I'm thinking beautiful thoughts; if anything can make this experiment fly, that will." But despite her light answer, she called on the power of positive thinking. She called upon the Cup's undeniable—and unpredictable—talents.

And her thoughts were, if not beautiful, at least nostalgic. The earthy smell smacked of games of hide-and-seek under the Island's sumac bushes, ruddy with autumn. She would burrow among penicillin-scented ferns fanning low and luxuriant, hoping that Petey and Demaris wouldn't find her, her heart thumping against the ground like a drumstick about to betray her hiding place.

Somehow they always caught her, because they were older, because they knew the game and she didn't, and because what she considered clever and safe was never quite good enough. When she was finally wise enough to outsmart them, her brother and sister had outgrown the childish games she had mastered and had gone on to other, more mysterious games she had yet to imagine.

Alison realized that her fingers were stiffening, that the Cup had grown colder than chilled aluminum in her grasp. Dirt etched her knuckles. As she looked down, she suffered a weird hallucination—or maybe it was a touch of Rowan's twain-sight. Her wrists were bound with tough, viney cords; shadowed flowers trailed from her hands like a funereal bridal bouquet.

She was more than ordinarily cold in the channel between the mounds, the valley of the shadow of death. Or Dearth. The Cup dribbled its liquid bounty on the ground behind her, but before her lay only an endless trench of destruction, like those in World War I, with bare hands and booted feet and helmets like coconut shells protruding from the broken ground. . . .

"Alison!"

The voice was like an echo in the mountains—faint and irrelevant. She was Here, and it was There.

"Alison!"

She looked up. Rowan sprinted along the sunlit bank, glittering like a rooster with a red comb.

"Come up!" he shouted, gesturing broadly. "Come up!"

She dug her boots into the sloping dirt, but it shifted beneath her weight with the eagerness of quicksand. She pedaled upward; then Rowan leaned down to grab her hands and the Cup as one unit, urging speed. Her wrists strained against their living bonds of vine, and her ears roared with the effort of climbing as if an artillery shell whined overhead. Then the roar became a rushing at her feet. The dirt melted to mud and was sucked away like sand by the tide.

Rowan strengthened his two-fisted grasp and yanked her atop the bank hard enough that her arm joints ground against their sockets.

"Hey!" she protested once she stood on the bank.

He pointed behind her. She turned to look.

The former trench boiled with black water that ate away at the mounded dirt they stood on, forcing them to retreat to level ground beyond the mound. They watched; within a few minutes, where the field had been riven as by a bomb furrow, there now lay a flat expanse of mud. Behind them, the farmers moved forward with seed. The sowers nodded their exuberance. Sunlight would soon dry up the excess water, leaving the fields tendable again. Alison examined her wrists. The illusion of dead-weed shackles had peeled away. Apparently freeing the land required some symbolic binding. No gain without loss, however temporary.

The Firemayne smiled for the first time in two days and nodded to the next dry furrow.

And so it went, the mystical ceremony—muddy work one step ahead of a rising water table. The Cup's pristine surface vanished under a diarrhea of dirt. Alison was wet, cold and muddy to her hips, Rowan no better, for his length and youth made him the obvious choice to serve as a rescue rope.

But when the sun impaled itself on a mountain peak and the air turned as cool as the mud bathing Alison from sole to rib cage, the lands below Desmeyne had lost their worried frown of furrows, and fragile green stems poked through the muck. Alison sneezed, surprised that she wasn't too exhausted to do so.

"Enough," the Firemayne declared in the slanting sun's rays. "In a few weeks' time, tubers will grow that we can process to feed Desmeyne for months. Now we will return to Desmeyne and discuss the next business."

Alison silently clutched the Cup to her bosom like a poultice. Rowan, as weary as she, kept silent, too. They plodded across the fields.

"Maybe this Heart of Earth," she suggested to Rowan on the long, inclined road back to the city, "will bestow its talisman on you, making you the equal of any Cupbearer."

"I am the equal of any Cupbearer now," he retorted.

"You know what I mean," Alison mumbled through her fatigue. She longed for a hot Desmeynian bath in a deep pewter tub. "You've already tapped long-lost powers of twain-sight. Even I can't see your Crux-people. You don't need me now; I and the Cup can go our own way. When you find the Heart of Earth, which sounds damnably distant, it'll probably be time for the next Wellsunging, and I'll still have laryngitis from this joyous tramp through the mud, so you can easily capture the Cup and go on to make many, many happy returns to Questland. And I can . . . try to get home."

They were almost at the gate to Desmeyne by the time Alison finished her speech.

"You are weary, Taliswoman," the Firemayne commented with uncharacteristic mildness. "You do not know of what you speak. We will discuss this again in a day or two. Now my son and I will leave you to rest."

They all left—guards, Firemaynes, the stray farmers who'd accompanied the party back to Desmeyne. The exercise's ending felt as anticlimactic as one curtain call too many at a play that hasn't quite gone over. Alison staggered down the exalted halls, dripping mud on the glorious inlaid floors.

She slunk into the Lofts like a bad smell, and by now the drying mud did indeed perfume her vicinity. The Cup looked as if it had been hammered from tin by an excessively filthy smith. She tromped past the niches, hearing the eternal flutterings silence as if she had drawn a rank shade over the gleaming apertures.

Sage received her in youthful guise, which depressed Alison further. "Sage, I need a bath; I need to look at a real human being, not a glamour-puss—"

"Shhh!" Sage admonished. "You'll frighten the little one." Sage had never referred to the Littlelost so tenderly. "I donned my younger self so I could bring her in when she came cringing to the Lofts."

"She? Camay?"

Alison bent to the huddle of rich brocades near Sage's bare feet and drew back the cloths. Fold after fold collapsed before she glimpsed the child's curled form. Camay stirred kittenwise, still asleep but basking in the sensed attention.

"Let her rest," Alison urged, compassion in her voice.

Sage bent to shake the child awake. "You must hear the tale from the source, the better to judge it."

Alison sank back on her stinking boot heels. "Sage, I can barely tell black from white at the moment." But her objection was stifled by the way Camay awoke: first with sleepy contentment, then with rising alarm as she recognized the two around her, the rich chambers of the Loft. Whimpering, the child crawled like an infant to bury her face in Alison's mud-caked shirt.

"What's the matter? Camay? Sage, for heaven's sake—"

Camay's panting little body was expelling words now, almost singly. "They have . . . locked . . . the others . . . up."

"Locked up? All the Littlelost? But not you? Where?"

Unshed tears magnified Camay's eyes to pale star sapphires; her mouth puckered with distress. "In a bad place in the Webbings. Like the Taker's wagon, dark and hard."

"This is ridiculous!" Alison eyed Sage. "Why?"

Sage bent fluidly on her twenty-year-old knees to whisper in the child's ear. "Tell her what you told me."

"They said . . . because they were sleeping together."

"Oh, honestly!" Alison rose abruptly, fatigue vanquished by anger. "The Littlelost always pile together like a litter of puppies. This notion of everything in its place and a place for everything gets carried too far here, to the point of hysteria." She caught Camay's clean little hand in her own filthy one. "Come on, we'll go to the Webbings and straighten this out."

"I should come." Sage spoke with the firmness of her elder self. It did not sit well with her ravishing features.

"As you like. But I don't need a backup for this one."

Sage nodded obliquely. Alison knew she was coming and was tempted to challenge the wisewoman's air of restrained knowledge, but Camay yawned beside her. Well, she'd settle this latest ludicrosity, tuck Camay in with the only family she'd ever known, and then return to the Lofts for bath and bed . . . in that order.

Her slow-moving brain was still forming the agenda when they wound down the last stone stairs to the Webbings. A line of the grim grayladies awaited them; actually, it was a cluster of consulting grayladies, who broke into battle formation when they saw the trio coming.

One stepped to the fore, a woman with a face as plain as rain. "She ran away," she accused, staring harshly at Camay.

Alison wasn't about to have these colorless nursemaids turn the tables on her. "She was driven away. What is this incredible story about the other Littlelost being locked up?"

Bland-eyed, their silence was an admission.

"So it's true? You've actually confined them someplace?" Alison looked beyond them into the faintly lit Webbings, where children had settled into sleep as separate as stars. "The Littlelost are a community, a *family;* they're not used to an adult-ruled life. You can't separate them just because they don't suit your socialization plans."

"This is what the child told you?" the headwoman asked.

"Yes. And I demand to see her friends. At once!"

A long pausc. Then the gray woman smiled maliciously. "Very well, Taliswoman."

The women led them lower than Alison would have believed possible. The stairs narrowed and turned tighter.

"Where are we going?" Alison asked.

"You wished to see your Littlelost," one graylady spat back with uncharacteristic passion.

It was so creepy down here that Alison wondered if the grayladies were escapees from some horror movie and about to do them in. She remembered that Lorn had vanished from the Webbings; could the feared Earth-Eaters have somehow gnawed through solid rock to burst in and snatch that heir of Desmeyne?

These dungeonlike depths encouraged dark thoughts. Alison twitched with impatience to think of the Littlelost being so badly treated in the very place she herself had urged on them as a haven.

A sound like screeching bats shrilled in the stairwell, and then they rounded a bend to enter a large cave where phosphorescent water in the center of the floor made the walls look like they were sweating rainbows. The whole place glowed with eerie neon arcs of light. And when she spied the cages swinging from the constantly protesting chains—several of them holding faces she knew, faces that recognized her with suppressed cries of her name—she turned on their grim guides.

"What kind of people keep such a place as this?"

"The occasional Earth-Eater has intruded on our privacy in decades past," the spokeswoman answered. "We had to confine them."

So the dreaded Earth-Eaters were small? "But *children,* for heaven's sake! You confine your children here?"

Several grayladies had the grace to shuffle at Alison's incredulity. A carnival of phosphorescent color from the damp walls cast itself on the perfect gray scrim of their garb and faces, turning them into serious-featured clowns on whom brightness seemed unnatural and sinister.

"Not our children," one answered sharply.

"Not . . . children," the spokeswoman echoed even more grimly.

Alison tried to be conciliatory. "Some of them may be a tad old for the Webbings, but they've been abandoned and on their own for who-knows-how-many-years. You have to go back and treat them like younger children before you can expect them to act their ages. I know their litterlike sleeping behavior might seem babyish to you, but not all cultures are as disciplined as Desmeyne, thank God, and—"

The women were watching her curiously.

"We did not intervene," one said, "because they were sleeping as one, but because they were sleeping as two."

"What difference does that make?"

"Together," the spokeswoman muttered in a contralto undertone, "as is done in Desmeyne only between wedded men and women."

Alison couldn't seem to understand. She turned to Sage to find a look of sad comprehension on those exquisite features. "As between wedded men and women," she repeated, to give her weary brain time to compute a new formula. "I suppose you mean that when Rowan and Darnellyne wed, they would live together, or at least sleep together?"

Alison turned to see the Littlelost in the gently swaying cages. The chains' shrill grinding clawed at her nerves. She saw the same small, fiercely independent faces—minus dirt—that she had pulled from the Takers' wagon on the Island that was now Island-Not.

The graylady pointed. "That one—and that one. We thought it best to restrain them all, except the littlest, who may not be tainted."

"Tainted?" Alison eyed those named: Twist and Faun. "Sleeping together?"

"We d-d-did in the woods!" Twist burst out defiantly.

"Not with me around!" Alison insisted.

"With the Takers," Faun said as softly as ever.

"While you were with the Takers or . . . with the Takers themselves?" Eyes dropped for the first time.

"Some Takers—" Faun began.

"Oh, my God." Alison sank down upon a stone. "Not . . . all of you? Not Camay?"

"Camay is too new," Pickle said with disdain.

Alison protectively clasped Camay's slender frame to her side, clutching this frail straw of a child as one normalcy in a world turned devastatingly upside down. Now she could understand the grayladies' actions.

"You will no longer urge us to release them, I hope," one graylady said a bit smugly.

"Yes, I will! One doesn't lock up the victims, and these children are not to blame for their behavior. Better to lock up the Takers and the world that lets Littlelost wander unclaimed, unsought. These are *your* children, don't you see that?"

"Our children lie safe in the Webbings—or did until you brought these unholy creatures here."

Alison sighed. "I can't say that what happened is wholesome, but it is understandable. We must decide what to do, but not until the morning, when I can talk to—" She stopped. Who could she talk to about such a shocking subject? Who in Desmeyne was not already prejudiced against the Littlelost to the point of callousness? Who would help her help them?

"They stay here, where we know what they are doing, or are not doing," the spokeswoman declared. "And the littlest—"

"Stays with me." Alison pulled Camay closer, then got up on one knee. It seemed that her joints would buckle if she tried to use them, but she finally stood, weary beyond exhaustion. She glanced up to the cages. "I'll come back for you tomorrow, I promise. I'll figure out what to do. Maybe we'll leave, I don't know. Tomorrow."

The gleaming walls left an afterglow of spots before her eyes all the way up the dark stairs. The journey back to the Lofts was an out-of-focus pan on a screen as dead and ashen as the Webbings grayladies' garb.

Sage briskly donned her old self once the niche curtains had wafted shut behind them. She bedded Camay again and went to draw Alison's bath. Alone later, Alison peeled her stiff clothing from her even stiffer body. Her thoughts were less easy to doff. She sank into the hip-high tub, clothing her naked self in a sheath of hot, limpid water that offered little of the usual comfort. The earth that had seeped through her clothing muddied the crystalline water, and nothing could rinse her mind free of the knowledge that clouded it.

In the foul, cage-hung cave beneath the artificial wonder of Desmeyne, Alison had confronted an evil more powerful than even the dread lord, Dearth, a land viler than the poisoned realm she had glimpsed through Rowan's twain-sight and the eternal pull of evil on her sleeve.

But all of that alien, exotic evil was as nothing next to the evidence, the results, of twisted human lust for the rare innocence of a child's mind, body and soul. She'd seen and listened to the evidence of that before.

26

Alison awoke to the sound of arguing in the Lofts. For a moment, the lacy train of sleep clouded her memory. Then the previous night's shocks descended upon her like a stone.

She batted her way out of the richly embroidered covers and past sheer bedcurtains and quickly donned her jeans and shirt. She wanted no . . . taint . . . of Desmeynian thought or clothing to muffle her intentions, or her obligations.

Beyond the veils of Alison's niche, the raised voices lifted and fell as rhythmically as a teeter-totter, no doubt heard all through the Lofts. Alison was startled to identify the combatants: Darnellyne and Rowan.

"I cannot tell you, Dar," he was repeating. "I am here on another matter, and that involves her alone."

"If she carries the Cup, nothing involves her alone, and I notice that you are ever nearby."

"If she carries the Cup, I must guard it."

"To preserve it for your next attempt."

"For my next attempt."

"Rowan, should you not forget this vain striving? Lorn is lost already—"

"That had nothing to do with the quest for the Cup—"

"You cannot know that it did not."

"I know that my brother's loss so long ago has no bearing on my own pilgrimages."

"Had he not been lost, you would have stayed in Desmeyne."

"Had he not been lost, you would have faced the prospect of wedding him, and you and Lorn were never friends as we are."

"He was older than we, Rowan; you and I were even better friends with each other than either of us was with Lorn."

"Then why are we quarreling?"

"Because some terrible trouble is knocking at Desmeyne's

gate. I hear it even in the silence of the night. If only there was something that I could do—"

"Wait. And do nothing," he returned. "That is how you can offer the greatest service. I cannot understand, Dar; you were always the most dutiful daughter of Desmeyne. Now . . ."

From her doorway, Alison studied them—a couple from an Arthurian illustration, perhaps: young, sincere, pleasant to look at, if not easy to listen to at the moment.

"What am I doing here?" she muttered aloud. This lovely scene struck her as more unreal than Dearth's desolate realm. The Littlelost. . . .

The quarrelers sensed her presence at the same moment; they stopped their debate and spun to regard her.

Rowan looked relieved to see her. "You must accompany me to the Men's Quarters. We have much to discuss with the Firemayne."

Alison nodded, not wanting to risk an argument with either Desmeynian. She was well aware of Darnellyne's anxious—almost envious—gaze that followed her as she accompanied Rowan into the passage. Amused, she watched him eye her old clothes askance, trying to read what had made her dress in her former way again.

"I have changed my mind," he announced en route.

"About what?"

"My father is right—"

"Well, he'll be happy at least."

"I must seek the Heart of Earth as soon as possible. You and the Cup must accompany me."

"What changed your mind?"

Rowan's long strides shortened. "I saw yesterday how the Cup responded to your possession."

"It almost tried to drown me."

He shook his head, his hair shimmering in the strong light lancing through the curved crystal walls. "A light tongue cannot disguise the heavy matters we face. Taliswoman you are, for what remains of the year, yet Desmeyne—or Veil—cannot wait so much as another week before taking action."

"Terrific! But I'm not going anywhere with you, Rowan. I said so yesterday, and I most certainly say so today."

He stopped and turned to confront her, looking most heroic and gloriously dense. "You would refuse the role you claimed before all Desmeyne but two nights ago?"

"I had another role before I ever possessed the Cup, Rowan. You told me yourself in the woods that it was upon my head."

He studied her bare brown hair, seeking that of which she spoke. Alison explained. "You said that I was responsible for them, remember? Now I really have something to be responsible for."

"Them? Who?"

"The Littlelost. You haven't heard?"

Rowan waved his hand, a gesture that set his supple sleeve in graceful motion. "That. Of course. It is known throughout Desmeyne. You have much to answer for in bringing this abomination among us. But that is unimportant now. The quest for the Heart of Earth is paramount. Do you realize that no one has ever before found this mythical place? That no one has any notion where it lies? We may have to search until the next Wellsunging to find it."

"You're wrong. The Littlelost *are* important—to me and to all of you, if Desmeynians had any sense. What's the matter with you people? These children have been forced to labor in body and soul for brutish men, with no one to care for them. Haven't you come to know them even a little? You're hell-bent on seeking out mystical sites to counter the distant evil you fear, when another evil stands before you. Can't you try a little understanding? Ask me to go root out the Takers, close down the etherion pits and rescue all the Littlelost! That I might do. But I'm afraid that this Heart of Earth is just another illusion to distract your minds from the true ills of Veil."

"Did you not see the Cup heal the gashed earth yesterday? Have you not stood in Dearth's desolate halls? Can you still deny the reality of the Cup's power, of my wondrous, newfound twainsight? The Littlelost were ever a debased breed; they have only once more proven it here."

Alison sighed impatiently. "What will you do with them?"

"I do not know!" He saw that she would answer his questions

only if he satisfied hers, and sighed. He was too action-oriented to enjoy argument for the sake of it. "They must be kept apart, of course."

"In *cages?*"

"A temporary necessity. We are not cruel. We will give them a separate area of some sort. Perhaps, with time, they can be persuaded to abandon their . . . habits. I have argued this position against my father's inclination to release them to the forest, for I know you fear that they are not safe there."

"So your 'enlightened' solution is to create even more prisoners within Desmeyne!"

"What do you mean? We keep no prisoners."

"What about yourselves? You're kept from each other and from everyone outside Desmeyne. Stranded on such an island of your own kind that you learn nothing of others, or of yourselves. Sorry, but that's not what I want for the Littlelost!"

"The others will either loose them there"—he pointed to the landscape beyond the crystal walls—"or bind them here. At least I offer them some chance for reform."

Alison nodded reluctantly. "Listen, so much damage has been done to these children by the Takers—and now you Desmeynians do more in rejecting them. I have to get them out of those awful cages—now! Even these miserable Earth-Eaters can't be debased enough to deserve that."

She glanced, troubled, to the repaired fields that she had transformed the day before. Perhaps the Littlelost's psyches could be smoothed in a similar fashion. Perhaps the Cup—

Some motion on the deserted flatlands between Desmeyne and the Earth-Eaters' sinister cliff caught her eye. Beau and the wolves? If she had Beau again, trekking through Veil wouldn't seem so daunting. She'd take the Littlelost and leave Desmeyne this instant.

Alison pressed against the wavy quartz, trying to see precisely through the clouded medium. She spread her hands on the pebbled surface, surprised by its intense cold emanating through her fingertips. What moved—she saw now—was not wolves, but something two-legged.

"Oh, no! The Littlelost! They're leaving Desmeyne on their own!"

Rowan rushed to stare through the crystal. "They cannot be. They are confined."

"Not now!" She couldn't help grinning at the Littlelosts' reviving independence.

Something else struck Rowan. "On that ground, they are meat for the Earth-Eaters. They will be taken by their Womb-bats."

"No! We made it through."

"By repelling the Womb-bat. They are not armed. And your Slinkers saved us; they are not here now."

"No, they aren't. And—oh, no. Camay!"

Alison raced back up the hall, her boots thudding on the stones. She streaked through the Lofts, shadow-boxed past the entrapping veils to her chamber to find only Sage there, looking puzzled. "Camay! Is she here?"

Sage leveled a slightly palsied finger to the bundle huddled before the fading fire.

Alison slid to her knees beside it and began drawing back petals of brocade. The fabric gave way like unraveling origami, and gave way and gave way. . . . There was nothing—no one—within. Alison settled onto her heels in sick silence.

"What is it?" Sage asked.

"The other Littlelost have gone, escaped. They must have collected Camay first. Oh, Sage, what have I done by bringing them here? They were just children—"

"Were they?" Sage's voice was sharply seasoned with her wisewoman tone.

Alison searched her face but found only the fierce, uncompromising expression Eli Ravenhare had donned when he expected her to think something out for herself.

She sighed again, in no mood for thinking too hard about anything, least of all about these wronged children. "Rowan was right, you were right: I'm responsible for bringing them here to their ruin."

"How have they been ruined? Did the corruption the Desmeynians despise begin here?"

"No, but it was discovered here. And the Littlelost have run away."

"Did they run when you first found them?"

"Heavens, no. I had to pry them from the innards of that filthy Taker wagon. They'd barely talk, and were so sullen and dirt-caked you might have mistaken them for a set of overgrown walking toadstools."

"So they were dirty and dispirited?"

"Yes."

"And they had accepted their bondage?"

"I suppose so."

Sage's smile ironed the wrinkles into her skin. "Now they have not."

Alison sat up straighter. "That's right. They escaped those awful cages somehow and slipped through the city gate. But if they came here to collect Camay, why didn't they awaken me, tell me, take me with them?"

"Because they are again fearful and ashamed, when they had been growing secure and proud. They may not understand the uproar, but they understand that they are not understood. They dare not trust anyone not of themselves."

Alison nodded numbly and reached for her backpack. "And now they are bound toward the territory of those whom the Desmeynians fear almost more than Dearth itself. The Earth-Eaters."

Her hands patted the empty cloths, the nearby carpeting. The gun. She'd take the gun and go after them. One hand snagged a familiar strap and she dragged the backpack over the floor to her. In her haste, the pack overturned and its contents tumbled out. Just as hastily, she began stuffing them back willy-nilly—and froze in dismay when a viscous sticky substance coated her fingers. Her irreplacable contact lens fluid! Spilled. Alison stared at the cornucopia of belongings blurring before her eyes. Ridiculous! A serious loss, but nothing to get teary over. Water might do for a while, as it did in an emergency . . . except she *wasn't* teary. She seized the fluid bottle to read the directions. She couldn't focus on the tiny print. Come to think of it, everything had been a little hazy since the trek to the brink of Desmeyne: the splotchy forms behind the

Earth-Eaters' cliff-wall, the perpetual soft-focus view through Desmeyne's rock-crystal walls.

She picked up the contact case, opened it and popped out her right lens. Squinting with one eye, then the other, she tried reading the minuscule print again. Yes! Out with the other lens. Yes, she did see better without them, as if the world around her had been rinsed clean. Ever since . . . since she had washed the lenses in the Cup, she hadn't seen as well *with* the lenses. She saw better with*out* now. Wow. Alison wanted to jump up and shout, "I can see, I can see!" But she didn't know how to explain it to Sage. Or herself. And now wasn't the time to contemplate minor miracles.

Sage appeared before her with the Cup. "You cannot leave this."

"Oh—thanks, Sage." She took it with real reverence. Maybe it *was* a Grail. Just holding it was soothing. Alison stowed the vessel in her pack with her suddenly irrelevant contact lenses, then rose and embraced the old woman. Words were unneeded. She ran from the Lofts and returned to the hall with a new confidence. Rowan still watched the Littlelost growing small and wee. If only there were a balloon man here, a false Wizard of Oz, Alison thought impulsively, who could hand the fleeing Littlelost hope and helium on a string—or give them wings of etherion that would waft them over the distance between Desmeyne and the cliff-side entrance to the Earth-Eaters' realm.

They were hardly visible now, dust motes driven across the land. Alison found this defection even crueler than Beau's loss.

"I have to go after them," she told Rowan, turning to do just that.

He caught her shoulders in hands of steel. "You forget; you cannot!"

"You forget that I can." Her voice was as thin and lethal as a garrote at his throat.

Rowan stiffened, knowing that she would resist physically if necessary, and would likely be as successful as before. "I must stop you," he warned.

She shook her head, easing the backpack off her shoulder to the floor. Their bodies instinctively began circling in the measured orbits that would permit the most surprising and swift action and reaction. She had already angled him to face the window-wall of bright light.

Rowan wasn't afraid. Alison had to credit him for that. And then his face changed to unguarded consternation. He was staring at something behind her. She was certain that he was truly shocked.

She turned. A distant, dark cloud hung smoglike over the cliff face. Then it dropped, an attacking, wide-winged Womb-bat troop diving at Littlelost crawling across the naked land like bugs. Shadow after shadow swooped down from the ebony mouths of the rock wall to engulf the valley floor below.

The Womb-bats lifted in swift unison, pale prey wriggling in their thin, prehensile legs. Their leathery wings beat as they rose against the sky like those elusive floaters that hover at the edges of clear vision. Then they glided the downdraft back into their unholy caverns.

It transpired so silently, an aerial ballet choreographed for a slow-motion nature program on PBS. Nature in the raw. The eaters and the eaten. Alison's hands pounded the cold, clear stone, but the blows were soundless, impotent.

"They took them alive." Rowan's voice sounded distant behind her. She heard a strange shuffle over the floor, then whirled to see that he had retrieved her pack.

"I have the Cup," he said carefully, his eyes narrowed with a resolute cunning she'd not seen in them before.

Heart pounding with panic, Alison grew cunning in return. "So what? I'm not supposed to care about the bloody Cup, remember!"

"If you want to find the Littlelost, the Cup you call bloody may aid you. But you will have it back only if you accompany me to the Heart of Earth. Now we will finish what we began, and go speak with my father."

27

"So this is the strange woman you found in the wildwood, Rowan."

To Alison, the "strange woman" was the sole occupant of the Firemayne's quarters who lifted her outermost veils and approached, the better to study Alison.

Rowan made immediate obeisance, setting down Alison's pack as he dropped to one knee. The woman acknowledged his gesture by lightly passing her hand over his bowed head but never paused in gazing at the object of her fascination.

Alison noticed that the woman's hand bore no metallic talons as it rested on the burnished pillow of Rowan's hair. This woman also radiated a self-confidence so far unglimpsed in a woman of Desmeyne.

"My mother, Zormond," Rowan explained shortly as he rose. And he was a little ruddy in the face. Why, he was embarrassed to be caught being mothered, especially in front of her. Poor baby. Alison grinned to herself.

Zormond's eyes smiled through the sheer web of her inner veil. "You need no introduction," she said. "Alison of Island-Not presented herself most memorably the other evening."

Caught off balance, Alison only nodded. She hadn't encountered subtlety in Desmeyne until now, but perhaps that was because she hadn't yet met a woman of such position and experience. At first glance, Rowan's mother looked hardly older than Darnellyne. The tendrils of hair that escaped her headdress were the same sallow blond common to the Lofts. Red hair was obviously a Firemayne genetic trait, unique to the family males.

"You also," Zormond went on, "continue to cause memorable events in our city. The Firemayne is in the Deeps, tracing the means of these most . . . adult . . . children's escape. Nor has so much scandal touched our city until your arrival, Taliswoman."

Rowan's mother tasted her words as if they were delicacies fraught with some lethal risk, and thus even more tasty.

"Alison is a stranger to our ways," Rowan explained. "I warned her from the first that the Littlelost were treacherous, though even I did not suspect the depth of their degradation."

"The Littlelost aren't to blame for their behavior," Alison said hotly. "They were cast out into the world with no one to care how they lived or into whose hands they fell. They've been abused too long to understand what they've done that you consider wrong."

"Strange ways indeed pertain in Island-Not," Zormond murmured, but feeling flared in her eyes. Alison could have sworn it was guilt. "Why do you claim that these Littlelost were cast out into the world?"

"They must have been! No responsible parent would allow children so young to simply wander off and vanish. They can't remember their past, not even the circumstances of their casting-out, so they must have been terribly young at the time. If humane people had taken them in, instead of fearing and shunning them, they would never have been exposed to the Takers . . . and . . . to what they obviously have been."

Zormond turned her back on Alison and her son. A thread of unease wove through the silken shuttle of her voice. "I have never considered the Littlelost in that manner, as someone's long-separated children. My own lost son—"

Rowan interrupted, his voice husky. "Lorn was taken by the Earth-Eaters and is beyond retrieval. They have a great appetite for children; we know that from Desmeynian history."

"Yet still we trade with them!" His mother's tone betrayed an emotional intensity Alison had seldom glimpsed in Desmeyne.

"We must." Alison almost missed the matching strain in Rowan's voice. "We sit upon mountains of piled wealth, yet are barred from delving into it by the Earth-Eaters' presence." He glanced at Alison. "Lorn is . . . was . . . the only Desmeynian they have taken unwilling in decades. It will not happen again."

Unbelieving, Alison broke into the charged exchange between mother and son. "Rowan, are you implying that there are, were, Desmeynians who were given *willingly* to the Earth-Eaters?"

The pair turned from each other, as if fearing to read any reflection of Alison's question in the other's eyes. Rowan finally answered. "I do not know why I put it that way."

Zormond lifted her oddly etherion-naked hand as though to distance herself from the issue. "The Earth-Eaters have a great appetite for children. We used to place those infants burdened beyond survival by some terrible birth-bane in the deepest cellars of Desmeyne. They always . . . disappeared."

"No wonder the Earth-Eaters are loathsome to you." Alison mulled over another disturbing implication. "But why establish the Webbings so deep within the mountains, then? Why set those awful cages even deeper? And why imprison the Littlelost there, closer to the Earth-Eaters?"

Rowan stirred impatiently. "There was no danger. We have not even seen an Earth-Eater in decades. They do not violate our places any longer."

"Then how do you trade with them?"

"We use . . . agents."

"Agents? And where does this trading take place?"

"The agents' identity is secret, the Firemayne's special knowledge. And they trade in the Deeps of Desmeyne, down below, where the Earth-Eaters' domain abuts ours. But that is not your concern. Even I do not know the details."

Alison eyed Zormond, who was looking away. "You know nothing of these agents, either?" Zormond shook her head so violently that Alison pressed forward on another front. "And is it possible that Lorn might have survived? That Lorn, too, might be merely . . . lost, like these other little ones?"

"No!" Rowan roared, resembling a bloody-maned lion in the firelight, his hands fisted into blunt but powerful paws.

Poor Rowan! Preserving an identity based on his brother's loss and destruction was not easy. His rejection of Alison's probing questions had propelled him closer to his mother and away from the backpack. Alison darted stealthily forward to snag her pack while he was busy mouthing the party line to his mother, and most of all, to himself.

"The Littlelost are as alien to us as the Earth-Eaters," he was insisting. "Many inhabitants of Veil are fell or bizarre. You have observed that yourself, Taliswoman. We must not attempt to see ourselves in such monstrous kinds. We must keep separate from them."

Zormond wrung her hands, as no other Loftlady could do without clawing herself with her decorative hand armor. "I have not forgotten Lorn as well as I might have," she admitted. "Now this matter of the Littlelost, seeing them, and the new thought that Lorn might yet live, in some unknown condition, and even perhaps"—she bit her polished lips—"his sister . . ." She stopped suddenly.

"Sister?" Alison asked sharply.

Rowan stood thunderstruck. "Sister?" he muttered. "There is no sister. You are distraught, Mother. These Littlelost have upset you." He cast Alison an accusing glance—then really saw her, standing with Cup in hand, an expression of cool determination on her face.

"Sister," Alison repeated narrowly. "What sister?"

Zormond's intertwined hands trembled. "Rowan is right. The excitement of the past hours has agitated me. I mis-spoke."

"No, Rowan, stay put," Alison warned, watching muscles tense in his arms and neck as he prepared to lunge for the Cup. "I'll smash this precious chalice of yours to smithereens on the stone floor if you provoke me."

A lengthening silence showed the power of her unmeant threat. Rowan stood frozen in indecision. Zormond sank onto the Firemayne's massive chair. Her apparent weakness drew Rowan's eyes.

"I have questions," Alison said, edging away from Rowan just in case, "that need answering." She approached the veiled woman sitting upright in that ungiving chair. Zormond's eyes were lowered, but her paper-pale lips had tensed. "There *was* a sister, one that even Rowan was unaware of. A girl-child of yours. An older—oldest-born. Where is she?"

"No!" Zormond looked only at Rowan. "No, no . . . never was. She . . . she . . . no sister. Never. Never born."

Alison lifted the Cup, the gesture threatening to dash it down.

"No!" Zormond rose as if jerked upright by a force outside herself. "Everything Firemayne is for the Cup. It must be so. It is tradition. It is foretold that a Firemayne will give his heart and soul to save the roots and roof of Veil. 'His,' not hers. His. Firemaynes for generations have lived by this obligation and this honor. If you destroy the Cup, you crush decades of sacrifice, and future decades of hope. You must not!"

Rowan, too, wheeled on Alison. "I will destroy you if you harm the vessel," he promised with the cold control of arrested fury, the sincere vow of vengeance. "No creature of Veil, no honorable Cupbearer, no man, could contemplate such perfidy."

"I am no creature of Veil and no man, but the Taliswoman, and I have more questions." Still, Alison's voice wavered a little, and she backed against the wall, too near the beating flames for comfort. Yet here she had a wide enough field of vision to watch both mother and son. "Zormond. What of the sister? Rowan's sister. Lorn's sister."

"There is none!" Rowan roared again.

"Be still," Alison cautioned. "You might startle me into a clumsy gesture." She regarded Zormond once more. "Tell me of the sister."

The woman drove her fingers under the veils, as if to cover or claw out her eyes. Rowan tensed at that driven, innately feral gesture, as did Alison. Neither dared move.

When Zormond spoke, it was from behind the more opaque veil of her own flesh and blood. Her voice was a soft monotone, evoked from some far, untouchable place in her mind. "It has always been done so in Desmeyne, and especially among Firemaynes. The eldest son must undertake to win the Cup and make the quests to the Four Quarters. There must be no question that his existence fulfills the prophesy. That is why if Lorn—but, no, Rowan is right. Lorn does not live. *She* does not live."

"She?" For the first time, Rowan sounded shaken.

Zormond's lips parted to emit a sigh as poignant as a smothered sob. "Some are unkindly born, with birth-banes too terrible to permit. Some are kindly born, but ahead of their times. An eldest son who is the eldest of all is always a good omen for every family of Desmeyne, in honor of the Firemayne prophecy. So those who come too early or too damaged are left in the Deeps and never seen again. The Earth-Eaters have a great appetite for children."

Alison lowered the Cup, overcome with horror. Rowan's rage had paled to ashes, and she felt as limp as when she had listened to the grueling testimony in the Blue Earth child-abuse trial a world away in Minneapolis: afraid of what it would be, afraid it was all too true.

The long silence forced Alison to again ask the unthinkable. "Are they dead? When you abandon them, are they dead?"

Zormond's veiled head shook, so slightly it seemed to shimmer. "I do not know. We of the Lofts do not ask dangerous questions. It is the custom. The Earth-Eaters have a great appetite for children."

Slowly, painfully, Rowan went down on one knee again—not in respect, Alison saw, but simply because his mind could not absorb what he had heard and still exert the energy to support him upright. "Why did my father not tell me of my sister, of the custom?"

His mother spoke softly, her son's distress distracting her from her own long-buried pain. "You are not wed, are not about to be wed. There was no need."

"So when Darnellyne and I wed, we will surrender any . . . inappropriate offspring to the Deeps? How can you be so certain we will do this terrible thing?"

"Because *I* did it," his mother answered in a voice of beaten metal.

Rowan suddenly sprang up and struck at Alison like ninja-lightning, snatching the Cup from her grasp. He lifted it high above his head and turned toward the fire.

"Rowan! No!" This genuine danger to the Cup gripped Alison by the throat. It tore at something deep within her, as if he threatened an unseen, unsensed child. Her own threat, she had known, was empty. This one was not. "Rowan . . . no. The Cup is not the cause, but the excuse. You mustn't destroy it. You are bound within it until you grow beyond it. You'll destroy yourself. You'll harm Desmeyne—and me. Please." Her argument was instinctive, but rang true. Where had these convictions come from, she wondered. Panic still clutched her throat.

Her intervention worked. He turned on her with focused rage. "You have called the Cup 'bloody' from the first, but I never suspected how truly you spoke. If this other, this unheard-of sister, was *given,* how can I believe that my brother Lorn was truly taken and not given also? There is too much I have not been told. I would never have sought something I would attain at the cost of my brother's life. Nothing thus . . . tainted . . . can produce good."

"The Cup *can* be used for good, Rowan." Now she spoke the convictions of a dedicated reporter. "It healed the fields. It may help heal the Littlelost, and they need our help! We can't save those lost years or decades, but we can still aid those in danger of the same fate today. The Littlelost—those we know, those who trusted us to shelter them, no matter the wrongs they suffered or the wrongs they came to accept. Now will you help me find a way to the Earth-Eaters?"

He lowered his arm at last and thrust the Cup at her brusquely, almost carelessly. He did not look at his mother. "Yes, Taliswoman. I will."

28

"A spoon!" the Firemayne raged. He stood red-eyed with weary anger among the empty cages in the dark belly of the mountain, his guards standing useless on the perimeter. The spoon in his fist had been painstakingly honed against the cage bars into a rapier-pointed lock pick, then passed from cage to cage.

Here in the torch-lit dark, the iron cages swinging above like unmelodious bells, Alison felt preversely proud of the vanished Littlelost. Sage was right; they were no longer passengers riding the coattails of their own fate, mere Taker-bait. They were survivors. Thus far. . . .

Alison kept silent; it was Rowan's turn to ask questions now. She withdrew into herself as he tried to lead his unwilling father into sharing information they needed. She didn't envy him the task.

And while she waited, she totaled her own losses: her sister Demaris, drowned so young; her brother Peter, semi-estranged since college, and she hardly knew why; Eli, missing; Beau, running wild, running away. And now the Littlelost, fleeing into the maws of the Womb-bats. She pursued her dark thoughts while near her, Firemaynes argued like mumbled thunder.

Rowan observed Alison's mental absence with approval. His father would not abet an enterprise that he knew to be the notion of a foreign female, no matter how many Cups she carried. So he led the Firemayne into the dark near the cave wall for a masculine conference.

"I must know more of our intercourse with the Earth-Eaters," he told his father.

"Why? Such matters are reserved to the office, not fitting for the heir to it. It is forbidden to tell you more than you need know, and until my death, you will not be the Firemayne."

"I must know more," Rowan repeated. "She"—he nodded

toward Alison, standing among the silently tolling cages—"has forced troubling admissions from my mother, among them that we trade with the Earth-Eaters. Is it true?"

"Zormond told you that?" The Firemayne shifted uneasily. "She should not have, but one cannot keep everything from a woman, especially from a wife of many years. Yes, we trade. How do you think we get the rarities of earth we do have? The Earth-Eaters occupy caverns not only beneath this mountain, but under our farmlands and the neighboring peaks. If we want anything from the earth below, we trade."

"And what of these agents?"

The Firemayne scowled. "That, too? The Earth-Eaters have chosen agents of an . . . an odd nature. But the dealings have been satisfactory, if unpleasant."

"Who speaks for us in this? Have you ever seen an Earth-eater?"

"Myself, and a few chosen men who accompany me to make certain that no treachery occurs. And no Desmeynian has seen an Earth-Eater, though we've glimpsed their creatures, the Wombbats, and have seen the Harrow-worms' tracks."

"And the meeting ground lies here in the Deeps, where Desmeyne's lowest caverns and the Earth-Eaters' realm meet?"

"Enough, boy!"

"One more question. *What* do we give the Earth-Eaters?"

"Why—" The Firemayne seemed at a loss for words. "Food from our fields—"

"The Earth-Eaters consume dirt. I have been told that since I was a lad."

"Not . . . always. Cloths, we do trade cloth. And . . . candles. For the darkness."

"Father," Rowan rebuked, "even we use the glowing stones from the Deeps to light some of our lamps. Surely the Earth-Eaters have even more such rocks in their domain. Is there not something else we trade, something secretly left for them?"

"What has Zormond been telling you?" The Firemayne had become pale, guarded.

Rowan fixed his eyes on his father's face as if to read every nuance there. "She spoke of the . . . the babes we leave in the Deeps for the Earth-Eaters. Of my lost sister, your daughter—"

"I have no daughter! One who is Earth-Eaten is gone as if it had never been." The Firemayne nervously eyed Alison. "How did this so-called Taliswoman so undermine Zormond's good sense as to make her speak of such things?"

"By dint of half-guesses and endless questions. She has a gift for such pestering. Alison is determined to breech the Earth-Eaters' realm to rescue the Littlelost, whom we saw snatched from the plain by Womb-bats."

"Taken? You are sure?"

"By my own eyes, I swear."

"Earth-Eaters and Littlelost grow overbold together: One flees openly and the other takes even more openly." The Firemayne's heavy features curdled. "But what concern of yours are these missing abominations? Good riddance, say I and all Desmeynians. We were divided on what to do with them, in any case."

"True. But the woman is adamant, and she carries the Cup."

"More ill luck. The honor of our line, the fate of Desmeyne, ride with you, Rowan. If you cannot eventually win the Cup, you will not wed Darnellyne, and she risks remaining Cup-maiden forever. You would not want that."

"I may have no right to seek the Cup. I may not be the heir. From what my mother said, other Firemaynes may survive."

"I tell you, no! *Gone is gone.* It has ever been so. You should not have known this until you were ready to accept my office. You would have had the necessary wisdom to conceal it then. You must forget it, as Zormond has done all these years."

"Has she forgotten, Father? Or simply remembered to pretend to forget? But I must know the truth about the Earth-Eaters before the woman and I penetrate their domain; you must show me where you trade. An entry must lie there—"

"Risk yourself to rescue these worthless Littlelost? No. I will tell you no more of the Earth-Eaters! It takes a hoary head to hold such truth, a man whose age has dampened the Firemayne passions."

"My passions have been well dampened by my abstinence for the sake of the Cup," Rowan snapped.

His father shook his head. "Rowan, you do not even suspect the burden of full knowledge. It is something you will earn in time, not shake from me for small reasons."

"What of a big reason then? One that threatens the completion of my quest . . . indeed, its very beginning?"

"This is—?"

Rowan stepped into his father's shadow, which fell fat and distorted by the torches far behind them. Alison looked small and moth-pale under the ominous circle of empty cages. He recalled his mother's face: evasive, and creased with painful recollection. Only one argument would convince his father to impart knowledge he meant to keep until his deathbed. Rowan's hand rested on the Firemayne's shoulder, linking them in secrecy and sorrow.

"I care not for any Littlelost," Rowan insisted. "Nor a sister lost before I existed. But I also do not care to think that the true next Firemayne—the only Desmeynian the Earth-Eaters have taken, not at birth or at death, but in his boyhood—may yet live. This would void my right to seek anything, including the Cup of Earth at the next Wellsunging, or the Heart of Earth now. If, in any . . . condition, Lorn lives on among the Earth-Eaters, I become a false pilgrim, a usurper unworthy of the Cup, or of anything more. You must tell me of the Earth-Eaters' realm or I cannot continue my quests!"

"Your quests?" The Firemayne's expression hardened as he glanced at Alison. "You have not succeeded in the first quest thus far, having been beaten by a foreign woman at that."

Rowan felt a salt-bitter wave of the childhood shame that only a parent can evoke. His father had dealt him a hard, even a cruel, blow, but he answered calmly. "The Wellsunging's success is judged by others; the remaining feats are deemed successful merely in the finding, the getting there. If you wish me to continue to strive for the quests, I must be certain that I am the one eligible for the role."

"Wish you? By the teeth of the mountains, boy, you make nice distinctions. You *must* do these things, because you are the Firemayne's eldest and only son. Because I tell you so. You dare question me?"

"I question myself," Rowan said in deliberate, quiet contrast to his father's choler. He had learned that much from the Taliswoman: Let others rant and burn; remain cool and control the outcome. "And if I question myself, I will not be fit to quest for anything."

"Hmm." The Firemayne's hand scrubbed his goateed chin. "If I instruct you early in the secrets of my office, *she* must not share them."

Rowan nodded. "I agree, but you will have to arrange that with her." He smiled at his father's sour face, then watched him stomp over to Alison.

He could not hear their words, but the import was only too easy to read. First his father, gesturing, set limits and conditions. Alison's bland abstraction sharpened. Her head shook. She moved about less than his father, and also conceded less. The Firemayne began pacing before her, his aspect threatening. Rowan's lips parted when Alison lowered the backpack that dangled from one shoulder to the wet floor. Some of his father's words floated to him: "do as you are told . . . meddling . . . Desmeynian matters and my son . . . you will not go, then, but occupy a cage without the services of a spoon!"

The Firemayne caught Alison's arms and called his guards. Rowan tensed to assist her, then paused. He could better visit the Earth-Eaters' domain alone, with Alison in custody and the Cup unrisked. . . .

For no seeming reason, the Firemayne abruptly sat hard on the cavern floor, clasping his midsection and coughing. Alison, whirling before the fallen man, caught one oncoming guard in the throat with her heavy boot. The second guard slid into the first and cowered against the rocky cavern wall.

Rowan watched his father flail on the floor. Alison's ubiquitous foot simply kicked from under him whatever prop of arm or leg he tried to use in rising. Her motions were supremely fluid, even gentle. He doubted that his father was much hurt, save in the deepest, darkest wells of his Desmeynian soul.

Rowan sighed and went to help the Firemayne up. Alison retreated just enough to have at Rowan should he turn on her. He knew better now. He was rapidly growing the wise head that his foolhardy father had so recently sworn took years to acquire. But then, his father had not traveled with the Taliswoman through long days and nights.

Upright again, the Firemayne avoided their eyes. "How, my son, can you trust such a one on the hazardous journey you propose?"

Rowan met Alison's steady gaze. "I must. And she must trust me, or we will never find our way back from the Earth-Eater's realm. Now. How do we find our way to it?"

An icy draft sliced like a giant ax blade along the stone wall at the farthest reach of the cavern. The Firemayne withdrew his hand from the chill stone, then flattened himself to the rock and edged sideways. A passage, so narrow as to be invisible from the cave's entrance, swallowed the Firemayne inch by inch.

Rowan's eyes flicked significantly to his father's disappearing figure. Alison hesitated, then held the pack out beside her and slithered into the rock passage after him. Rowan went last, thankful for his limber leanness.

The natural fissure undulated between sheets of solid rock. Alison's pack jammed occasionally; Rowan could hear her grunts as she struggled to ease it through. No light fell upon them. They edged farther into this crushing alleyway on faith.

Soon a fetid smell slapped their nostrils, the odor of deepest, darkest earth. Next came a sharp, rhythmic noise, like an instrument chinking on stone.

Something cool and scaled brushed Rowan's hand and undulated away. Revolted, he almost stopped, but he heard the others' feet shuffling forward and kept going. Despite the close, cloying dark, he did not rejoice when he saw a sliver of light glowing ahead. The colors were too unearthly to reassure him: luminous violet and empyrean blue, the orange of a moribund fire, and a bright, diseased saffron—all of them intermixed with putrid shades of green not found above ground.

The chinking sound became the drip of water; then he was plunged ankle-deep into a thick, icy current that lapped at his legs. He heard the others' boots suck free with each step, heard the Taliswoman's shallow, anxious breathing as she waded through unseen water in the dark.

The liquid clung to his feet like a Womb-bat tongue, agile and ensnaring. Rowan shoved his boots ahead step by step, the muck thickening around him. Then they were on dry . . . ground. He stood in a velvet dimness illuminated by myriad motes of air-borne phosphorescence that painted the once-familiar faces with him into fiercely alien visages.

The Firemayne had turned back to stare at his son as at an apparition. "Your hair! It glows blue in this place."

"Yours is striped blue and green," he told his father. "And Alison's is orange! Have the go-betweens you meet here never commented upon the effect?"

"No." The Firemayne sounded disconcerted. "They are not ones for trivial conversation."

Alison returned from pacing the cavern's dimly lit perimeter. "I suppose they don't remark on the stench, either. Rotten eggs mixed with a delicate overture of stinkweed. I see no exit or egress—beyond the alleyway by which we entered."

"That is true," the Firemayne said with some complacency. He was, after all, the only one to have seen this place before. Nothing restores a humbled pride like prior and exclusive knowledge.

"Not even the guards have been here?" Alison asked.

The Firemayne shook his head.

Rowan posed the next question. "What watery substance oozes on the floor between the rock walls?"

"I know nothing of it, save that it stinks."

Rowan turned from his father. Alison was surveying the phosphorescent walls as restlessly as her Slinker had sniffed out camp sites. At the cavern's center, a rock plateau had been carved into a pedestal table and its top darkly polished. Rowan studied it, drawn by the play of glimmering veins through the sleek surface. Hummocks of raw crystals glittered like constellated stars scattered here and there. Amid the furtive colors that changed as he moved around them, Rowan recognized the most dazzling powders and dyes of the Desmeynian ladies.

"Does this remind you of anything?" Alison had paused at a particularly gaudy portion of wall, where the lurid ores scribed a drawing on the black background of rough rock.

Rowan nodded. "The cavern we slept in on the way to the Wellsunging."

Her hand passed over the vivid surface. "I wonder how much of Veil's life is subterranean." When she held up her palm, a faint impression of the veins gleamed on her flesh, reminiscent of the designs embroidered on the Loftladies' protected palms.

"Do not touch the stone!" the Firemayne ordered. "We stand upon the edge of the Earth-Eaters' cursed domain. Even the light may sear us if we go too near."

"Is that why you use agents?" Rowan inquired.

His father joined him in gazing at the bizarre tabletop. "We must. I do not sleep well for a week after coming here, and my appetite is destroyed. My hands blister and bleed."

"What do you take from the Earth-Eaters?" Alison wanted to know.

The Firemayne stared at the stone table as if visualizing it heaped with bounty. "Rare ores, some so brittle they flake into powder; metals adamant enough to make into edged weapons; small sheets of etherion. Crystals that bleed color; these are much prized in the Lofts and are distilled into rare tinctures for beautification."

"How do you transport this treasure?" Rowan asked.

"Carry it out through the gash in the walls. Why do you think my hands blister afterward? I can carry only small quantities, but the dead fruits of the Earth-Eaters' domain are concentrated and supply all of Desmeyne's needs."

"You mean 'wants,' " Alison corrected.

"I am not used to contradiction, not by a woman, and not even by a Cupbearer."

"But, Firemayne, so far you describe taking only materials for cosmetics and weapons from the Earth-Eaters. What of foodstuffs, medicines? And why doesn't your agent bring them to you above, instead of bringing you here?"

"There is no food worth eating in these depths," the Firemayne barked. "And the Earth-Eaters consume just that—loose dirt they claw from the crevasses of these rocks." Rowan moved restlessly, as if about to speak, but his companions failed to notice. "Desmeynians do not descend to such habits," the Firemayne went on. "We seek beauty from the dark depths of earth, not sustenance and shelter."

"Sustenance and shelter are needs. Why blame the Earth-Eaters for finding them in places you scorn? In my land, people who eat dirt are ill, not evil. I'm not convinced that these unseen neighbors of yours are the monsters you make them out to be. They strike me as ingenious, not as degraded."

"May you see one in the flesh and decide then!"

"*Have* you seen one?"

The Firemayne's head shook vigorously. "I doubt I would be yet alive if I had. It is enough that I must come this close. But I am compelled to, for their agent is not . . . mobile as we are, and I sense that the Earth-Eaters take some dark delight in forcing a Firemayne of Desmeyne to such menial duties. Do you still insist on crossing into the Earth-Eaters' dread country?"

"If the Littlelost are there—"

Rowan stepped between his father and Alison. "We will soon solve the nature of the Earth-Eaters if we are successful in going there, but I want to know who negotiates for Desmeyne. Who would willingly go regularly among Earth-Eaters, and for what gain?"

"And how," Alison put in, "does the go-between arrive here—or go there? This cavern is a last cul-de-sac of Desmeyne. Unless the Earth-Eaters melt through solid rock . . ."

"They come and go," began the Firemayne, "in no manner known to man—"

At that moment a bar of blue light rose from the tabletop: a straight, slender reed of unearthly illumination.

Their faces sickened in its reflection. The rod widened and blossomed to brilliant hue, and Rowan's eyes were forced aside until its brilliance softened again. A draped figure sat upon the table like a mountain birthed by the light. Its presence was more an absence, an opaque negativity impossible to see through. Rowan was reminded of the blasted plain he had twain-seen from the Arcade dance floor. He was reminded of Dearth. But that was all, reminded. This was not the same entity. There was even an insouciance about the way the blade of blue light twirled in its fire-blackened grip.

"Greetings, Firemayne," the apparition said—or sighed, rather. Its voice was as wispy as veils, each word a rasp of varying tones. They all leaned inward to understand that frail, ominous sound, though closer contact with the speaker was the last thing any of them wanted, Rowan thought. "You bring me company at last."

"Not company." The Firemayne sounded apologetic, his tones almost cringing. Rowan hated to hear his father speak thus. The trader—for such Rowan took him to be—poised coyly atop the table. "There is nothing festive about our presence. We seek admittance to the Earth-Eaters' caverns."

"No cause for joy, no," the wand-wielder agreed. Its robes—or their apparent outline—shuddered as it spoke, making Rowan wonder if the outer form masked not the whole being as one would normally expect, but merely the mouth and throat, or whatever apparatus it used for speaking.

Alison spoke suddenly. "Why do you act as a trader between Desmeyne and the Earth-Eaters? What do you gain?"

"Trade of my own," the robes thrummed. They rustled like taffeta, each word a brittle gem dropped from their folds.

She persisted. "What goods?"

"The same that Desmeyne seeks." A pause. "Only more."

"What do you gain from Desmeyne for your services?"

"Nothing."

Alison regarded the Firemayne incredulously, but he nodded.

"Then why serve Desmeyne?" Alison asked the presence.

After a silence, the quiescent robes rasped like a string of dying breaths. "It is the price of our own trade."

"Demanded by the Desmeynians?" she asked.

"By the Earth-Eaters."

"They will not trade you goods unless you act as intermediary with the Desmeynians? But why?"

"They wish the Desmeynians to pay."

"What do you pay, besides the unspoken—the unspeakable?" she asked the Firemayne.

For the first time, he looked truly uneasy. "Simple things. Wool and linen cloths. Sometimes wood, if we have recently sent parties to the forest to gather it."

"Yet you have never seen an Earth-Eater face-to-face?"

He nodded. Alison turned to the scintillating darkness huddled on the tabletop. "And you?"

Can a rustle be said to smile? The creature at least audibly smirked. "I have seen Earth-Eaters' faces. Whether the reverse is true remains debatable. I would not wish to deceive you."

The peak of the robes, which could be presumed to contain a hodded head, shifted. Rowan had not interrupted Alison's interrogation; he was interested that the trader would deign to speak to a woman. Perhaps it knew, or sensed, what she hoarded in her pack. His impulse was to seize that mound of crackling darkness and shake loose whatever hid within it, but he did not move.

A series of subtle shudders agitated the form, as if it were a storm cloud harboring internal lightning. The blue wand hummed shrilly.

"I must cease," the creature slurred silkily. "If you would broach the Earth-Eaters, take the door that grows upon my departure."

Then the black form was crumpling as if crushed by an invisible fist. As it shrank, the wand swelled, stretching to the floor and broadening into a portal of vivid light.

"You are sure—?" The Firemayne was dithering like an old man, Rowan realized with shock.

Alison bent to sling her pack over her shoulder. The light's maw widened to engulf her. Rowan glimpsed opaque darkness at its center, like the concentrated iris of a Slinker's eye in sunlight, and then Alison—and the Cup—were gone. Rowan had no choice.

The Firemayne's hand grasped his son's arm. "How will you return?" he asked in alarm.

Rowan saw the slit narrowing and shrugged off his father's hand, plunging into the light, finding it as warm and enervating as bathwater. He shut his eyes against the brightness, against the slow sensation coagulating around him, a sensation of blackness seeping and spreading. He could not move, and breathing seemed a function that occurred only in his memory.

Rowan forced his sticky eyes open. The blue light was gone. Glimmers of subterranean phosphorescence lit the surrounding abyss like distant candles. In their flicker he found Alison nearby, her eyes moving to acknowledge him.

She was now robed, wrapped like the trader in midnight cloth, her face webbed by a veil. She was draped, as was Rowan himself, in a wall of translucent coal that had formed around her, freezing motion in limbs and blood in veins. Only thoughts moved in that eerie, enshrouded state, and they were blacker than the darkness.

29

Once, when she was a freshman reporter, Alison had been assigned a story at the state school for the mentally retarded. That had been true terra incognita. When she was barely past the doors, the residents had swarmed her and the photographer, hands reaching out to touch them, unfocused faces like wilted sunflowers following the passage of these uneasy ambassadors from the "normal" world outside.

The photographer, a bluff veteran tending more to belly than hair, had shot a few pictures (to be carefully screened for obvious abnormalities before appearing in the newspaper) and fled to his car. Alison had stayed, finally overcoming her fear and guilt enough to get a story, a real story filtered through her honest impressions, not the usual sentimental bow made to anomaly before it is swept under the community rug again.

There, she could have fled as the photographer did. Here, in another world's socially forbidden zone—the Earth-Eaters' realm—she was a fixed exhibit.

Through the smoky layers of quartzlike coal that sealed her and Rowan into separate but equal sarcophagi, Alison watched groping extremities shadow the glassy lid of her upright coffin. She felt like Snow White in a Hammer film, wondering what kind of prince would awaken her from this nightmare. Dearth again?

Remnants of blue light swirled around her, cushioning her from the rock she sensed hardening behind her. She was vertical; she could breathe and see. Otherwise, she was sealed within a scentless, soundless isolation. Her eyes flitted to Rowan's behind his smoked-glass barrier, as his sought hers.

And still the blind, reaching . . . limbs . . . undulated beyond the murky darkness, tentacles eager for touch. As much as Alison yearned for freedom, she dreaded their contact.

Her muscles and nerves produced the impulses of motion—her fingers curling, her head turning—but nothing stirred except her eyes and the bellows of her chest. She inhaled to aerate her terror. A wreath of blue light within the space slithered past her mouth like cigarette smoke.

Was it poison, that eerie light? The empty figure had carried the same light. Whether or not, she had to breathe. So did Rowan. She could see tendrils of blue smoke wreathing his head. She had a sudden sensation of falling, all the more horrifying for her immobility. Then a topaz fissure streaked across the translucent mineral barrier in front of her face. The fissure engendered another branch, and another, until the entire surface had crackled . . . to shatter like a caramel-sugar glaze and crumble to the floor.

Air, alternately chill and warm, and definitely damp, cocooned her. A finger twitched, and then a nerve in her thigh jumped. It was such a relief to move again that Alison took a forward step without thinking, her heavy pack dangling from her hand.

Immediately figures engulfed her, white and dumpy, draped in the darkness of hoods and robes. Arms like raw dough that sunlight had never warmed, much less baked, ended in ever-yearning, flared fingers blindly seeking to touch.

A crunching sound made Alison turn. Rowan also had stepped into this chaos. Pasty hands were pulling on his trousers and tunic, patting his body, straining for his hair and pulling him down so their stubby fingers could tangle in its strands.

Just as they were her own. But Rowan's red locks and bronze skin attracted the greater number of pawings. Alison gasped as the many faces—no higher than her shoulder—were turned up, the better to pursue their benign attack. Some were smaller, like the littlest Littlelost; others crawled, hummocks of fabric whose size and shape were lost against the dark rock floor. Hoods draped fish-white faces dotted with shapeless holes for nose and mouth . . . and for eyes that were filmed as if with cataract growths.

The smallest figures were humped behind, like dowagers; others were humped before, as if pregnant; and some were merely runty . . . children? Children not unlike those Alison had seen years ago at that state home, save for their scar-white eyes.

Rowan approached Alison by a great effort, dragging a contingent of dogged hangers-on, his expression dazed, until he was close enough to speak. "Where have you led us?"

She studied their surroundings. The flickering distant lights had swelled to the glow of a rainbow filtered through black chiffon. Slick-sided tunnels led away in all directions. Clusters of raw ore twinkled in the rocky firmament above them. The ground was soft and aromatic, like freshly turned dirt. Phosphorescent fungi bloomed at their feet.

"Where we wished to be, I think," she said.

Rowan snorted. "Unfortunately. What of the Cup?"

She turned. A knot of Earth-Eaters writhed around the pack a step removed from her feet, chirping and drawing it away from her with questing fingers entwined in its straps and buckles. And other restless, greedy hands were stroking her clothes to the accompaniment of satisfied humming.

Alison inched toward the pack, her feet barely able to shuffle through the crowd. No one interfered as she bent to reclaim it and lift it to her shoulder, but a clot of Earth-Eaters remained attached to it, hung from it, crowded against her.

"Enough!" Rowan flailed his long arms, pushing away pale, parasitic limbs. The Earth-Eaters fell back voicelessly, then poured inward again in a tide, clinging, claiming.

"We must speak to someone," Alison said as the flock gently surrounded her and pulled her away from Rowan. "There must be some means of communication."

Only the gentling coos of the Earth-Eaters answered her, the inarticulate murmurs of those who perhaps could not speak. She and Rowan, separated by a squat, bobbing flotilla of Earth-Eaters, were wafted down the slick-sided tunnel like ocean liners towed into port. The dark rainbow light ebbed behind.

"Harrow-worms," Rowan said out of the blue, or out of the blackness, rather.

"What?" she asked.

"These tunnels were formed by Harrow-worms. I recognize the ribbed impressions left in the worm-furrowed fields. That same pattern scores these rocks."

"Then the worms' ancestors must have made these tunnels ages ago, before the inside of the earth hardened to rock."

"Rock is rock." Rowan unclamped a doughy hand from the neck of his shirt. "Earth is earth. One is not the other."

"All rock was once dirt. And all rock will erode to dirt again, given wind and water and enough time. That's why dirt is only a layer over solid rock, as in these tunnels."

"Nonsense! Harrow-worms still ravage our lands today."

"Probably not the same Harrow-worms. That's why the worms venture from the mountain depths into your fields, in search of more earth to eat."

"To despoil!"

"In Island-Not, worms benefit the soil—though they are not, I admit, nearly as large as the worms that must have drilled these tunnels and those that drove those furrows into the fields."

Their argument had relieved the tension of their strange floating progress amid a murmuring tide of inhumanity. Now that they, too, kept the peace, Alison could hear the plink, chuckle and ripple of flowing water and realized that a stream must snake alongside them.

The stream's sound suddenly coughed and shattered into a chattering waterfall. She and Rowan were as abruptly stuttering down an incline, kept upright only by the strangling swarm of forms around them.

Before them, the claustrophobic worm warren opened into a vista: an imposing gash, a deep, yawning valley in the rocks. Its cavernous roof was as black as midnight, except for the glimmer of rich lodestars, but its distant walls reddened toward the bottom, as if bathed in some subterranean sunrise, or sunset.

Alison had resolved to experience her genteel captivity as a form of group therapy and was actually relaxing, recognizing that the press of bodies prevented her from falling.

Rowan was not, predictably, so laid back. He flailed again at the encroaching forms, his face ruddy with resistance as it reflected the growing heat and light. His efforts were to no avail.

Alison and Rowan were being herded toward the floor of this rocky cavern. In a channel cut into the rock, the stream tumbled noisily alongside them, sizzling over boulders and simmering past the few level spots, its boiling whitewater tinting a deeper pink as the party probed deeper into the gash.

Water tendrils oozed down the cavern walls like a legion of snail slicks. Sweat, turning to the color of blood in the sunset glow, beaded Rowan's forehead. Alison felt sweat meandering down her own cheeks and wondered if she looked as gruesome as he did.

And then they were gradually coiling down a circling ramp. An awning of hammered, rusted metal fringed the cavern, which was narrowing like the end of an egg.

Earth-Eaters chirped and cooed with excitement, and the swirling motion around them stopped. The figures ebbed away so swiftly that Alison felt disoriented at abruptly standing on her own two feet again. Rowan also swayed to recover his balance.

In the scarlet light at the cavern's bottom, rows of humped figures sat on massive stones in a rough, rocky amphitheater that hellishly mimicked the Valley of the Voices. Dwarved, monkish forms, whose pale faces, shadowed but not hidden by their hoods, shared the featureless similarity of bowls of Cream of Wheat.

"I am Speaker." Who addressed them was impossible to tell. A moving mouth in those puddles of blandness was little different from a blinking, white-pupiled eye. "You come by the Crux-gate."

"The Crux!" Rowan was astounded. He turned disbelieving eyes on Alison. "My father dealt with a Crux-master?"

"Apparently," she said, "and unknowingly. So have we, or we wouldn't be here."

"You are Desmeynian." The Speaker's voice was as featureless as the faces, but disdain colored the word "Desmeynian."

"I am—" Alison and Rowan began in unison.

"—not," Alison finished solo.

A hood turned toward Rowan. "You are Firemayne."

"Not yet."

The hood shook dolorously. "Firemayne is . . . and was . . . and ever will be the Earth-Eaters' enemy. You wear the headdress of Firemayne." A white worm of a finger emerged from a baggy sleeve and tapped the owner's slack hood.

Rowan had straightened in defiance at the word "enemy." "I am Rowan Firemayne," he threw in their shrouded faces, "and if I live—and when my father dies—then, yes, I will be *the* Firemayne."

The Speaker's hood swiveled toward Alison.

"I am Alison of Island-Not," she said hastily to undo Rowan's foolish bravado, "and *my* quest has brought Rowan Firemayne among you. You mustn't blame him for his father's wrongs, whatever they are, until he has committed some of his own against you."

"You, a woman, speak for a Firemayne?"

"I speak for myself, but he accompanies me, and therefore I am responsible for his safety."

Chirps and twitters stirred the hooded figures.

"Besides," Alison went on, less certainly, "the Earth-Eaters have wronged Desmeynians by churning up their fields with Harrow-worms."

Twitters became hoots . . . apparently of laughter.

"The worms require exercise," the bland voice said with an undertow of irony, "but they come and go as they please, and always have. There is peace and cooperation in our shadowed domains that the sunlit regions seldom attain. We share our space with them, and they with us. And sometimes they unintentionally serve our ends. What they take from the sunlands is little compared to what the Desmeynians have taken from us."

"You take our dead! Our newborn." Rowan's voice rang with the rigor of the recently enlightened. "If I were the Firemayne, I would end this foul, unspoken taking. No Desmeynian birth-bane can be baleful enough to merit consigning its victim to your dread regions!"

"If you were the Firemayne," the voice said, and now iron replaced irony, "you would do as each Firemayne before you has done. None has bothered to visit this below-land we find fair and you call foul. Yet none has failed to covet the rare jewels and minerals we claw from these dark corridors. And none has dared raise a hand against us."

"Why?" Alison asked, unable to help herself. "Who, what, when, where" was the journalist's daily credo, but *"why"* was the profession's true and only saving grace. "Why do you resent the Desmeynians so much, when you admit that they have little contact with you, that you have things they want and that you can use things they have, such as cloth? Why extract this terrible price in abandoned children, even if the Desmeynians are so foolish as to reject some of their own offspring?"

"A fair question, woman of Island-Not, but not for one to answer. Let these speak for all." A robed arm swung wide, like a gate. "Show yourselves, my children."

They crept closer again so Alison could see them, one by one, the dwarved, humped scarcely human figures. One whose head hung below the looming peak of a back lifted its weak hands to push its hood into the groove of neck that separated its grotesque anatomy. The pallid gray face revealed was old; skin like Silly Putty hanging from its bones, as its misshapen body hung from the distorted hanger of its skeleton. Eyes peered from distorted sockets of bone. The nose had been eaten to a mere bump in mid-face.

An incredibly small figure crawled beside it, and the ancient hand swept back its hood. An infantile face, slick with drool; its slack skin rumpled like a Shar Pei's, and a single pale lock of hair decorated its mottled bald head in an obscene parody of babyhood.

A third figure, its belly bowed out like a melon, dropped its covering: a young woman's face, drained of all color and blotted here and there with luminescent acne.

Again and again hoods dropped, and in that leprous company there seemed not one—young, old or in-between—who was not debased and broken. Most were recognizably female. Shock held Alison in place, unable to look away, yet unable to regard such ruination. She had cringed at each unveiling, expecting a Littlelost's visage among them. But every ill-begotten face was unfamiliar, a multiplication of anonymous agony.

"What has happened?" Rowan asked at last in sheer horror. "Why do you live here, like this?"

Sighs agitated the mobs. Alison was glad that they hadn't all dropped their hoods. Such mass misery would be more than sane mortals could bear.

"We live in darkness here," the Speaker intoned, "but prefer it to the darkness the sunlands dealt us. We delve in the dampness for our food, for our trade. We leach color from the earth, until all the color is bleached from us. We live long, very long, as do our memories. And we have grown content with our lot. When Vereleon was Firemayne, we were many. Now we are more."

"Vereleon?" Rowan asked alertly. "What do you know of him? That was centuries ago."

The hood nodded. "Some among us have not seen a Firemayne since Ganth."

"*More* centuries ago! You cannot survive so long!"

"Oh, but I will—for I am among the newest here. Up there, we are forgotten; here we live on, whether we wish it or not."

"Is that why you take the children of Desmeyne?" Alison asked. "Your numbers seem virtually all female; you cannot reproduce—"

"Not unless we take a man of Desmeyne, as stands before us now."

Rowan started uneasily.

The hooded one cackled like a witch in a children's play. "Fear not, young Firemayne. We all become sterile in the caverns. There is no longer any point in it."

Alison winced at this new revelation. "So the children the Desmeynians abandoned to the Deeps became yours, and the practice became a bargain. What of the young women, unlawfully with child, who fled here on the rumor that they'd find succor?"

The arm swung again to indicate the surrounding, hooded throngs.

"We had better have killed them!" Rowan muttered unwisely.

"Why?" the hood asked searingly. "They are alive, and will be so far longer than you, poor sunburned Firemayne. They are free."

"Free to decay—" he began.

"All things decay, and Desmeynians sooner than most."

"Is that why you despise us, because we live above ground in the light? Because we are upright . . . and handsome?"

"No!" At last deep emotion charged the dry, hooded voice. A matching hum of feeling thrummed through all the bent, dark figures. Even the exposed ones bowed their heads, so the hoods fell docilely into place. Alison guessed that the gentle vigil-light red glow haloing the cavern was still too violent for their dark-accustomed eyes.

The Speaker lifted trembling hands to the hood, then slung it back. The other faces had been blotched and puckered, even if baby-bland; this one was as pale as parchment and vacant of all expression. Though the features were not debased, they vanished into the overall waxiness of complexion. Yet one semblance of youth clung to this visage. The other Earth-Eaters had been virtually bald; this one was not. Thin, shining strands gleamed in the auburn light and more than reflected the sunset glow. The strands still retained some of their original color: red.

Alison's eyes jerked to Rowan, whose face was becoming a mask of shell-shocked stone.

"No, Firemayne—" The woman's voice thrilled through the cavern like the first murmurs of a deep, impending earthquake. "We despise you because we *are* you."

She let the hood conceal her head again.

Into the silence that infected them all like a virulent disease, there came a sudden thin and anxious cry in a familiar voice, "Camay . . . no!"

30

The child came skittering over the rough ground, shedding the smothering hooded robe as she ran. Healthy, pink-cheeked features shone, a wholesomc sun in that dark place. Alison couldn't help but smile. She bent to lift the tiny form above the damp earth. The milling Earth-Eaters' inarticulate uneasiness vibrated through the rocky chamber in an off-tune hum.

"At least *she's* not altered," Alison told Rowan in relief.

"Why should she be?" The red-haired Speaker asked. "*She* will not change for decades."

Other small, robed figures converged on Rowan and Alison, moving deliberately. As they reached her and halted, Alison pushed back the obscuring hoods: Twist, Faun, Pickle, Rime! She was so glad to see them!

Rowan frowned absently at the Littlelost, then eyed the Earth-Eater who had revealed a glimpse of red hair. Alison also turned to her.

"If you were ever like this, then Camay will change too; they will all alter if they remain with you," she said. "That's why they must leave."

"They are Littlelost," grumbled the voice. "No one claims them; therefore they are ours."

"I claim them," Alison returned. "I claim their freedom for them. Is durance with you better then serving the Takers in the etherion pits?"

"Durance?"

"Forced confinement here."

"Then durance is better than Desmeyne."

"Desmeyne is barred to them now, anyway," Alison said. "You don't know what you deal with, Earth-Eaters. These children have been hurt beyond the random blows of so-called birthbanes. These are not . . . ordinary children any longer."

"No." The red-haired figure's voice rang out hoarsely. "*You* do not know what you deal with, Alison of Island-Not. I cannot imagine where such a place lies, but it surely does not share borders with the world we know. Otherwise, you would perceive the truth about the Littlelost."

"If you mean their sexual abuse—"

"Abuse?"

"Being used unwilling by another."

"Ah! All sex is abusive; that is why we dispense with it, increasing our numbers by recruitment. Since we keep the Littlelost, we must . . . disabuse them of their practices."

"But to hold the victims here, to become pale and shrunken—"

"—and immortal," the voice crowed. "Or nearly so."

"But these children—"

"Children?" the Speaker challenged. Titters shook the mob. Alison glanced at Rowan; he looked as confused as she felt. "Children?" the Speaker repeated derisively. "These are no more children than I am, except for that littlest one. Abide with us, Alison of Island-Not, and in a year or so, you will see what we mean."

Sleeves fell back as nearby Earth-Eater hands and fingernails with dirty half-moons reached—for the Littlelost, for herself. Alison twisted to keep Camay from their touch. Perhaps the Earth-Eaters' leprous looks sprang from their close-keeping beneath the earth, but perhaps it came from actual disease.

"Leave the child alone!" she shouted, and evoked laughter.

"These are not children," the Speaker declared with something triumphant in her tone. "They are small in stature, true, but only because their size was frozen at the time of separation from their families. Years may have unraveled since their banishment. Decades. And every month, every year, they grew older within as they grew apart from their kind. Their bodies remain youthful, but their minds and inclinations are adult. If you claim their right to choose leaving here, remember that it is *their* decision if they choose to remain with us, not yours." The voice grew harder, and more indifferent. "You will withdraw to a place of containment while we consider your fate."

"*My* fate?" Alison blurted in disbelief.

"We have come here freely," Rowan said. "In all honor, you could not detain us against our will—"

The other interrupted with relish. "Perhaps there is something we wish in trade for a Firemayne heir. You may share your 'durance' with the 'children,' " the woman added as Alison began drawing the Littlelost closer.

The Littlelost, already adapted to this dark underworld, didn't seem to mind the surrounding Earth-Eaters' herding, their stroking, and casually suffered the shuddersome petting as they were all buoyed along the cavern floor, flotsam in a tide of gently prodding bodies.

Alison was busy shrugging off the encroaching hands until she saw the large metal cocoon awaiting them, huge tusks of curved grating poised high to slam shut on the cell's open front.

She started kicking out then, but the Earth-Eaters' size and misbegotten anatomy foiled her instinctive placement. Besides, they gave like waves of rubber. Rowan's less artful struggles were more successful. Hooded figures scattered, but more rushed in to take their place.

In the end, the sheer numbers of Earth-Eaters served as a shovel that scooped them into the chamber, half-falling, half-crawling. The Littlelost willingly scampered within just as the huge, ribbed portcullis slammed down behind them.

The Littlelost snuggled into a far curve, where rags and raw crystals made an uncomfortable-looking nest. They regarded Alison and Rowan with the bright expectancy of baby mice welcoming Mother and Father Mouse back to the family hole. Outside, the Earth-Eaters swayed and cooed, pressing against the massive bars.

Inside, Alison studied the circle of faces she thought she knew well. How had they had first struck her? As hard-bitten, hungry masks, like those of Depression-era orphans, suspicion squeezing eyes tight, caution folding lips tighter than twigs. Could she have been seeing, instead of abuse, the force of adult minds in children's bodies? And the Littlelost's gradual, endearing exuberance as they grew secure in Alison's company—had that been mature exhilaration at release from bondage, no more? And the sexual activity between them—was it only nature, not a violation of it? In the next few years would Camay, too, pass invisibly through puberty . . . yet fail to lose her fey, childish aspect? Whether mature children or childlike adults, Alison found comfort in their fresh self-esteem.

She clutched Rowan's sleeve. "Have we—you, I mean—wronged the Littlelost? Punished them for behavior that isn't what it seems?"

Rowan looked dazed. "Perhaps."

"What of these Earth-Eaters? They feel that Desmeyne has terribly wronged them."

"Perhaps them, too," he replied absently. His voice lowered as he leaned toward her. "The riddle of the Littlelost is not as disturbing as the reason why that . . . that woman has, or had, hair the same color as my own."

"Oh." Alison let Camay slide down her hip to the ground and run to the others. "Red hair. Must have been quite a shock to see it. Like no one else in Veil, you said once. Only among Firemaynes."

"Only Firemayne heirs," he corrected.

Alison nodded. "Then that explains why she was left for the Earth-Eaters!"

"She?"

"Your sister. Don't you see it yet? She was given to the earth not only because she was an elder girl-child. Her birth-bane was her red hair—hair that would not merely betray her house of origin, as yours might when on a quest, but hair that had appeared for the first time upon a female of the Firemayne line."

"That . . . creature? My *sister?* Never! My mother was half-mad when she spoke of those things, and this—this is some mummery of the Crux-masters. Obviously, the Earth-Eaters have collaborated with the Crux for some time."

"So has the Firemayne," Alison pointed out dryly.

Rowan looked pained. "Why did he never speak of such things to me?"

"You understand why your mother didn't, I hope?"

"About Lorn? Yes, a cruel loss from which she never recovered in her deepest mind. Her grief must have twisted her to imagine that other loss, that so-called sister—"

"Rowan, your mother 'imagined' no such thing, and I think you know it. You just can't face the truth. It's *your* imagination that's been blighted for twenty years. You can't even cope with seeing another human being with red hair."

Rowan scowled with great dignity. "My red hair is a burden, a birth-bane. That is why I must dedicate myself to pilgrimage and self-denial."

"But if others shared the burden, they'd share the glory, wouldn't they, Rowan? You wouldn't be so unique. What if you're just another pawn in a game others have been playing on a world-wide scale?"

His face took sudden fire. " 'Pawn'? No matter, I take your meaning." He looked around the cell, then whirled on her. "You have led me into the hands of the enemy! For what cause?" He twisted to regard the Littlelost. "Children who are not children, not victims even, who did not need our help. They are wanted here, whatever this place may be, and we must leave—quickly! These Littlelost do not ask for or need your help, Taliswoman. Nor do I."

"M-m-maybe we can give it," a small voice suggested.

They turned to see Twist sitting cross-legged at the forefront of the Littlelost.

"We are tired of being talked about," Faun added. "We would rather talk with."

"Who is the Crux?" Rime scrambled forward on her knees. "Is the Blue Man a Crux-master?"

"The Blue Man—the one with the blue light? You've seen him?" Alison asked.

Heads nodded. "He comes," said Faun with relish, "like needle lightning dancing in the place where the rocks are reddest. He talks with the Earth-Eaters and takes many stones from this place, carts and carts of them."

"Carts?" Rowan caught Alison's glance, eagerness in his face. "Drawn by beasts?"

More nods. "Like the farmer's field-beasts that we saw from the frozen waterfalls of Desmeyne," Faun said.

"Frozen waterfalls?" Rowan wondered.

"The crystal window walls," Alison explained.

"Only, these beasts are shrunken and blind, like the Earth-Eaters," Faun added.

Alison crouched beside the Littlelost. "Listen, do you really . . . really like the Earth-Eaters?"

Looks were exchanged. " 'Like'?" Rime asked.

Alison said, "The Earth-Eaters want you to stay; they say that you'll live long, but they'll . . . expect you to be like them, as the Desmeynians did."

"No!" Pickle leaned into the curved dark corner, knobby knees drawn up, elbows braced atop them and his hands holding his turban-scarf to his head. Alison wondered if an Earth-Eater had tried to pry it from him. "We want no more of those who expect things of us, not even you."

Alison sat back on her heels. "You're right; Rowan's right; the Firemayne's right; the Earth-Eaters are right. I've meddled in matters I knew nothing about."

Pickle accepted her admission with chilling complacency, but he glanced rather shyly at Rowan, then told Alison, "I did not understand all that you said to the Earth-Eaters. Is it true that . . . that red hair is only in *his* family? Why is that so important?"

"It's important," Alison answered, "only because it makes him *feel* important."

Rowan gave her a withering look and went down on one knee to speak to Pickle. "She is, as usual, mostly wrong. I am sorry, Littlelost, if my people have underestimated you. We are busy with our own ills. You can see that these Earth-Eaters have no love for Desmeynians. Now they may concoct some vile scheme with the Crux to do more than irritate us. I will not say that you must leave or stay, but I must know more about these Earth-Eaters for my own sake. You say that stones are taken from here in beast-drawn carts?"

Nods and murmurs.

"Then"— Rowan chose his words carefully —"there must be paths to the upper world that do not depend on the Blue Man's portal of light."

Animated nods, more of them.

"Could you show us such paths?"

Nods all around. "Yes," Pickle said, looking proud at being spokesman, "but we must start at the red rocks."

Alison had gone to the curved bars to watch the Earth-Eaters scuttle about on their vague business. She sighed pointedly, and when she had everyone's attention, curled her fingers around a bar the thickness of a broomstick.

"Any idea of how we're going to pass these, in full view of a cavern crammed with Earth-Eaters?"

Rowan joined her and ran his hands over the formidable bars. "These are not cold, like iron." He looked up at the ribbed roof yawning overhead and then down at the adjoining cells tunneling away. "This is no ordinary prison! This is the desiccated shell of a Harrow-worm! And these are"— his hands released the curved bars with distaste —"their bones."

"No wonder those furrows in the fields drove so deep," Alison said with a shudder. "If worms this big have delved here for centuries . . . the Earth-Eaters realms are no more than huge worm burrows these creatures made before the caverns had hardened to rock!"

"Mere dirt and clay could never form rock and stone," Rowan insisted again. "But Harrow-worms *could* have tunneled through solid rock."

"If it's easier to conceive of a monster tunneling through solid rock, fine," Alison told him. She turned to the Littlelost. "What about it? Think these carts follow the worm burrows out of here? Will you stay, yet still help us leave? Or will you leave with us?"

The warm bud of Camay's hand blossomed in Alison's hand. "Go with Alison."

One by one the others nodded agreement, Twist most sullenly, and Pickle last, his eyes downcast.

An odd expression flashed across Rowan's face. For a fleeing second it resembled regret that the Littlelost's loyalty was so specifically hers, Alison thought. If it was, he had at last begun to respect their value!

She smiled and shook one of the ribs of mineral-rusted bone that confined them. It was as well-anchored as an elephant tusk. Imagine a "worm" with a skeleton! But this was Veil; many things were odd, as even Rowan had so recently learned to his very real and personal regret.

31

Night never fell in the Earth-Eaters' cavern. An eternal sunset glow leaked up from among the black rocks, tinting the interior the color of rare roast beef.

Yet those who lived here observed the conventions of a day-night cycle. Eventually, most of the Earth-Eaters withdrew to adjoining caverns. A few hunkered down among the rocks until they became one with them. In the warm, ensuing silence, rivulets of water dripping down every cavern wall ticked like a display of clocks.

That was when Camay accommodated her youthful spine to the sway of old bones and slipped through the well-spaced bars.

"They k-k-kept us here first," Twist whispered. "Camay got out and found the latches. Most Earth-Eaters are small like us; it does not take strength to t-t-trip the lever."

Soundlessly, the ossified ribs hinged upward like an opening whale jaw, the few complaining squeaks obscured by the syncopated chorus of the water-clocks.

Alison's hands capped her ears. "That plick-plick-plicking would drive me nuts! No wonder Earth-Eaters are odd—and they claim to live lifetimes in this dungeon."

"This way." Faun had sprinted out of captivity with the other Littlelost. Her figure was silhouetted against the reddish rocks.

Rowan noticed the effect and warned them, "We must not let the Earth-Eaters spy so much as our shadows. And no sound!"

So they ran crouched like mobile rocks, the soft-soled boots of Desmeyne as soundless on the stone as lynx paws. Pickle led; Alison took the middle, Rowan the rear. The two had negotiated the escape formation in a hushed conference while the Littlelost slept, awaiting the Earth-Eaters' time of dormancy.

"They trust you," Rowan had conceded, "so you must keep near the lead. I will follow. I have decided to trust you for the moment. I doubt that even you would relish aging like the Earth-Eaters."

"Yes, but do I trust you?"

"What can I do at the rear but defend against pursuit?" Rowan's voice had taken on a grimmer undertone since their descent into the Earth-Eater's hell. Alison sensed that he'd made decisions he wouldn't share with her.

"Do you trust the Littlelost to lead us to a Harrow-worm path?" she asked.

"Yes. I do not trust any worm-ridden viaduct that we may find in these abandoned regions, but I like it better than the blue-light doors of a Crux-master's wand. And there seem to be enough intersecting tunnels that we can avoid any enemies."

"Wherever they are, the Crux-masters know we're here, that's for sure."

"Because they opened a road to lead us here—and you were too quick to use it. We must depart before they decide that leaving us to the Earth-Eaters is not good enough," Rowan advised.

"At least you no longer seem to think that I'm a Crux-mistress in disguise. But what would the Crux gain from coming after us?"

"Besides the Cup?"

"Ouch!" As alien as Veil's struggles were to her, how could she have forgotten that the Cup was a major piece in the game? "What else would they gain?" she wondered.

A pause. "Myself." Rowan spoke with unshaken belief in his role. "And perhaps you."

"You concede I'm worth enough to be in danger?"

"You hold the Cup. And . . . since my twain-sight in the Arcade, I have been having dreams."

"Dreams? Great. In living color?"

"I do not remember if they were colorful, only that you were in them, alive, in a strange place, with two men not of Desmeyne, or even of Veil."

"Crux-masters?

"Twain-sight is potent only when it involves our enemies in the Crux."

"But were they Crux-masters? Was I . . . captured?" She didn't like the sound of that.

"You were among them," he said stonily, "whether willingly or no, I cannot say. You will be near the forefront of the escape party—"

"So you can keep an eye on me—and on the Cup!"

"The Cup is a thing of Veil. You are not."

"In my world, we would say that I was expendable—to both sides."

"In Desmeyne, we would say that you walk a two-edged sword barefoot. And I will guard the rear," he repeated.

"Yes, my Firemayne."

"My father lives! I am not Firemayne, nor do I aspire to the title. If ever I accomplish the quests to the Four Quarters, I will be more than a Firemayne, and less than one. I will be content."

Alison mulled the family revelations of the past twenty-four hours. She patted Rowan's knee as they squatted together in the flickering, bloody dark. "My guess, Rowan, is that you'll never be content again, but that's *my* twain-sight at work, otherwise known as reporter's intuition."

Now they crept out of the main cavern in the agreed-upon order, Alison feeling that she played a rather grimy Becky Thatcher to Rowan's Tom Sawyer. In the real world, her world, had she been given up for dead by now? If she ever returned to the uncomplicated peninsula, the sometimes-island that she had somehow left, could she fit right in again? Or would she be like the Littlelost, an exile in her own land, forever not what she seemed to be because she had seen and done more than she was supposed to have?

A shower of loose rocks sparked past her shoulder, glowing meteorite-scarlet in the ever-sanguine light. They all froze, hunched like Earth-Eaters. Alison looked back: Rowan's hair shone unreal and lurid. They all looked like they'd been trapped behind the red warning light of a photographic darkroom. Sleeping Earth-Eaters mewed like kittens and stirred. Breathless moments passed. When nothing stirred again, the Littlelost snaked forward with the caution of Lost Boys, or weekend campers, or neighborhood kids playing "Green Light, Red Light" in a Minnesota-autumn dusk.

Doubled over to avoid notice, Alison inhaled a smell of unadulterated dirt: earth sifted by rain and wind and fire through so many millennia that the odors of death and life fought for primacy in its perfume. She imagined eating such stuff—eating ancestors and enemies, animal and vegetable and mineral, in one dark feast. Might an elder kind of wisdom be consumed in this way? Or would one consume oneself in a reverse evolution, a dumbing down of the human species' rise from primordial mud?

She pictured actually dining on dirt—dirt patted into the form of suckling pigs and pumpkin pies and banana splits. Pregnant women sometimes resorted to this odd compulsion . . . poor pregnant women in the rural South. Was there a rationale to it, a mere nutritional deficiency, or was something to be gained in revolting against the social rules against the apparently revolting act?

Alison's head throbbed with too much dark and damp and earth-smell and heat beating through reddened rocks. She tightened her grip on her pack and edged forward.

And stumbled. The path had abruptly turned upward. Again the party froze until it felt safe to move forward. Then they were in a passage: a coiling burrow that was cool compared to the overheated cavern, despite the red-reflected aura that defined its narrower walls.

The passage resembled a fossilized alimentary canal, with corrugated, endlessly convoluted rocky sides. This space could have been gouged out by a gigantic, wayward spiral drill-bit or by one of Rowan's rock-excavating mammoth worms; or the party could be traversing the intestines of a Gulliver, Alison thought. What if she hadn't entered another world from the Island, but had merely *shrunk* to fit a world always there, unseen?

They had all—slowly—begun walking more upright. They felt less vulnerable in this intimate, curving path out of cavern-sight that led them so gently upward. Littlelost had forsaken their line to bunch ahead of Alison, leaving Rowan now directly behind her. She could feel his breath on the back of her neck.

Alison turned another coil—into a sudden draft from an intersecting passage. In the mouth of that passage, a rending yellow web melted like cotton candy into strings.

Glowing eyes on stalks loomed over her. She glimpsed a furred—hairy?—body, like a great velvet cape, bunched just behind the webbing. Those gleaming bronze eyes and structures that might be mouth or maw, pincer or snapping turtle jaw . . . Something huge burst from the passage, struggling free like an infant fighting down an ungiving birth canal. It was a massive and mindless form, pouring into their escape route—and then Rowan was standing like a mirror-image of herself, struck dumb, on the other side of its burgeoning body.

"Womb-bat!" he cried,

Or worm? she wondered. Weapon? What would work on this?

The Littlelost had scattered against the walls in disarray. Alison stepped backward, the pack she'd hand-carried for control in the main cavern banging her ankle. Rowan, bare-handed, watched the beast's emergence with horrified disbelief.

Then he leaped—and not for the ghastly glowing eyes, not for the tusked mandibles, not for the clawing, saw-toothed propelling limbs, but for the wet, rustling yardage of collapsed wings. He began to rend them in a frenzy.

The yardage ripped with the sound of taffeta torn against the grain. Alison flinched. None of the fifties' sci-fi films with their machine-gun volleys at the creatures from Beyond Belief were as revolting as this raw attack upon a monster's most vulnerable aspect.

Glowing Womb-bat eyes dulled to the verdigris patina of copper. The limbs still flailed, but as they did, the unfolded wings shredded further. Alison felt as if she watched a preadolescent boy ripping the wings from a moth. Despite the Womb-bat's advantage of size and surprise, despite its deadly danger, the struggle seemed unequal.

Aware that he had wounded the creature, Rowan sprang back, now apparently weary from his efforts and expecting Alison to perform the next step of this deadly dance.

She fumbled in her pack for the revolver. At least it could put the beast out of its misery. Its ungainly head swayed from side to side. Wedged in its narrow tunnel, it lay helpless, although once free to spread undamaged wings in the larger tunnel, it would have been undefeatable.

Alison's fingers found a smooth, chill surface in the pack's interior jumble. Cold steel or icy stone? She tussled the object free—it was the Cup. She slung the pack over her shoulder and faced the beast.

The Cup felt colder than a gun in her hand but held nothing to fling, either in destruction or succor. And then a decision was moot. The creature crawled a few feet forward and collapsed.

"Is it dead?" a small Littlelost voice asked.

"Dying." Rowan edged closer to Alison. "I thought we were about to be devoured."

"They never hurt us." Rime pushed the pale hair from her eyes as she came nearer. "Even in their . . . mouths, when they brought us into the mountain, it was like being carried in clasped hands."

"It seemed we had been carried like that before," Faun added. "I felt so peaceful."

Rowan shook his head, bewildered. "We appeared to be in danger of death. Yet, for such a horrible thing, it was too easy to kill."

A shudder racked the dark creature on the tunnel floor. The huge, tattered body eased forward, leaving bits of wing strewn like fallen leaves. And then opalescent light tickled the edges of Alison's vision. Neonlike glows grew everywhere in the passage, painting the circled faces a dozen unearthly colors. The tunnel that had ejected the Womb-bat still dripped shredded webbing, looking like a torn cocoon.

The creature's ugly carapace was dropping away like a candy wrapper, brittle and thin. Something glorious throbbed within. Colors in a swirling, marbleized pattern intensified on the unprotected surface. Inner wings stirred and unfurled, and now the hues were moving, circulating in myriad, diamond-dusted veins over the body. The same hidden dazzle that streaked the Earth-Eaters' dark stones sprang to living, phosphorescent light, illuminating a creature of supreme brightness and beauty. The eyes caught fire last and radiated the same tranquil lavender color used in Minnesota plant lights. That such a dark and menacing casing could conceal this beautiful new life was a wonder. They stood speechless . . . until the gorgeous new Womb-bat stirred.

Alison almost laughed. "Rowan, your attack only hastened its metamorphosis. You've freed the beast, not wounded it."

"I have never seen such a thing," he admitted. "Where does the creature go after such an alteration?"

"Perhaps it remains here. It looks just like the ladies of Desmeyne's rarest powders and fabrics. It must be their source."

"It is killed for its beauty?"

"Or periodically harvested by the Earth-Eaters, just as Desmeynian farmers reap the fruits of the fields." Alison brushed the edge of a trembling, Technicolor wing. Her hand came away coated with transferred glitter—rose and aqua powders in an abstract pattern.

From far down the passage, a murmur drew their attention. Light radiating from the fallen Womb-bat colored the tunnel archway into a luminous pastel rainbow. Beyond this alley of luscious reflection, more dazzling than a kaleidoscope interior, lay a dark, untidy Rorschach blot. It enlarged as they watched, and resolved into a group of Earth-Eaters on the march.

"Quickly!" Rowan rounded on the Littlelost.

They hesitated, loath to leave the hypnotically pulsing carousel of unsuspected colors, the wings that rustled and unfurled, theatrical curtains garnished with iridescent graffiti, glittering against the dark rock.

Then Alison grabbed her pack and they were pounding down the passage. Behind them, the Womb-bat spread its incandescent wings into a barrier of light and color before the chittering onrush of Earth-Eaters.

An exhalation of warm air drew them blindly into another intersecting passage. Even their muffled footsteps seemed to thunder in this narrower space. Light had ebbed. The Earth-Eaters' distant noise—even they, especially they, wouldn't rend the shimmering, translucent wonder of the Womb-bat's wings to follow so few—was amplified by the smaller tunnel into the roar of distant whitewater.

"Wait!" Over the Earth-Eaters' whitewater din, Alison heard a peculiar far rumble. Her soles were tickled by a faint oscillation. She'd once visited New York City, had been underground there, had taken the subway. . . .

"Oh, my lord! Wait!" Alison looked around frantically. Yes, another tunnel, off to the right! But where was it coming from, that advancing vibration, that earthshaking onrush of sound and fury, not quake, but—

"Harrow-worm!" Rowan blurted. He pushed them all, jammed them, into the yet-narrower tunnel to the right, which seemed to be only a shallow niche. They were barely inside it as rumble became roar became hurricane. Light winked out. Pure rattling motion sped past like a dark freight train at arm's length.

Heat smote them on waves of overwhelming scent—hot dirt and molten rock. Their skin erupted in pearls of sweat that trickled to the tunnel floor. The sound was beyond deafening; it drilled into their ears with the nasal whine of a gigantic electric screw-driver. They clung together, flesh facing a force that could rend rock.

At last the ongoing agony of sound and motion ebbed into plain pain, and finally into an afterthrob that ached like three hundred root canals.

In the larger tunnel, stone walls glowed red-hot, shifting shape in the heat haze that sizzled in mid-tunnel. Faces appeared in bas relief on the rock, masks of melancholy that melted lugubriously into tragedy and then softened into malformation.

Alison's first shaky breath hurt her rib cage. In the numbing silence, her inhalation was echoed all around her. Littlelost pressed against her knees and hips; she still felt molded by the terrible vibrations into one pulsing mass with her companions. They separated reluctantly, to see if flesh could still function with inches between itself and another.

Those moments of clinging together in the lee of melting rock had altered them. Rowan, she saw, had snatched up Camay in the split second before their world had become a long, howling storm. The child's head—and Camay, of all the Littlelost, was still really a child—lay on his shoulder, draped by strands of his red hair.

Rowan cleared his throat. "We cannot return to the passage; the rock still steams. Is there an exit behind us?"

Pickle reached up for Camay.

Rowan, startled, eased her into the Littlelost's scrawny arms, resting his hand for a moment on the cloth that swaddled Pickle's head. He had grown fond of them at last, Alison saw.

It was silent Rime who finally found an exit: an Alice-in-

Wonderland-low archway into a hands-and-knees tunnel. Alison doffed her pack. She hated enclosure almost as much as she abhorred water. She watched the Littlelost squirm into the dark, then stiffened at Rowan's prod in the small of her back.

"I will bring up the rear," he offered.

She turned. "Aren't you worried that this . . . chink . . . will fail to accommodate you?"

"I am more worried that another Harrow-worm will find my body in its pathway," he said.

Alison's cavalier shrug was more like a shudder, but she eeled down on her stomach and wriggled into the dark unknown. The analogy of a birth canal was all too apt. Her elbows and knees rubbed raw as they windmilled through the rock-lined aperture. The gasps of the Littlelost ahead, and the grunts of the Desmeynian behind, kept her going.

The air remained warm. She imagined them all paddling upward to fresh air like deprived infants. The journey would be worth it if they were finally hiccupped into the cold, crisp atmosphere of the mountains cradling Desmeyne.

Only when Alison could see the silhouettes of crawling Littlelost ahead did she realize that light had begun leaking into the tunnel. None too soon; she was tired of dragging the heavy pack after her. When she didn't draw it along fast enough, Rowan ran into it and the guttural sounds of Desmeynian curses rained upon her hapless heels.

The light increased—until a scarlet sun dominated the end of the tunnel. Everyone speeded up.

Suddenly the first Littlelost screamed: a scissors-sharp screech that swiftly dimmed to a wail. Alison paused in shock, only to hear more ear-shattering howls. She could see nothing ahead but the backs of the Littlelost, silhouetted against daylight.

"Retreat!" Rowan urged from behind her.

But it was already too late.

The rocky earth beneath her palms, the earthy rock beneath her knees, broke into loamy clods. It didn't crack but simply crumpled, collapsing into itself and sucking Alison along with it. She was swallowed by the yawning maw of red sun that was not the *end* of the tunnel, but the mouth of a new tunnel speeding toward her.

Then she sank into a dirt devil of swirling clods, her eyes necessarily shut, one fist clamping the pack's strap. Solidity had evaporated. She fell through a blizzard of agitated earth, buffeted by random pebbles but plunging harmlessly through an aerated, insubstantial element.

The fall ended as insidiously as it had begun. Earth thickened, piled, compacted. At last Alison's spinning senses felt anchored, but now she was drowning in dirt. Clods pelted her like reeking, semisolid raindrops. She flailed to keep from sinking under their pattering weight, her eyes still sealed shut. Thank God she no longer needed her contact lenses, she thought. At least if the earth-rain stopped, she could open her eyes. *When* the earth-rain stopped, she corrected herself.

Isolated mewlings cheered her. The Littlelost had landed.

She waited until the hailing earth had ebbed to an intermittent drizzle, then cracked open a dirt-caulked eye. She shut it immediately. The sun at the end of the tunnel had gone nova in a bright bloodbath. Its afterimage painted sunsets inside her eyelids, against which tiny silhouettes cavorted—the floaters in her eyes upon a flaming backdrop.

Shielding her vision with her hand, she looked again. Searing scarlet light flared all around. She was sweating, and muddy rivulets covered the palm she wiped across her forehead. In the lurid light, the streaks looked like blood.

Around her, the Littlelost and Rowan, resembling bloodstained survivors, were digging out of the mammoth dirt-slide and brushing off faces and clothes. The backpack was virtually buried. Alison clawed at the crumbled dirt to free it, releasing an earthy spoor that intensified to the pungency of incense. Rowan lurched over to her and bent to help her, his incandescent hair swaying in the hot, humid air and licking at his filthy shoulders like flame.

Alison surveyed the Littlelost's sweat-shiny faces. "We're a sight," she commented. "Where do you suppose we are? I was sure we'd break free of the mountain soon."

Rowan looked up, and so did Alison. Sheer rock walls—dull red with heat—extended higher than the hubris of a cathedral nave. Forever. Had the dirt not cushioned their landing, they'd have died from such an endless fall.

"We're deeper than we were!" Alison exclaimed in sharp disappointment.

Rowan nodded. "Deeper than even the Earth-Eaters delve."

He stumbled upright and moved—navigating on the still-settling earth was like walking through warm, sticky oatmeal—toward the still-mired Littlelost and plucked them one by one from their earthy impalement. Alison had to admire his pluck.

She levered herself upright, dredged her pack from the mound and slung it over her shoulder. It had gained about half a pound of dirt.

Slipping and sliding, they climbed down the shifting pile until their feet touched solid rock—and jumped back onto the dirt. The rocks were warm . . . hot. In fact, the rocks were oven-baked red.

"Indian earth," Alison murmured.

Rowan waited to be enlightened.

"In Island-Not, some land is mostly red clay, from which the Indians made pottery for centuries. I always think of red clay as Indian earth. There's even a cosmetic called 'Indian Earth.' These red-hot rocks remind me of that."

"In Island-Not, women paint their faces red?"

"No, but they dust them with reddish powders."

"Why?"

"To . . . look healthy, I guess."

"Why should women wish to look healthy?" he asked incredulously.

Alison sighed. "To demonstrate that they are strong."

His face stiffened. "Much is odd in Island-Not."

"Not as odd as elsewhere," she muttered. She had seen, beyond the red rocks, an outcropping of gray ones. If she moved fast, maybe . . . Skipping over the hot rocks was like fire-walking; but the heat was fleeting, and the gray rocks were of normal temperature. The Littlelost scampered after her, giggling. Rowan finally followed, his long strides keeping his contact with the hot stone to a minimum.

From the prominence of the gray rocks, Alison surveyed their situation. She was not encouraged. Neither was Rowan when he bounded up beside her.

"This place is odd beyond Island-Not," he admitted, shielding his eyes from the overheated rock walls rimming the horizon.

They stood within another enclosed world within the mountain. This one was far less hospitable than the Earth-Eaters' domain. Beyond these cooler rocks, a serpentine river of molten lava undulated between banks of hard red clay. Heat radiated from the lava as if from the heart of a star. It would soon become debilitating, then damaging, then deadly.

It was already making Alison thirsty.

She sat on the gray rock—even it was lukewarm—and pulled out the Cup, which felt cool and soothing. Time for a magical communion. Her canteen was half full of water. A cup of water for all of them? Well, the Cup had multiplied water before now. She returned the empty container to the pack. The Littlelost sipped in turn, beginning with Camay and ending with Twist. Rowan tried to insist that she drink before himself, but she sensed that she must offer the Cup to all before she could partake.

The frost-cold water mimicked the glacial stem of the Cup, and her first swallow clove her mouth and esophagus like an ice-sword. When she had drunk all she wanted, the Cup was empty—and dry. Its veins had darkened to crimson. Drops condensed on its smooth white sides like blood and ran down until the stem was as slick as ice in her grasp. She wrapped it in flannel and tucked it away in her pack.

"This place reminds me of something," Rowan said.

"You're better traveled than I."

He studied Alison with a frown. In the red-hot light, he resembled a Native American warrior, his bronze skin darkened to burnt sienna, his long hair blooded in the furnace of the inner earth. Alison had never noticed that in him before, that faint reflection of an ancient race from Mother Earth. It reminded her of Eli and northern Minnesota and past and present wrongs. It gave her a shiver that had nothing to do with cold, clear water from a Cup of Earth.

Rowan was all business. "We must leave this heat-struck smithy. I propose that we follow the—" He pointed to the snake of slithering lava, lost for words.

"River?" she suggested. For some reason, this carmine stew of liquid stone—chili con carne on the rocks—unnerved her less than a river of its shifting, translucent sister element, water. Perhaps because it glimmered like a moving sidewalk of molten gold, signaling a vast, living alchemy hidden in the bosom of the planet. Warm and radiant, it throbbed like mineral lifeblood. It was the antithesis of cool, treacherous water.

She began walking alongside the flow, leaping from gray rock to gray rock, basking in its vibrancy. The others followed. Alison didn't know where they were going, but she felt suddenly certain that the river of liquid rock would take them to where they should be.

32

The path led ever downward, no doubt about that.

Rowan grew restless, complaining that freedom lay in the opposite direction. He was probably right; freedom always felt like something different from whatever you were doing at the moment, yet Rowan knew as well as Alison that they had no choice. How could they backtrack when a sheer cliff face blocked any return to the Earth-Eaters' domain? And did they really wish to return there, anyway?

"Look!" Twist bent to lift something from the rocky riverbank.

The Littlelost puddled in amazement around the object. Alison walked over: Twist's find looked like a conch shell.

"Oh, Twist. How nice! This shell once housed a living creature."

"In this blood-hot river?" Rowan interrupted.

"No, long ago, when a huge expanse of water, an ocean, covered all the land above. These passages were burrowed by long, subterranean fingers of water."

"O-shan." The Littlelost chorus made the word sound like a cuss phrase.

Rowan hooted at this, to him, unlikely tale. "Mildwater comes from below, it is true," he conceded. "From springs and wells that may destroy as well as bless. And wildwater comes from above, in showers of rain and snow, or it is squeezed between the fingers of the clouds and plummets to earth as waterfalls, which are benign enough, considering that they begin as the gods'—" he looked askance at Alison "—urine."

"What a quaintly vulgar concept," Alison put in.

Rowan shrugged sheepishly. "It is thus written in children's Rimes on the winter-frosted window walls of Desmeyne, and has been so forever. Such a thing is far likelier than this tale of water so vast that it lies wherever the eye can look. So much water would be demon-ridden."

"What is this, then?" Alison indicated the spew of melted rock. "Thickened water or liquid land?"

"It is a wound of the earth, never meant to be seen. Some violation by the Earth-Eaters."

"Sure, blame them for everything, including natural wonders," Alison groused good-naturally. "Primitive man always needs a nearby scapegoat. What else are neighbors for? But I say that the earth's center is hot and flowing, like this river, and that water forms great oceans over much of the earth's surface, whether Rowan Firemayne or any other Desmeynian has seen them or not."

Shy Rime whispered, "Near the Rookeries where the Wild Littlelost dwell there lies an endless road of sand bordering a liquid horizon as bright as beaten copper."

"More fancy," Rowan insisted, but he sounded doubtful.

"What are the 'Wild Littlelost'?" Alison wanted to know.

After a glower at Rime, Twist said, "The Wild Littlelost serve no Takers and dwell in no Desmeyne. If we knew the way, we would go to their country."

"And I'd go with you," Alison said. "I for one am sick of Desmeyne."

"You would be welcome to go," Rowan said crossly, "if you would leave the Cup."

"We travel together, the Cup and I," she retorted, "and I'll take it where I want to."

"At this point," he said grimly, "you will take it where you can."

The Littlelost had darted ahead to scoop up more shells. The way beyond was shadowed and uncertain, but the lava's illumination always overpowered the featureless darkness by the time they came to the unknown stretch.

The scenery had an eternal sameness. If they weren't trapped in an obvious dead end, neither were they assured of any limit to the caverns they traversed. Camay had dawdled again beside the riverbed to pry some prize from the bank, perilously near the searing flow. Rowan and Alison started for her at the same moment, just as she lifted her find from the hot silt.

"Careful!" Rowan reached Camay first and snatched her up.

Camay didn't mind the sudden swooping; she proudly extended her trophy to Alison. Alison looked, and couldn't believe her eyes. The piece had the contradictory heft and fragility of a shell, but it also had a human-imposed shape.

"Pottery," Alison mused aloud. "An old pot. I've seen its like on the Island. I'd swear it's Ojibwa."

"More exotic tales," Rowan said scornfully.

Alison ignored him. "This pottery is done by a . . . by an ancient people from my land. Long, long ago. It shouldn't be here; nothing else of Minne—of Island-Not is, except me. And Rambeau."

Rowan frowned politely over the crown of Camay's head. He looked incongruous, his handsome face and melodramatic hair looming over the head of a child-who-was-not-a-child, or who soon would not be one. Yet it was comforting to have him stand and listen as she made an uneasy discovery.

"Rowan, this is like—no, not like—this *is* the pot I was carrying when I fell and scarred myself! See the marks scribed in the clay plain as a cattle brand, the same symbols that mark you, that mark me!"

He put Camay down, then took the pot.

Alison breathed, "Then my scarring really wasn't an accident."

The pot filled Rowan's hands as he turned it like a ball. "The marks are similar," he admitted at length.

"The same."

"A mere coincidence, some lines scribed into the pot by the rocks."

The flat of Alison's hand pounded her chest. "I fell on just such a pot; the marks . . . seared . . . my skin. So neatly. Nothing smudged. And then, here, someone else—you!—walks around with the same marks, deliberately cut. And so do chosen others. You think that's coincidence? How did Veil come by symbols from my land, which it has never heard of, and vice versa? Why must young quest-heirs have those same marks knifed into their chest?"

"These things are mysteries better left unexamined."

"Not when the evidence of a link rests in your hands."

He turned the pot again, as if to reshape it on the wheel of his churning mind so that it no longer challenged reality. "I will ask my father," he finally said.

She rolled her eyes. A good Desmeynian looking only far enough ahead to see the next step, not the entire seven-story flight he was about to fall down. "When?" she asked.

"When we return." Rowan's eyes shone blood-brown in the brightness of the fiery river.

"With the pot?"

He nodded, then extended it to her. "If you can carry it in your pack."

She crouched to Camay, pulling down the child's pathetically flimsy, wrinkled skirt. Neither Desmeynian women nor children were dressed to negotiate red-hot rapids beneath the Earth-Eaters' den. Alison punched room in her pack for the pot. More travel weight.

"I can carry the pack," Rowan suggested with a spurt of unexpected chivalry. Yeah, and the gun and the Cup, too, she thought. The discovery of the Indian pot had made her wary again.

"No, thanks." Alison stood to adjust the weight over her shoulder. "Might as well find out what's beyond the next bend."

That was easy. More bends, more rock. More heat, and more red light.

And they moved more slowly, hindered by the high temperature. Another communal round from the apparently bottomless Cup refreshed them like a passing breeze.

Pickle scratched at his turban—it must itch in this heat—and nodded to the lava. "I have watched and counted steps. The fire-water goes slower."

"Slower?" Rowan turned to the flow, then consulted Alison. "Do you think so?"

She looked, then nodded, very slowly. "See the patches where it turns more gold than red? And some of the eddies that swirl backward? It must be pooling."

"What does that mean?"

"That Pickle's right. The river is becoming a pond."

"You mean that it . . . ends?"

"Yes, or soon will."

They turned—Littlelost, Rowan, Alison—to regard the next length of cavern.

In the pregnant, swollen silence, Alison heard only the muted thump of their heartbeats in unison, of an *earth*beat in rhythm. She stretched out her hands. She didn't have to say a word. Camay grabbed one hand, Faun another, then Twist took Camay's fingers and Rime's, who took Pickle's. Only Rowan had resisted Alison's impulse. He stood apart, looking as if he suspected that participation might make him appear foolish. Poor Rowan, Alison thought; heroes can afford any risks but that.

Alison could feel blood pumping in her own warm fingers, could sense the same pulsing in the small hands linked with hers, joined to hers via one intervening body, and another. It was the oddest feeling, amplified by her exhaustion.

Then Pickle lifted a sweaty, grimy hand and Rowan looked more foolish for ignoring it than taking it. He reached out at last, just as Faun captured his other hand. So they made a circle of hearts, all drumming to a single beat, even the rocks beneath their feet echoing that steady rhythm.

Why?

Alison sensed, and somehow knew at the same instant everyone else did, too, that *something else* set the pace of their matching pulses—something beyond the next visible stretch of river and rock.

Of one accord, their hands dropped. Without a word or a common look, each moved toward what every instinct said was the journey's end, now that they sensed it had always been a journey, and had always had an ending.

There was no hurry. Like the ruddy molasses river, they, too, moved to the ponderous beat reverberating from the earth. And when they passed the last looming shoulders of rock, they found that the river had stilled into a sun-bright pool of pure gold. The surrounding rocks perspired bloody rivulets of lava into the golden basin beneath them.

The party edged around the dazzling pond until it reached

higher ground. The gilded surface seemed absolutely still, but the pools' center still moved, so subtly that motion seemed its reverse. Yet the small, spinning center drew into a whirligig of force, a dimple in the creamy, glittering soup. As they watched, the gyre widened until the whole pool surface trembled like pudding—always shaking, always in motion, yet solidifying even as it spun away down the vortex into the navel of the earth.

"Perfect stasis," Alison said, needing to hear something human in this remotely inhuman place.

"Stasis?" Rowan spoke with awe-inspired patience.

"Never changing and always altering. An eternal drain of the elements into the true center of the earth, so that motion becomes immobility. In Island-Not, that is one way of describing God. Eternal balance, but invisible."

"You have gods in Island-Not?"

"Yes, a great many, and some even believe in only one."

Rowan had moved beyond theological inquiry. "If this is ever-moving and ever-tranquil, what did we hear? What heard us?"

"Come!" Pickle called. He had ventured farther around the pool to a ledge of rocks. As they looked, his figure shivered and then trembled, as if rejecting their focus.

They moved after him. That same vibration afflicted them now, so that Pickle seemed sharp-edged and the cavern around them was blurred. He waited by a depression in the cavern's clay floor; it formed a cavity that seemed to expand both in and out, its breathing jolting the loose rocks within with a bone-shaking, soul-quaking rhythm.

"Heart of Earth!" Rowan knelt to peer into the rough bowl of clay carved from the rock. He eyed the bright, tremulous cave framing the vibrant rhythm before them "Heart of Earth is found only by long, arduous journeying, at the end of everything."

"Perhaps we've come farther than we know," Alison suggested. She rummaged in her pack until she extracted the Indian pot. "Look at the rockface behind you! Isn't it marked by the same scars that scribe the pot?"

Rowan snatched the pot to compare its inscriptions with the slashes writ large on the wall. Unconsciously, the fingers of his free hand traced the ancient pattern on his chest.

Ancient, Alison reflected, startled to find that her hand was tracing her own scars. She dropped it self-consciously. Ancient meant more than merely old; it promised a pattern spanning distance and time—a pattern embracing both the Island in Swan Lake and the wilderness surrounding Desmeyne. Was inner earth the same, no matter the skin upon it? Were what people called myths and history only so many onion skins of time wrapping the same core, sometimes invisibly overlapping?

She took the pot from Rowan. "This *is* the Heart of Earth. What must you do here?"

He seemed startled. "I had no time to prepare myself at Desmeyne—to study the old maps, read the elder legends, memorize the rimes of Heart of Earth. My quest had not yet begun."

"I'm not sure that quests accommodate themselves to our schedules and expectations. You'd better do something; you don't want to return to Desmeyne empty-handed."

He was about to retort in kind when she saw him realize that she was looking beyond him toward the marked wall, and smiling. He turned quickly, as if to forestall an enemy. So much for mutual trust, Alison thought wryly. Then he saw what she had noticed: a tunnel leading from this cavernous cul de sac, its floor slanting sharply *up*, back to Desmeyne, perhaps . . . perhaps back to open air.

Rowan wheeled on Alison. "This I know. I must gather the stuff of earth, its essence, to be made into an amulet that will embody the power that these scars of ours merely symbolize. But . . . what is earth's essence? Should I dip the pot in the fiery water and carry it back to Desmeyne? Is that the lifeblood of earth?"

"Perhaps the Earth-Eaters are not so wrong," she said. "Perhaps you need actual dirt, some clay scraped from this beating pit, from the heartbeat of earth."

He glanced down, not liking it. Those pounding rocks could pummel a man to death faster than a plunge into the lava stream would boil him alive.

Alison understood Rowan's dilemma. How maddening to stumble upon this unreachable place without knowing how to seize its magical essence! Thinking came hard under the rocks' constant pounding, in the glare of the lake of white-hot lava.

Then a sizzle stung the heavy air, like a hot branding iron striking a block of ice. And another. They spun in different directions, so that each saw the straight and narrow lightning rods of bright blue light impale the path rimming the pool. A particularly thick rod drove into the ground before the exit tunnel and widened into a door—a closing door. They were surrounded.

"Crux-masters!" Rowan shouted, "drawn by the smell of a quest fulfilled."

"Guard this." Alison thrust the pot at Twist, who took it. "I'll get the Cup."

She knelt to search the pack, her hair falling forward, blinding her to all but her frantic search. The electric tang in the air grew overpowering as she snatched the Cup from the pack.

"That's why they let us through to the Earth-Eaters," she told Rowan. "They *wanted* us to lead them here."

His empty hands were fisted impotently. "To have come without even my staff, with no weapon—"

"Try this." Alison dug in her pack again and clapped the pistol into his hand, molding his fingers to the cold steel. "Point it only at what you mean to kill. Hold it as steady as a crossbow and pull back slowly with this finger, here, to use it."

Rowan had tensed at the instant the cool black metal touched his palm. "This foul amulet is forbidden."

"But it will kill."

"Even Crux-masters?"

She eyed the widening portals of blue light, each now haloing a shadowy black form. Eyes like those of light-pinioned, night-ranging animals glared at them—animated metallic red, green and blue marbles. A particularly eerie pair was comprised of one red and one blue iris.

"It may not kill Crux-masters, but it should surprise them," Alison said.

"What will you do?"

"First, I'll try the Cup. Then I'll try *taekwondo.*"

Alison pantomimed a swift kick in the *taekwondo* manner. Rowan eyed her dubiously. "Against Crux-masters?" he asked.

"It surprised you."

The Littlelost had drawn into an anxious knot. Alison nodded encouragingly to them before crouching over the golden pond. Her reflection, as bright as Midas's daughter, gleamed back at her. The Cup, mirrored into a twenty-four-carat chalice, dipped toward the hot lava. The substance coated and filled the vessel, which felt amazingly heavy again as Alison lifted it out. Perhaps the river truly was molten gold—a broad, unmined vein that would harden and reveal itself to the miners on a world other than Veil—and fresher than her worn and war-torn earth.

Now the Crux-masters' elongated wands danced over the pool's turgid surface, rigid electric eels buzzing and snapping, tilting to probe the spinning central vortex.

Rowan lifted and aimed the revolver, but a lucent rod flailed high above the pond and spat to earth at his feet, blasting rock into hail. Rowan retreated, forearms guarding his face.

"Afraid of disfigurement, Firemayne?" A Crux-master's voice taunted. It came hollow and cold, as if broadcast from a loudspeaker unthinkably distant from the dark forms gathered there. Alison thought the words were cleverly calculated to sting Rowan's pride into overreaction.

Rowan kept silent, gingerly examining the weapon he held. He was not about to engage these inhuman forms prematurely.

She herself had little idea of how to combat these encircling light-masters with their gaudy laser rods. They hid behind the thrusting wands and their own too-vague presence, yet they must be vulnerable in some way, or they would have simply zapped everyone dead.

"You may leave," a stentorian, arrogant voice reverberated. By some artifice, the odd-eyed Crux-master appeared beside the only exit. "That tunnel leads to light and air and all that Desmeynians hold dear. Go, and meddle no more in matters that do not concern you."

The voice's steely mockery grated on Alison's nerves; it grated even more on her suspicions. "They want something here," she whispered to Rowan. "Something that they *don't* want us—you—to have."

He nodded. "Not the river," he said softly. "It is too vast and mysterious to be turned even to the uses of the Crux."

She wasn't sure she agreed, but she didn't spare the breath to say so. "Let the Littlelost leave first," she suggested to the tunnel guardian.

A silence. Rods raised and clashed together, buzzing in conference. Then a Crux-master floating above the river seemed to speak. "They may go"— Alison nodded at the Littlelost, her eyes prodding them toward the tunnel's opening —"all but one."

Alison and Rowan exchanged a wild, questioning glance. Why would the Crux want . . . one . . . Littlelost?

"Which?" Rowan demanded.

A Crux-master shrank into a shaft of black drapery, then was swallowed by the blue snake of his rod. The staff levitated toward the Littlelost like a shepherd's crook. It circled their huddled formation. It . . . sniffed . . . from feet to heads, its sickly blue glow draining Littlelost faces of youth and energy. It probed them, delicately searing the edges of their clothing to ashy tatters.

"This one," a voice echoed from all the Crux-masters' forms. The rod leveled at a single head, a single frozen, fearful face. Pickle's. "Leave, and leave this one insignificant creature as token of your good faith, and you shall go from this place unmolested. You shall breathe cool air and stand in the warm light you so worship. You shall see mountains from without, as is proper, and you shall live to quest again."

"No hostages," Alison said.

The rod left Pickle to lash toward her. En route it crossed blades . . . with the barrel of Rowan's gun.

Contact crackled like cold lightning, and as steel engaged the airy menace of laser light, the rod snapped into a vee, broken. One portion struck the rock wall like an arrow and impaled itself there, gouging out chunks of rock in a brittle spray. The other plunged into the golden firewater.

An anguished wail rattled against the rocks, and blue rods dimmed to white. The black, negative images of the Crux-masters developed the hazy, halftone pointillism of black-and-white photographs that show subjects as an abstract blur.

Rowan regarded Alison's revolver with a new reverence.

Rods and figures blazed to full strength again, but one was definitely absent. "—six, seven! We've got a standoff," she murmured.

"Will you try to speak Desmeynian?" Rowan snapped.

" 'Standoff.' We aren't stronger than they, but we're not as weak as they'd like."

"Ah." Rowan nodded sagely. "Stasis."

"Stasis."

"Does this mean that the gods support our cause?"

"The gods don't always relish stasis. It bores them. But we can't surrender Pickle."

He turned to the clustered Littlelost. Pickle's face was grim and noncommittal. He watched Rowan with an odd expression, half-defiant—as if to say he didn't care if Rowan wrote him off—and half-hurt. Even a quest-myopic Desmeynian could see that.

Rowan turned back to the Crux-masters. "No Littlelost," he told them. "Besides—" he grinned "—this devil-weapon is steel but not edged. An ingenious place, Island-Not."

"Not ingenious, just homicidal," Alison cautioned. "And remember to point only at what you mean to kill."

Rowan focused on the odd-eyed tunnel guardian.

"There is nothing here for you," the voice insisted. "You will not leave unless we permit you to; without food or water, you will soon perish."

"Apparently you don't need food or water, or sleep," Alison said.

"Our needs are not yours, that is true. We can wait."

"What of the Cup?" She lifted it. "Perhaps you don't need it, either." She thrust it over the lava, its pale exterior absorbing the red-gold flicker.

Seven rods remained poised, lofted in midair but motionless. She saw that the Cup was not what they wanted. Destroying the Cup would accommodate the Crux, not defeat it. Alison brought the vessel to her chest as a shield.

"We will go," Rowan said, "but none stays behind."

"Why should we accept? That gives us nothing," hissed the voice in tones of soft thunder.

"We have nothing also," Rowan said. "My quest was to find this place and bring forth the wherewithal to form a new talisman for Desmeyne and all of Veil. I will leave empty-handed; that should suffice, since we have a . . . a standoff."

Tension resonated from all the rods and rocks around them. "A standoff is not enough, Taliswoman," snapped the one voice that spoke for them all, and from them all, ignoring Rowan. "That one remains. That insignificant Littlelost there."

Seven rods formed a vee that pointed at Pickle. The other Littlelost instinctively tightened around him, as much for self-protection as to defend him against the Crux-masters' terrible fascination.

"I will stay." Pickle's thin voice came from their midst.

Rowan looked hopefully toward Alison. So much for his burgeoning compassion. "No," she answered all of them again—friend, rival and foe alike. "By the Cup, I will not permit it. We all go, as we all came."

The rods unleashed in a flurry of blinding strokes. Where their luminosity touched clothing or skin it gave a cold, cutting pain that froze and burned equally. She and Rowan, both hurt, staggered back toward the Littlelost and the wall inscribed with their common scars.

The revolver's discharge nearly deafened all of them, its sound ricocheting like a weapon from every wall. Rowan had fired into the dueling rods. They broke, a shattering fireworks that stung the far walls in an azure sleet, arcing sparks like a steelworker's welding tool.

Fractured, the rods doubled back to reassemble and again lash toward an astounded Alison and Rowan. Alison swung the Cup in a wide arc, its hot contents of lava spewing a lacy contrail into the air, spitting metallic embers onto the oncoming lances of blue light.

The lances seemed undamaged, but a stench of burning flesh blossomed in the air like an unhealthy, unseen orchid. A Littlelost wailed, and Pickle broke from the group and ran toward the tunnel and the waiting Crux-master. "Rowan!" Alison screeched in warning.

One of Rowan's long arms snapped out to intercept the Littlelost, but he missed. His hand closed on the fleeing head and tightened—and came away with a scrap of twined cloth.

Pickle stopped in mid-gallop. Rowan and Alison froze in horror. Even the rods hovered, as if shocked, and the Crux-masters kept silent.

The fulcrum of the universal immobility was Pickle's head—or, rather, the long red hair that had been hidden by the turban. Alison blinked. What had the Earth-Eaters said of the Littlelost? Never growing up, only older. No beard, no facial growth. No need for a rubrock, only a head-wrap. Hair was Pickle's birthbane, one he could hide, and did. Especially when he encountered another of the same scarlet stripe, a Firemayne of Desmeyne.

"What obscene illusion is this?" Rowan whispered. He lowered the gun.

Alison took advantage of the Crux-masters' inaction to dart to Pickle and yank him back to the other Littlelost.

"Do you remember anything about the time of your losing?" she asked him quickly. "You were older than most."

"Some things. Earth-Eaters. And escaping through a Wombbat tunnel."

"Do you remember Desmeyne?" she asked.

He shook his astoundingly red head. "Almost nothing before the Earth-Eaters' caverns."

"I don't understand—" Rowan began.

"This is your elder brother, Lorn. The Crux has some use for him."

"No." Rowan stepped back from one last, unacceptable fact. "No."

"The Taliswoman speaks truly," the Crux-voice thrummed into the silence, "and now you have forfeited all mercy. See what the price of defying the Crux will be, and wait for your doom."

Rowan and Alison spun. Two rods had fattened into broad swords of light, and those formidable blue blades slashed toward their throats, pausing just a centimeter away from their skin. They could feel the weapons' icy heat pulsing in time to their heartbeats.

"Watch!" the odd-eyed Crux-master commanded, echoed by the gaunt shadows encircling the cavern.

A rod fractured into quarters, which whipped at Pickle like fencing foils. He retreated alone against the inscribed rock. The other Littlelost were now ringed by a rod that had stretched into a noose of light.

A length of light underlined Pickle's terrified face and pressed against his throat. Two others forced his hands to the rock wall behind him. The fourth burned the tunic from his body in hissing strokes. It poised to strike—then drew along his hairless chest as delicately as the tattooist's needle. A jagged mark burned azure on his skin. Pickle screamed, "No!" as the scent of burnt flesh flared into an obscene incense of sacrifice.

Rowan jerked as if his own body had been assaulted, his throat spasming under the waiting scalpel of light, recoiling in his own, unuttered pain.

They watched, helpless, while the scribing rod hesitated above Pickle's flesh, then pressed to make another mark to match the first—the mark of Quest-right. Alison shut her eyes. She had been scarred in one bloody instant, with shock the anesthetic. Rowan's scarification at knife point had been different, a ritual ordeal by blood, yet undergone willingly. Now poor, innocent Pickle—Lorn, she must call him—felt the defacement of a poisonous light infected with unknown evil. The blue bar at her throat was a blade too horribly contaminating to touch, yet she . . . *they,* someone . . . must do something!

"Why?" The word wrenched from Rowan's throat as the moving blue rod wrote again. Pickle's screams escalated into an unholy counterpoint to the Crux's insistent, disembodied power. "No, no—!" His eye-whites grew blue and phosphorescent, as if the Crux-masters' weapons were unleashing a rising alien tide within him.

"An . . . *anti*-Talisman!" Alison murmured with dawning horror. "Lorn was destined for it. He pre-dates you, Rowan. He *is* the Talisman and he will soon be theirs!"

Rowan's features tightened in grief and fury. His hands pushed at the blade of blue light, his palms pausing only a centimeter from its cold heat as if to break it, even if closing his fingers on it would melt the bone from his body.

"No!" Alison shouted, equally desperate to rush to Pickle's defense, her hand fighting to elevate the Cup toward the razor of light at her throat. Across from her, the Crux-masters clustered in a clump of unseeable shadow, lurid irises gleaming from their midst. They didn't even bother to guard the tunnel . . . how near that escape route was, merely seven or eight bounds away.

The blue light sizzled even closer to her skin as the Cup lifted, searing thought as well as breath. Alison felt a rising fog in her senses and hallucinated an oncoming tidal wave of cloud, clogging the throat of the tunnel opposite, rushing toward her like a lacy spume of spin-drift. Her surf-blood pounded in her ears, white horses thundering on the wave crests, Eli's underworld ghost-buffalo stampeding, the Bone Buffalo at their fore, and in her hands not a Cup, but a terra-cotta pot. For a moment Alison hung by her neck from a thin, radiant thong, a deer dressed after the slaughtering.

And then the huge, Viking-horned head and hunkering shoulders of the white Bone Buffalo were thundering into the tunnel archway, front hooves clad in buckskin, mane combed into pennants of long, flying white hair, and domed head a crown atop a ghostman, a faint figure with Eli's features.

Alison opened her mouth to greet him, but Eli dropped to all fours again. The buffalo's horns became pointed ears, and the beast grew a pointed nose. Rambeau! He was shooting the rapids of the oncoming fog, a half-dozen pale, wolfish forms boiling behind him.

Blue lights sprang upright before the tunnel like bars. Rambeau leaped—his whole white glistening cloud-form airborne—and flew through them.

Alison screamed, her senses clenching to shut out the piercing whimpers, the burning fur and flesh, the shape-shifting forms. It worked, for she saw, heard, smelled none of that. She looked again to see Rambeau, wrapped in an aura of lurid blue light—and then blue rods breaking as if they were twigs.

Someone did scream, a dreadful screech that was hardly understandable—a last, defiant "No!" Oh, no—Pickle. . . . From the corner of her eye Alison watched Rowan's fists tighten on the blue light at his throat. Her own hand pushed the Cup across her laser barrier. Both blades winked out before they were touched.

The Crux-masters faded behind an aquamarine-pale haze until only the afterimage embers of their eyes glittered against the gray rock. Even as they did so, Rambeau charged forward.

"Beau!"

But he trotted past, five black-eyed wolves behind him. She turned to see what Rowan had already seen. The space before the runic wall was empty.

"They took him!" Alison approached in disbelief, but Rowan's hand caught her wrist, stopping her. A thin tattoo-blue line sliced across his throat.

"No." Rowan's soft answer echoed his brother's. He neared the spot where Pickle had . . . vanished, then went down on one knee.

Rambeau's nose sniffed where rock wall and level earth met. Then he lifted his head and howled. The cavern magnified the sounds like an echo chamber.

Rowan's shaking hands—and Alison saw that they weren't damaged—curved protectively above the spot where Pickle, where his lost brother Lorn, had stood. His fingertips touched something gray piled on the ground.

"Ashes and dirt," Rowan said, reverently gathering the grayness into a pathetic little heap. "Essence of earth. The heart of a Firemayne. An amulet of human clay. The very heart of Veil. Bring me the pot."

Twist brought the vessel Camay had found. Alison watched Rowan brush what remained of Lorn into its dark earthen mouth. Somber Littlelost surrounded him, bewildered. Rambeau howled, the wolves howled, and Alison's temples pounded.

"Mystical mumbo-jumbo! Is that all you can say?" she demanded of Rowan's back, her rage and loss boiling like a lake of lava. "The Crux destroyed your brother before you even knew him, because Lorn wouldn't let them use him! Yet *you* will use his remains for your own doomed and ever-overriding quest? I tried to save the Littlelost, but not for some wrong-headed human sacrifice. I won't watch you dishonor the remnants of one you and your parents surrendered too easily. Veil is a nightmare world, and I want no part of it! Rowan, do you hear me? Stop! Or I'll take the Cup and run so far that not even Rambeau can find me!"

"You do not understand." Rowan spoke without looking up, his voice husky but calm. "The Crux-masters haven't won. This . . . apparent loss fulfills the terms of the first quest. All is as was meant to be; even Lorn knew it when he shouted 'No' and cheated the Crux of their victim:

> *"He is who is first shall be at last*
> *Unmade in the Crux of a too-present past.*
> *The heart that is human, born to Dearth,*
> *Will beat for all time in an armor of earth."*

The words, without meaning, flowed over Alison in a drowning tide. Rowan's hands were busy, busy, brushing the ashes of his brother into the gaping mouth of the clay pot. Pickle was gone. A Littlelost she had fought for and loved, a brother Rowan had never known and was just learning to like. . . .

"Lorn would not object," Rowan said.

"*I* object! I object to all of Desmeyne's misguided and lethal notions. I renounce Veil and even being here! If I cannot walk far enough to leave it, I will walk to the end of it and throw the Cup into the deepest ocean I can find."

Feeling mortally wounded, though the blue light had never touched her, Alison turned and ran for the mouth of the tunnel without a look back. The Cup was in her hand; her pack dangled from her shoulder; she felt no weight, no burden, nothing but revulsion for the horribly unreal thing that had happened. She charged toward a vision of ultimate daylight, toward a scene that would not wrench her sense of right and wrong, of reality, so out of joint.

Fog still foamed in the tunnel. Alison vanished into it, into the pounding pulse of the sky-herd. Her feet stumbled over rocky terrain she couldn't see. There was no light left except the ghostly ambiance of the fog. She ran blindly on.

Later, she heard the click of trotting feet and felt the wolves brush her knees and heard their unflagging panting. She ran now with the pack, the herd, and her separate pain was a small thing on such a vast scale. The mindless act of running established a rhythm and a welcome sense of removal, of distance in both time and spacc.

Her emotional pain became physical, became a blue light twisting in her abdomen, then a recognizable womanly ache.

The Bone Buffalo's disembodied hooves thundered beside her, its passage throbbing out the rhythm of a powerful heart.

"Why?" she beseeched it. "Why Pickle? Why death? Why me—here, where I can do nothing but witness the unthinkable?"

That, answered a voice like the drumbeat from the Heart of Earth, *which cannot be made into something else is not cherished.*

"Eli—?"

A thigh-high form jolted her leg—Rambeau there, too, in the fog and the hunt. They were hunting, all three—Alison, Dog, and Buffalo. For what? Answers?

She felt pendant blood gathering in her like a gravid tear, ready to flow free from the vortex of her pain. She suddenly saw. *She* was the bride-price, the scarlet swan, fleeing the slaughter . . . And if her period came now, the mundane pull of her own world was asserting its natural cycles again. She was leaving Veil, as she had so often wished.

"Why now?" she asked the Bone Buffalo.

You have found the Red Swan, it answered.

Rowan's instinct was right, she suddenly thought. Pickle—Lorn—had to be remade to redeem himself and his world. He had to become the sacrificial red swan. Blood was both end and beginning. So there was reason behind the loss and the pain, the helplessness and the villainy always waiting? There was reason in Veil and Desmeyne and the ways of them both? And the reason required a witness, except that she was now fleeing the scene of this fore-ordained accident, as she had another once before. Too soon, too soon. Too late and too soon.

The Bone Buffalo, hooves thrumming beside her, murmured that she, too, fulfilled and evaded her destiny and her death by running, that she would find the direction she had always desired when her task was done.

Home? Alison wondered numbly to the monotonous drumming of animal feet. Was she finally going there only because Veil didn't need her anymore? But how could it be enough?

33

Her blue jeans were wet and stiff with cold. Her fingers were icy, and so was her nose . . . as was Rambeau's when his black snout inquiringly touched her face. Alison looked around. The darkness softened, like a withdrawing fog.

She felt as if she'd been shot through the gun barrel of her own narrow focus.

She was in the woods. Again. She froze to see the circle of wolves edging a thicket. Gray, gold, black, their wary, lean intelligence was so different from Rambeau's.

Alison got up. Grass stains marked the backpack, she noticed as she pulled it over her shoulders. Her nose was running. When she began walking, her left leg limped, and she didn't know why.

The forest creaked and chirped with hidden life. Rambeau paced beside her, his coat tangled with burrs, his eyes apologetic—that guilty, gauging sidelong look of dogs who know they've been derelict in some human-decreed behavior.

Alison patted his shoulder, where the thick, white fur curled slightly, and felt a sudden wash of relief. The wolves followed discreetly, yellow eyes winking warning from the underbrush. They were wild, she told herself, just ordinary wild wolves with nothing better to do.

The wild asparagus was unfurling lacy shoots against the leaf-bare fences of winter saplings. Whips of brush already blushing green with buds. Dead leaves—not crisp, crackling fall ones, but soggy, long-gone spring ones—clung like milk-sodden Frosted Flakes to her boot soles.

She walked through the trees, glad that they obscured the world she wasn't quite ready to see again. As if her thoughts had evoked it, something glimmered blue through a stand of pale birch trunks. Alison stopped, letting the pack sag on her back, feeling her throat close with panic. Rambeau sat beside her, alert, relaxed, silent. Did she expect him to talk, or what?

Edging closer through the birches, she saw more blue: open water. Once identified, the element called to her, her usual fear muted by the fact of its presence and a return to a normal world. She began trotting, then ran toward the shore. Once she stopped and turned suddenly. The wolves were gone. Or hiding.

Rambeau kept pace with her. Good dog.

She came upon the lake. Swan Lake. She'd seen it a hundred times. It was *the* lake. Her lake. Her . . . Island? Not far away, the cabin hunkered under the pines, its weathered log sides as gray as the tall trunks. Eli's cabin.

Alison approached it with an uneasy blend of awe, hope and fear. Her knock sounded puny in the open air, against the busy chatter of all outdoors and the far, hooting laugh of a loon. No answer. She finally pushed, and the wooden door opened.

Inside, the front room was the same. Fishhooks glittered in their Mason jars. A rifle lay angled on the wooden tabletop. Her fingers hesitated over the cold barrel. Again? Should she take it and go to the woods and kill the Taker/bear and take the children and eat deer meat? Again? No.

She slung the pack to the tabletop and rummaged for what her world so delicately called "feminine protection." Like Veil, it had its own self-deceptions. Her menstrual cramps were a constant, aching echo of a recent but unimaginably distant emotional miscarriage—the pain of Pickle's loss. Her fingers brushed the Cup's smooth side as she replaced the tampons. Her jangled emotions soothed at once, as if she had stroked a favorite pet. Her eyes studied the mosaic of fishhooks in their jars. She could see the grain of every feather as clearly as through a magnifying glass, with perfect, unaided vision. She may have taken the Cup from Veil, but did its magical potential come with it? Come with her? Would her world ever be the same now? Would Veil? Before she could worry about the future, she had to make sure she was in the proper present again.

She left the rifle and the cabin and began circling—she hoped—the Island. A pile of dumped trash—bones, fur—festered where she'd seen such garbage before. Now she harbored no rage toward trespassers, just a numb hope that there was no one else on the Island. No Takers, no Littlelost, no wolves. No Veil.

Rambeau whimpered at something in the woods ahead. She patted his shoulder. "Good dog."

His whimper became a warning growl. Alison approached what drew his gaze, aware suddenly that she had no revolver in her pack, just a Cup that would look like a theatrical prop to people in Minnesota, and would be of no use against a trespasser. A twinge of guilt almost stopped her in her tracks. She had never meant to take a thing of Veil—an empowered thing of Veil—from its world before it could fulfill its purpose. What would be the consequences—to her, to Rowan and Desmeyne? And the gun—! She dare not think of where the revolver was, and of what use might be made of it.

So she walked to where Rambeau looked because she knew he could sense things she might not. He didn't accompany her.

"Rambeau! Come on, boy."

Sitting on his haunches, looking so intelligent, so . . . sorry. Disobeying. Not coming. Alison stared at him. Again? He would not come with her again? Was it all to repeat in an endless round like "row, row, row your boat"? Maybe Rowan could win the Cup singing that little ditty . . .

Something snapped in the woods ahead, a large branch. Someone was coming. She turned back to beseech Rambeau one more time, but he had vanished. No dog sat on his haunches in the woods. No wolves haunted the underbrush. No Eli waited at his cabin. Footsteps came—bold, undergrowth-crushing steps that acted like they owned the Island.

Alison braced herself, not knowing if it was for the same thing or for something terribly, terribly different.

Two men crashed through the trees, stopping short as they saw her. Down vests, navy and khaki pants. Plaid shirts, boots. Pale winter faces. She stared at them.

"My God! Alison?" One moved toward her faster than she wanted, a bland, blond-haired, gray-eyed man with pleasant features: Mark McPherson. What was Mark McPherson doing up at the Island?

"Alison!" He said, and she was glad he was so certain. "We've been combing the Island for hours. There was a terrible storm last night. I'd come up Saturday to cover an environmental story, and got worried about you. So I got ahold of your brother, and when we reached the Island, your sleeping bag was there but your camp was deserted. We couldn't find you anywhere. How can anyone get lost on one square mile? Jesus, I thought you were . . . drowned, or something. Peter's been helping me search, but we were about ready to call in the National Guard."

Alison needed strong emotion to penetrate the fog still smothering her. She glanced at the second man, realizing that his face was deeply familiar, if not often seen.

"Gosh, Peter."

The stranger was her brother. How had she forgotten the hockey scar on his cheekbone, his odd eyes, one hazel, one blue? It had been too long. A brother shouldn't be a stranger, no matter what. He hugged her awkwardly. "I told you this Island was no place for a woman alone. You should have sold it, like I said."

She shrugged. There was no answer to that: there never was with Peter on the subject of the Island. "You came to help Mark find me, though?"

"Sure. You *are* my sister, even if you're too stubborn for your own good."

"Or maybe just sentimental," she said, aware that sudden tears were sheeting down her face. She couldn't believe that she was really seeing Mark McPherson and her brother—that she still had a brother, no matter how estranged, and that the Island was just like it had always been. "When . . . when did you come to the Island?" she asked Mark.

"This morning." He looked at her oddly. "I was planning to surprise you with the first copies of your big Sunday front analysis piece. It was going to get dark soon—where on earth have you been?"

"Then it's . . . Sunday. Sunday afternoon?"

"Yeah, sure." The two men exchanged glances the way men do when women seem a little confused. "You okay?"

What could she say with the tears flowing like a river and no sobs accompanying them, just buckets and buckets of running saltwater? "Rambeau's missing," she blurted out. That was a loss they might understand.

"He'll probably turn up. Just lost, like you."

She shook her head, scattering tears as a dog sheds water drops. "No. And I couldn't find Eli—"

Peter's arm weighed on her shoulder. "Hey, we better get out of here before it gets too dark to cross over to mainland. Eli's out fishing, that's all. And as for the dog—you must have gotten hysterical looking for the damn dog, Alison. I've always said you were too attached to that thing. Look, you can get another one—"

At last he'd said something that let her sob. 'Cause you *can't* get another one, not another Rambeau, not another . . . no, she wouldn't think the name, wouldn't think of anything from . . . *there* right now. Not when she was safe here. Maybe.

Her brother, behind her, spoke to Mark as if she weren't present. "—always been too attached to things, and to places."

"I'll make sure she gets back safely to the Cities," Mark promised. "If you hear anything about the dog, let her know."

"Sure."

At the campsite, they paused. She picked up the paperback she'd been reading, the lantern that was cold and extinguished, and put them down again. She lifted the sleeping bag to roll it up, but Peter wrinkled his nose.

"Whew! Something stinks! Some beaver came up and whizzed on the bag, I guess. That's outdoor living. Leave it, Allie. You don't want to smell up your condo with that. Keep it up here in the storage shed as a spare."

She didn't argue, but went with them, wiping the wetness from her face over and over, until they reached the lakeshore. Then she stopped, dead. "The water's down."

"Usually goes down about this time," her brother said in his blandest, know-everything voice. "You're not going to get unglued about just walking across now?"

She eyed the tongue of land leading to the opposite shore and the whole continental United States of America. Her Blazer stood under the pine tree where she'd left it, and the boat was tied up near it, where it should be once the water was down. The idea of walking over and getting in her vehicle and turning the key and driving onto the dirt road and the paved road and the Interstate and back down to the city gave her such a wild sense of freedom that she couldn't cry anymore just now, Rambeau or not.

Alison started across the land bridge. Her boots stamped on something hard with a crackling sound. She looked down to see a piece of thin, rusted metal about the size of a dragon scale.

"Somebody's been dumping on the Island again," her brother complained. "Looks like part of a fender. Sure worn thin. I'll complain to the sheriff tomorrow. I'll tell him Eli's missing, too. You just get back to the city, Alison, and don't worry about a thing up here."

She nodded and stepped onto the soft earth linking mainland and ex-Island between lapping aisles of water. Maybe behind her a strange, half-seen Veil shimmered in the spaces between the budding leaves. Maybe behind her a flash of red wasn't just a male cardinal on a birch branch. Maybe the Cup in her backpack wouldn't become a docile trophy in a case or an everyday receptacle for tomato juice and burgundy. Maybe Veil wasn't done with her and she with it. Maybe.

Certainly she was no longer what she had been. Nor was the Island. But for now she needed it to be just a peninsula, an empty, uninhabited peninsula, and she was leaving it.

For now, Alison of Island-Not did not look back.